The Rancher's Callous Heart

A Ranchers Hot & Cold Duology: Book One

By Jazz Matthews

ISBN: 978-1-7367518-1-7

Edited by Michelle Morgan
Proofread by Stephany Esposito
Cover Design by LJ Anderson
Vector Graphics by Pixabay & Canva
Published by Lone Lady Press

Lone Lady
PRESS

"Stop," she whispered, a demonstration of how much of her will remained. "This is wrong."

"To who? You?" His voice was mocking. "I know this goes against the grain of your moral fiber, honey, but I'm not going to sit here like a damn monk and play off that your body has no effect on mine. Not when, after all this time, I've thought of little else."

His hard mouth set into a mutinous line, his quicksilver eyes scrutinizing a body he had already seen naked and trembling at his whim.

"It's hard to forget the essence of a woman. Your moans sounded so sweet, your juices even sweeter as you came. For days, I swear, I could still taste you." He paused, a glimpse of his tongue skimming across his lips followed by a small, impish smile. "Sometimes, I still think I can. But that came second to the moment I was inside you. God, I've almost gone crazy in the last few weeks. You have no idea how many nights I've wanted to come to you. I've surprised myself at how much restraint I've shown so far. But no more, Andrea. I've waited long enough."

Dedication

This is dedicated to all the readers who had believed in me and never gave up.

Thank you for patience and support. This is for you.

Note from Jazz

This story has been about fifteen years in the making for me. That being said, this book has a callous alpha male who worships his fierce lady love to the *fullest* extent. Mature themes apply for strong language in and out of bed, sexual violence, and death.

Chapter One

Unwanted eyes had tracked her on what was the worst day of her life. A day that she had no preparation to steel herself from. A day she hadn't imagined would come for years. Now suffering through the unimaginable with the very eyes that had invaded her dreams and roused her fear. It only complicated what was an already taxing moment.

Andrea's entire state was mechanical, her mind on lockdown as she bore through the task of ushering the last guest to the door. Her aunt, who had insisted on staying with her, glanced back at her with concern.

"I'll be all right, Aunt Gloria."

Solemn brown eyes regarded her. They reminded her of her mother's. One of only a handful of things she could remember.

"You sure, honey? Your cousins want to go back to Alabama tonight, but I'll stay for as long as you need."

Andrea shook her head. "I'm tired. I plan to go to bed after I soak in a nice bath. That always does me some good."

The older woman smoothed Andrea's hair behind her ear, pity occupying her face. Andrea's gaze diverted down. Pity. It was handed to her like candy she didn't care for, and she was sick from stomaching every piece. She just wanted to be alone, wrapped in her own thoughts and feelings. Away from the sympathy she hadn't been able to avoid for over a week.

Aunt Gloria took one of her hands and squeezed. "Be sure to call if you need anything."

"Okay," Andrea whispered before watching her aunt turn to descend the stairs and step out into the cool downpour of the mid-autumn rain. It was when the midsize sedan pulled from the limestone paved driveway that Andrea shut the door, restoring the house to the unusual quiet she wasn't accustomed to.

For the past few days, someone was always there, providing her with food, comfort, and lending their opinions on how her father should be buried.

The thought broke the already fractured dam that held her tears back. Andrea sagged against the door as a sob broke from her. "Oh, God!" she wept as she slid to the cold, marble floor of the foyer. She still couldn't believe it, even when she witnessed him in peaceful repose during the viewing at the church for what would be the last time.

This was the worst day she could ever fathom. Andrea had dreaded the day she would have to bury her father, but this was too soon, too sudden.

The police had come to notify her, and her feelings remained locked inside ever since, despite the goading from her family and friends to release them. Now she was crumbled in an inconsolable heap on the floor. Darren Banks had not only been her doting father but her everything. It had been just the two of them since Andrea's mother died when she was seven.

With her father gone, so was her safety net despite the gaping holes that had been in it. But it had been there, nonetheless.

She knew her father's "accident" was no such thing. The police cued it up to Darren's alcohol consumption for the reason his Bentley took a dive into Lake Travis. From the empty liquor bottles in the car and their dwindling finances, the evidence pointed to either suicide or a freak accident. Her request for an autopsy and toxicology report was ignored, and the case was closed.

She could feel injustice in the very marrow of her bones. It was obvious who was responsible. The man who possessed eyes she detested. Andrea could never bring herself to hold that immutable gaze, terrified of what she would find within them. But she knew when they were on her whenever he had come to visit her father, lingering far longer than they should in a mental caress that repulsed her.

She thought she had imagined him in fleeting glances at the gravesite, but her paranoia was affirmed when he had somehow slithered his way into her house during the repast. Andrea couldn't believe the blatant audacity of him as he managed to trap her in a corner of the living room, despite her family and friends conversing nearby, oblivious to it all.

Andrea had glared into the piercing green eyes of Edward Gaines, wishing she could condemn him to hell with just one look. Being over two decades older, he was menacing as he loomed over her, but the man was magnetic and persuasive. He was handsome with a rumbling timbre that could charm a nun to breaking all her vows. However, Andrea found his lifestyle as a loan shark a turnoff, not to mention his shady dealings with her father before and after his death.

Rolling her eyes, Andrea had attempted to swerve around him. Gaines placed a firm hand on her forearm. The look he gave her then dared her to cause a scene, but fearing what he could do, she remained subdued.

Gaines cleared his throat, his fingers rubbing the tender skin on the inside of her arm. She would have to soak in her tub for a week to feel clean again.

"Miss Banks," he purred. "You have my condolences on the passing of your father. He was a good man."

Dark brown eyes flashed at his daring. She withdrew her arm from his grip, her body humming with the intense, unnatural black fury she felt.

"Don't give me that," she seethed. "You're the one who killed him."

Her voice remained low for only him to hear the charge she leveled at him. Gaines smirked, undaunted by her accusation. "Why would I kill your father? He owed me money, and he still does. The tab is still running at two and a half mil, and congratulations, sweetheart. You just inherited his debt."

If Andrea could turn green, she would. She never knew how much her father owed. Hearing the amount sickened her. "I don't have that kind of money."

"I'm sure you do, little one. If anything, you can put your daddy's life insurance policy to good use. Relinquish his bank account, put the house up for sale. I don't care how you do it. I want my money."

"Or what?" she goaded. "You'll kill me, too?"

Gaines stepped within an inch of her, his gaze trailing down her body and up again. "Would you prefer that, or some other, more beneficial arrangement?"

"I'd rather have a venereal disease," she breathed as she moved to walk around him, and again he detained her, his demeanor serious.

"If there's two things you don't mess with it's my money or my time, and both have been wasted. Pay me what I'm owed, and for you, sweetheart, I can take all kinds of payments you're willing to make."

Despite his face hardening with the menace he presented, the smoldering within his eyes was irrefutable. Bold, his left forefinger traced down her cheek. Andrea flinched away before he could do anything else.

"You'll get your *money* without any other interest or incidentals," she stressed. "More than that, I don't owe you a goddamn thing."

He grinned, as if he found her anger cute. "We'll be in touch," he promised before leaving. The look she had exchanged with Aunt Gloria told of the older woman's misgivings of what took place, but she didn't bring it up when she left. Even if she had, Andrea would've denied anything was awry. She didn't want anyone to have any more knowledge than what was already apparent. It was her father's mess, but she had to clean it up to ensure that no one she cared about would be hurt by Edward Gaines ever again.

Andrea had no idea how long she was on the floor, but she managed to get to her feet, renewed with resolution. She glanced around the foyer of the place she had called home for years. She always thought it was too big for just the two of them. They had moved in after her mother had passed from cancer, and only because her father had a dream. The house, nestled in the opulent neighborhood of Tarrytown, was what Darren Banks had considered as one of his crowning jewels in his road to success. A thriving Black man who had been a high-paying executive at Cisco Systems. He had the flash and the cash to treat his only child to a life of affluence and security.

Now those illusions were empty just like the sad, quiet foyer she stood in. Just like much of the house, once lush with life, now glum and hollow. Since she had been eighteen, her father had them sell numerous items to pay down the debt. Five years had been spent peddling off aspects of her life that had meant something to her parents and herself. From vases her mother had collected, her father's books, designer clothing and paintings. Now that her father was dead, more items would follow. Every single bit of what remained would be gone, including the house that had been her home since she was a child. It didn't make sense for her to keep it, nor did she want to stay somewhere that held painful memories. Andrea needed to start fresh after she cut off the bindings of her old life. Only then would she be free.

"I can't believe you're doing this!" exclaimed the astonished woman across from Andrea.

She had taken her best friend and roommate out to lunch at a Mexican restaurant to lessen the blow, but she knew Ella wouldn't condone what Andrea was about to do.

"I'm dead serious," Andrea answered. "I'm going to do it. I'm going to take a job on a Wyoming ranch as a cook."

The fetching features of Ella flickered with suspicion. "Whatever, girl. You're going up there to be a housekeeper. A housekeeper! You haven't even graduated from college yet. You still have a year and a half to go."

Andrea shrugged. "I don't know if I want to be in business management anymore."

"Change majors."

"And put in another year or so than I already have? No thanks. I'm so mentally through with everything from the last few months it's hard to concentrate on school. But who knows? I may come back and finish my degree, but right now, I just want to go off and do something worthwhile."

Ella ate a forkful of rice. "Going to New York for a business internship is worthwhile. Getting a job in Milan for a fashion career is worthwhile. You chose…a horse ranch."

Leave it to Ella to be forthright. It had been five months since Andrea had moved out of her childhood home. Since then, she had been crashing on her best friend's couch. Ella, who she had met during her freshman year at UT, knew more than anyone about Andrea's hardships in paying off her father's debt and had kept it in confidence.

Andrea had paid the rest of the money a couple weeks ago. She was finished. Gaines' other intention toward her had been ambiguous. She had seen him a couple times in the last few months, and it was business-related. Granted, he never again attempted to touch her when she had to be in his presence. Still, she could feel the way he would study her profile when her eyes were eager to wander elsewhere. She wanted out before he revisited that issue of wanting her, and she had found a way in online ad a day after she had met with him. It was an extreme idea, even for her, but Andrea saw that she had a far better chance in Wyoming than waiting around for the other shoe to drop. She just had to disappear until he forgot about her.

"To each their own. I've seen pictures of it. The ranch is situated on good land with acreage for days, and the homestead is just ideal and homey."

Ella appeared as if she wasn't buying it. "Uh-huh. No one in their right mind would give up the comforts of home to go to a state where there are just three Black people, you included." Despite herself, Andrea couldn't help but smile at her friend's jest. "Admit it. You want to get as far away from here as you can, and you're willing to take any means necessary, even disregarding your God-given common sense."

"Do you blame me?" Andrea asked, seriousness taking reign.

Ella eyed her before gazing down at her half-eaten chimichanga. "No, but there are other ways to go about this. How do you know this place is legit? I mean, who hires a *cook*, of all people, sight unseen?"

"It's not like I didn't do my research. I made sure the place exists. In fact, it's won awards, one of the best in the US, not to mention the owner is the best horse breeder and trainer in the biz. A lot of owners have brought their champions to South Land to sire and breed. I saw that the last Thoroughbred who won the Triple Crown was trained there. At any rate, the housekeeper appeared nice when I talked to her over the phone. I explained to her what all I can do. It'll feel like it's always been, except this time, I'll have more people to worry about."

"Mm-hmm, you mean more *men*. I can assume you'll be cooking for the hands, the owner, and his family?"

Andrea's brow furrowed at the memory. Maybe it was just her, but she felt that when she talked to Gemma Upshaw, she had zipped through the part about the owner, covering parts such as the man's name and that he was out in the field most of the day. "The owner's a confirmed bachelor from what I understand."

Ella shrugged. "He's probably an old hermit or a conceited ass." Andrea's eyes widened at her directness. "What? You know it's probably true. A man like that is irresistible to us females unless he's too difficult for even his mama to deal with. Or maybe he's gay. It's one of the two."

"Him being gay may actually work in my favor," Andrea reasoned. "I've already been hounded by one man in my life. I could use a break. Plus, the man's not here to defend himself on why he chose to remain single. Regardless, I'm sure his mama loves him just fine."

Ella gave an unladylike snort. "I'm sure he's safe thousands of miles away from where his precious ears aren't ringing from me talking about him. But to be honest, you know how I love dark meat, but there is some fine white meat too that I wouldn't mind saving a horse to ride."

Andrea giggled. "You're such a freak."

"I know it, and men love it. I'm praised all the time for my numerous talents." She proceeded to hint at one of her talents by twisting her dexterous tongue both ways, then forming it into a three-leaf clover.

Ella wasn't the customary size two. She was voluptuous, gorgeous, and had the seductive allure and smile down pat. Andrea was introverted for the most part, speaking to someone if she had to. However, there were times when her temper came to the surface. One cocky boy who picked on her in the fifth grade could attest to that.

Andrea stirred her strawberry lemonade with her straw. "I wouldn't know from experience. All my experiences have been from living vicariously through you."

"You've just been sheltered by your father," Ella pointed out. "But you're a closeted freak, girl. You just need the right man who'll unlock your closet to let you out or just fuck the hell outta you inside it. Either way, I'm sure it'll make for an exciting time for you."

"That's a little extreme, even for me," Andrea replied with a nervous chuckle. "I mean, I have no experience with the opposite sex. The one person I've managed to attract is an obsessed loan shark who offed my father."

"And that's the real reason you're leaving?" Ella seemed to intuit. "Has he made a pass at you?"

Andrea shook her head just as their server came to check on them. Once she was gone, Andrea pushed her plate aside and took a sip of her drink. "No, but it's there. I'm tired of looking over my shoulder every second waiting for him to make a move. I just want to disappear for a while. Maybe in a couple years, he'll forget about me and move on to someone else."

"And if not?"

Andrea blanched at the thought. She wanted to get away now. She didn't want to think about what could happen down the road. The waitress came back with their separate tabs. Andrea took out her debit card, wrapped her receipt around it before placing it on the edge of the table. She rested her head upon her hand. "I have to try. Going to Wyoming could be no worse than staying here. As far as I know, he has no land up there, and I'll be in a corner of the world where no one will know who I am. I can start fresh, get a new outlook on life. And maybe, just maybe, I can find my true purpose. I mean, I was so used to looking after my father since my mother passed. Now I have to find out what to do with just me."

Ella nodded. "Understandable." She sniffled and lowered her thick lashes as if to hide tears. "When are you leaving?"

Andrea fought back the desire to shed tears of her own. Ella had been her lean-to in this time of grievance and fear, but she didn't want to be a burden. Ella had her own life to live. Andrea just prayed she'd have the strength to leave her best friend behind.

"In four days. I'm not bringing much with me, but I'd appreciate it if you can keep up with my storage fees. I'll send the money to you on whatever app you want."

"Agreed." Ella studied Andrea. "Now that I think about it, this little journey to Montana—"

"Wyoming," Andrea corrected.

"Whatever," Ella replied with a teasing smile. "Anyway, this might turn into a good thing. With all those handsome men up there, you'll probably call me in a month saying that you're married and pregnant."

Andrea scoffed. "I doubt that."

"Honey, the thing most of the men up there can do is work with a few women every one hundred miles. Don't worry. As soon as they look at you, they'll come running in packs."

That was the last thing Andrea wanted, to be hounded by a bunch of horny men whose first reaction to a new woman would be to jump and hump her.

"I'm not like you. When I open my mouth, charming things never come out on their own. You can seduce any man into wanting you. I'm not that talented."

"Oh, yes you are. You're a Pisces. All you gotta do is bat those pretty, long lashes of yours and look at them with those bedroom eyes. You'll have them eating out of the palm of your hand. Better yet, eating your—"

"Don't say it."

Ella laughed, amused by the way her best friend's face registered mortification. "You're so modest. I'm sure a man up there will find you appealing and treat you like a princess. It's high time somebody did. And you might find your rugged Prince Charming up in Colorado."

Andrea smiled. "Wyoming."

"That too." Ella leaned in. "The question is, are you ready for this? It's a big step."

"Sure," Andrea answered with a confidence she wasn't sure she felt. "What do I have to lose?"

She almost lost her mind. It seemed like she had been driving forever. She had left Austin just before daybreak the day before. Andrea managed to drive twelve hours before she stopped for the night at a motel. She must have soaked in the bathtub for the longest time. Waking up and starting all over wasn't met with enthusiasm the next day but by twelve thirty that afternoon, she made it to Rock River.

She was ecstatic, almost enough to fall to her knees and kiss the ground in reverence. The ranch wasn't within the city limits. Her GPS had her circling the outskirts of town so much that she was starting to memorize the different avenues and streets. Both her gas tank and her stomach nearing empty, Andrea decided to swallow her pride and ask for help. She spotted a diner just north of town.

When she exited her car, she received a couple of curious stares from patrons leaving the establishment. Others she'd rather not revisit. Andrea gave them a timid smile, her nerves in shambles. Texas had plenty of farm and country land, but it still felt different. The slight chill of the late-April wind whipping through made her long for the warmer climate back home.

Maybe this wasn't a good idea. She was far from the usual sort that lived in Wyoming, her skin shades darker than what was the norm. But she had nothing to run back to. She was doing this for a reason. The least she could do was follow through, despite the regrets beginning to surface.

She walked into the diner and took a brief glance around. Andrea just missed the lunch-hour rush, if such a thing existed. She spotted a stool out of many unoccupied at the counter. Andrea had to lower her brown eyes when a lady, the "head honcho" of the place, gave her a brief perusal while conversing with another customer about to take their leave.

Andrea made her way to the vacant stool. Once seated, she wished she could pull the disappearing act of the century. She felt so uncomfortable and out of place, feeling the crush of unwelcome stares aimed at her.

Light cerulean eyes focused upon her once the waitress had bid the customer good day. The woman, maybe in her late fifties, wore a yellow button-down dress and a white apron that had seen better days. Her honey-colored hair was done up in a makeshift bun held together by a pencil. She had another one behind her ear, which she plucked and scribbled something on her notepad.

"Something I can help you with?" the lady drawled.

Andrea took a second to peek down the counter at a man eating something brown, but that was about it.

"What kind of stuff do you serve here?"

The lady blinked, staring at Andrea as if she had said the sky was falling in Mandarin.

"Food."

The response was dry, and Andrea wasn't sure how to take it.

"I'm aware of that but what type?"

The lady sighed, sticking the pencil back behind her ear. "Tell you what. How about I give you a menu and a few minutes for you to figure it out?" She fished beneath the counter for one, but this time, she also served Andrea with a kind smile which helped her relax. "Let me know when you're ready. Name's Shelley."

She went to assist another customer as Andrea studied the menu. Almost everything on it dealt with a bucket full of grease for the main course with a side of grease. Not her favorite delicacy. The safest thing she could find was a salad and a glass of water, but she hesitated to order.

At any rate, it made her hunger worse, and even that bucket of grease they were serving at every turn was starting to smell good. What little she had gotten from a convenience store earlier that morning had burnt off, and her stomach was letting her know just how it was feeling.

Shelley came back once Andrea had closed the menu, her mind still indecisive. "You ready to order, honey?"

Andrea rubbed her arm, a small, simple smile tipping a corner of her mouth. "I'm still trying to decide, but in the meantime, I was wondering if you can help me. I have an appointment at the South Land Ranch. My GPS is useless in getting me there. Do you think you can help me?"

"That happens a lot. But sure, I can get you there." Shelley proceeded to give Andrea directions through the southern part of town and which county road to take. All the while, Andrea drew a crude map along with it. During her impromptu creative session, the waitress studied her with an inquisitive gaze, and she waited until Andrea was done before she probed.

"I don't mean to be nosey, but why are you going there?"

"For an interview with a Mrs. Gemma Upshaw. Do you know her?"

Shelley smiled. "Yeah, I know her. She often plays bridge and canasta with my mother after church on Sundays. But I heard she's retiring and going to live closer to her kids in Nebraska." She leaned in closer, her smile fading as she neared. "Does the owner know you're coming?"

The introduction of that subject made what little of the happiness Andrea exhibited fade. She tucked a dark strand of her long hair behind her ear, her gaze returning to the menu. "I don't know. Mrs. Upshaw says it shouldn't be a problem since he's hardly at the house. It gives me the impression that I should avoid him."

"As you should. Not many females travel up that way and for good reason. They know not to."

Andrea gave a short, nervous giggle. "I guess no females allowed, huh?"

"That's exactly what I mean. Hardly any women have been up there since…" Her blue eyes wandered over the younger woman. "You're from out of town, so I'll spare you the details."

Andrea had never been so terrified to meet someone in all her life. The way they were painting him made it seem like he was a serial killer. She had been listening to too many true crime podcasts.

"I guess you know a lot about the owner. Mrs. Upshaw didn't say much besides that I would need to stay out of his way." Not to mention, she told Andrea this the day before she left Austin. She was just hoping the older woman was overreacting, but it seemed her employer's temperament was legendary.

The waitress gave her a pat on the hand. "He's fine once you get to know him. I used to babysit him years ago. He might be reserved, but he's hardworking. He's our own local celebrity, and he has the best horse ranch in the state." She paused. "However, if you're going to the ranch, maybe you can ask to follow him there."

Andrea had a sense of dread of what that insinuated. "Why?"

"Because he's over there in that corner," Shelley confirmed, gesturing her head in that direction.

Andrea's entire body tensed, and the feeling of dread sank to her stomach. However, her curiosity rose to the occasion. She just had to look.

Her eyes scanned the emptying diner and landed upon a man sitting in a booth in the corner. The low lighting made him appear so threatening but appealing. Andrea studied him as much as lighting and his gray Stetson would allow. He was absorbed in a newspaper while nursing his pie and black coffee. The paper was flat on the table, but with his bowed head, Andrea could see the form of masculine lips and the scruff of a dark five-o'clock shadow.

She browsed the outline of his body, seeing the muscles several years of working had done for him. The sun-kissed bronze of his skin was apparent from the well-sculpted arms the rolled-up sleeves of his shirt presented. She marveled at him turning the page, executing such strength in just his forearms. Andrea never thought an arm, muscled, veined, and dusted with hair, could ever turn her on like this. To imagine such power and strength embracing her, loving her…

Andrea forced her gaze away from him, resisting the potent temptation to stare longer. Taking a few breaths, she glanced at the waitress, who wore an amused smile on her face as if she had seen this kind of reaction before. Or felt it herself.

"*That's* Braden Sutherland?" Andrea managed to squeak out. "What's he doing here?"

"He comes in the same time every Wednesday for the usual blue plate special of cherry pie and coffee. It'll be a miracle if he orders anything else. But if you want to get to the ranch, I'm sure he won't mind if you follow him back. Wouldn't hurt to ask."

Andrea peered over her shoulder again. Just sitting there in the booth, the man seemed so formidable. Unapproachable. She was petrified to talk to him, afraid he might reach out and snap her neck before asking questions.

"I'd…rather not," she stammered. "I don't want to intrude."

The waitress placed a slender hand upon the slight flare of her hips. "Take it from me, honey. It's better to ask him here in public where it's safe than meet him later at the ranch. At least you'll have a fighting chance. He can be mighty surly in private."

He seems mighty surly in public, too. Each comment made Braden Sutherland out to be a hard-nosed bastard. Still, he didn't seem as dangerous as the threat she had left at home.

There was one way for her to be sure.

Andrea swallowed her anxiety as she stood and strode over to him. The walk took ages. Almost as if time stood still. She reached his table and waited for him to acknowledge her. But he didn't. An entire minute passed, and he was still absorbed in the paper.

The gray Stetson continued to do its job of keeping much of his face covered with its brim, but the whiff she caught of him was all male, a tantalizing combination of earth, sweat, and leather. She bit her lip, either out of impatience or to fight the urge to rip his hat off to feed her curiosity.

Standing there, she was growing more self-conscious by the moment. She refused to appear foolish a second more.

"Excuse me, Mr. Sutherland?"

No answer. He did manage to take a sip of his coffee.

"You *are* Braden Sutherland, right?"

"Depends on who's asking."

If Andrea weren't wearing a jacket, she would have quivered from the coolness lodged in that deep tone.

"I am. My name is Andrea Banks." She threw her hand out for him to take, but his head turned just enough to glance at it then return to his paper. Her confidence slumped. Andrea was embarrassed about the position he was putting her in. She could just feel a few pairs of interested eyes on them, since their conversation, one-sided as it was, was the only communication throughout the diner.

"You're the owner of the South Land Ranch, right?"

"You're asking an awful lot of questions, lady, when I don't even know you."

Andrea bristled at his callousness. It was no wonder people avoided him like the plague. "Maybe if you'd look at me instead of burying your nose in your paper, you wouldn't have that problem."

He paused, staring at one spot of the paper but not reading the print. He held it still, and she could have sworn she saw him clench his jaw. It was as if he were restraining himself, his body taut. She could feel her will dissolve into nothing, and part of her wanted to bolt from the diner. But he did something just as shocking before she could.

His head tilted, and gleaming back at her were two impassive, quicksilver eyes that didn't seem to just look at her but penetrated her very soul. Even with those hard, gray eyes that flashed with vehement intent, he was so good-looking. Andrea's breathing stilled as she studied his strong, masculine jaw peppered with scruffy hair for that rugged, unshaven look. He appeared to be someone who wouldn't put up with anyone's shit.

Andrea shivered as his eyes took a brief perusal down her body and up again. But his interest was short-lived, for he soon returned to his paper as if she were nothing special, which made Andrea's nostrils flare. She gritted her teeth so hard, it was a wonder they didn't break.

"I wanted to see if you didn't mind if I followed you to the ranch," she said, schooling her temper. She had to remember why she was here.

"I don't know what the hell for."

"I have an interview with Mrs. Upshaw, your housekeeper?"

It seemed as if it wouldn't have mattered if she were on a soapbox with a megaphone aimed at his ear. He turned another page and kept reading. This man was aggravating! He was either blowing her off or attempting to make her mad, which he was doing a good job of both.

"She told me to meet with her to see if I wanted the position."

"We ain't hiring."

"Excuse me?"

Out of the corner of her eye, she saw someone at the booth next to them throw down a few bills on the table and leave. She refused to be bullied by Braden Sutherland.

His gaze returned to her, cooler than before. "Read my lips, honey. We ain't hiring."

Despite that she found his lips appealing, she was far angrier than aroused. Andrea placed a hand on her hip. "I've come a long way to see her."

"Not my problem."

"Come on, Braden."

Andrea glanced over to the person who intervened on her behalf, leaning over the counter and leering at Braden.

"You know you're going to need a cook after Mrs. Gemma leaves."

He pointed in her direction, but his light eyes remained fastened to Andrea. "Stay out of this, Shelley. You know it's a general rule that no women are allowed on my ranch."

Shelley mocked Andrea's stance, placing a hand on her own hip. "And what? Mrs. Gemma's one of the guys?"

Braden's eyes flashed to her. "She's the *only* exception."

"Your exception needs to change," Andrea replied as she crossed her arms. "But you know what? I don't even know why I'm talking to you anyway. My appointment is with Mrs. Upshaw, and I just thought I'd break the ice beforehand, but I see your mother lacked in teaching you some manners."

It was out of her mouth before she could stop it. And Braden showed her just how much he didn't appreciate her comment. Andrea backed away a couple of steps as he rose out of the booth, clearing six-foot by a couple of inches. She wasn't the sort to seek out trouble or say anything she would regret, but this man riled her, and for no reason at all. As he towered over her, he appeared like he was about to give her the set-down of the century. Despite her trembling knees, she stood her ground, willing to take every abrasive word.

"You tell me, lady," he countered, his tone cold. "You can talk all you want about me, but I'll be damned if you bring my mother into this. And if you set one foot on my ranch, so help me, I'll personally throw you off."

"That's no way to treat a lady."

Everyone was so preoccupied with their confrontation, no one had heard the diner's door open. They all turned to see a man standing at the threshold before closing the door and approaching them with a confident gait. Andrea was awestruck. This man, who appeared to be a rancher like Braden, was a pretty boy compared to him. He had a boyish face that accompanied twinkling hazel eyes that gleamed at her in mischief. The smirk he wore was never ceasing, turning up one corner of his mouth. He wore a brown Stetson that wasn't low on his brow like Braden's, revealing his wavy blond hair interwoven with chocolate-brown curling at the nape of his neck.

Oh, yes, this man seemed to be nothing short of every woman's fantasy, and to be situated between two good-looking men, she couldn't stand it.

The man glanced over to the waitress and nodded. "Afternoon, Shelley."

"Caid," Shelley acknowledged.

"What the hell do you want?" Braden asked, not hiding his dislike.

"Saw your truck out in the parking lot. Thought I'd come to confirm the rumor that you turned down the sire and mare Andalusians from the Spanish royals."

"That's right. You know I don't do dressage horses or even warmbloods, no matter where they're from."

Caid feigned surprise. "That's right, because you're interested in racehorses. But I'm here to let you know that they came to me when you turned them down, and I've accepted their very generous offer."

Braden's face remained deadpan. "Good for you. You come to gloat?"

"Maybe. I think it's in order since I sealed the deal of a lifetime, it seems."

Braden smiled, although humor was lost on it. "But I bet it'll forever stick in your craw that they came to me first."

Andrea witnessed Caid flinch at the barb. Nevertheless, he recovered, retaining his ever-glowing smile. He then turned to Andrea, looking her up and down as his hazel eyes reflected curiosity.

"Well, well, Sutherland. Who's this pretty little creature?"

Braden didn't satisfy him with an answer. Caid took hold of her hand.

"I don't believe I've had the pleasure. Caid Marshall."

Andrea was speechless, her heart fluttering. The man had infinite charm, unlike his brooding counterpart who had done nothing but glare at Caid since his arrival.

"I'm—"

"Just leaving," Braden said and grabbed her arm to usher her outside.

Caid stood in their path. "Hold on. You can't herd her outta here like cattle. She has a right to be here just as much as anyone." His gaze moved to her. "You new in town?" he asked. She nodded. "What brings you here?"

"I *was* here for an interview at Mr. Sutherland's ranch, but he's outright determined to ban me from it because I'm a woman."

Caid chuckled. "Yeah, that seems about right. Some things never change, huh, Sutherland? Forever the woman-hater."

Braden's face remained expressionless at the taunt. "I *don't* hate women," he gritted. "I just don't want them on my ranch."

"You hear that? To me, that sounds like a man who hates women. Now, if you're looking for a job, I can find you one at mine. What can you do?"

"I can do anything if someone will give me a chance," she responded. "I can cook, clean, keep your books if someone's not doing them."

Caid's interest in her heightened, and with an ironic twist of fate, so did Braden's.

"Really?" Caid rubbed his stubble. "You any good?"

Andrea shrugged. "Should be. That's part of what I had gone to school for."

"Well, I've been struggling to keep up with them since my bookkeeper left a few months back," Caid explained.

"That's because Alicia was tired of keeping them *and* earning her living on her back."

Hazel eyes clashed with gray ones as Andrea cringed from the insult. "That's hitting below the belt."

"Gotta call it as I see it," Braden countered, evidently thirsting for a fight.

Caid turned his attention back to her, glaring sidelong at Braden. "Look, honey, you have nothing to worry about. I won't touch you. I'm a man of my word. Now, how about I give you a starting salary of four-fifty a week, room and board included?"

"Four-fifty?" Braden scoffed. "Hell, I'll make it an even five."

Caid flustered, and soon Andrea was forgotten as the two men became occupied with outdoing the other. "Six!"

"Seven twenty-five!"

"Eight—!"

"A thousand a week," Braden snapped as he fished his wallet out of his back pocket and plopped a few bills on the table. "Room and board with paid time off, and whatever benefits she wants, within reason." He grabbed her hand and touched the brim of his hat. "Afternoon."

Braden didn't leave without giving Caid a stern glare before dragging her outside. She resisted so she could collect her things from the counter as he continued to pull her behind him. Outside, Andrea fought against his firm grasp.

"Wait!" She stuck her heels into the rock-lain parking lot. "Wait a goddamn minute!" She jerked hard, getting her hand back.

Braden turned to scowl at her.

"I don't know who the hell you think you are, but if you think I'm going *anywhere* with you just because you think you've just won a pissing contest, you can shove it!"

Braden stepped closer, his gleaming gray eyes glaring down at her. "Lady, I've probably just made you the richest housekeeper in the whole damn state. Don't throw a fit with me. You might not realize it, but I've just done you a favor."

Andrea's brows shot up. "Oh, really? How?"

"I wouldn't trust a woman within fifty miles of Caid Marshall. He might be a man of his word, but believe me, he'd have you in bed come nightfall. So, if you want to be his next bed warmer, go on back there and take his offer. I dare you."

She didn't dare. She couldn't afford to. Andrea folded her arms, shifting her weight onto one foot. "Can I trust you to keep all those promises you just spewed in there?"

"I've broken many things but never my word."

He studied her as indecision crossed her features. No doubt one of the many things he'd broken was someone's face. From the way he acted in there, the slightest statement could set him off. Could she risk her life against a man of his consequence?

"Where did you say you were from?"

"Austin."

He frowned, pensive. "That's a long way from here. Any particular reason you chose Rock River to seek employment?"

Andrea fought to keep her face stoic, not wanting to relive the hell she had gone through. "There's nothing but painful memories back home. I wanted to move on, get a fresh start."

He was still suspicious of her. She could just tell by his stare and the mounting moments of silence between them. She had to glance away, which probably made her seem guilty. But it was his eyes. They were intimidating. He could strip her bare with just a look.

Braden shrugged. "Fair enough, but if you're coming to work for me, you better not let your personal life interfere. Is that clear?"

Andrea gave a tight smile. "Crystal."

"Good," he murmured. He started toward a burgundy GMC Sierra. "Stay behind me. If you get lost, don't bother trying to find the ranch. You can just keep driving to wherever the hell you want."

Andrea bristled as she returned to her car, but she hadn't closed her door before Braden backed out of his parking space and took off, his truck disappearing in a cloud of dust.

Chapter Two

Andrea was so angry she was seeing red, and it wasn't just from the red dirt on the country road. She knew Braden Sutherland was doing everything in his power to lose her. However, she managed to follow the faint clouds of dust he left behind and double-checked herself with the crude directions she had received from Shelley.

She didn't even have time to take in the splendor of the ranch sitting on acres upon glorious acres of land. Braden didn't react when she pulled in behind him, but he headed for a corral off to the left of the house. Andrea grabbed her bag, got out, and slammed her car door.

"Who in the hell do you think you are?" Andrea yelled. "You did that on purpose!"

He didn't respond. Nor did it seem like he cared to. He kept walking with a purposeful, masculine gait to get away from her.

She glanced up to the porch, her eyes coinciding with the warm, brown ones of an older woman smiling down at her.

Andrea stopped herself from running after him and pitching her shoe into his direction. She took a couple of deep breaths to collect herself. Andrea tucked a silky strand of hair behind her ear as she approached.

"Mrs. Upshaw?"

"You must be Andrea." The woman offered her hand. Andrea took it after she had mounted the stairs leading up to an expansive porch. Mrs. Upshaw patted it with her free hand. "I'm so glad you could make it."

"No thanks to him," Andrea huffed. She took a moment to glare in the direction he had gone. The breath caught in her throat at the way he was staring at her from the threshold of the stables. Their gazes locked in a few intense seconds before he disappeared inside. Both missed Mrs. Upshaw's grin as it widened until Andrea glanced back to her.

"Is he always like this?" Andrea inquired.

"He never used to be," the older woman said but left the vague explanation at that. Although Andrea was an outsider, she had a hard time imagining that man ever being nice to anyone, even as a little boy. It just appeared that the joys of childhood were lost on someone like that.

The housekeeper placed a gentle hand upon the small of Andrea's back but paused before ushering her inside. "Do you want to get your things from the car, dear?"

"I'm not sure how long I'll stay."

Mrs. Upshaw disclosed a look of shock. "Why, you've just got here."

"Believe me, if *he* has anything to do with it, he'll make sure I'm thrown off in the next few minutes."

The elder chuckled. "Well, it'll give you plenty of time to enjoy some chicken casserole I have heating in the oven."

At the sound of "chicken casserole," her stomach grumbled loudly enough for them both to hear. Andrea wrapped her arms around her waist, shame appearing on her face. Mrs. Upshaw laughed again.

"Come on, my dear. If we have a few minutes, then we're going to enjoy what time we have. After all, not many women come this way, and you've already met the reason."

It was no wonder no one of the feminine persuasion wanted to spend more than two seconds on the place. The two possible reasons someone would put up with his attitude was because of his rugged good looks and his ever-expanding bank account. Neither was worth it to Andrea.

Andrea allowed Mrs. Upshaw to lead the way into the sprawling mansion. Despite the few hallways that branched out from the foyer, Andrea could almost tell how to get to the kitchen blindfolded. The fanatical aroma floating through the air was a dead giveaway. When they arrived in the kitchen, Andrea was taken aback by its old-fashioned décor that had a woman's touch. It was what she would call refreshing and cheery, with a canary-yellow wallpaper of happy daisies. Lace curtains covered the window over the sink and two windows in front of the kitchen table.

From the white marble countertops and cabinets to the clean linoleum kitchen floor, the room was spotless. There was even a vase of daisies to brighten up the kitchen even more, although Andrea didn't think it was possible to do so. To say the least, it was a kitchen far from drab and dreary.

"Go ahead and have a seat at the table, Andrea. I'll serve us."

"You don't need help?" Andrea offered as she set her bag in a chair adjacent to her. "I'll be more than happy to since you prepared the meal."

The older woman declined the help and proceeded to bustle about. In a way, Mrs. Upshaw reminded Andrea of her maternal grandmother. Her father allowed her to stay with her in Bastrop in the years following her mother's death. She was her influence, and until she had turned thirteen, her grandmother was her world. She was the one who taught Andrea to cook, passing along the family recipes. Andrea didn't dare compare her own cooking to her grandma's, but she got along okay.

And like her grandmother, Mrs. Upshaw exuded the same homey feel that made Andrea want to go up to her and embrace her. She had longed for the effortless comfort her grandmother always gave. If she hadn't passed a decade ago, Andrea would be a little better off.

The emotions must have been displayed on her face as plain as day, and the ever-present smile Mrs. Upshaw wore dissipated a little once she had turned away from the stove, two plates of steaming, delicious casserole in each hand.

"What is it, dear?" she asked with concern.

Andrea glanced away, aware of some tears forming at the bittersweet memories. "Nothing," she replied. She rubbed her eyes in the pretense that she was tired. "It's just that you remind me of my grandma. Just dawned on me how much I miss her."

A plate was settled before her. The delicious smell tantalized her tastebuds, and she felt her mouth water. Mrs. Upshaw offered her some tea then settled at the table beside her. "If I may ask," she prompted, "what happened to your grandmother?"

"She had diabetes, bad to the point she had her leg amputated. Then after they brought her into recovery, she started to go into heart failure. Grandma had a weak heart from a childhood illness, and I guess the traumatic strain of the amputation took its toll. It was the first operation she ever had, and she never got to come home after it."

Mrs. Upshaw's face displayed her sympathy. "I'm sorry to hear that. It's never easy, losing a loved one. I lost my mother not too long ago, and my husband longer than that, so I understand." She took a moment to take a couple of bites of the casserole. "What about your parents, dear? Did they mind that you came so far from home?"

Andrea had paused for a second but then continued to fork a piece of chicken. "Both my parents have died. My mom when I was little and my father a few months ago."

"My Lord. You don't have anyone, do you?"

Andrea shook her head. "No, ma'am. I do have an aunt, my mother's sister, and her kids. They live in a different state, and I see them for life's tragedies. No. I'm afraid it's just me against the world. But to be honest, I don't know what I'll do if I can't get this position. Is there some work in town?"

Mrs. Upshaw took a long sip of tea. "Some here and there. Not all at once. A lot is gone before you know it."

"I have to find something if I don't get on here."

"What'll stop you, dear?"

Andrea snorted. "Two words: Braden Sutherland. Had it his way, I wouldn't even be here right now."

"I was surprised when I saw you pull up after him and start screaming at him. No one stands up to Braden."

And it was no wonder. If Andrea had to decide between Braden and a rattlesnake, she would rather take her chances with the rattlesnake any day of the week.

"I was wondering," Mrs. Upshaw began, "how you managed to follow him here?"

Andrea proceeded to fill her in, all the way up to screaming at him from the driveway. The older woman's shoulders shook with mirth. "So, he gave in, didn't he?"

"Too easily. I'd like to be here on my own merit, not because he had a bravado moment due to too much testosterone."

Mrs. Upshaw was about to respond when the kitchen door swung open. Andrea's eyes widened as Braden's tall frame lumbered into the kitchen. His eyes collided with hers, and though his gaze was hard and unwavering, she found it almost impossible to look away as if her gaze were pulled by a magnetic force.

Out of respect, he took off his worn but much-loved gray hat, displaying the dark, chocolate-brown hair matted to his head. Even though it was cropped within an inch from his scalp, Andrea could tell that his hair had a natural curl. There were a few curls that refused to lay dormant from him wearing a hat or perspiration.

With Stetson in hand, he pointed his forefinger at her, his face set in a stern fashion. She waited for him to tell her to get off his land, but at least she was able to enjoy a meal and a good conversation beforehand.

"Starting right now, you're on trial. You show me your skills in the kitchen, with my books, and around the house, and if you got what it takes, I'll let you stay. If you're not cut out for it, then you're outta here. Do you understand me?"

Even for him to budge for a trial basis was surprising to her. "For how long?"

"Could be a week." His eyes glimmered. "Could be an hour. Who's to say? But before you go into a tirade of how unfair I'm being, you'll still get paid for what you've worked. I'm not a complete bastard."

No doubt that could be debated. Andrea shrugged a slender shoulder with an uncaring air. "Fine."

Two dark eyebrows shot up. "Fine? No questions? No screaming? No comebacks?"

Her lips parted, wanting to respond with all the fire and brimstone he expected, but she clamped her mouth shut. The way he was staring at her, the gleam from those intense, gray eyes made her aware of what he was doing. He was welcoming a fight, and he could, in his own sick, perverted way, be enjoying the banter or was searching for an excuse to throw her off the ranch. Well, she wasn't going to give him the satisfaction either way.

Andrea licked her lips and sat there silent as she continued to hold his gaze. Braden rested his forearms on the back of the chair across from her and leaned forward. The wood of the chair groaned beneath the strapping weight of him. That same, humorless smile he wore at the diner resurfaced. His eyes became cooler.

"What, honey? At a loss for words? Huh?" He edged closer, his demeanor intriguing and holding her captivated. "Where's all that fire you were flaming at me at the diner?"

"Braden," Mrs. Upshaw cautioned.

"It's okay, Mrs. Upshaw," Andrea said, finding the will to break free of his gaze. "Since he's the owner of this place, it's not wrong of him to want to test my skills. After all, it is kind of weird to hire a cook when you haven't seen what all they can do. I could say that I can cook and be lying. So, I agree with Mr. Sutherland." Her eyes then returned to his. "If he wants a demonstration of my skills, I won't disappoint."

"Good," he concurred but had stated it in a way that he couldn't care less. "In that case, how about letting our new cook throw together tonight's dinner? There's still plenty of daylight if you wanna run into town to pick up anything you might need…" He cocked his head as he eyed her. Andrea's stomach dropped as she saw the devilish twinkle in his eyes. "On second thought, Mrs. Gemma had just gone to town yesterday to pick up some things from the store. Any *true* cook can make a meal out of what's already here."

The bastard! He reveled in being a complete ass and it appeared that other people's pain was his pleasure. Braden replaced his hat low upon his brow so that the shadow of the brim returned him to the look that made him appear so dangerous.

"I want dinner on the table by seven. Not a second later. If so, you can just chuck what you've made and get the hell off my property."

Andrea glared at him as he walked toward the door. He rested his hand upon the doorknob before glancing over his shoulder.

"And enough for us. I don't want any of my men getting sick." He walked out, leaving her in a mess of emotions.

Andrea had never been so angry at someone in her entire life. It was something about Braden Sutherland that just made her want to lash at him. And yet, beneath the hostility, there was something that had ignited her interest in him as well. She hadn't known the man for two hours, but that didn't cancel out the thoughts she was having. Intimate thoughts she had never had of any man. Wouldn't Ella be proud of her ability to respond to the idyllic essence of a man? Even one with Braden's callous attitude?

She stared at the door seconds too long. Andrea was drawn out of her reverie by the sound of a chair scraping across the floor. Mrs. Upshaw rose from her seat and collected the dirty plates. "Seems like you have a lot to do before seven," she said as she carried them to the sink. "Let me know what you might want to cook, and we'll see if I can deliver."

Andrea rested her head upon her hand. "I'm glad he didn't tell me I had to make something out of two crackers and a turnip." She sighed as she rose from her seat and scooted her chair in place. "If he ever decides to get married, I'd give the bride the Medal of Honor. But I think no sane woman would do it even if you paid her."

Andrea was too preoccupied to notice how the older woman paused while rinsing the plates. She resumed, placing them on the drying rack.

"Mrs. Upshaw, what about the guys?"

The older woman turned to her, wiping her hands off with a cup towel. "No need to be so formal with me, honey. You can call me Gemma or Mrs. Gemma like everyone else. *Mrs. Upshaw* makes me sound like a stuffy old maid." She chuckled. "As for the hands, you don't have to worry about them. I'll take care of that. You have your hands full with trying to impress Braden."

She didn't want to think about it. Andrea had no idea what she was going to cook. Perhaps once she assessed her available ingredients, she'd get a good idea.

Andrea smoothed a wayward strand of hair behind her ear. "Well, we don't want to keep Mr. High and Mightiness waiting on his meal, do we?" She meandered over to the fridge to open the freezer door. "Now to see if I can make something he'll choke on."

Andrea seemed to have gotten her wish except he didn't keel over. He just glowered at her from across the table with a look that had "damn you" written all over it. This time, she couldn't hold his fierce gaze. She was ashamed of herself. She could cook better than this, but he wouldn't know that. Not with what she had to show for it.

This was just one of the instances where she didn't familiarize herself with her appliances and didn't pay attention to what she was doing. Not every stove was made the same. She knew this, yet nerves and negligence had her at fault.

Andrea had decided on something simple: fried pork chops, rice, and string green beans. She had set the pork chops in the sink to thaw then left the kitchen for Mrs. Gemma to prepare dinner for the hands. After she got her things from the car, she was shown to her room upstairs. The room almost reminded her of her bedroom back home. The lavender color of the walls, the long lacy curtains, and white furniture made everything seem so pristine and untouchable. But once she sat down on the downy bed, Andrea passed out for what she thought was a second until she woke up and realized that it was approaching six thirty.

She had thirty minutes. Andrea rushed downstairs to see Mrs. Gemma wrapping up her cooking, toting a large pot outside. Andrea proceeded then to whip together her dinner. She floured and cooked the chops, all the while multitasking with the green beans and the rice. These things she could make blindfolded, but the way the pork chops and rice turned out, it seemed as if she had worn one. Turning her back on the pork chops for what appeared to be a minute was enough to have them burn. The rice soon ended up like the pork chops, burnt and overcooked. But at least one thing turned out okay.

"Well, the green beans are good," complimented Mrs. Gemma. "You put some butter in it, didn't you?"

Andrea nodded, a slight smile displayed upon her lips as her eyes returned to Braden with hesitance. His glare hadn't wavered. The single thing that moved was his chest as he breathed, but it appeared as if he was restraining himself from leaping over the table.

He then pushed his plate away, glaring down at the charred contents. "My men can't live off of green beans," he grumbled. His gaze locked with hers, retaining the same, subzero stare. "What do you call this?"

"Not my best."

Braden scoffed. "That's yet to be seen. This ain't edible. Hell, not even a hungry stray dog would eat this. Couldn't even bribe him to."

Andrea bit the inside of her cheek to refrain from saying anything. She'd love to smack that look off his face. "I can do way better than this. All I'm asking is for another chance."

"To do what? Try and kill me with this…stuff that you call cooking?"

"No," she replied. "To show you that it won't happen again. Now, if you want to kick me off the ranch, you can go right ahead. Most of my things are still packed, but I'd rather you reconsider. Please."

The last thing she wanted to do was beg, but she needed this job, and if she had to beg for another chance, she'd do it to buy more time.

He took the napkin from his lap and tossed it upon the plate. He leaned in, making the 'okay' sign with his right hand, holding up his last three fingers. "You get three strikes," he forewarned. He lowered his middle finger. "Strike one."

Braden then got up from the table. She heard his footsteps retreat down the hall until he closed the door to his study. Andrea glanced at Mrs. Gemma, whose face displayed nothing short of worry. Andrea reached across the table and placed her hand on Mrs. Gemma's. "Please say you won't leave for a while. If you're not in the house, I swear it won't be my so-called bad cooking that'll kill him."

Mrs. Gemma patted the younger woman's hand with assurance. "Don't worry. I won't leave unless I know for certain that you have the position. Call me crazy, but I'd rather you have it than a lot of people in this town who I've known for years. I've never met someone so sincere."

Andrea snorted, leaning back in her chair and crossing her arms. "Too bad he doesn't have your point of view." She growled in frustration. "That man, I swear! How can someone be so...so...cruel?"

Mrs. Gemma stood from the table and began collecting plates. Andrea did the same and followed her into the kitchen. She sighed as she placed the dishes beside the sink. "All I can say is that he's his father's son. And I was praying that Braden wouldn't turn into the exact person his father was. He hasn't, but..." She shook her head, her brow wrinkling as she ran warm water into the sink. "Every time I look at Braden, I hurt. Hard to accept that he used to be the most loving little boy." She added soap and placed a couple of dishes in. "I suppose with the way life has treated him, I almost expected it. But I'd take this over another outcome any day."

Andrea rested her hip against the kitchen counter, pensive. Part of her fought against feeling sorry for him, though she couldn't subdue the fact that she was curious. "My life hasn't been a frolic through a field of flowers either. But I'm not taking my frustrations out on anyone else."

The older woman gave Andrea that luminous smile that made her return the gesture. "That's why I've taken a liking to you already. You haven't let the hand life has dealt you get you down."

"Because there are more things to worry about." Then Andrea noticed what Mrs. Gemma was starting to do. "No, no. It's my mess. I should do the dishes."

"You've had a long day, sweetie. Me getting the dishes just this once won't hurt. Why don't you go ahead and go to bed?"

"You sure?" Andrea questioned.

Mrs. Gemma nodded. "You have to impress Braden in the morning so every minute of sleep will count. I can finish here."

"Thank you, Mrs. Gemma. Goodnight."

"Goodnight," said Mrs. Gemma.

Andrea strode down the hall, but her footsteps slowed as she approached Braden's study. Just like its owner, the door was broad, hard, and impossible to penetrate. Mrs. Gemma had given Andrea a little insight into the man who was Braden Sutherland. It made her wonder if life hadn't been so cruel to him, would the harsh lines of his face be softer due to smiles? With all the cold looks, it was a frightening thought to picture him smiling at all. Still, was such a man capable of emotion? Were those icy gray eyes capable of melting due to warmth? Humor? Or even for the passion of a woman?

Her body throbbed at imagining such a man with her, demonstrating to her an ardor he could show her. And God played a joke on her while she was conjuring up images that made her blush, for she was far from composed when Braden swung the door open. Andrea jumped, her heart damn near leaping from her chest and scurrying down the hall.

Braden leaned his well-structured body against the doorframe, eyeing her with those damnable eyes that had all but stripped her stupid during dinner. They remained aloof and unreadable, even as they roved down her body, stopping at her breasts. Andrea flushed, feeling nipples peaking to make themselves known. She folded her arms.

"Can I help you with something?" he drawled.

She stared at him a couple of beats before continuing down the hall and made her way upstairs, feeling his gaze on her the entire way.

Andrea thought the next morning was going to turn out better. She woke up, showered, dressed, and headed downstairs. Mrs. Gemma was already up, making pancakes, eggs, and bacon for the guys. She smiled as Andrea, still half asleep, dragged into the kitchen.

"Morning, sweetie," she chimed in her usual cheerful mode. Andrea was glad that someone was happy it was five thirty in the morning. "Did you sleep well?"

"Pretty good, thank you," Andrea replied. "I'm not used to getting up so early, not even when I had to go to class."

"I'm sure you'll get used to it once you find your sleeping pattern." She placed the eggs on a serving plate. "Can you do me a favor and put some coffee on? I'll get out of your hair in a moment."

Andrea made the coffee and Mrs. Gemma put the finishing touches on breakfast before taking it outside. Andrea washed out the skillet and started making breakfast for the three of them. She made omelets with bits of sausage and cheese. Then she made some hash browns to go on top. By the time she had set their plates on the kitchen table, Braden made his appearance.

"Good morning," Andrea remarked as she moved about the kitchen. She felt his gaze follow her as he stood poised in the doorway, probably trying to get accustomed to this strange woman bustling around. "Grab a seat. Breakfast is ready."

He trudged in just as Mrs. Gemma came back with the empty serving dishes. She sat in her usual seat on one side, Braden at the head of the small table. Andrea retrieved and lifted the coffeepot. "Coffee?"

Braden grumbled something along the lines that he wanted some. Andrea poured him a cup. She poured Mrs. Gemma some then filled her own. Putting the pot away, Andrea returned to the table to find Braden glowering at his plate.

Lord, what now?

His unbendable gaze lifted to drill into her. Andrea got edgy and shifted uncomfortably in her chair. Talk about putting the fear of God into someone.

"What the hell do you call this?"

Andrea balked, but she couldn't help shooting off a smart comment once she regained her tongue. "Breakfast."

"What the hell do you call this?" he repeated even louder as if she hadn't heard him the first time.

"What? It's an omelet. I'm sure even you have seen them before."

Braden leaned closer to her. "Around here, you have to cook things in mass and be quick about it. You can't just take your time in putting love and care in every little fluff."

Andrea could have strangled him. Instead, she stared at him, incredulous. "Are you kidding me? You're getting all in a huff over how I did the eggs? They're still eggs!"

His face became sterner. "I take my eggs one way: scrambled." He took a sip of the coffee, and his taste buds didn't approve. Braden looked as if he wanted to spit it out on Mrs. Gemma's polished floor; however, he decided to be a man about it and swallowed. He held up his hand, his fingers in the same 'okay' sign before lowering his middle and ring fingers.

"That's two strikes, honey," he murmured. "One more, and you're gone."

He scooted back his chair and rose to his feet. All Andrea could do was stare daggers at the man as he went over to the counter, took the coffeepot, walked over to the sink, and proceeded to pour it down the drain.

"Coffee's terrible, by the way," he critiqued. "Not strong enough."

If it weren't for the tender hand Mrs. Gemma had on Andrea's arm, she would have hailed Braden with a barrage of words and fists. "Just because it's not made like the sludge you're used to, doesn't mean it's not bearable to anyone else," she gritted out.

Braden pretended as if he hadn't heard her. Once the kitchen door slammed behind him, Andrea popped to her feet.

"The man's impossible! This is the best I've ever cooked an omelet, and he acted as though it offended everything he stood for."

However, she did place a lot of attention to make sure they were done right, from grating the cheese to the little pieces of sausage in between.

"Forgive him, dear. He's used to doing things his way. Once you get into a habitual routine, it's hard to break it." She rubbed her tired brow. "Perhaps I was setting you up for failure. I should have warned you before you drove all this way…"

Andrea sat down and placed her hand upon the other woman's. "There's no need to apologize. It's not your fault. He's just an insensitive ass—" She gulped when she caught the look Mrs. Gemma gave her. She cleared her throat. "He's just insensitive to other people's feelings. If I screw up lunch, I'm done."

Andrea tucked her hand beneath her chin, losing herself to her thoughts. *What recipe would help Braden change his mind?*

It then came to her. One of the rare recipes she could claim came close to her grandmother's. And if Braden Sutherland could resist what she was planning to whip up, she could kiss her chances for a new start goodbye.

There was one option Andrea refused to acknowledge, though: it would be a cold day in hell before she went back home. A cold day indeed.

Chapter Three

Andrea made sure that what she made for lunch would be something he couldn't resist. Despite having gone upstairs after breakfast and packing her things, it wouldn't hurt to give it one valiant effort before he chased her off. But she could say her grandmother was smiling down from heaven. She nailed her granny's homemade chicken pot pie. Since the weather was a little cool, it was a good thing to have to warm the insides. And a way to distract Andrea from how she wanted Braden to warm hers.

She knew the man was on his way to the house, but each time he filled that doorway, or any doorway for that matter, Andrea's breath caught in her throat. Despite how he acted toward her, she couldn't dismiss that she was attracted to the belligerent ass. Why in so short a time, Andrea thought of him bending her to him and stretching her wide in different ways. So...so many ways. Her body flooded with heat to the point she had to hold onto the counter, feeling herself get wet at the thought. What would Ella think of her now? She was lusting after the man who was doing his damnedest to get rid of her.

How far would she be willing to go not to leave?

Braden strode into the kitchen like he was the lord of the manor. He washed up at the sink, took off his hat, then sat at the table without a word. Andrea served him and Mrs. Gemma before joining them. They ate in silence. She stole a few sly glances to see if Braden had face-planted into the bowl. But he had his head bowed over his meal, his eyes not straying far from it.

Due to nerves, Andrea didn't have an appetite, but it wasn't long until she heard the scraping of Braden's spoon against the sides and bottom of the bowl, scooping up the last bit of pot pie. He wiped his mouth with a napkin, got up, and left the room. Andrea stared at Mrs. Gemma, dumbfounded.

"Don't tell me he's about to get his shotgun?"

Mrs. Gemma was about to answer when he reentered, placing his Stetson back upon his head. He didn't glance her way as he headed straight toward the door, but he did manage to toss behind him, "Hope dinner's just as good."

Andrea and Mrs. Gemma exchanged a look. Braden's concession was so surprising, Andrea sat stunned for several moments. She was so convinced that he would for sure toss her off the ranch, she hadn't even thought about dinner.

What a baffling man Braden Sutherland was.

Once they had finished lunch, Andrea followed the veteran housekeeper and assisted with chores. She learned specific ways things were to be done and what time to be finished by. She then prepared dinner of Salisbury steak with gravy, garlic mashed potatoes, and salad. And like before, Braden sauntered in, washed up, ate, then left the table with neither compliments nor warning that she had less than three minutes to get out.

Growing accustomed to his uncaring attitude, Andrea cleared the table but was shooed from the kitchen when Mrs. Gemma insisted on doing the dishes. Andrea walked down the hall, but slowed as she approached Braden's study. The door was wide open, but he was nowhere in sight. She didn't even think about it before she crossed the threshold into the very masculine study.

Every facet of the room bespoke of a man, from the leather couches to the dark mahogany of his furniture and floor, and walls painted a dark gray. Brooding and foreboding just like the man who occupied the space. She was almost intoxicated being there. Braden's unique smell seemed ingrained in every square inch. The combination of everything made her head swim.

Andrea's attention caught on a portrait that hung behind Braden's desk. A man with a cold stare much like the man she often dreamt about, a knee raised and his left arm bracing on it. But his gaze was merciless. She surmised he must be his father, and something about him didn't sit well with her. It was as if her intuition told her that he was the reason Braden became the hardened, imperious man he was now.

She bent her eyes to his desk, noticing how everything on it was in disarray. Haphazard stacks of folders and papers lined the outer edge of the desk. The inner space wasn't much better, but smack in the middle of it was the huge leatherbound ledger. Curious, Andrea sat down at his desk and opened it to browse the detailed numbers that were written by a masculine hand.

"What are you doing here?"

He asked the question in a deep, grating voice. Andrea didn't show how much it stirred her, setting goosebumps along her skin as if he had whispered it in her ear. But she kept calm as she turned a page.

Out of the corner of her eye, Braden neared her and went to stare through the blinds at the window. She kept her eyes on the page but read nothing. This was the closest she had been to the man in such a confined space. She glanced over at him as he stood there. He had changed clothes, the scent of cleanliness about him from his shower. His dark brown hair was wet, slicked back from his forehead, a few renegade tendrils curling at his nape. How she wanted to play with his curls, grabbing onto them as she kissed him, and letting him kiss her anywhere and everywhere...

Her gaze flitted away when he caught her ogling him but pretended to appear indifferent. "Your books are a mess," she pointed out.

He sighed, turning so his back leaned against the window frame. "I've noticed."

"You know, they have software that'll make this a lot easier."

"Why should I let a machine do something I can do myself? Believe me, honey, I'm just as capable of doing figures."

Andrea rolled her eyes heavenward before directing them back to the books. "It shows. There hasn't been a notation here since three months ago. If you don't have the time to do them yourself, why didn't you hire someone to keep them for you?"

"Because no one wants to deal with my temper."

"Small wonder there," Andrea muttered under her breath.

Braden remained quiet for a beat. "Something you wanna say to me?"

After such a rough start, the last thing Andrea needed was to say the wrong thing to make him change his mind. She thought of how she was going to respond before opening her mouth. "Look, this is your ranch. You're good at running the place, so you can do things as you see fit. I'm not going to challenge your authority. I'm here to do a job. We can go a whole week without saying fifteen words to each other, but if you have a problem or concern about the way I handle things, we'll deal with it." Her gaze diverted from his. "I don't think it'll hurt us if we never get along on a personal level. We keep this professional and above board and things can run smoothly. Don't you agree?"

He made her nervous by the way he scrutinized her now. Andrea connected her eyes with his again. For the longest minute of her life, he held her gaze before pushing away from the window. "Mrs. Gemma says you have a fairly good grasp on how things are here. Except you have one more test before I hire you." He turned toward her as he rounded the desk. "Cooking breakfast for everyone tomorrow will determine it. The strikes still apply. No negotiations if you don't make the grade. Understood?"

She saluted him. "Sir, yes, sir!"

He showed no sign of irritation or humor, which would shock Andrea if he had the latter. Instead, Braden stood there, those gray eyes piercing and incisive as they gazed down at her. She quivered, closing the ledger as she got to her feet.

"Well, I'll go over these again in my free time." She went around the right side of the desk to avoid having to brush his body to pass. "Goodnight," she replied as she stepped out and toward the stairs, her nerves racking within her.

The next morning, Andrea came with her "A" game. There were bowls and serving platters stacked with pancakes, two different kinds of sausages, bacon, oatmeal, biscuits, and scrambled eggs. She made everything except the coffee, which Braden had already made to suit his tastes. Andrea would stick to orange juice.

Mrs. Gemma collected them all and served the men, then came back to join Andrea in the kitchen to eat. Braden ate outside with the guys. Part of her was relieved not to have those silver eyes of his glaring at her from across the table. The other part, in a twisted way, missed the way he did stare, although she had a feeling he wasn't looking at her because he was attracted to her. Even when he had noticed her heaving chest the other day, he didn't show a flicker of interest. He appeared, as always, impassive and unimpressed. That knocked her a bit, but he seemed to be a self-proclaimed woman-hater. What did someone like her have to prove to someone who wouldn't want her even if she was gold-plated with diamonds?

The two women ate and cleaned their plates. Then, for the first time ever, Mrs. Gemma had Andrea follow her outside. She hadn't left the house for almost a couple of days, opting for the porch swing to rest at times during the day. But other than Braden, she hadn't seen any of the other men up close and personal, and no wonder. When they saw her, none of them hid their curiosity.

Mrs. Gemma gathered the plates while Andrea collected the serving bowls and utensils. All the while, they murmured among themselves until someone asked, "So, Mrs. Gemma, who's this sweet little thing?"

"Someone who's not interested in dates with you, Cooper."

The group of men laughed and taunted. Even the man named Cooper, a burly man of about forty, laughed, despite the delivered set-down by Mrs. Gemma. Andrea kept her eyes down on what she was doing. When she collected a dish beside Braden, she could feel his eyes on her, but she didn't dare meet them.

"Who said it was Mrs. Gemma hiding her?" said another. "Could it be Braden who realized his dick is going to explode from not having a woman in a while?"

"Dane!"

Andrea's wide eyes went to Braden who looked murderous.

"She's not accustomed to how we do things around here, so I'd recommend easing off until she does…if ever," Braden said.

Her gaze narrowed on him. "Colorful language doesn't scare me, especially coming from a man, I'm sorry, a jackass like yourself."

Some "*ohhh*s" came from the table, along with a hearty round of laughter. She may have jeopardized everything by calling him out like that, but the look on his face was priceless.

He sat there silent, as if his mind were searching for a suitable comeback. None came, but his eyes spoke volumes.

"I knew I'd like her," Cooper guffawed. "Any woman willing to tell off Braden Sutherland is all right in my book." He stood and extended his hand to her. "Sam Cooper. Cooper to closer acquaintances and pretty women."

Andrea smiled. "Nice to meet you, Cooper. I'm Andrea."

Another hand, not much older than Andrea, stood and took her hand. "Oh, Andrea, where have you been all my life?"

"Put a sock in it, Kel," Mrs. Gemma teased. "As you can see, that's our little charmer, Kel. And his outspoken brother, Dane."

Dane nodded in greeting. Around the table, she heard the rest of the names: J.D., Buddy, Sal, Quentin, and Handy, Braden's oldest hand. There were four others who worked for Braden, but they were married and ate breakfast with their families before coming to work.

"Pleasure to meet you all."

Handy cleared his throat and glanced in the direction of the older woman. "You sure are looking mighty fine today, Mrs. Gemma."

"Don't you start in on me this morning, Handy," she scolded, but Andrea could see the faint blush that came upon her face.

"I have to compliment a beautiful woman when I see her," he replied. "Unlike some of these younglings around here, I know how to talk to a woman."

"And when was the last time you had a woman?" Dane retorted.

Handy cleared his throat. "I'd respond to that, but since we're in the presence of a pretty young lady, I won't insult her with being vulgar."

Andrea grinned. "Thank you, Handy, but as I told Braden, it'll take more than Dane's mouth to run me off. Unless your boss fires me after today."

"Why would he?" Cooper responded. "If he's going to fire you for calling him what he is, then he's a flat-out coward."

"I agree," said Quentin. His eyes, she noticed, never strayed far from her. It already filled her with alertness. "So, are you the one who cooked all this for us?"

"Not unless you guys didn't enjoy it, then I won't own up to it."

"It was very good, Miss Andrea," Handy complimented. "Helped myself twice."

"Three times here," Cooper chimed. Andrea was glad she had cooked enough. Judging the redheaded, two-hundred-and-something pounds of muscle, Cooper looked like he could have inhaled it all without leftovers.

Braden glanced around the table at each of the men whose attention was upon her. He took a slow sip of his coffee, his customary scowl in place. "If you're done ogling, I suggest you get to work. We got less than two weeks to break in that Thoroughbred before his owner gets antsy. Donovan still wants that mare brought here next week, so we better get a move on."

To each of them, Braden issued orders that weren't repeated twice. They each left the table, saying good day to Andrea and thanking her for the wonderful breakfast. Braden finished off his coffee, and without a word, followed his men to the corral. Andrea shrugged as she collected the rest of the dishes and returned to the kitchen.

"So, it seems that Handy's pretty sweet on you."

The older woman waved off the suggestion. "He's always been, but I'm afraid I'm too old for romance and being chased after. After I lost my Turner, I haven't wanted to be in love again." She sighed. "Anyway, it won't matter. If things here become stable enough, I hope to be out of your hair by the end of next week."

"Oh, not so soon?"

"I've been around this place for most of my life. My father worked here, as did my husband. But now I need a change of scenery. I will miss this place."

Andrea rested her hands upon the counter. "What if the day after you leave something happens here, like homicide?"

Mrs. Gemma dried her hands on a cup towel before patting Andrea's cheek. "You'll be fine. If you can stick up to Braden as you did out there, I know you will."

Weeks had passed since Mrs. Gemma had left, and so far, no homicide had been reported. However, Andrea had some close calls of wanting to bash Braden over the head with something out of pure frustration.

Although Andrea stayed connected with the former housekeeper, not having another woman at the ranch made it difficult to pass what spare time she had. Outside of Ella, she had also befriended Shelley, the waitress from the diner. Andrea saw her about once a week when she went into town to buy groceries. A little bit of female companionship was better than none.

Andrea didn't lack in her duties either. She cooked and cleaned on a tight schedule. The first week by herself, she soaked in the bathtub, her muscles aching from all the bending and straining, but now she had become accustomed to the work. And after dinner some nights out of the week, Braden would sit down with her to go over the ledgers. She did her best to keep everything professional, but she couldn't manage a coherent sentence without getting a whiff of him or studying his handsome features in profile.

Other than the books, they barely said a word to each other. A few grumbled "good mornings" or "good evenings" was the extent of what he had to say. She didn't push for conversation because she found it pointless. For all he cared, she could go live on the farthest moon in the solar system.

Some peaceful evenings that weren't too cold, Andrea would go outside and watch the guys wrap up for the day or spend time to herself on the porch swing. Sometimes, a few of the guys would come up and chat before going to the bunkhouse or out to a bar on the weekends. Quentin Doyle talked for what seemed like forever. She obliged, though looks he'd give between gaps of their conversation unnerved her. But when Braden came around, he couldn't scramble away fast enough.

She stayed close to the ranch because of feeling safe. For the first time in a while, Andrea felt at peace. The thoughts of Gaines and her father were still on her mind, but it wasn't as prominent as it once had been. But she couldn't get accustomed to this feeling of ease. The first turbulent burst from her past could send her fleeing from this place she now called home. She prayed she could stay for a little while before Gaines found her. She hoped to hell he never did.

One Friday night, Andrea found herself walking to the huge stables and corral. Some of the guys had gone into town to the local bar, affording her the peace to explore.

Andrea walked into the stables for the first time since her arrival. Many stalls were occupied with horses for either breeding or training. There was one elegant stallion she had seen Braden ride often.

His dark, illustrious ebony coat shone as he held his head while peering down at her. Andrea reached her hand out to pet his snout but almost jumped out of her skin when she heard a door slam. Her eyes followed the sound, witnessing Quentin Doyle exiting the stall next to her. He greeted her with a cocky gait and a smirk upon his face.

"I wouldn't recommend petting Samson. He doesn't take kindly to strangers."

Andrea set herself a foot away from the stall door. She placed her hands into her jean pockets. "Oh, thank you for the warning, Mr. Doyle."

"No need for formalities. Call me Quentin."

She nodded. "Quentin." Her eyes toured the stable, growing more uncomfortable with each passing second. The way he stared at her was akin to a man who hadn't had meat in years and was about to enjoy his first meal of it. Her experience with men was limited, but she'd recognize that lascivious stare from anywhere. She had received it plenty of times from Gaines.

Andrea cleared her throat. "Why are you here? Didn't want to go to the bar with the guys?"

"I had some things I needed to finish, preparing the Arabian mare we got some weeks ago. She's in season and it appears she's receptive to Samson. Tomorrow we'll place them together and we should have something to brag about in a few months."

"What's her name?"

A corner of his mouth lifted. "Delilah. Ironic, isn't it?"

"Yeah, it is."

He gave her a sly glance, gesturing her with his head. "C'mon and take a look at her."

Hesitant but not wanting to betray her uneasiness, Andrea moved over to the stall. She beheld the magnificent black Arabian mare who neighed and shook her head when Andrea came into her sights. As she moved closer to the stall, she felt his presence behind her. He hadn't grabbed her, but he pressed himself against her. She started to struggle, but he wrapped his arms around her.

"Mr. Doyle, what are you doing?" she gritted.

"Shh," he hushed into her ear. "It's Quentin. Friends should call each other by their first names. And we are friends, aren't we, darlin'?"

Her hands tried to pry his arms apart to loosen their hold. She tried in vain. She jerked against him to get loose. "Let go."

He did, but to spin her around and push her back against the stall door. She could hear the panting of Delilah right behind her, but her attention was upon a man who was desperate to get what she didn't offer.

"You look like a woman who's needing to be fucked," he burred while he swept her long hair to expose a side of her neck to his wandering lips. She gasped and pushed hard against him, repulsed. He raised up, his eyes full of licentious intent. "Is that what you want?"

"If that's what you think I want, you're out of your mind, you bast—"

He silenced her with his lips. The stables filled with sounds of her muffled protests and her struggles against him. His mouth transferred to her neck to sample it again when they were startled by one of the stable doors being slammed shut. Quentin glanced to see who it was and dropped his hands, then moved a couple of steps away from her.

Dread filled her. Andrea knew who it was. When she had the will to lift her dark brown eyes, they clashed with the unrelenting grays of Braden, his face hard with anger. She was innocent of any wrongdoing, but that glare alone could make her apologize all the same.

Since she was greeted with nothing but hostility, Andrea narrowed her eyes upon the hay-lain floor. Quentin, however, started moving toward Braden. "Boss, I—"

"Goodnight, Quentin. I'll deal with you in the morning."

Stalling a second, Quentin then walked around Braden toward the exit, but not leaving before giving Andrea a solemn glance-over. Once the door closed behind him, Andrea was left alone with Braden. She quivered beneath his scrutinizing glare.

What seemed like an eternity had passed, Braden didn't make a move nor sound. The way he was standing there, seething, he didn't appear to be in the frame of mind to listen to what she had to say. Unable to bear his glaring and saving herself the aggravation of trying to explain, she turned to leave out the back entrance, not wanting to walk past Braden to exit.

"Where in the hell do you think you're going?"

Andrea stopped dead in her tracks, and halfway turned to stare at him. "To bed, but I don't see why you'd care to know."

Braden took a few steps toward her. "If it's to frolic in bed with one of my hands—"

"Stop…right…there."

The weeks dealing with his abrasive attitude were coming to a head. She was frustrated enough now to say screw the job and let him have it.

"Who in the hell do you think you are?"

"Employer over you and Quentin Doyle," he returned, "and if you think I'll tolerate you messin' around with my hands, think again. This is the reason I don't allow women near my ranch. They distract my men. Just like Quentin Doyle's been distracted since he first seen you," he scoffed. "What were you gonna do out here, hmm? Let him feel you up before fucking you in the stall?" She said nothing but continued to glare at him. "Seems mighty sad for a woman to drive so far because she was desperate."

Andrea was shaking with rage and couldn't stop herself from walking up to Braden and slapping him hard against his stubborn, proud jaw. He reeled, but as his roiling, silver eyes returned to her, death was the sole thing she read within them.

She shouldn't have hit him, but he had been out of line with his words. He had no idea who she was or what she had gone through.

Andrea rounded him to leave, but was snagged by him, his hand capturing her wrist. His anger was still apparent by his narrowed eyes and heaving shoulders. Braden reeled her measuredly toward him like a fish on a line until his livid face was all she could see.

"We're not done," he fumed.

"Yes, we are," Andrea countered, her gaze blazing. "If you think I'll tolerate being manhandled by you or anyone, you're wrong. I didn't come here to be pawed at."

"Then why are you here?" There was an odd shift in his demeanor. His anger faltered, and there was a curious gleam in his eyes. Curiosity with a hint of heat. "I still find it strange that a city girl like you wound up in the middle of nowhere to work on a horse ranch. A pretty woman like you...hiding away up here..."

He had latched onto the word as if he were a dog picking up a scent. Now he was going to follow the trail until he discovered her secrets. Alarms sounded inside her as he kept hinting at what had driven her here. She was unsure of how well she schooled her features to give away nothing.

Braden leaned closer, Andrea feeling his hot breath wafting across her face. "Whatever secrets you're hiding, Andrea Banks, I'm going to find them out."

Andrea had no idea why she felt both petrified and aroused. She had no desire for him to find out about Gaines, and she wouldn't break now.

"I'm not hiding anything. Now if you'll excuse me..." She attempted to pull away but he refused to let go, keeping her secured to him. "What—"

"Did you want him to kiss you?" he said.

The question wasn't accusatory. It was spoken with intimacy. With a warmness from him that was foreign to her. It was coupled with his eyes staring down at her lips, prompting a silent question. Her body reacted, shaking involuntarily as her gaze studied his mouth. His bottom lip was a tad plumper than his top, and Andrea had the compulsion to latch onto it without letting go.

Yes, she wanted to kiss him so much. Something she never thought would happen considering how antagonistic he had been. He wasn't that way now, and as if to answer both of their needs, Braden dipped to take her mouth with his own.

There was such a maelstrom of feeling rippling through Andrea as her lips parted to the conquering of Braden's tongue. He plunged inside her, over and over, leaving her so wanting. God, he tasted better than anything she could imagine. Better than her favorite ice cream. Better than her favorite pasta dish. Better than her favorite anything. Each time his tongue dipped into her mouth, she cradled it like she wanted to keep it inside her. Like the part of him that she felt firm and impenetrable against her. Feeling his cock made her shiver as well as confused. It was a clear sign that he was hard...for her. She moaned into his mouth, feeling such a deep throb within her as she rubbed against him.

Still keeping his arm around her, his other hand cradled the back of her neck, angling her head enough to drink from her deeper. Everything in her was throbbing as she melded against him, dueling her tongue with his. His masculine scent enveloped her, dragged her under. Made her weak. He was her air supply and the usurper of her own. But they seemed to be fused together, like two sources that would die out if separated.

Braden broke the kiss, peering down at her with eyes filled with hot intensity. His rough thumb stroked her swollen bottom lip, his gaze intrigued. Her hands grasped his chambray shirt, her dark brown eyes showing him everything. Her vulnerability and desire, and that she'd take every thick inch of him that he would love to impale her on.

Braden lifted her, her legs going around his waist and the hardness of him rubbing against her already-soaking pussy with each agonizing step. Braden groaned as he kissed her again while he moved with her to an empty stall. He released her as soon as they were inside, closing the stall door behind him. He pulled her back into his arms, damn near bending her backward as he assailed her with his passionate kisses. They inched backward until her back met a wall. His mouth moved to her cheek before smoothing down to sample her neck, zeroing in on weak spots Andrea didn't realize she had.

Her pulse strummed faster beneath his kiss. She swallowed the moan that attempted to escape her throat. Andrea was trying to collect her scattered wits. What was she doing? Who was she doing? She couldn't be here fucking around with her boss. They were both grown adults and if she wanted to ride him until she came, that was between them. But she needed this job. Andrea hadn't had much traction with men, and she was afraid of her being a convenience to him. Or that he'd take what she had then kick her off the ranch. What then? What would she do? She had been so secure that she hadn't thought about a plan B.

Braden's hand cupped her breast, his thumb caressing her nipple. She gasped at the pull the stroke made to her center. Her body reacted, seizing at the sensation that assailed her. That irrepressible moan, however slight, came from her. Almost like a white flag to ensure her surrender. That she would endure anything to keep being touched like that. She wanted more. So much more.

But she couldn't afford to. She was afraid of the consequences if they went further.

"Braden...Braden...wait."

He stopped, his hands still on her hips and his forehead resting against the wall over her shoulder. His breathing was ragged, his shoulders heaving with great effort. It was hard for Andrea to contain those same lusty emotions. Not while his hot breath stirred the hairs at the base of her neck, keeping her passion on a low, simmering heat. Braden's fingertips flexed into her hips, as if it were taking everything within him to not haul her over his shoulder and carry her back to the house. Andrea wasn't prepared for that.

They had already gone too far. It seemed as if there was no going back. The line between employer and employee was blurred, and Andrea feared the repercussions of it.

Braden exhaled long, then pulled back to stare at her. There were no words. There wasn't a need for them. His gaze projected all the desire consuming him. But she couldn't answer it. She wasn't going to be a slave to her passions no matter how much she wanted him. She couldn't work with a relationship like this. She couldn't.

Andrea moved, but his hand shot out by her head to stop her. "Where are you going?"

His voice still retained a passionate roughness that made everything within her curl.

"Inside," she replied.

"In a minute. We need to talk about what just happened."

She wouldn't. She couldn't. "Not now. Please?"

With her plea, Braden eased from her. Andrea didn't wait for him to drop his arm, ducking beneath it before exiting the stall and heading to the house.

Oh, my God, what have I done? She had been in the most delicious lip lock with her boss. Andrea had to remind herself of why she was there. What drove her there. She couldn't lose sight of that.

As she ascended the porch stairs, Andrea's mind was resolved on what she had to do.

Braden loitered minutes after she was gone, dazed from the ordeal. His body was raging and felt at a loss. His arms were filled with the most sensual fire… He felt it in her. Smoldering and the potential to be all-consuming. And he wanted it to burn him alive.

He had kissed Andrea, and through that kiss, she might have realized how long his drought had been. Her lips had quenched the aridness of his need but made him thirst for more. The taste of her was intoxicating and now an instant addiction.

This addiction had been brewing before this happened. From the first, he found her so beautiful. The way she stood over him at the diner, appearing warrior fierce and not willing to put up with his shit. It was so attractive next to seeing her figure that curved with a handful of breasts and a luscious ass that made him react.

Despite the two of them acknowledging each other at the house, each time he saw her, his eyes lingered. Being near her when they went over his books conditioned his consciousness of how much this woman was unraveling him. The magnolia scent drifting off her skin had him almost wanting to dive his nose into the deep shadows of her shirts.

All those little things added up to this one explosive moment. Braden had lost his ever-loving mind the second he saw Quentin Doyle kissing her, touching her. Unexplainable jealousy had taken hold of him despite that he had no claim to her. Their relationship was professional between a boss and his employee. She wasn't his, but it didn't quell the burning curiosity to test the velvety softness of her pretty mouth.

A heavy sigh blew past his lips. He had been fascinated by the plump, dark pink hue of them, and he had wanted to see if they tasted as sweet as they looked. Hell, if *all* of her tasted as sweet as she looked. And now he'd had a sip of this intoxication, and he wanted to plunge headfirst all the way.

He might come off as a bastard to her, always staring at her with indifference, but it was to mask a secret: the intense need for her. He had felt confident that the reason he wanted her was because it had been a while since he had been with a woman. Now he wasn't so sure. He had been so adamant for years to keep women away from his ranch, and this was one of the reasons why.

She was a distraction. A damn beautiful distraction.

Braden cursed, his mind replaying her hardening nipple urging him to keep her attuned. Focused on him and this moment. It was hard as hell for him to stop. Not after having the sensual curves of her body against his, feeling her damp heat through their jeans as she rocked against him. Jesus, he could imagine how wet and tight she'd feel around his cock thrusting deep inside her. Seeing her come undone…

Despite how he wanted Andrea Banks beneath *and* on top of him, she was still a mystery, and she seemed adamant to keep it that way. But why? What had driven her here? Andrea did her job without complaint, and if there was any drama, besides the one between them, she didn't show it. Regardless, Braden was going to peel back each layer until she was naked for him in *every* sense.

Filled with determination, Braden walked to the house, still rock hard. He mounted the stairs with heavy feet, his eyes journeying down the hallway to her room. The room light was still on, so he assumed she wasn't in bed yet. Now wasn't a good time for their chat. Not when he should go and take a long, cold shower to send all his unbridled lust down the drain. Tomorrow was a brand-new day. He would breach the topic of what happened then.

Braden headed for his bedroom, knowing a sleepless night awaited him.

As soon as he closed the door, the woman of his all-consuming thoughts snuck from her room, down the stairs, and out the front door. She loaded her suitcases and maneuvered her car away from the house.

Andrea drove down the country road. If Braden knew where she was going, he'd lose it. She turned into the long driveway of a sprawling two-story mansion. Andrea couldn't appreciate it much in the dark and didn't waste any time as she grabbed her things and shuffled to the door. She waited until someone answered.

Caid didn't hide his shock at seeing her on his doorstep. "Andrea?"

"Is that position still open?"

He blinked but didn't say another word as he stepped aside to let her in.

Chapter Four

Eight hours and a handful of minutes had passed when Caid had ambled to the front door. He was allowing his new housekeeper to sleep in, still in disbelief that she was now under his roof. He had seen Andrea around town. Caid had conversed with her on many occasions and found her…refreshing. Not many women could retain his attention for long. This one was not only attractive but could hold a decent conversation. She didn't fawn over him because of his looks or money.

True to his playboy ways, Caid would have comforted the little darlin' as much as she'd allowed him to, and if that happened to include a tumble or two in bed, he'd be happy to oblige. However, just by the passing conversations, Andrea didn't seem to be the sort to fall into his bed because his charms willed her to. She seemed the kind of woman who would want the husband, the kids, the dog, and the dream house with the white-picket fence.

The scary thought that had reared its ugly head was that Caid, the confirmed bachelor and perpetual heartbreaker, was thinking about what it would be like to have just one woman to satiate, giving her children and loving him despite everything. And the more he thought of it, the worse this...strange yearning grew.

Andrea had divulged that she had quit Braden's place after an incident with one of his hands, and Caid had a feeling that another part of the reason behind her leaving was the one ringing his damn doorbell.

Caid didn't hide his scowl as he opened the door, finding Braden there with a menacing glare of his own.

"Where is she?" Braden asked without preamble.

"What difference does it make? You won't see her."

Braden sized Caid up, not at all intimidated. "And who'll stop me?"

"Me, if I have to. Don't think I won't."

Caid didn't get to make good on his threat. He had been on his guard for Braden to try something, but his alertness failed him. Braden charged forward, shoving Caid hard in the chest. The momentum of it made it hard for Caid to keep his feet beneath him and he fell flat upon his back in the foyer. It was the opportunity Braden needed to rush past him and up the stairs. Gritting his teeth, Caid rose to his feet to give chase.

Andrea was startled awake when her door was forced open, thinking it was Caid losing his mind. But her sleepy eyes widened as Braden swept into the room.

The blankets were snatched off her, Andrea gasping as Braden reached down to haul her into his arms. She struggled, kicking her legs and screaming at him at the top of her lungs.

"Put her down, Sutherland," came a low threat from the bedroom door.

"Or what, Marshall?"

Caid explained with his actions, charging toward him like a linebacker. Braden tossed Andrea upon the bed. Her body bounced once, twice, before landing upon her bottom on the other side of the bed. She watched in astonishment as Caid tackled Braden to the spot he had thrown her.

Punches flew, most of them hitting their marks with a few agonized groans thrown in. Andrea edged around the outskirts of the fray, gathering her things into her suitcases and sneaking out when she was done. Andrea scurried down the stairs when she heard the animalistic roar of her given name. Her shaking knees sustained her in making it down the stairs without breaking her damn neck.

At the bottom of the stairway, she glanced over her shoulder, colliding with the heated mercury eyes of her former employer, marred a little by a bruise already forming around one of them. Before she could reach the foyer, he grabbed her upper arm. He swung her around, the force of the action sending her into his lithe, strong body. Andrea dropped her suitcases and lifted her gaze. The turbulent ferocity he projected was enough to send her eyes back to the floor. She heard Caid's heavy footfalls thundering down the stairs, matching Braden bruise for bruise, a murderous scowl competing with his aggressor's.

"Release the lady, Sutherland," Caid demanded.

Braden glared back for a split second before heading toward the door, his hold on her arm unbreakable as he willed her to follow. She picked back up her suitcases. Caid balled his fists at his side, and threw a glare at Braden filled with loathing. He advanced behind them with every intention of continuing the brawl. Andrea implored him with her eyes and shook her head. Caid stopped, his gaze bewildered.

Other women might have been flattered to have men fighting over them, but Andrea wasn't one of them. There was an underlying dislike between Caid and Braden that ran so deep, Andrea believed that was why they scuffled. She couldn't have Caid fighting this battle for her. No, this was a fight she had to face on her own, even if it meant dealing with Braden one on one.

Braden shuffled her out the door. He turned to stare at a venting Caid over his shoulder, muttering, "You come near her again, Marshall, I'll break your face."

Slamming the door behind them, Braden marched to his truck, dragging a fuming Andrea behind him. She pulled against his hold, resistant and screaming at his back.

"Why did you threaten him? He didn't do anything but try to take up..." She hesitated as he jerked open the passenger-side door of his truck. "My car—"

"I'll have someone drive it back." He took her suitcases from her and gestured with his head. "Get in."

Seething, she obeyed, buckling her seatbelt just in case he decided to make a sudden stop at high speed and send her sailing through the windshield. Braden tossed her things in the back, got in, and they were soon on their way. Andrea, with her arms cross, stewed in the passenger's seat, refusing to give him the satisfaction of tears that formed. She refused to let them fall. They were tears of anger and pure frustration from dealing with such a man. She could fight him, but Braden gave as good as he got.

They turned down the road going back toward the house, but Andrea's body language changed from indifference to uneasiness when Braden turned onto a side road. They trucked along until they reached the edge of a field he apparently owned and sat there. Braden didn't say anything for moments. He leaned in his seat, his wrist draped over the steering wheel, staring down the winding dirt road ahead.

Andrea refused to be alone with him anywhere, let alone off a small road far from help. She released her seatbelt and opened the passenger-side door to jump down. She got the door open before Braden reached over her like a flash, slamming the door. He sat upright before leaning back into his side of the cab as Andrea beheld him with astonishment.

"It's time that we had that talk," he burred in his usual rough tone.

"The hell we do." She forced open the door again but was soon pulled back inside, shutting it. She heard the locking mechanism, signaling her doom. Now draped halfway across his lap from the momentum, Andrea stared up at him, shocked.

"We need to talk."

"Sure, we do," Andrea quipped. "How about you start since I know this will be a one-sided conversation where you talk, and I listen, which I *refuse* to do, so you can let go of my arm right now."

She tugged on her captured arm, but his fingers remained secure. She'd have to do nothing short of gnawing it off to get free. It perturbed her that his visage remained hard, her resistance an issue to him.

"Why did you go to him?"

The sudden question caught her off-guard. The last time she had checked, this man didn't care if she pranced around him naked with a bottle of oil in one hand and a can of whipped cream in the other. But that all changed last night when he kissed her with a promise of fucking her through the stall wall. Was it possible something else was fueling his ire?

Could he be…jealous? Jealous because of her?

She almost laughed at the thought of it. Caid was a catch, but she considered him an acquaintance. Surely there were plenty of women lined up to see how acrobatic Caid was in bed. She may have been one of those curious souls if Braden Sutherland hadn't caught her eye first.

Andrea lowered her eyes, choosing her words to test her hypothesis. "What difference does it make? It's none of your business what I do with my personal time."

Braden didn't answer for a couple of beats, and she felt the way his hand curved around her arm. "But it is my business when you're doing your personal time on mine. Hell, according to my watch, you're still on it."

Andrea flexed her arm, testing his grip that still refused to give. "Like hell I am. I've already quit as of last night."

He scoffed. "You can't quit."

She freed an unladylike snort. "Too late, cowboy. I've already done it."

"Not according to the contract you signed. I believe I had you read it and gave you a copy. It states that you can't quit until you've trained someone to take your place for at least two weeks' time."

Andrea's chin dropped, almost forgetting about that clause in their agreement. How could she argue against that? The rules were simple, set in black and white. But Andrea was determined to find a way to get out of this situation, even if she had to crawl on her belly to do it.

"That could take forever!"

"Not my problem. You put your signature on the dotted line, honey. I didn't force you to."

"But you can't expect me to go back there like everything's honky dory. I also refuse to go back if he's there."

"I fired him," Braden supplied.

Andrea lifted her gaze to study his always-serious features. "You did? But when?"

"Early this morning. Right before I got in my truck to come after you. He won't be there to bother you again. Promise."

The smoldering fire in those hot mercury eyes almost made Andrea believe that he was angrier about what Quentin had done. However, she felt that he, being the reserved, angry creature that he was, was fuming for dealing with the situation in its entirety. She had heard that Braden hadn't fired anyone in a couple years. He didn't have to. He had gotten on some honest men who were willing to work, but a few had quit when their work ethic couldn't meet Braden's expectations.

And then she came along, interrupting the solidity amongst them. Not a day went by when one of the guys hadn't brought her fresh wildflowers. Braden didn't hide his contempt each time he saw a new bouquet in a vase in the kitchen. Everyone tried to get to know her, except her employer. Andrea supposed it didn't matter to him since his pride forced him to hire her in the first place.

"I don't understand. You've wanted me off the ranch since day one. I just gave you an out. Why the sudden change of heart?" Her brown eyes gleamed with daring. "Was it because your precious pride got hurt because I went to Caid?"

"There was *no* reason for you to go running to him!" Braden snapped.

"If we had fucked last night, what would it have been? A one-and-done, or would I have to give a two weeks' notice for that too?"

The extended cab seemed to echo as silence fell upon them. His body became at ease, though Andrea didn't to jerk her arm away. The tension was still there, humming.

"I wasn't expecting that kiss to happen. I don't know why I reacted like I did…" He sighed. "Apparently, you ran because I had crossed the line when I shouldn't have. I was a bastard for taking advantage, and I'm sorry."

Shocked eyes focused on him, meeting the incisive silver ones that had lost a little of their austerity. "You, Braden Sutherland, apologizing? That's rich."

Those eyes took a split second to harden again. "You better accept it, 'cause that's the only time you'll hear me say it."

He was right about being a bastard. After he ruined an earnest moment, Andrea jerked her arm away from his grip, placing herself as far away as the cab would allow. A continent wouldn't be enough.

"I don't have to accept that half-ass apology. And tell me this, why was it okay for *you* to kiss me? By your own logic, *you* should also be fired this morning."

Braden didn't address the accusation. He relaxed his tall body in his seat, his silver eyes peering off into the distance. "You'll come back to the ranch," he asserted in a low voice. "If you want to leave, fine, but you better make damn sure you get someone to replace you. Else, I don't want to hear another word about it." He cut a glance to her, almost nailing her to the passenger door. "Do you hear me?"

Andrea stared back at him, confusion on her face. "I still don't understand why you're going through all this trouble to keep a person you hate. Why?"

Braden's answer was to make a wide U-turn and drive them in strained silence back to the ranch.

Once they got home, Braden told Andrea to take it easy for the day before disappearing into his study. He tossed his Stetson, watching it twirl until it landed onto his couch.

The day was already off to a rough start due to his lack of sleep from dreaming about divine lips kissing him everywhere. Then he discovered the owner of those lips were nowhere on his land, and his mood cratered. He felt like an ass, unsure of what had frightened her from the night before. Was it because of Quentin or his kiss that had her flee into the night?

Braden had her number. He could call her, but he knew she wouldn't pick up. She was gone, leaving Braden with a bad temper, a raging hard-on, and an unquenched thirst for more of her.

Regardless of the reason for her leaving, it was the fuel Braden needed as he stepped outside to where the hands were gathered for breakfast. With his eyes narrowed on Quentin, he said that they were on their own and were allowed a late start because of it.

He excused everyone except Quentin. While his men walked away, he overheard someone mention Andrea's car sitting in Caid's driveway. If he wasn't livid before, his anger consumed him to where he spat nothing but fiery vitriol at Quentin, cursing him nine ways to Sunday. After Braden finished his tirade, Quentin headed to the bunkhouse to collect his things, no longer in Braden's employ.

Then Braden was heading toward his truck without a second thought, determined to get her back. And he did, by forcing his hand and creating conditions that would make it difficult for her to find a replacement.

Why had he done all of this when he had just destroyed Quentin for doing the same?

Because for Braden, it was him who wanted his hands on her. Him who wanted to kiss her. To be inside her in all the ways her body would allow him. The signs from last night had all been there. Her trembling body, her staring at his lips with eyes keen with interest. Braden hadn't imagined it. In that moment, she was just as hot for him.

The potent Miss Banks had no idea what she did to him. The scale of it would unbalance her. Perhaps even frighten her. Would it scare her to know how he craved to strip her and have her beneath him? How his every waking thought was consumed with the need for her?

He had to dial it back though, because she was right. He had acted like an ass because he was hard up and jealous over her. And he didn't know where things would go next if they had done the deed. This was nearly uncharted territory, something he hadn't explored in a long time. Perhaps in comparison, this was nothing like the relationships he had before.

He was a caveman, beating his chest and claiming what he perceived was his. But she was a woman with her own mind and choices. And despite how their bodies were drawn together like magnets, the reason why he now knew how good she tasted was that he didn't want anyone to have what he yearned for. Not before nor after.

Jealousy slithered in his gut along with intense lust. She said they were friends, but that didn't stop the imaginings he had as he drove to Caid's place, and he didn't like what he thought up. She wasn't his. She *wasn't* his. But he wanted her to be in whatever capacity he could have her, and he sure as hell didn't want Caid Marshall to stake his claim on her. If she wanted to be satisfied, why wander elsewhere when he'd satiate her need as well as his own?

Undone. This woman had undone him. With a single glance from those bewitching eyes of hers, she stirred him like no other. If he wasn't careful, they could affect the rest of him, controlling him into giving her any and everything.

Braden needed time. Time to explore what this was. It had been forever since he found himself so ready for a woman. He wasn't sure he had any other feelings apart from anger, lust, or indifference. But the prospect of her opened so many other emotional avenues. Braden hadn't felt more alive in years.

He wanted to be reckless, to see how far a boundary she could push. He would have to be brave enough to let her.

Even though Andrea had spent what was left of Saturday trying to get someone, anyone, to fill in, it wasn't happening. She would have had an easier time convincing them the sky wasn't blue. Most of the locals and in the surrounding parts knew of Braden's legendary black temper and valued their lives enough not to come within a hundred miles of it. She couldn't even beg Shelley to take over for her.

"Oh, no ma'am," Shelley remarked when Andrea had addressed her on the phone. "Just putting up with it on Wednesdays is enough. Sorry, babe. You're on your own."

It had been a few hours, and Andrea was disheartened by the prospects. No wonder Mrs. Gemma had posted an ad online. Now Andrea had fallen into a hole she couldn't get out of.

The more she ruminated over her situation, the more her head hurt. She couldn't figure this man out for the life of her. Braden insisted that she rest and not worry about tending to the house until tomorrow. She didn't believe him, but when he had spotted her attempting to do the laundry, one look from him sent her flying back upstairs.

She had given him the perfect opportunity to allow her to quit, and he wouldn't let her. She didn't think it was because he wanted her. The thought made a rush of fever flood her body. That was a joke. Him wanting her? Despite dismissing the notion, the facts were there. He consumed her as if being deprived of her would kill him. She felt the hard ridge of his cock in his jeans. But it was unclear if it was meant for her or because she was convenient. Andrea didn't know, and she wasn't sure she wanted her worst fear confirmed: That she meant nothing to him at all.

By the next morning, she was still trembling with the new emotions that she had tried to avoid. The peace that he had allowed her made her realize her immense curiousness of him. That's how he found her when he came into the kitchen, picking at her food as she stared down at her plate. Andrea felt his presence as he watched her, but she never acknowledged him.

He shuffled past her to the counter, getting coffee and joining her at the table. Her eyes caught the broad, muscular chest covered with fine, brown hair that made her wonder how it would feel to have the sensitive tips of her breasts rasp against them. His skin was bronzed, and muscles undulated beneath strong, sinewy skin from years of hard work. A renewed sense of awareness flooded her as she became receptive of this man displaying his wares and tempting her to buy what seemed forbidden.

She couldn't pull her gaze away. He was mesmerizing and gorgeous. Andrea's eyes drank their fill, touching on the tight, corded muscles of his abdomen, to nipples that seemed like they would enjoy being touched like hers, caressed, licked, and worshipped.

Her daydream shattered when he cleared his throat. Brown eyes rose to the quicksilver of his and diverted away. Andrea almost died when she witnessed the brief, slight upturn of the corner of his mouth. He was good-looking when he smiled, if even for a millisecond.

She continued to pick at her plate, her appetite growing for something different. Out of the corner of her eye, she watched him partake of his coffee in absorbed silence. She licked her lips, feeling brave enough to talk while the tiger was subdued.

"Breakfast?"

He murmured, "No," as he continued to stare into his cup.

"You put something on your bruises? Make them heal a little faster?"

He shook his head. He had a dark ring on his right eye that wasn't swollen as badly as it had been yesterday, paired with a bruise on his left jaw. It seemed like he wanted to display his war wounds.

They returned to awkward silence. The sounds echoing in the kitchen were her fork scraping across her plate and him setting down the cup. Sitting for five minutes more and taking a couple of bites was all she could bear next to him, eaten up with lust. Andrea stood, emptied her plate, and began washing dishes. She felt him glance at her, and she tried to play off the emotions he enabled in her.

"You didn't sleep well either, did you?"

Andrea looked over her shoulder, witnessing eyes that were bloodshot and dull from weariness. She turned back to the sink, her head bowed. "No."

Again, silence. Andrea continued to wash the dishes but kept her ears alert of every move he made. The one movement that made her knees buckle was him scooting back his chair. Good thing her hands were immersed in the water or else he would've seen them shake, vibrating like the rest of her. He strode up beside her, setting the coffee cup on the counter. Her dishwashing became slower, her senses filled with him. Lord, it was never this bad! Just the other day she was avoiding him like hell, now here she was being seduced just inhaling the enriching essence of him that screamed utter masculinity.

He moved to turn his body so that he faced her. Leaning against the counter, his gaze lingered on her profile. Andrea licked her lips, a nervous habit. She didn't notice the heated stare he gave her when her tongue peeked out from its hiding place. If she had, it would have burned her alive.

"What do you have planned today?"

The question, as the last couple had, caught her off-guard. She cast a quick glance at him before it returned to the soapy water. "Why do you want to know? You usually don't care what I do on my own time." She looked at him again, a slow, simmering blaze of anger within her eyes. "But I'm not planning to fuck every man in Rock River, let alone the whole damn state of Wyoming if that's what you're getting at."

"I know you're not. God, I let you have it, didn't I?"

Andrea shrugged. "I was warned that you were a woman-hater. I should've taken the hint and ran while I still had the chance."

"I don't hate you."

Her eyes lifted again to study features that were nothing but serious. She freed a small laugh. "Oh, yeah, because we've been buddy-buddy since I got here."

He rubbed his hand against his chin, the grating sound of stubble against his rough palm sending tingles down her spine. "I guess I deserve your sarcasm...and your hate, but perhaps, one day, I can earn your forgiveness."

Andrea was in awe. Whatever happened to the bigger-than-life asshole who had been negative and condescending from the first? She never expected that he had a soul and by a contrite demeanor, found the right words to start tearing down the defenses she had built against him.

She didn't respond as she continued with the dishes. He didn't move. Just stared at her with his arms folded. He stayed until she had rinsed off every silverware, cup, and plate and placed them in the draining board. Andrea dried her hands on a towel then turned toward Braden, who still stared at her.

"Would you like to go to church with me?" Braden asked.

Andrea's brows lifted. "You? Go to church?"

"I might be a hard son of a bitch, but I do believe in God. I don't go as religiously as some, but I go when I'm not out of town." He regarded her when she remained quiet. "Look, no pressure. Tell me yes, no, or go to hell. Your call."

Andrea tossed the towel aside and placed a sassy hand upon her hip. "You can go to hell later," she responded, "but I have to see for myself that Braden Sutherland doesn't burn alive setting foot in a church."

The church wasn't quite around the bend. They remained quiet for the twenty minutes it took to drive to a church on the route to Medicine Bow. The church almost reminded her of the small, country churches she went to with her grandmother back home.

There were twelve pews for the congregation, six on each side. Braden directed her into the last pew close to the middle aisle, and he settled in next to her. had recognized people from around town. Julius Clark, the person she got her groceries from. Shelley and her mother also attended. And someone else she didn't expect to attend. Sitting across the way was Caid Marshall.

As Braden's bruises were apparent, so were Caid's. Everyone in church gaped at them, and didn't take a rocket scientist to figure out that mixing two volatile entities could equal an explosion. They seemed curious if this new young woman had anything to do with it.

Every time Caid's hazel eyes would cut into their direction, Braden would glare back, not afraid of being in church, and threaten harm with just a look. Andrea paid attention to their silent war. She was too focused on the way Braden sat in the pew like he was at home. His right arm lined along the back of the pew, and the sleeve of his suede sports coat would brush her back close to the nape. Too close. She found herself sitting straighter to avoid the touch.

God, she felt like a downright sinner. The almost fatal combination of cologne, leather, and earth entranced her. She couldn't help but inhale him. Here, another part of him bewitched her—his singing voice. When they shared a hymnal for a congregational song, she heard his strong baritone sung with clarity and strength. Andrea's own voice wasn't a powerhouse, but light in its mezzo-soprano quality. Even still, they exchanged glances as their fingers brushed while holding the hymnal and shying away like they were inexperienced teenagers stimulated by a simple touch.

But everyone paid attention to the sermon. It was shorter than what she was used to, but the pastor was able to get his point across. Before she knew it, she was outside the church as the congregation dissipated. She waited on Braden, who was inside talking to the pastor for a couple minutes. Shelley had just left, needing to take her mother home. Then she found Caid walking up to her, rotating his brown Stetson in his hands. Andrea checked to make sure Braden was still inside. After yesterday, Andrea didn't feel like dying due to association.

"Andrea," Caid acknowledged when he reached her.

"Caid."

He studied her, concern on his face. "Are you all right? I mean, did he do anything to you after you left?"

"No. He gave me the day off when we got back." She didn't proceed to tell him that she had spent a good deal of it searching for a replacement.

"I'm surprised you stopped me," he replied. "I'm even more surprised that you went quietly after it was said and done."

Andrea crossed her arms, discomfited by his questioning. "I just didn't want you to fight over me. I can fight my own battles."

Caid's face hardened. "Yeah, waving the white flag is one hell of a way to fight."

Her eyes flashed at him. "You fought because you didn't want to lose to Braden. It's always been competition with both of you. It never was about me."

"It was yesterday!" he exclaimed. "To hell with the reasons why we've always been rivals. If memory serves me, you're the one who came running to me. I took you in, and it wasn't so I could sleep with you. I wanted to help. And when it came time to protect you, you gave up. Just what kind of power does he have over you? How could you be like a wildcat one day and sitting next to him in church like a saint on another?"

She faltered for a reply because she didn't know. Andrea didn't know what to say on how she felt about Braden. She did hate his abrupt manner, but she was also attracted at the same time. It was a double-edged sword. What she felt for Braden was unlike anything she had felt before and part of her wanted to stay to see just what power he did have over her.

Before she could answer, she stared up to see the subject of their discussion standing on the top stair of the church. His mood was dark as he watched them and began making his way over. Caid glanced back to see Braden marching, closing the space between them.

"As a friend, I'm willing to protect you if you need it. All you have to do is ask, but you have to be willing to take what's offered. You'll let me know if you do, won't you?"

Andrea nodded, a split second before Caid was turned around by Braden.

"Didn't I warn you about coming near her, Marshall?" Braden threatened.

Despite it all, Caid had the audacity to grin. "I was doing nothing but talking to her, Sutherland. Just talked, didn't touch. Even though for a woman-hater, you're going through an awful lot to protect her from me. Almost like you have feelings for her."

Braden didn't take the bait. "I'm feeling lenient this morning, Marshall. I'm willing to spare you since we're at church, but I'll have you know that anytime and anywhere else, I'll rip your damn spine out."

"Then let me know time and place." He put on his Stetson, running his fingers along the brim. "Caid Marshall never misses an appointment." He tipped the brim of his hat to Andrea. "Good day, Miss Banks."

They both watched as Caid made his way to his truck and pulled away. As soon as he was out of sight, Braden herded her toward his truck, and they departed for home. The trip back started off in silence until Braden broke it.

"What did he say to you?"

Andrea knew Braden wouldn't be willing to just let it go. "Nothing. He was just concerned."

"Define concerned."

She watched the passing scenery out her window. "I told him that he shouldn't fight for *or* over me. I just don't want there to be more of a reason you guys hate each other."

Braden scoffed as he drove with casual ease. "We'd hate each other even if you weren't in the equation, honey," he answered. "I have nothing against him. Nothing personal. It's just something bigger than both of us. Something that got handed to us without us asking for it. Funny how things can go on from generation to generation until it gets pointless, lacking in reason."

"So, you're saying you hate Caid because of a family feud? Like the Hatfields and the McCoys? The Montagues and the Capulets?"

"Something like that."

He didn't elaborate any further. Andrea bit her lip to restrain herself from asking. She didn't want to push an issue he wasn't willing to tell her more of.

"How did you enjoy the sermon?"

Andrea glanced over to him. "It was good," she replied. "It's been a while since I've heard a sermon about the Beatitudes. Not since I was about eleven when I used to go to church with my grandmother. My grandma was a saint, holy and sanctified. She went every Sunday until her health failed. But she was the kind of person who always sat in the front row, had a Bible that was as old as Texas. And she had this singing voice that was perfect in praising God, almost outdoing everyone in the choir." She looked down at her folded hands in her lap. "God, I miss those days. Miss being innocent and unaware of the ways of the world."

Braden glanced her over. "How long have you been alone?"

The admission came after she freed a sigh. "A few months, but it seems so much longer than that. Grandma died ten years ago. She meant a lot to me since my mom passed. After that, it was just me and my dad."

"You didn't get along with your dad?"

"Oh, I got along with my dad at first," Andrea divulged with reflection. "I was his little girl, but things had changed in the last few years. Then when he died last year, my world shattered. Now I'm trying to pick up the pieces, but I couldn't from where I was." She lifted her eyes to him. "That's why I came here. I was offered an out, and I took it. So, I guess I came here for my own selfish reasons."

"There's nothing selfish about needing a place to go to recuperate from your wounds," Braden responded. "We all need to do it, or we'll never get past it. We're human, and we can only take so much at a time. Better to deal now than let it accumulate to the point you'll regret later that you hadn't."

"And do you have something in your past that you regret?"

She watched as his jaw tightened, his eyes unblinking. "Every damn day." He glanced at her with eyes that appeared heavy but still retained that ever-present intensity. "Some wounds from this life run too deep to heal. Sometimes a lifetime isn't enough."

That was the last of their conversation as they neared the ranch, but what he had said weighed upon her thoughts. For weeks she had tried to build up defenses against him, passing him off in her mind as an ill-tempered man who was hateful to everyone. But now, for the first time, she was beginning to see and understand that even big bad wolves had wounds and feelings they tended to hide. She saw a mere glimpse of what was behind the stony façade Braden often wore. It made her wonder if he'd ever show her or anyone else what had hurt him so much. He'd never ask for help or desire to talk it over. His will was too strong to let anyone watch him be vulnerable.

However, Andrea was optimistic. His small confession was a step in the right direction. Maybe her big, bad wolf could be redeemed after all.

Chapter Five

The next day started off uneventful. Andrea cooked, caught up on chores, and put away the laundry. She had just prepared a casserole for dinner and placed it in the oven to cook for a couple hours. Taking a break, Andrea walked out toward the corral and stables. She leaned against the fence and watched some of the guys try and break in a couple of horses they received the week before. One was kicking its hind legs, bounding and doing its best to send J.D. flying into the dirt, which it did. Several times. And the rest of the men laughed every time.

"Not so cocky anymore, are you, boy?" Handy guffawed.

J.D. continued to defy them all by getting back onto the feisty mare. Buddy, one of Braden's more experienced hands, walked over to her once he realized she was standing there. "Evening, Miss Andrea."

"Hey, Buddy. What's going on?"

"Trying to tame this mare," he replied, leaning his back against the fence. He crossed his arms and his legs at the ankles. "So far, she's doing pretty good."

Andrea watched as J.D. was tossed once more. "Oh, because nothing shows progress like getting constantly thrown into the dirt."

Buddy chuckled. "Well, Miss Andrea. Sometimes you have to train more than the horse. J.D. is confident he could break her in his own way. We're letting him."

"But won't he hurt himself or the mare?"

"He's too hardheaded to get that thick skull of his to crack. And as you can see, the mare can take care of herself, just like any woman in our neck of the woods." He winked and smiled at her before directing his attention back to a battered J.D. Buddy smiled. "Had enough?"

J.D. got up, grabbed his hat, and dusted himself off. He ambled over to where they were, sighing as he eased himself down to lean against a post. "I'm about to break every damn bone in my body." He beat his dirty baseball cap against his palm, his eyes narrowing at the animal that bested him. "Damn horse."

Buddy chuckled. "Don't be sore because the horse taught you a lesson. It ain't like the movies, boy. You have to woo her like she's your true love. It'll make all the difference."

J.D. snorted. "Sorry. I ain't into horses like that."

Andrea giggled and started to make small talk with them just as Braden came striding out of the stables. She could have fainted from the sight of him. He was sexy and shirtless, displaying a strapping upper body that had her saliva glands on overdrive. God, jeans shouldn't fit a man so well! And the way his skin shone in the sun from perspiration didn't help. Andrea had never seen a man more comfortable in his surroundings and skin than Braden Sutherland.

He walked up to them, glaring at first the mare and then his defeated ranch hand. "What's the problem?" he asked with his usual straightforwardness.

"J.D. thought he'd teach this mare a lesson. Looks like he's the one who got schooled," Handy replied, still chuckling in amusement.

Braden's gaze slid over to J.D., then Buddy, and then stopped on her. His stare was so penetrating and measured, it made her forget how to breathe. She grabbed onto the fence tighter to steady her quivering knees as he made his way closer, unwavering and determined.

Buddy cast a quick, sly glance at her and smiled. He helped J.D. to his feet, giving the younger man a pat on his back. "Come on. Lemme show you how it's done."

Buddy guided J.D. away just in time for Braden to stand where he had. Andrea had to draw on everything within her to keep her eyes focused on his. He strutted around with confidence and surety that signaled he was the one who ran things and knew his business well.

"Never thought I'd see you out here," he said as he leaned against the fence. "Not many people take a fancy to sweat and horses."

"Just goes to show there are a lot of things you don't know about me," Andrea countered. "After all, I'm from Texas."

Braden lifted his hat to run a hand through the curly, damp tendrils of his hair. "Just because you're from Texas doesn't mean you know everything about horses." His gaze took a brief perusal down her body. "I bet you've never touched one, let alone ride."

"But isn't it a common misconception? A lot of people believe that everyone in Texas is nothing but country people with ten-gallon hats, horses, and pickup trucks."

He didn't smile, but his eyes twinkled. "I guess that's so, but we both know that isn't always the case."

Andrea climbed the fence until she sat perched upon the top rail. Braden glanced up to her, thoughtful. "What? Are you going to say that a city girl like yourself would like to learn how to ride?"

Her eyes simmered at the underhanded challenge. "What if I said I did?"

He rubbed the corded muscles at the back of his tanned neck. "I'd say no."

"And why not?"

Braden held up a couple of fingers. "Two reasons. One: I don't have the time to teach a three-hour crash course on how to mount a horse. Two: there's not a horse here I'd trust you on without getting thrown."

"You wouldn't care if I did."

"I'd care quite a bit." Her eyes went to him, astonished. "Truth is I hate dealing with accident reports and the bullshit of insurance companies. They're a pain in the ass, so I'm hoping you'd spare me the trouble."

"You know, there're other people on this ranch, too. Maybe Handy will teach me. Or even Cooper."

If he was going to take the bait, he didn't say. He blew it off like everything else. "Then don't come crying to me when you break your ass." He then marched back to the stables.

Andrea sat idle for a few moments, waiting until Cooper had stepped away to take a break. She hopped off the fence to ask him if he could show her how to ride. With his rugged, wholesome smile, Cooper obliged, but as soon as they turned their attention toward the stables, Braden was stalking out of them, leading two Arabian horses by their reins.

His glare dared anyone to ask what he was doing. No one would even dare. His glower shifted in her direction. It almost made her wish she hadn't asked.

"Cooper!" he boomed, jerking his head. Cooper jogged up to his boss, taking the reins of both animals. Then Braden marched up to her. Andrea looked from side to side to see if there was any place to run, or if anyone would dare to help her. The men, though pretending to be lost in their work, cast the occasional stare at the events unfolding between their boss and his housekeeper.

Braden stopped in front of her, eyeing her for a few beats before taking the helmet he had dangling from his fingers and settling it hard upon her head. He drew a little nearer, saying the next words so that only she heard them.

"You wanted your lesson, honey? You got it."

He walked away with that slow, confident gait toward the other horse he had Cooper hold. "Step one: never walk right up to a horse you don't know. Sneaking up on him could earn you a trip to the hospital. Now, approach Samson from the side so that he can see you. Make a little noise to let him know you're coming, but don't overdo it. And if he starts to get skittish, just wait for him to calm down."

Braden waited as she approached Samson with caution. The stallion shied away a couple times, and her footsteps had faltered when he did, but she kept steady eye contact.

"Another thing," Braden threw at her. "Never look a horse square in the eye. Predators do that. The wrong look could send them flying. Remember, you want to be in control of your horse but not intimidate them."

"But they're very intimidating."

Braden stroked the ebony mane of his horse, whose lineage, from what Andrea understood, was the same as Braden's favored horse, Samson. Except this one, who was named Daredevil, had a demeanor that was as menacing as his owner's. Daredevil wasn't the kind of horse recommended to amateurs if they valued their life. Neither was he for an expert rider. Braden was the exception. She had seen them ride away from the house as they tore off into the distance but riding with such fluidity. A true horseman like Braden could be at home in a saddle, even with a horse such as Daredevil. She supposed that because of their parallel demeanors, in a peculiar way, they understood what the other needed and shared that wild streak.

"They're only intimidating for those who don't know what the hell they're doing. Just keep coming toward him."

Andrea wasn't sure if it was plain fear, but her body shook all over as she approached the horse. She appeared as if she was on her way to her own execution.

"Don't do that!" Braden barked, sending both horses sidestepping. "Get yourself under control. They can sense your fear, and they'll use it against you. A horse needs a gentle but confident rider. A nervous rider can endanger both themselves and the horse."

"Understood, but you don't have to yell," Andrea gritted between her clenched teeth. "I'm standing right here."

Braden sighed. "Honey, it's taking you two minutes to walk twenty feet. If you've lost your nerve, then we can forget the whole thing. I've got other shit to do with my time, and my time, like my patience, is short as hell. So, what's it going to be?"

His challenge strengthened her resolve to be defiant and unyielding. She took a few deep breaths, her mindset and her body composed and under control. She reached out to pet Samson. Her confidence grew when he didn't rebel but awaited her next move. Her eyes went to Braden. He gestured for Cooper to release Daredevil to concentrate on holding Samson still for her.

"Now, the proper side is for people to mount the horse on the left. So, left hand upon the pommel, right hand on the cantle, and left foot in the stirrup. Bounce a couple times to get momentum and pull yourself up. Once you're up and over, ease yourself into the saddle. And, by the way, when you try to mount, horses move, which is expected. Don't be scared if he does."

Andrea just stared at him. The man said the whole spiel and didn't take two breaths.

Braden rolled his eyes. "I hope you got all of that 'cause I'm not repeating it."

"Let me see you do it," she dared.

The boss-man shrugged, and the next second, he had mounted Daredevil with unbearable ease. The horse didn't move at all. Braden made it look so easy, and by the arrogant smirk positioned on his lips, there wasn't a doubt in her mind he did it to make her appear foolish.

"Showoff," she mumbled as she positioned herself to mount Samson. She held onto the places on the saddle she was instructed to. As she attempted to mount, Samson shied away just as she got her right foot to leave the dirt. Next thing she knew, she was on the ground, staring up at the clear, blue Wyoming sky.

"Miss Andrea!" Cooper came to her side to help her to her feet. "Are you okay?"

She nodded, dusting off her bottom, eyes glowering as they lifted to Braden. His face retained that same, damnable smirk. "Dare to try again?"

That ass! Andrea, after counting to ten in her head, tried again. This time, she got up with success. Cooper handed her the reins. Braden clicked his tongue and began Daredevil off at a slow walk. Andrea emulated him, and Samson did the same. She followed him as they made it around the corral at a gait. After a turn or two, Braden nudged Daredevil into a trot. Again, Andrea emulated but ended up having Samson rear upon his back legs and sending her to the ground yet again.

The air stole out of her, and a few precious seconds passed until she got her lungs back in order. As she eased into a sitting position, Andrea let out a painful groan and rested her arms upon her knees to catch her breath. Cooper went over to help her, but Andrea held her hand out and shook her head. She gritted her teeth as she rose to her feet, then she turned around when the soft neighing of a horse alerted her. Braden sat in his saddle with confidence, his mercury gaze glimmering.

"Had enough, honey?"

Her eyes narrowed into slits, and with a clenched fist, she marched over to Samson to try again. *That pompous bastard,* Andrea fumed as she mounted the horse with better ease this time. The result turned out to be the same, although, with each attempt, she managed to stay on a few moments longer. After a couple more ungraceful falls, the men started to get worried, each casting a concerned glance toward Braden. He had already dismounted after his jab at her and now just watched her. His face was unreadable, but after another fall, he stepped toward her as she mounted Samson again. Braden seized the reins, stilling her.

"What are you trying to prove?" he asked in a low tone. She said nothing, glaring down at him from her elevated height. "If you're trying to show how brave you are, all right. I'll give it to you. You're a ballsy little thing, but you don't have to break your damn neck to prove it."

She detached the reins from his fingers and nudged Samson onward. Braden shook his head and walked toward the corral gate. Cooper called after him. "Boss, you gotta stop her before she kills herself."

"Let her since she's so hell-bent on doing it!" he threw over his shoulder and continued to march toward the house.

Braden was seething, pacing in the kitchen as he put on another pot of coffee. His Stetson was off his head and damn near balled up in his fist. He had warned her but that damnable pride of hers was outright determined to prove him wrong. And it would weigh on his conscience for the rest of his life if she succeeded in breaking every precious bone in her body.

Braden stopped pacing for a second before he strode back to the corral. But by the time he got to the fence, he watched her in complete awe. This young woman, who had been tossed into the dirt time and time again, was now riding his horse with confidence. She managed to get Samson into a trot, holding the reins with ease. Her carriage in the saddle was regal, her back straight, her head poised, wearing smudges of dirt like slight badges of honor.

Braden felt the seeds of pride plant and grow within him. He was proud of her, even if part of him was seething that she'd risk her life to get him to feel that way. He leaned against the fence, resting his forearms on the top railing as his gaze followed her around the outskirts of the corral.

"Well, I'll be damned," he murmured in astonishment as Cooper strode over to him.

Cooper glanced over his shoulder, a similar seed of pride apparent in his own stare as they both looked on.

"Isn't she somethin', boss?" Cooper asked.

Good thing everyone's eyes were preoccupied or else they would have caught the slight grin that tugged at the corners of Braden's mouth.

"She sure is, Cooper. She sure is."

It was difficult for Braden to concentrate on drafting a new contract later that evening. Not while his mind was focused on something else. Someone else. His mind kept returning to feminine legs bracing his horse. The way her jeans had stretched across her fine backside. God, he was jealous of his own damn horse! Jealous for the simple fact Samson was able to get her in a position Braden had dreamt about. How he wanted her to ride him like that, her nimble thighs braced around him as he buried his cock so deep within her, she could choke on it.

His fingers flexed, crushing paper that happened to lie within reach. He was wound so tight. If he didn't relieve himself soon, he was going to snap. There were a million and one ways he could find relief, but he wanted to gain his gratification through one. Between the thighs of the young woman who had him in knots since day one.

He glared down at the crumpled pages of what used to be an immaculate contract. He shoved them to one side. At this rate, he'd crumple and tear every damn thing in his office. Braden's frustrations were mounting. He couldn't do any more tonight if he tried. He should take a cold shower. And maybe after thirty minutes to an hour, he could get his erection to ease a bit.

He headed toward the stairs, unbuttoning his shirt to ready his body for the long, cold baptism he needed. He was glad that no one except for Andrea was in the house. Even still, she was closed behind the safety of her bedroom door. Braden's mind went back to the events of the day and the way she displayed her grit. After she was done, she rode up to him, dismounted with little trouble, and handed him the reins. Braden watched as those lush hips swayed back and forth as she walked back to the house, her back straight and confidence intact.

Even when she served dinner, she still wore her smudged marks on her face. Braden's gaze kept following her as the guys chatted about her with praise and adoration. He had the image of her smiling at all the guys except him, her eyes sparkling. She made a pretty, little picture, appreciating the way the dirt enhanced her sweet features. It looked as if she belonged. Perhaps that was one of the reasons why he wanted her back. He couldn't imagine not finding her in a corner of the house, keeping it clean, or avoiding his company. Then again, how was she to know how much he appreciated all her hard work when he never acknowledged it? Most of the time, he came down on her for the couple of things she did wrong, ignoring all the things she had done without error.

After ascending the stairs, he stood there as if at a crossroads. His eyes journeyed left down the dark hallway that led to his bedroom before turning right, seeing the light that projected from Andrea's door. It was cracked. His feet carried him toward it. He was going to tell her how much he appreciated her and her courage at the corral. He neared the door, his hand poised to knock. It never met the wood. Braden remained motionless, mesmerized by the sight in front of him.

Her back was to him, her sweet body wet from the bath she was soaking in. Skin so soft, creamy, and beguiling. Braden could have sworn the lights from the bathroom were playing tricks on his eyes. Deceiving him into thinking someone's skin could appear so appetizing. A few, short tendrils of hair had escaped her pinned-up hairstyle, matted to flesh where the water touched.

Goddamn, she was beautiful. Ethereal and enchanting. And this goddess was in his house, naked and so, so wet. What Braden would give to join her, to have his rough hands trail along supple flesh that seemed forbidden for him to touch. How he'd love to lay her down and worship at her altar like the gods and goddesses of old. What rewards would she give him for proper tribute? A pleased sigh or her wetness christening his tongue as he drank from her?

Braden was the hardest he'd ever been in his life. To say he wanted her was an understatement. He got harder at the thought of laying her down beneath him, her eyes wide and curious but expressive and hungry. Hungry for something he could give her. He wanted that so damn much, he ached all over.

A lathered towel smoothed up one of her arms, leaving a trail of soapy white fluff along her shoulder. Her arm moved just far enough from her body for him to see the opulent swell of her right breast that appeared full and high. Braden could imagine the majestic dark brown tips that crowned them and wondered if they'd respond faster to his tongue than his fingers, and how loud he could make her scream because of it.

On impulse, Braden gripped the side of the doorframe, his fingers tense as they contracted. The noise of the crackling doorframe beneath his fingertips alerted her. Dumbfounded, doe-like eyes connected with his. Her arms went up across her chest like he could see them from where he was standing. But for what seemed like years, she didn't tear her gaze away. And Braden could have sworn that in that window of time, he saw a glimpse of a yearning that reflected his own dire need.

He sure as hell wasn't going to get any sleep tonight. Although it wouldn't be the first time he had lost sleep thinking of her, now he would be haunted by those bedroom eyes that harbored any sort of desire toward him.

But as soon as he thought that, the desire she had shown him was eclipsed with anger. Her pretty brow furrowed, her eyes alight with a new fire. Braden backed away from her door and retreated to his bedroom. It wasn't because he was spineless. Oh, no. If he knew her by now, he suspected that he wouldn't be alone for long. She'd come running to confront him, tell him to go to hell a couple times before she was done. All in all, he'd be waiting for her.

Braden turned on a bedside lamp before peeling off his shirt as he waited for his pretty opponent to show. She might have wanted to start a battle, but the little lady would soon learn that some of the best battles were won on the home turf.

Andrea stopped to dry herself off before she whipped on her terry-cloth robe. She was so angry! How dare he spy on her like that! Then again, why did she have to be so responsive? Andrea's pussy pulsed at what she saw radiating from his eyes. His desire was laid bare in those brief moments, his hunger unmistakable.

She knew this. Then why in the hell was she confronting him? Andrea was still asking herself that when she barged into his room, startled by a bare-chested Braden. She was at a loss for words, her mouth opening several times, but nothing poured out.

He used the weapon of his body well, displaying his muscled goods to muddle her brain. From the sweep of dark brown hair across his broad chest, to his tapered middle. How even his corded abs seemed to jump when her eyes landed on them as if she had touched him. Her gaze drew down his body in an intent study before zooming back to his eyes. Even they were smoldering, boiling like hot mercury as he waited for her to respond. They were both breathing slow and heavy. The air in the room was thick, palpable, and enough to suffocate. Andrea licked her lips, almost forgetting the reason she pursued him.

"Cat got your tongue, honey?" Braden asked, a cool smile touching his mouth.

Andrea cleared her throat, attempting to gather some of her scattered wits. "What the hell do you call that?"

"What?" was the cold return.

"That voyeuristic stint you decided to pull back there."

Braden's face hardened. "It wasn't like that."

"Really? Enlighten me." She rolled her eyes when she received silence. "You've got some nerve. You had the audacity to accuse *me* of sleeping around with every male beneath the sun when *you've* been the worst out of all of them! You bastard…"

"Don't," he muttered. It was almost enough to make Andrea shy away. His gaze was still searing from the way it oozed from heated desire to hot malice. He began to narrow the distance between them. Andrea took precautionary steps back, unable to tell what he may do.

"I came with the honorable intention of telling you how proud I was of you." Andrea eyebrows shot up at that confession. "Or how much I appreciate what you've done around here. Done so much, but I hadn't given you the respect you deserve. And then I see this beauty bathing, looking like a goddess amongst us mortals." His eyes detoured down her body. He swallowed and paused a beat while those very eyes got heavy again with yearning. "A goddess so lovely that it took all my strength not to join her."

He stopped mere inches from her. Andrea's body ached everywhere as his eyes and words caressed her. "If I didn't know better, I'd say you meant for me to see you that way." She started to shake her head to deny it, still backing up until he seized her right wrist to still her. "A man can only take so much when tempted at the sight of a beautiful, naked woman."

Andrea tried to pull her wrist from his solid grasp. "You could have looked away," she whispered, her voice quivering at the nearness of him.

"Look away? No man in his right mind could, honey. Not when your eyes told me you'd enjoy all the things I'd do to you."

Andrea reacted before thinking, her free hand coming to pound at his hardened flesh. Braden, unaffected by it, seized her other wrist. "Why do you fight me? Always trying to fight or run away."

Andrea lifted her chin. "I'm not running away."

He bore her closer to the intimacy of his body. Not even the thick layer of her robe could protect her from his warmth.

"You aren't running now. Not while I've got you."

Andrea couldn't repress a shiver at the way his thumbs stroked the sensitive inside of her wrists. He studied her for a second.

"I believe I read your eyes right, and your body's reaction reinforces it. I can wager that the only thing separating your skin from mine is this." He moved, with her wrists still encased in his hands, to the lapels of her robe. He lifted his forefingers away to part the thick material, faint fingertips brushing her skin. "All I have to do is move it out the way..." He moved down to the belt that was her only salvation. He flicked one of the ends of it. "...or pull this free..."

Andrea flinched away, pulling against his hold. If he managed to part her robe in any shape, form or fashion, it would be over. "Let go."

"What is it? You're the one who came in here itching for a fight, and as soon as I return attack, you run. Not a good tactic."

"You're not fighting fair," Andrea replied, her voice quivering.

"Neither are you. Coming in here with that on is asking for nothing but trouble. Was this your war plan? Hmm? To distract me by letting me know that your body is naked and trembling beneath here," he indicated, his fingers brushing against a clothed nipple, willing it to life. Andrea shuddered. "Tempt me to surrender everything if given the chance to strip you bare and put you beneath me." He stepped forward, closing the gap she had tried to make between them. "If I could have you screaming my name as I fuck you, then I'd happily lose the war." He gave her a wolfish grin. "But we'd know who the true winner would be if I did, wouldn't we, sweetheart?"

Her pulse skyrocketed. Part of her yearned to hear more. To hear more of his rich, deep voice telling her how much he wanted her. The other part of her was afraid of where this was going. It was to a place that was beyond her dreams, and unlike her dreams, this was something she couldn't control.

She freed her left arm from his grasp and struggled to free her right one as she retreated for the door. "Let go! You shouldn't say that to me. God, I work for you!"

"Which doesn't matter a damn to me."

Andrea's eyes narrowed. "Is this how it's going to be? Prove you're superior because you're my boss?"

His eyes gleamed. "Boss or not, you can't deny that you want me. Want me so badly your body's quivering for it."

Andrea started toward the door, despite that he still had her wrist encased in the warm manacle his hand presented. She should have known better. She was ill-equipped to play games with a man like Braden, who had been around the block more than a stroll or two. He had thirteen years more of living than she, and no doubt ten times the experiences she had ever had. A girl like her had no business fooling around with something out of her understanding.

But that understanding came too late. As Andrea wrenched her wrist out of his hold, Braden attempted to grab onto her again. He managed to snag the sleeve of her robe, pulling it just enough to unveil the supple silk of her carnelian-hued shoulder. The struggle went out of her. She turned to gaze back at him. Her heart skipped a beat. His gaze burned into her skin as it zeroed in on her shoulder, eyeing it with such voracity.

If he had snatched her, Andrea would have fought him with everything she had. But Braden reached for her, his hand going to the robe to expose more of her shoulder. He guided her until her back met the wall, and she was trapped. But now, she didn't want to escape. The way his eyes held her transfixed made her push all reason aside. They veered from her face, back to the sweet section of flesh that was revealed.

The single stroke of his thumb sent irrepressible shivers through her. His arm wrapped around her waist, bearing her closer as his head bent to sample her skin. His lips trailed from the end of her shoulder and made their way to the supple column of her neck. His mouth fastened against her strumming pulse. If it weren't for the strong arm secured around her, Andrea would have fallen to her knees. A small, dulcet sound broke from her throat, and that alone seemed to be Braden's undoing.

His passion spiraled out of control. He suckled her, applying zealous open-mouthed kisses anywhere her skin was bared. She held onto him, her fingers digging into his sinuous shoulders to keep her anchored. Braden reached between them, pulling more of her lapel aside to reveal one of her smooth breasts. Andrea shivered at the introduction of cold air to her sensitive skin and cried out when he engulfed the enflamed peak into his mouth.

This time, her knees did buckle, but he held her fast. Her hands cradled his head to her as Braden continued to lave her sweet nipple with his tongue before sucking hard on it and scraping it with his teeth. The moans came, and Andrea was past caring about her pride. Her mind was whirling. These sensations were new to her, and the kindling Braden fed to her fire burned her alive. The strong suction of his mouth made her ache with such need that she squeezed her thighs together to ride the overbearing sensation.

In the breadth of a second, Andrea felt a tug at the flimsy belt around her waist and the robe parted. There was a hesitation and a sharp intake of breath. She opened her eyes and the breath hitched in her own throat. The way his blazing gray eyes ran down the soft curves of her body made her burn.

His hand smoothed up from her waist, cupping her left breast. He teased her hard nipple with his callused thumb. She emitted a moan, sagging against him as he continued to tease and stroke. Then his hand ran up to her shoulder, pushing the robe off to fall around her feet. Andrea exchanged a heated glance with him before he lifted her into his brawny arms and carried her over to the bed. Braden laid her down like she was precious. She rested there on display to him. The appreciation on his face was enough to make any woman feel sensual and wanted. But as soon as his eyes strayed down toward the apex of her thighs, she became shy and attempted to cover herself. Braden moved, holding her hands still, and shook his head.

"Never cover yourself," he muttered, his voice thick with desire. "You're so damn beautiful. So sweet lying there, waiting for me to taste every inch of you."

He drew back, taking a moment to whip off his belt and toss it away. But when he reached again to unfasten his jeans, he stopped. Her gaze stayed on his that was curious, but still unsure.

Braden smiled. "You little innocent." He eased down on the bed, his eyes lingering on every enticing, smooth curve. Though she was an introvert, there was an underlying hum inside her to know he found her attractive.

She jumped as his hand started at her stomach and worked its way to a breast. She gasped, arching her back against his hand as it cupped and rolled the straining nipple between his thumb and forefinger. His head dipped, inhaling her nipple back past his lips. Her body arched, her fingers curling into the dark tendrils of his hair, holding him there. With each deep draw from his hot mouth, she squirmed, and the more she squirmed, the more she cried out at the desire he fed her.

He released her lathered nipple with a pop before gracing it with a single lick. Andrea's hazy eyes opened to find his watchful but blazing with heat. She inhaled when he dipped down to cover her lips with his. Her tongue reached out to meet his, striking against it like a match that flamed the bonfire between them. She felt like she was at sea, set adrift by the combination of her clean scent and his sweaty, earthy one. Her upper body lifted from the mattress as Braden continued to ravage what she offered.

Braden's hand traveled down her body, going straight for the treasure of her being. Her hips rocketed off the bed and she moaned into his mouth, her fingertips digging into the structured mass of his arms. His thumb circled her engorged, slick love button. Andrea began acting like she was having a panic attack, her hips surging against his hand as he encouraged and stoked the flame to blaze wild. She broke the kiss to bury her head into the crook of his neck. When his thumb ran over her again, she sank her teeth into his neck a little to keep from screaming.

"Braden…" she panted. "Braden…I…"

"I know what you want, baby. I hear you," he endured. And he proceeded to move down her body, leaving a burning kiss here and there. Andrea shivered as she felt the tip of his tongue dip into her belly button, causing her to clench. He chuckled against her skin, and Andrea waited in anticipation of what he would do next.

She felt her thighs being parted to his eyes. She heard the throaty groan, feeling the air hit the coolness of her now-spread, soaked slit. Braden parted her further to see the captivating pink beyond. A finger stroked along her seeping sex before inching inside.

"Bra-Braden!" Andrea panted. She was strung so tight. Her every neuron was alerted and in anticipation of what he would do next. She trembled as she felt his digit baptize itself in her snug tunnel before withdrawing. Andrea felt the loss. She was craven, needed any part of him to fill her. She heard him sucking his finger and a hissed "fuck" coming from between her legs. "Braden?"

She felt his searing breath at her saturated threshold before his tongue reached up to tease her folds. She jumped, simpering as she arched her hips against him. His arms coiled around her thighs to keep them still and spread. His lower lip stroked her swollen flesh, then delved deeper inside. Braden lapped her up as if she were like a delectable, ripe peach. Slow and languid, then avid and ravenous. He sought her clit and suckled hard upon it, the sweet, succulent juices of her being racing down his chin.

Andrea bucked against him, unseating his mouth as the pleasure became almost too much for her to handle. Braden was hell-bent on enjoying every precious drop of pleasure her core released. By now, Andrea was screaming, not caring if the hands or the whole town of Rock River heard her. The pleasure she was achieving with Braden's skillful mouth was unlike anything she had felt before.

Her thighs began to tremble as he alternated between licking her throbbing bud and burying his tongue as far as he could inside her. Andrea couldn't hold back any longer. It was too much. "Braden," she cried. "Oh, shit, Braden!"

She was almost there, and Braden sought out her pleasure, his hold on her thighs intensifying as he drew out more of her saccharine honey. Andrea thrashed, her entire being tensing as something akin to fire burned her. She arched her back, calling his name as she came with such a force, she almost passed out.

Braden was relentless. He took her inflamed clit into his mouth again, sucking upon it. Andrea didn't have to wait long after her first orgasm to experience her second. She tugged, screaming louder than before, and pulled at him as she came back down from her ultimate culmination.

"No more," she said as he continued to work on her, nudging her little nubbin with the flat of his tongue. "Please, Braden. No more. I can't…"

He administered a few lingering licks before he eased back, giving the downy softness of her inner thighs kisses before he hovered over her. His eyes bore into her with a passion she had never seen before. He claimed her lips in a kiss driven by passionate frenzy, tasting her singular flavor. Then he placed hot kisses along her throat, bestowing them on every inch of her skin.

"Oh, baby," he whispered as he bore her closer to him. "You tasted so sweet, especially when you came on my tongue." Braden then took her hand and guided it down to the hard essence of him. "You feel that dick, Andrea?" She couldn't speak. She gave him a slight nod. "This dick wants to be inside you. Do you want to fuck it?"

Braden released a hiss of air as Andrea felt the cumbersome size that was on the verge of busting free from its prison. His cock swelled and throbbed under her exploring touch. Braden stole her mouth in another turbulent kiss, his hand pushing hers aside to undo his jeans. It wasn't long before she felt the sweltering tool notch against her weeping pussy. He began stroking it as he prepared for entry.

Braden kept his weight on his elbows as the tip of him nudged into her. Andrea waited on hitched breath as he moved an agonizing inch, Braden cursing into the delicate curve of her neck. He slid into her until he met with the resistance of her hymen, the delicate barrier that was the difference between being a virgin and a woman possessed by a man.

He was so thick. So encompassing. Braden inched out, his breath coming out choppy as he crawled back into her. "God, I'm about to come just getting the tip in." The eyes staring back at her were feral and turbulent as if it took his entire willpower to give her one moment of lucidity even if it was fleeting. "Want it? Say yes."

She did want this, wanted to feel him to his fullest, balls-deep capacity. But those fears resurfaced from before. They hadn't been able to explore what this was or what this was destined to be. What they wanted from each other besides jumping each other's bones. What else did he want from her? How would they deal with the aftermath of whatever this was? Andrea wasn't brave enough to ask what that unknown was. And she couldn't bear it that she would feel nothing but used. She hated that she couldn't face that outcome yet. Not yet.

She started to rebel, unable to push him away. Braden gritted his teeth as Andrea moved up, his cock slipping from her. He tried to grasp her wrists to still her flailing arms.

"Baby, stop. Baby, baby, don't!"

"I can't!" Andrea cried out, giving him a final push. "I can't!"

Andrea moved upon her side, her arms wrapping around a pillow like a lifeline. Ninety-nine percent of her was screaming at her! The back-to-back orgasms she had achieved by his diligent mouth had her yearning and curious for more. The way her body felt against his was nothing short of everything. She felt like it was the most natural thing in the world to lie beneath him, saturated in profound pleasure. But that one percent of her, that paragon of virtue and everything good, became the voice of reason.

She was in bed, without a stitch of clothing on, with her boss. Even though she had a ton of dreams involving him in scenarios like this, she never thought it would become a reality. There wasn't an ounce of protection between them. She never had the inclination to get birth control. Not like she was saving herself for marriage, but at least for someone she loved. She didn't love Braden. She was attracted to him, yes, but that's where she should have drawn the line and never crossed it.

Andrea had noticed how he had just unzipped his pants. The romantic notions inside her head wouldn't let go of that concept. He had let his dick out with just enough space to get inside her. He'd fire her after the deed was done. He might fire her for denying him. Either way, this was precarious.

Braden, whose panting had subsided, released a heavy sigh. "I want you."

Andrea grasped the pillow with shaky hands, still quivering from the sexual passion he had given her body. "I know."

Braden rolled until he was right behind her. She felt him prod against her backside, his skin still slick with sweat. She had to fight to not give in to that warmth. Braden's hand reached around her and found the ever-hard tip of her breast, plucking at it. Andrea bit her lip to keep from moaning because she still wanted it, wanted him so much.

He released her nipple, his hand running along her waist and resting on her hip. He kneaded the soft flesh. "Tell me what you want. Whatever it is, baby, I can adapt, and I won't go further than you want me to."

"But you're my boss, and outside of being my boss, I know nothing about you. Then you just…seduced me—"

"I wasn't feeling that before, Andrea," Braden countered. His voice was taut and cool, almost as if it had not been warm and intimate a few seconds prior. "You've got a will of your own and want it as I do. No seduction required. But if you think differently..." Braden rolled onto his back, his air now of indifference. "...then you can just get the hell out."

Andrea was shocked by his cruelty, but it was expected. She'd had the audacity to pretend that he had all but forced her into his bed, though she had dreamt of being there.

She rose to sit on the side of the bed, glancing over her shoulder. Braden kept his eyes directed to the ceiling. He wasn't having any of it. But she wouldn't apologize. If he could act indifferently, so could she.

Andrea went to where her robe remained discarded on the floor. She shrugged it on, almost afraid to gaze at Braden before she left, engulfed in shame. As she went back to her room, she reflected upon the situation with sadness. If it weren't for her moral outcry, she'd still be in his arms, being loved by him, if only for the night. But now, what ground she had gained with him was lost.

She closed her door behind her and sagged against it. Regardless of everything, their relationship had changed. She knew the choice she'd made to abstain would make her the target of Braden's everlasting hatred. Andrea slid to the floor as tears formed behind her eyelids, wishing she could turn back time.

Chapter Six

Braden didn't fire her, but Andrea was almost wishing he had. Before, when he didn't talk to her, he had at least grumbled a good morning or some other salutation of the time of day. Now his demeanor was so hostile, Andrea avoided him.

Their behavior was juvenile. Apart from the nonverbal form of communication, if Braden came across her in a room, he'd mutter some expletive before he left. However, she couldn't call him out because she behaved the same way. If there was something she had to do while he was in the room, she'd avoid eye contact, do her work and leave. Even then, she could feel his eyes digging into her back like daggers.

This was how it went down for days. Andrea was in a torturous way. It was difficult to be so disliked by a man who made her body burn at night. Braden invaded her dreams now that she had an inkling of what passionate heights she was capable of reaching with just the intimate sweep of his tongue inside her.

By that Friday, Andrea had resigned herself to this new status of their relationship. She had hoped Braden would soften, but she knew he wouldn't. He wouldn't admit guilt. She knew when he had apologized last time that it took a lot of eating crow just to say it. He was more than capable of holding a grudge for decades without a second thought. Caid could attest to that.

She might have been a virgin, but she knew what going into his room would involve. She recalled that searing stare he gave her through the cracked door of her bedroom and how those stunning eyes of his glimmered with profound appreciation and yearning. And for once, it was from a man who didn't repulse her, a man whose looks alone could set her on fire.

Late that morning, after she had finished with the kitchen, Andrea walked out toward the road for the mailbox. On her way back, she sorted the mail according to their importance. One particular envelope stopped her in her tracks. Andrea's heart thundered in her chest. It just had her name and address. There was no indication of who had sent it, no return address. But Andrea had a perturbing inkling of who it was.

"Hey, Miss Andrea!"

Startled, her eyes flew over toward the corral. The guys were there, some waving their hats at her. She smiled, masking her unease, and waved back. Her gaze followed along the jovial features of each man except for one in the background whose silver eyes glowered at her from a distance. Andrea's smile disappeared at the sight of him and she walked toward the house, hoping he hadn't kept his eyes on her the entire time and witnessed her brief moment of distress.

Andrea went back into Braden's study, placing the envelopes in their respective piles before she ripped open the one that came for her.

It was a message printed on a slip of paper that had been cut then taped to an index card. It was just a sentence that made her legs unsteady, and she plopped down in Braden's executive chair. Andrea closed her eyes, her apprehension rising as she saw those five words behind her eyelids.

I know where you are.

She knew her happiness wouldn't last, what little bit she had left. But she had to go. Andrea frowned at the despondency that surged within her at the thought of leaving. She didn't understand it. There wasn't anything here worth staying for. It wasn't like Braden would die of a broken heart if she left. Knowing him, he'd throw a party at her departure.

Even still, Andrea hated the thought of leaving South Land Ranch, but now she had no choice. It was her fault for getting too comfortable, knowing there wasn't a guarantee it would last forever. Was it always going to be like this? Would she be on the run for the rest of her life?

Fighting back the stinging tears that formed behind her shut eyelids, Andrea prayed for a godsend.

Later that evening, Andrea placed the last pot in the draining board and wiped down the countertops. Upon one of them was an envelope addressed to Braden. She eyed it with trepidation. He wouldn't be happy with its contents, knowing how he'd reacted to something like it before.

After she put up the dishrag, she picked up the envelope and made her way down the hallway. Andrea was resolved to just leave it on his desk and not say a word about it. Perhaps by the time he found it amongst his plentiful piles of papers, she would be out of dodge come tomorrow morning.

Andrea tried to ignore the nervous tension in her stomach. She hated to be a coward and run, but she just couldn't bring herself to tell him the truth. Her pride would rather take the brunt of his everlasting hatred than to let him know.

She was partway into his study when she heard a shuffle of papers. She glanced up, startled to see his dark head bowed over his paperwork. She had hoped to leave the letter unnoticed. Perhaps it would be best to leave it in the morning when he was out at the corral.

She turned on her heel and slinked toward the door.

"Always running, aren't you?"

The dry, blatant remark made her pause. Those four words were the most he had said to her in days. It was amazing how they had managed to survive on gestures and glares alone.

Andrea glanced over her shoulder at him, but he didn't even bother to look up, his eyes still on his work.

"I haven't been the only one," she said. "If I was in the room, you couldn't get away from me fast enough." She scrunched her nose at him before continuing her way toward the door.

"What's that in your hand?"

Andrea froze again, turning halfway. Those gray eyes were sharp, penetrating, and relentless as they now had her undivided attention. "Nothing that you'd want to see since it appears you have other things to tend to. It can wait."

"Bring it here," he demanded in a hard voice. His face was even harder, devoid of every emotion but aloofness. She had the stupid notion to hide the letter behind her back like a child hiding a broken vase, but that would raise suspicion.

Braden's gaze traced her curves to the envelope before traveling back up again. "What? Is it something illegal?" he derided.

Andrea held up her chin. "Depends on how you look at it."

"Can't look at it if I don't have it. Bring it here."

He held out his hand, impatient. If Andrea continued to stall, Braden would snatch it from her. Drawing on courage, she marched up to him and handed him the envelope.

He studied his name written on the face of it. Braden's gaze went back to her as his brow furrowed. "What the hell is this?"

"Read it and find out."

Braden's face relaxed before he proceeded to tear into the envelope and open the letter. He scanned its contents before focusing on her again, incredulous. "You can't be serious."

"As a heart attack, cowboy. As of ten o'clock tomorrow morning, I quit."

Braden tossed the letter down, leaning back into his chair. "Without putting in your two-weeks' notice. You understand I could sue you for breach of contract?"

Knowing Braden, he could make good on that threat. "Understood. You can dock my pay to make up for the two weeks I'm skipping out on, but I can't stay here. I *refuse* to stay here," she emphasized.

Braden's head jerked back almost as if she had slapped him. Just as well. The look he gave her now was nothing short of murderous as if she had. "And why's that? As your employer, I have the right to know."

"I have my reasons," Andrea evaded.

He was quiet for a measure. "Do those reasons involve what happened between us?"

Andrea didn't deny it, nor did she confirm. Her mouth remained shut, unwilling to disclose anything. Let him think whatever he wanted. The less he knew of the real reason why, the better.

"I deserve at least some sort of explanation."

"I don't owe you anything except an apology. You needed me to fulfill a duty. I failed in that, and I'm sorry. But if you want to get your rocks off by suing me happy, you're welcome to. I wish you good luck."

She turned to leave, to give him time to chew on her words.

"My God, woman, you're something else."

Andrea turned back to him. "What?"

"You have some goddamn nerve to just stand there and act as though I've desecrated your 'holier than thou' virtue and dragged it through the mud." His lips curled into that smirk far removed from humor. "But we both know that's not true, don't we? You wanted it."

Even when stated in a reproachful tone, Andrea's nether regions pulsated at the words. But she couldn't let him get the upper hand.

"And that's a good enough reason for me to stay? Just because you're able to…to…"

"Make you come with back-to-back orgasms?" he supplied. Her heart thundered against her ribcage at the dauntless grin that appeared on his kissable mouth. "And that was with just my tongue. I can only imagine how it would be if I ever got the chance to really be inside you and feel you quiver around my cock as you come. And you'll come hard, baby. I guarantee it."

He wasn't playing fair. It was obvious by the malicious gleam in those eyes that he was aware of what his words did to her state of mind. To her body. If she didn't get a grip, Andrea knew his wicked tongue would be caressing her clit, not just her ears.

"What would people think?" she inquired, determined to stay focused on the issue at hand. "What'll they think about how I've gone from being someone you hated to your fuck buddy?"

"Let them think whatever the hell they want. They'll talk whether or not something's going on between us. And you know they already have."

She knew. Word had gotten around town by Monday about how Braden had rushed to Caid's house to get her. The bruises they sported at church confirmed what everyone was speculating. She couldn't go to the store without people staring at her and whispering amongst themselves. Andrea cursed at the stupid move she had pulled over the weekend. No doubt others were linking her to not only Braden but Caid as well.

Even at the prospect of her taking them both at once. No. It was better that she was leaving before the speculation blew out of proportion like an overran soap opera.

"Then why feed into it? A rumor will always be a rumor if it's not true."

"What we did that night would put all those rumors to rest, wouldn't it?"

Andrea was grasping for straws at this point. The man was more than magnetic to her, but she couldn't let the thought of being in his arms sway her from leaving.

"We both know the real reason why you've decided to pounce on me. You've gone on without a woman for a while now, and I happen to be the one who's fallen into your lap. So, you're willing to forego all the hate and animosity you feel toward me just to have something to occupy that cold space next to you in bed. Well, I'm letting you know here and now that it won't be me. *Ever*."

His eyes flashed at the placed challenge. "I already told you. I don't hate you, so you don't know what the hell you're talking about."

One of her eyebrows cocked. "No? Prove me wrong."

"I wouldn't recommend that. Not when the result could be you flat on my desk telling me how deep you want it."

The air stole out of Andrea for a moment. As much as she had grown accustomed to his directness, she was defenseless with this sensual approach. Now she was trying to fortify herself against the husky, carnal assurances that flowed off his articulate tongue. She was fighting hard to keep standing on legs that felt like they could buckle at any moment.

"And you've just reinforced what I was trying to say. It's apparent that you don't give a damn about anyone else but yourself and your own gratification. No wonder nobody wants to come up here. With the hospitality you give everyone, I can see why people would go out of their way to walk a mile around you just to avoid contact."

Andrea was on a roll as she said the words that came to her mind and out her mouth. Even when his visage displayed a pained expression from her well-placed jabs, she couldn't stop.

"And God help any woman who's willing to put up with your bullshit. Anyone who's willing to be with you must be crazy or suicidal. Either way, they have my sympathy."

When she had said her piece, Braden said nothing in his defense, but his quicksilver eyes displayed what he thought of her, and it was nothing too keen.

Andrea didn't deem it necessary to say another word, and she left the brooding Braden to his own demons. Hell, she had her own to battle. But as she ascended the stairs, she wondered why it bothered her to see his brief look of pain.

The next morning, Andrea woke up, gathered her things, and went downstairs to start breakfast for the final time. When she served the guys, they all smiled and conversed with her, all ignorant that in a couple hours she would be gone from their lives forever. It would be best to keep them in the dark. It would be less painful if she didn't hear their pleadings for her to stay. And no doubt Braden would tell them she went to hell in his own, brusque way.

He was still MIA. Andrea recalled witnessing from her bedroom window the silhouette of a well-made form she knew to be his riding off to the north not soon after their confrontation. As far as she was aware, he hadn't come back. Even though he hadn't been in the house all night, Braden was present in her dreams, arousing her body, but from time to time, she would see that same agonized look he'd worn the night before.

She regretted what she had said out of anger. Andrea thought about leaving him a note to tell him how sorry she was but thought better of it. Knowing Braden, he'd tear it up before reading it, damning her and the contents with her. Perhaps it was better he continued hating her. From this moment on, she wouldn't be a problem to him anymore, and she would be just known as a woman who had stung his pride. But for Andrea, she would forever remember him as the man who had aroused more than her passion and touched her in a way no man had. Perhaps ever would.

With the last of her things packed up and ready to go, Andrea's glanced around with profound sadness, not wanting to say goodbye to a house that held so many memories for her, even if it was only home for a little while. But the small envelope in her hand reminded her of why she was running in the first place. It was for the good of everyone, and she'd rather have Braden hate her than to be around and see something terrible happen to him because of her. Over something that wasn't his fault.

Andrea dragged herself to her car, glimpsing toward the corral to see that none of the guys were out. Just as well. She didn't want them to know, but she couldn't help feeling depressed that in less than a minute, she was going to leave this ranch life behind and attempt to move onto something new. Whatever that was.

Her attention was caught on a sleek, black Lexus pulling up behind her car. Andrea slowed her steps, her eyes curious as two opposing guys got out of the sedan, dressed in black suits like they were spies or the Secret Service. Her heart was pounding so hard as they neared her, it was hard for her to form a single, coherent thought. These imposing gentlemen hadn't come to see Braden. This was a personal visit for her.

"Miss Banks?" the smaller of the two inquired.

Andrea stalled a split second before dropping her things and rushing toward the corral, the house. Anywhere. But Andrea, before she could run more than five feet, was grabbed around her waist, the air rushing from her lungs. She fought like a wildcat against the gargantuan who had been victorious in capturing her. She buried her fingernails into hands that refused to release her. A brutish hand reached around to cut the scream that was a split second from piercing the quiet air.

Her gaze went to the corral, still not a guy in sight. They were in the stables grooming the horses as they did every weekend. She squealed against her aggressor's grip, trying to make enough sound that someone would rush out of the stables to come to her rescue.

That hope expired once Andrea felt a blinding pain at the back of her head as the leader demanded her to be placed in the car. And the last thing she thought before losing consciousness was how she wished Braden were there to save her.

Samson trotted back toward the homestead. His rider wasn't in any hurry to get there.

It was already past the time Braden should have arrived to start the day with his men and to see Andrea leave the ranch. Leave him. He could have ridden faster to see her before she left, but he wasn't sure how he would have kept his mouth shut from convincing her to stay.

But stay for what? Upon reflection, Braden realized he hadn't given her a reason to. All he had been thinking about was the different ways he could have her. Reliving the way she came alive in his arms, and how he relished every sweet sound of her surrender. At the end of the day, what did that make her but a woman of convenience?

Braden didn't give a damn what someone else thought of him, but as much as he didn't want to admit it, what she had said last night got to him. In her eyes, he was nothing but a sex-craving bastard who wanted to have her not only make up his bed in the mornings but lie in it with him at night. He was almost abusing his power when it came to her but feeling her soft trembling body against his as she came undid him. Ever since that night, he had been dying, burning each time he closed his eyes and saw the image of her there, undulating and moaning as he took her.

Braden had spent the night away at his secret retreat that he had since he was a kid. He couldn't bear being at home with reminders of her. Lingering on the bed where he almost had her. The stables where he almost had the same. And she was still there. For her last night, she was just a couple of rooms away. And everything in his being was urging him to claim her body like he'd been aching to.

Instead of giving in to those urges, he left the house to sort his mind and feelings for this girl who had turned his life on its head. Not many women would tell him where to go without blinking a lash. She didn't hold any punches with him instead of bowing and scraping like a subservient little miss. No. Andrea gave as good as she got, and Braden had never found anyone more refreshing or desirous.

Nevertheless, he couldn't help himself when he was around her. Hell, just trying to sleep that night after she fled from his bedroom was damn near impossible. Not with her heady aroma loitering in the air, reminding him of what had taken place and what hadn't. He had drifted between ecstasy and anguish to have the divine taste of her on his tongue and her exotic perfume still on his fingers long after it was done.

There was something more, more emotional that tied him to her. He knew that night seeing her engrossed in the loving he was giving her. Observing that rocked him to his very soul. Her burning passion was what haunted him every night, and he felt bereft without it.

No woman had ever done that. Not even...

His eyes set with poignant despair as he neared the ranch. Braden rode over to the stables to dismount from Samson and passed his reins along to Dane as he exited without uttering a single word. Nor did Dane ask if he was going to come back. He started toward the house, but not before he caught a sleek, black blur flying down the driveway out of the corner of his eye. Braden's attention drifted toward the driveway and he froze mid-step.

Andrea's champagne-colored Toyota Corolla was still sitting there with her items in what seemed a haphazard pile beside it. Apprehension resided in him as Braden jogged over the rest of the way, noting the careless way her things were strewn about as if thrown down in haste. Perhaps before a pursuit?

He took notice of the little white envelope buried halfway beneath her suitcase.

Braden took it up and inspected it. It was postmarked a few days ago from Austin. He whipped out the index card and read that brief, cryptic line. His eyes hardened as he lifted them. He didn't like the feeling that poured over him. But Braden could bet his ranch that the black car that appeared too fancy for anyone he knew, and the note dealt with the same thing. And no doubt the reason why Andrea was determined to leave.

He raced inside to his study to fetch his twelve gauge from the gun cabinet. Amid the chaos whirling in his mind, he dug out his phone and called in a favor to the local sheriff's department. Braden then described what he saw to the best of his ability and what direction they were heading, no doubt taking the road into town before hitting the interstate going south if these men were from Texas.

Once he hung up, and with his shotgun already loaded, Braden ran to his truck, cranked it, and barreled down the driveway. He might have been going into something that could very well cost him his life, but he'd be damned if he didn't try and find her. And he was determined to get her back. Come hell or high water, he was getting her back.

They were still on the rutted, twisting dirt road that led to the lane going to South Land's sprawling acres. Even with all its class, not even the Lexus they chose could withstand the turbulent potholes in the road as the driver took no time to avoid any of them. The other two occupants in the car held on as the car's shocks caused them to rock. The one sitting in the back seat with their unconscious charge held onto the girl as best he could without dropping her onto the floorboard.

The leader struck the driver across the back of the head. "Slow down, you idiot! This isn't fucking NASCAR."

"I'm trying to get us the hell outta here!" the driver yelled back. "What if someone spotted us?"

"Even if they did, they won't find her," their boss replied. "We'll be long gone before they can do anything about it."

"I saw someone," the muscle confessed, staring into the eyes of the driver reflecting back at him in the rearview mirror. "He was coming out of the barn or whatever it was."

Despite that news, the leader refused to be deterred in declaring the kidnapping of the girl an easy mission. "He won't matter. By the time he realizes it, it'll be too late for him to do anything. We have the girl, and in about a few minutes, we'll be far enough away from here, so stop whining."

But two seconds later, they all had a reason to whine. A sudden *pop* sounded from the right rear, then the Lexus slumped on that side. The driver slowed the vehicle to listen to a sound they all regretted to hear before pulling off to the side of what little man-made shoulder there was.

"What are you doing?" the frustrated leader asked. "Keep going!"

The driver gaped at him. "On a flat? Are you out of your mind?"

The leader was damn near there. He peered behind him to see the muscle of the group staring through the back window with trepidation before his dark eyes fell down on the young girl still comatose from the blow. He had been instructed by his employer, Edward Gaines, that he had a package he needed to retrieve in buttfuck Wyoming where he and his crew would be paid handsomely for the girl's delivery. And nothing, not even a flat tire, was going to get in the way of him collecting that payment.

He forced his passenger-side door open, going to inspect what seemed to be a blowout. He growled in frustration and proceeded to kick the deflated tire several times. "Fuck this godforsaken place!" he shouted. "How in the hell do blowouts happen nowadays?"

"I don't know. Probably karma when you're in a hurry after a kidnapping," supplied the muscle as he exited from the back seat.

The leader wasn't in the mood for a smart remark. "Get over here and change it! I want to get the hell out of here as soon as possible."

"What about the girl?" the driver asked.

"Leave her. Holding her while she's unconscious will raise nothing but suspicion." When the muscle still hesitated, the leader damn near threw a temper tantrum in the middle of the road. "Hurry up!"

The muscle took off his suit jacket and proceeded to work on the flat while the leader and driver waited, all the while inspecting about their unfamiliar surroundings. They would peek into the car to check on the girl who was still passed out. Just as the muscle was twisting the last two nuts off, a burgundy-hued truck pulled up behind them, and they all froze with recognition. It was the same truck parked beside the girl's car back at the ranch. And as the man peered out of his window, the telling expression on the muscle's face made sense of who he was.

"Do you gentlemen need help with something?"

They all wagged their heads in a negative gesture, trying to stutter out a full sentence but getting no further than saying no.

"I see you got a flat there," the stranger replied as he climbed down from his truck, drawing a long, double-barreled shotgun with him. "Here," he offered as he cocked the gun and marched toward them. "Let me help you with that."

And before they could take off a hat, he placed two slugs each into the rear and front tires on the left side of the car. The vehicle shifted upon the jack as the other side became lower. Their wide eyes went to a man leveling with intimidating proficiency a weapon into their direction, with eyes no friendlier than the two barrels pointed at them. The driver moved his hand toward the gun inside his jacket, but their adversary was sharp in noticing.

"I wouldn't recommend that unless you want your hand blown off. And believe me, the lessons from my father and a tour in the military can vouch for my good aim."

The driver listened to what little sense he still maintained and eased his hand back to his side.

The man's eyes narrowed as they inspected the inept trio. "Where's the girl?"

"What girl?" came the leader's reply.

The man's jaw ticked once, and once was enough to get across that whatever patience he had was gone. He cocked the shotgun. "Wanna try again?"

"She's in the car," the muscle answered.

A slight, wry smile creased the man's mouth. "Smartest one out of you boys, isn't he? Now, march that way," he indicated with the point of his head. The leader nudged the driver as they, with their hands up in surrender, walked in front of the car. The man followed just enough to peek into the back seat. Even at seeing the girl, his features remained grim and blazing with vehemence. As much as they had boasted at how easy it would be to kidnap a girl, none of them anticipated locking horns with such a formidable enemy.

Then, almost as though it was timed to the very second, a sheriff's patrol car came from the direction of town. He rolled down his window, his brown eyes following from a firm standing vigilante to the long gun aimed toward three unfortunate individuals.

"Braden," the sheriff acknowledged.

"Sheriff Duchene," the armed man affirmed as the lawman exited his vehicle.

The rancher caught movement out of the corner of his eye, his gaze locking onto his targets like a heat-seeking missile as they attempted to flee. Without thinking twice, he lifted his shotgun and fired. The bullets flew a couple of inches past the head of the muscle and blew out a huge chunk of a tree nearby.

The three of them skidded to a halt, all of them looking at how close they had come to getting their heads blown off by someone who didn't care if the sheriff was watching him do it.

"Wanna push your luck?" the man asked. The trio turned to face him again, their hands up high again. "Brightest thing you guys have done all day."

Sheriff Duchene moved toward the group, his service revolver drawn. "Put your hands behind your head," he ordered and got instant compliance. The sheriff cuffed them with zip ties and proceeded to read them their rights. Meanwhile, the man addressed as Braden checked on the girl. When they were led toward the sheriff's car, those silver eyes blazed like hell and damnation, and they were aimed straight at them.

Before the back door closed on them, he came toward them with a threatening scowl. "If I find that there's more than that bump on the back of her head, jail will be heaven compared to the hell you'll get from me." His quicksilver eyes shifted to the lawman. "Sheriff Duchene," he acknowledged, touching two fingers to the brim of his Stetson.

"Braden," Duchene responded.

They all stared at this true son of Wyoming as he slammed the door and the car drove off. While they were still processing what had just happened in a matter of minutes, they realized with utter dread that they had failed their employer. Though fearful of the call they would have to make, a major part of them would take the wrath of their boss than the wrath of the man they had just left behind.

An almost unbearable throbbing at the back of her skull was the first thing Andrea felt as she drifted back to consciousness. She flinched at the pain, though grateful to feel it. It was a good indication that she was still alive.

She held her head as she attempted to sit upright. The pain intensified, and she squeezed her eyes shut as if to wish it away.

"Head hurts?"

Andrea's eyes popped open, elevating to see Braden standing over her with a grim expression. Her own face varied in emotion, one of surprise, confusion, then complete relief to be waking up on the couch in Braden's study instead of elsewhere. Or not waking up at all.

Her pretty features flinched as another excruciating throb racked her head. "Stay there. I'll be back."

Andrea bore the pain with as much tolerance as she could manage before he came back a couple minutes later. Her head, as much as it hurt, was still full of questions. The most prevalent was how in the world did she get back to the ranch?

"Here."

He offered her a glass of water and a couple of caplets. Andrea took them, popped both pills into her mouth, and washed them down. She tried to hand the glass back to him.

"Drink all of it," he stipulated in an unmovable tone.

Andrea drained the glass of its contents with a glaring Braden looking on. Once finished, he took the glass from her then got onto his haunches in front of her. He then rested a bag of ice against the back of her head and held it there. The cool compress, along with the medication, did its job as it numbed the pain. Andrea could feel his gray eyes staring hard at her, despite the tender gesture. All the while, she kept hers directed elsewhere. But a throbbing of a different kind went straight to her core when her eyes lit on the dark chest hair visible where his shirt was unbuttoned at the collar. She was sure he felt it. Felt the charge that shot up her spine as she remembered how it felt to have that chest graze against her engorged nipples as he moved over her.

An awkward silence settled between them. Andrea's headache had dissipated enough to allow the few logical thoughts in her mind to formulate. She lowered his arm away. "I don't want to get brain freeze." She graced him with a small, darting smile. "Thank you."

Braden said nothing as he plopped the bag upon his desk, followed by the glass placed with way more finesse. Andrea was edgy, unable to tell what he was thinking, but the deep lines on his face were huge indications that he wasn't happy. Then again, he seldom was.

"How did you find me?"

"By pure luck. If it hadn't been for the flat, you'd be long gone by now."

Andrea couldn't shake off the despair of where she would have been if it weren't for him. She owed this man her life because he'd risked his own to save her. She felt nauseous at the thought.

"The sheriff would like for you, once you're feeling better, to come down to the station to give an account of what happened."

Alarm bells sounded within her, and she couldn't restrain the panic lodged in her voice. "They've been arrested?"

"Yeah, but you don't sound relieved."

Braden watched as Andrea became restless, her eyes straying from him. He placed his booted foot on the left side of her, his gray eyes blazing down at her as he braced his arms on his thigh. "But now that you're conscious, I think it's about time you give me an explanation."

Her eyes widened as she popped up from her seat. "I can't," she said, fighting disorientation as she lumbered toward the door. She was frantic. She didn't want anyone to know. No one. Not even the man who had just saved her life.

"Where are you going?"

"I have to get out of here," Andrea stressed, stretching her arms out to keep herself balanced.

"Like hell, woman!" Braden grated as he reached for her. His arm wrapped around her waist to still her. Apart from the shock that was tearing through her from what had happened, his touch, as seldom as it came, unsettled her. Andrea's knees buckled. Braden supported her, picking her up into the masculine security of his arms, and placed her back on the couch.

His arms shot out to each side of her thighs, and he leaned in. Andrea retreated as far as the cushioned couch would allow, but Braden was so close, she could see the gray flicker in his eyes.

"I see whatever this is has you scared shitless," he began in a low murmur. "No doubt I've probably just signed my death sentence stretching my neck out to help you. Now, you're not going to move an inch until I know what the hell I'm about to die for."

Andrea hesitated. This was all her fault. As grateful as she was for him saving her, she was now filled with dread that he was involved in her troubles.

Braden whirled to grab the note off his desk and held it up. "Where did this come from?"

Andrea cast her gaze to the floor, ashamed to let him see the tears brim. "A debt collector."

"A loan shark?" he clarified. She nodded. Braden didn't stifle the raw blaspheme that tumbled out of his mouth. He was quiet after that, observing her and the meek way she kept her eyes lowered as a tear slid down a cheek. "Your father?"

Again, Andrea nodded. "My father loved my mother. He couldn't imagine life without her. But when cancer took her from us, he was filled with such…grief. Even though he pretended he was all right to me, I knew something within him died with her. After a while, he found an outlet to his grief: gambling. At first, it started off small. A friend of his had introduced him to gambling online. Then he started playing all the time after work, all hours of the night. I often had to bring dinner to him. But after a while, that wasn't enough. He started to go to the boat at Lake Charles every chance he got."

"He brought you along?" Braden asked.

"Sometimes. He'd leave me in the hotel to my own devices while he went and spent all the money he had earned. Even my college fund. After that was gone, my father was desperate for more money. Then *he* showed up."

Braden's jaw clenched at that foreboding note. "Who?"

"Edward Gaines," she remarked with a great deal of contempt. It left a bitter taste in her mouth. "He started coming around when I was fourteen. He supplied my father with the fuel he needed to keep going until an incident caused my father to shut off business with him except for paying back what was owed." She elevated her gaze to stare into his. "My father managed to rack up $5.3 million in debt. He proceeded to pay off half of it until the night he was found in his car at the bottom of a lake."

Braden's face hardened. "You think Gaines killed your father?"

"According to the police, I'm crazy for thinking that when all the signs pointed to just a horrible accident from drinking.

But I know better. My father knew one man who lived out there, and I believe in my heart that he had something to do with it." She laughed, despite the onset of tears that flowed from the pain. "The man even had the audacity to show up at my father's funeral, as bold as he pleased. He told me that because of my father's death, I had just inherited his debt to the tune of $2.5 million. I paid for it and then some. Sold off most of our things. Even a couple of heirlooms that broke my heart to sell. My father's insurance covered a good deal of the costs, and someone did buy our house, thank God."

"You said you paid it off. If that's so, why is he coming after you now? Exploit more money from you?"

"Possibly," she said, unwilling to reveal the reason why. "But he'll be disappointed. Apart from what money I had left over from my last semester in college, and what I've made from you, I have nothing more to give him. And I'm sorry I've gotten you into this. Your ranch was the first out I saw, and I took it. I don't want to deal with this anymore, but I never wanted to involve anyone else in this. I don't want to see anyone else hurt. Not because of what I've done."

Andrea, in her distressed state, saw the inferno rage in his gray eyes. "It wouldn't be yours to bear if it weren't for your father. Damn him!"

Her eyes flashed through her tears. "Don't, Braden."

He began pacing the floor before her, aggravation and anger flowing through him. "I know how it feels to go through grief. To be so eaten up with it, you can't function, let alone live the same way again. If I had a daughter, I'd *never* put her through that. And I don't understand how you can be so damn calm about it when I would be pissed as hell if it were me. It ain't right to be saddled with someone else's debt when it wasn't yours to pay."

"But I'm not like you. I can't be angry at the world for no reason."

"Oh, I have my reasons, honey. There's more to me than my bouts of hellraising and seducing unattainable virgins. Believe me."

Andrea raised her head, not willing to let him knock her pride. "I loved my father."

"Despite all he's subjected you to, I'm surprised you do."

Andrea flinched, not having the will to unpack all her emotional baggage. Not here and not in front of him. "I don't need this from you." She rose to her feet and walked toward the door. Her footsteps stopped when he grabbed hold of her upper arm.

"Where are you going?"

She stared at him. "I've told you everything you needed to know. Now I'm going to do us both a favor and leave."

"And go where?'

"Anywhere. I can get far enough away from here, they won't bother you again."

"I think it's a little late for that. I'm involved now, and I promise they won't get you. Not if I have something to do with it."

"You can't, Braden." She shook her head. "I can't let you risk your life for me. They'll kill you, and I couldn't bear it if you died because of me."

A portion of his mouth tilted into a rueful smile. "Stop it, honey. You'll make it seem like you care about what happens to me."

Her gaze darted away, almost unraveled by the devastating effect of that gesture. "I would care, even if that person is you."

There was something unreadable in his eyes when she said it, but she had a second to study them before she was swept into his arms. She struggled, kicking her feet as he made his way toward the stairs.

"Hush. I'm taking you upstairs to lie down and rest for a while."

"I don't want to. I'm not tired. I feel fine."

"Liar," he countered as he carried her into her room and placed her down on her soft bed. "You can't even keep your balance. Now, be good and rest. If you're still not feeling better, I'll take you to a hospital."

Andrea sat up. "Where are you going?"

"I have some things to take care of first, but don't worry. Someone will be here to look after you." His forefinger traced the soft curve of her jaw. "I'll be but a little."

It was funny how such a gentle action could mean so much. Outside of when he wanted to make love to her, this was the first tender feeling he had shown her since she came. She couldn't repress the way her wide eyes followed him out, yearning for him to come back, or how she had to restrain herself from leaning into that touch. Andrea shouldn't read so much into a gesture that didn't mean anything to him. But as her hand pressed against the place he had touched, that little act meant more to her than he'd ever know.

Braden was on a mission, slipping fully into the frame of mind he hadn't been in for fourteen years. Except when he was training in the military, he was taught to put feelings aside when it came to saving others. This time, his emotions were attached to this woman who now needed his help.

He had her back. Had a chance to protect her and, perhaps, explore these foreign feelings that stirred inside him each time she looked at him and the electric current that flowed between their bodies any time they were near each other.

The bastard who found pleasure in draining a young girl of everything she had didn't sit too well with him. Braden wanted to teach this heartless son of a bitch a lesson in terrorizing someone who was innocent in all of this. He couldn't blame Andrea for this misfortune. How could he? She was just a woman weighed down with a debt that wasn't hers to pay and sacrificed her livelihood just to be left alone. There was no telling how long she would have kept running, or by this afternoon's incident, how long she would be alive.

A troubling sensation settled in his gut. He didn't even want to think about what might have happened if he hadn't arrived when he did. Part of him felt to blame. If he hadn't left during the night, he would've been at the house to protect her. It was by providence that he had found her. He would be damned if today occurred again.

He strode out of the house and toward the corral. Halfway there, he gave a high-pitched whistle, resulting in his men herding out of it. In a terse speech, Braden proceeded to explain what all had developed concerning Andrea. The men, some sporting scowls as murderous as Braden's, were fuming that someone dared to threaten one of their own. And they were shamed that they hadn't witnessed her kidnapping or heard any commotion beyond the stables. When Braden suggested they rotate in keeping watch, they volunteered their services.

The first watch was Russ McShane, a married hand who lived some miles away and who had also done a couple of tours in the army. As Braden got into his truck, Russ had his rifle out and was carrying it toward the porch where he'd keep his post. As a precaution, he had a few backup pairs of eyes to keep watch on either side of the house for anything or anyone unrecognizable.

Braden departed from the ranch, taking the main road a couple of miles down to his destination. He got out and made his way to the front door and waited after he buzzed the doorbell. The person who answered the door wore a glower that mirrored his own, although his hazel eyes questioned.

"What the hell do you want," Caid breathed.

Braden ascended the last step. "We need to talk."

Caid was about to demonstrate just how much he was up for a chat by slamming the door in Braden's face, but Braden edged forward, splaying his hand on the door to keep it open.

"It's about Andrea."

Part of Caid's defenses lowered, but he still appeared on edge as he moved aside to let his rival step in.

Chapter Seven

Now Andrea knew how it felt to be guarded like the treasure at Fort Knox. She couldn't breathe without having someone nearby like the Secret Service. Her gazes out the window were marred by the constant patrol that circled the place 24/7.

After Braden got back later that evening when it all began, he laid down the ground rules for her. She was always to stay close to the house, and if she had to go outside for any reason, she was to be accompanied by one of the men. A good deal of the time, if she went to the stables to visit the horses, Braden was the one who was closer to her than a conjoined twin. It made for some awkward but soul-quivering moments when he'd be so close behind her, the hard essence of him almost brushing against her lush backside. It made her wonder if he did it on purpose; to let her feel the very instrument he'd almost used to take her virginity if she hadn't stopped him.

Even being said virgin, she couldn't help but notice how he was hard and ready to go each time she was around him. But he took care not to touch her. Perhaps this was out of precaution of what that touch might elicit if enacted.

A surprising change of fortune came the day Braden was going to upstate New York for a few days on business. He was walking toward his truck until another vehicle showed up. A person who Braden would have thrown off the ranch in ten seconds flat hopped down from his truck and shook Braden's hand. Both men's visages remained grim as Braden proceeded to inform Caid on items at hand before he left.

Andrea didn't question the sudden truce between these two men, but she supposed it was in her best interest.

Throughout the week, Caid would come over after all his affairs of the day were done. After dinner, he'd sit and make idle chat with her, even challenged her to a game or two of poker. One night he brought his books, and she promised him that if he brought them once a week, she'd keep them up to date for him. It seemed an amicable trade, considering he was willing to watch over her with his life while Braden was away. It was the least she could do.

Each night he was there, she'd studied his easy features that tended to be more carefree and untroubled than Braden's. His eyes would twinkle, either from mischief or mirth. He'd joke and tease to make her laugh, which she had done more times than she had ever done with Braden. In fact, she couldn't remember ever sharing a laugh with her brooding employer. Part of her wished she knew what his laughter sounded like. Or if he was even capable of such a thing.

Caid had the advantage of youth being about four years younger. But other than the indubitable quality Caid had in copious charm and heart-breaking good looks, Andrea wondered why she felt nothing for this man outside of anything platonic. Although appearances were deceiving, he had that wholesome, goodhearted personality that was the epitome of what she had always wanted in a man. And yet, Braden was the man she dreamt of at night. He was the one who set all her fantasies aflame. He was the one she wanted, despite he was the moodiest man she had ever met.

Perhaps it stemmed from Caid's numerous lovers Braden accused him of having, or maybe it had to do with the simple fact that she had become involved with Braden first. Trying to put a finger on the truth of the matter drove her mad, but she supposed it was just her luck to be attracted to a complete asshole.

Caid, during those nights at the house, was a perfect gentleman. He never came on to her but offered his company until she retired to bed. But then she'd hear him sometimes outside her door or pacing the hall during the night like Braden often did when he was home. And he did so when he returned home the following week, guarding her like she was one of the soldiers at the Tomb of the Unknowns.

Another routine that had changed was her going into town every Thursday to buy her week's amount of groceries. Braden accompanied her on those excursions. When he was out of town or unavailable that day, he asked Shelley if she could obtain whatever Andrea needed. Andrea went as far as to recommend someone else going in his stead, but Braden shot it down with a reproachful scowl that told her what he thought of that.

One Thursday came when Braden was out in the field and unable to break away. Andrea placed her request into Shelley. The waitress didn't get to come until after her shift was over, weary but still helped Andrea carry the grocery bags into the kitchen.

"I'm sorry about being late, hon," she apologized as she settled the bags onto the island counter. "I just couldn't get away. Hate to say it, but God bless broken buses. If it weren't for that, we probably wouldn't have gotten the business. Lord knows it's rare to see our diner packed for anything."

Andrea grinned. "You weren't the one who planted that huge pothole in the middle of the street?" she teased.

"God, no, child, but I thought about it. It's rare to have visitors pass this way. They sometimes wonder how us small-town folk thrive up here."

"Everybody has to live somewhere," Andrea said as she began putting things away.

"True," responded the older woman. "I wouldn't trade this small-town life for anything. I've got some folks who live in Denver. I only visit them ever so often but no more than I need to. Being with all those people just makes me claustrophobic."

Andrea smiled, but still felt a touch of sadness. Shelley went by her side.

"I'm sorry, honey. You're from a big place, and I know you miss it."

Andrea shifted her gaze down. "Austin was home. It'll always be, but I don't think it's possible for me to ever return there. Everything's still so painful."

The older woman laid a comforting arm across the younger's shoulders and gave Andrea an assuring squeeze. "It's only been a few months. The death of a parent is hard on anyone when it's unexpected. My father died of a heart attack at thirty-nine. I loved him. I was closer to him than I was to my mama. For years, the anniversary of his death, his birthday, Father's Day, my grief was still so strong, I couldn't handle those days when they came around until I decided it was time for me to move on. That's what he would have wanted. And I'm sure your daddy doesn't want the same for you, and he's glad there're people looking after you."

"I feel like an inconvenience to everyone." Unable to fight them any longer, tears streamed down Andrea's cheeks, fierce and warm. She grabbed an available paper towel to dry them. "Everyone's risking so much just to protect me. I can't even try to fathom how to pay everyone back."

"You don't have to worry about that. We're willing to help you out. After all, someone will have to catch hell from all us if they mess with one of our own."

"I guess that's part of my problem. I'm an outsider. I'm not accustomed to having people come to my aid like this."

Shelley snagged a bag and started to empty it. "Everyone considers you a sweet girl. I suppose such innocence is worth protecting."

Andrea moved from the counter to put her seasonings up in the cabinet. "Saying it like that makes it sound like I'm a bride trapped in a tower while a horde of bad men is coming for me."

"Isn't that exactly what it is? And for what it's worth, you do have your brave knight fighting for your honor."

Andrea's fingers fumbled with a small bottle of oregano as it went tumbling to the counter with a *clink*. She regained her composure and placed the bottle in its appropriate place. "Apparently, he's not the only brave knight I have. He's enlisted the help of Caid." She scoffed, though she couldn't repress a smile. "I have to admit that I was shocked when Caid pulled into the driveway like he's been visiting here for years."

"You're not the only one, honey," Shelley confided as she handed the next set of items for Andrea to put up. "Tell you the truth, none of us were expecting a truce between those two during this lifetime. Just as well. I guess life is still full of surprises."

Andrea leaned against the counter. "Braden told me once that this rift between them wasn't something that started with them. He had said he didn't have a personal beef with Caid. Is that true?"

Shelley glanced around to make sure the subject of her discussion was out of earshot. "Well, I'm not one to gossip, but you pour me a couple of cups of coffee, and I'll tell you everything."

"I hope you don't give in as easily concerning other things," Andrea teased.

"Only with good people I know. But as far as those people who are after you, honey, you don't have to worry about a thing."

Andrea carried two mugs to the table where Shelley was already seated. "You were right about the rift. It didn't begin with them, but with a couple of their ancestors back in the late 1800s. Their families came and settled, but both had their eyes on the same plot. The Sutherlands managed to outbid the Marshalls, but their rivals settled beside them. At least, for a while." She took a sip. "It started off as just pranks. Taking the horses' bridles from the stables and tossing them on the roof. Then piles of horse manure on the doorstep. The Marshall clan was known as practical jokers. And it went on for generations until someone came shopping around for trainers for his horse. Caid's grandfather, Cale, was the best trainer in the business. Rutherford Sutherland had a respectable operation on his own, but was the type of man who wasn't approachable, where Cale was the opposite."

"Sounds like a family trait," Andrea pointed out.

"You said it. Anyway, Rutherford Sutherland was nicknamed 'Ruthless' because he was ruthless when it came to his business, but he was good at what he did. But as I mentioned before, a prospective customer came shopping for a man to train his horse to be the next Thoroughbred champion. Rutherford Sutherland intercepted the man coming to see Cale Marshall and stole his business away. That man's horse went on to become the winner of the Triple Crown, the first-ever for the South Land Ranch, and certainly not the last." She scoffed. "Funny how trivial some feuds can be, even if it's over a horse."

But that horse was enough to cause an upset for a century. Now Andrea comprehended why that crucial part in her two knights' history had turned the tables of their fortunes. Her face then lit up in remembrance. "That's why Braden rubbed it in

Caid's face that the people from the Spanish royals came to him first."

She remembered how Caid had flaunted into the diner when she had first arrived, boasting his good fortune, but flinched at Braden's jab. As flamboyant as he was, she couldn't help but feel sorry for Caid. He did his fair share of business, but his prestige wasn't half of what Braden held. Caid had yet to breed a Triple Crown winner, although a few of his breeds did win a few Olympic gold medals in equestrian matches and dressage shows. Perhaps in the future, the winds of fate could knock things about and have them switch places or be equally successful.

There was something else that Andrea knew she wasn't going to hear from Braden. He'd rather glue his mouth shut than tell her anything personal, but it wasn't like she had been forthcoming about her past until her hand was forced. Still, she was curious.

"Did you know Braden's father?"

It was almost as if a dark cloud formed over the older woman's features. "I knew him. I did babysit Braden when he was a child for as long as I could stand it, not that he was a bad child." Shelley's cerulean eyes went off into the distance, searching back into her memory of long ago. "Obadiah Sutherland. That's a name I haven't said in a long time." Her face turned into a sour expression. "Haven't wanted to. Just saying it makes me want to rinse my mouth out with bleach."

Andrea's eyes widened. "Was he that bad?"

"If the devil had a son, it had to be Cash Sutherland. Ask anyone in town. They can't even say his name without making a face."

"Where did Cash come from?"

"He earned the nickname from his father. The man was born with dollar signs in his eyes but tried and true to his name, he made South Land flourish by any means, ethical or not. If there was a buck to be made, Cash would do it. And money was in the decision of marrying Braden's mother. She was a girl from a rich family. Young and bought the front he put up as this charming, loving man. He had the advantage since she wasn't from around here. Her father thought it'd be a good idea to invest three horses, his daughter, and her inheritance into South Land. All of that worked out in his favor and with the condition of whichever horse won either the Triple Crown or a ton of other derbies, Cash could keep it after its run to breed it. Her father got a couple of champs out of the deal, but too bad the investment of his daughter wasn't the same."

Shelley shook her head and continued. "Miss Gale is the nicest woman this side of the country and as sweet as can be, but only when she wasn't with her husband. With him, she was meek and mild. Then we saw she started to wear makeup to cover what he did to her."

Andrea's face didn't hide the revulsion residing there. "He beat her?"

"Like a damn man sometimes. We'd see a bruised cheek here, a black eye there. Sometimes it was for little things. Gone to town for a minute too long or talking to a man. The preacher, of all people! And he'd often accused her of cheating when he was the one running around on her like a cock on the loose."

"Why didn't anyone help her?" Andrea raged. "The police? Anyone? Someone should have saved her instead of letting that bastard abuse her like that!"

Her entire frame shook with the rage and passion within it. She would never understand how someone could treat another human being like that, without sympathy or remorse for their actions. She had never suffered the extent of abuse Braden's mother had, and she prayed to God that she would never have to, but her heart ached for Gale.

Shelley reached out and patted her hand, the contact bringing Andrea back from her troubled thoughts. "I understand, honey. But at that time, there weren't any laws that protected a woman from a man, especially if they were married.

But Miss Gale never once complained. She received a good deal of her beatings because she directed her husband's anger from their son to her. There wasn't anything Braden wouldn't get in trouble for. Every little mistake, he had to pay for it, and even with those little mistakes, Cash Sutherland beat that child without mercy. The older he got, the further Braden placed his feelings apart from him. Became so disconnected to the point that when his father would beat him, he wouldn't cry. He'd just take it. When I was babysitting him, his father had the decency to take him into another room instead of doing it in front of me, but when he came out, Cash had this look in his eyes. I'll never forget it. Those eyes told me what he's capable of doing if I told anyone, and I'd just sit there and cry while all this was happening to that poor baby."

Her voice broke toward the end, a couple of tears fell from her eyes and splashed upon the table. Andrea got up to retrieve an extra roll of paper towels and tore one off the roll to hand to Shelley.

The waitress dried the tears away, sighing as her hand wrapped around the coffee mug, fighting the tears that remained on the verge of falling like the ones before. She took a few moments to salvage her composure. "I was young and scared to death of Cash Sutherland, but I should have done something to help Braden. Can't help but look at him now and see the emotional scars his father left him. The day after his graduation, he signed up for the army with his mother's encouragement. He joined, went abroad, and didn't come back until three years later when his father died. His horse had bucked and trampled him. He's the only man I knew nobody cried for. The hour after they buried him, Braden's mother moved out and has lived in Cheyenne ever since. She never comes back here. Can't blame her."

"Why didn't she leave him while Braden was in the army?" Andrea asked. "He was grown then and didn't need protection."

Shelley shrugged. "God only knows why. I never understood it myself, and no one dared to ask. Toward the end of his life, Cash started to travel more, leaving her to her own devices. After he died, that was her freedom. Gale couldn't get out of here fast enough."

Andrea nodded, staring down into the coffee still in her cup, growing cold due to her lack of attention to it. Now she understood him. The reasons for the remote feelings, that perturbing coldness he demonstrated to everyone. Except she had witnessed another side of Braden no one else had. She knew how attentive he could be as a lover. That very coldness evaporated every time he touched her, and all she could feel was the enveloping strength of a warm-blooded male. His hands on her body that night were hot, possessive, and reverent all at the same time. He was burning up with the same heated fervor as she.

Andrea hid her shivering as best as she could. What flares of passion had he shown to lead her to believe there were redeemable qualities about him? Despite the wrongs his father had done to him, one question still resided in her mind. "Was this what led to him to hating women?" she voiced.

"Part of it," Shelley responded. "Cheryl made up the rest."

That was a new name. "Cheryl?"

"Yes, Cheryl. Braden's wife."

Andrea's heart almost stopped. "His what?"

"Andrea, you didn't know Braden had a wife?"

She felt sick. Here she was, believing he had been a bachelor. Everything around the house that she had seen gave no indication that he had married anyone. Mrs. Gemma didn't give any hints of that either. Part of her felt betrayed for not knowing the truth. Not knowing this crucial part of his history. Her knight had courted another princess.

"N-no," she whispered eventually. "I had no idea."

"I can understand why." Shelley glanced down to the table. "Probably wishes to forget it ever happened." She polished off her last swallow of coffee.

Andrea rose to get the coffee pot and poured some more into her visitor's cup, then got her own to take back to the sink. She didn't feel like drinking more of it. Not with the way her stomach was turning somersaults. "Was she beautiful?"

"Lord, yes," Shelley concurred. "And didn't she know it. Long red hair, porcelain skin, a perfect figure, and the bluest eyes you've ever seen. She could do no wrong."

Andrea turned off the faucet. She wished she could do the same to the tumultuous feelings that rioted inside her. "Did he love her?"

"I believe he had affection for her. As close to love as he could get. They had known each other most of their lives through their grandfathers. Her family's from McFadden. And everyone was shocked when he came back one weekend hitched."

"How long ago was this?"

"Almost fourteen years ago, when he was twenty-two. His father hadn't been buried for a year. We often wondered if that's why he got married. Being out here in this big house can get lonely. He believed Cheryl could fill the void. But for the first couple years, they were everything a happy couple would be. If she asked for the moon, he would have done anything in his power to give it to her encrusted with diamonds. Then, once he started staying away from the ranch more on business, her eyes strayed elsewhere."

Andrea wandered back to the table and plopped down in her seat. "She cheated on him? How could she?"

Andrea couldn't imagine how or why. Braden had a body that made her nether regions flood to biblical proportions, and she was aware that same body was capable of harm when it came to revenge.

"Every chance that…little bitch got," Shelley spat. "Any man who paid her a bit of attention, she'd paid them back in kind, if you know what I mean. If I didn't know better, I'd say she was running an escort service, catering to a good deal of Braden's hands when he was off on business. One hand gave her special attention and the two of them began an exclusive love affair."

"Did Braden not know?"

"I couldn't say. But I'd give it to Cheryl. She gave a brilliant performance. Attentive to his every need, as pretty as a picture on his arm every Sunday at church. Braden pretty much bought whatever lies she sold. Even passing off a baby that wasn't her husband's."

That one threw Andrea for a loop. "She what?" she asked.

"About three years into their marriage, Cheryl got pregnant. Braden was overjoyed about being a father. Then the gossip grew tenfold. Braden was stubborn, ignored whatever he heard. He found out the hard way, catching her and the ranch hand in the act when he came home early from a business trip. She did her best to save her pride, hurling insults against him and his manhood, and told him that she loved only two things: her lover and Braden's money. He told her to leave but not before telling her that he'd petition to get his child. She told him it would be hard to get custody of a child that wasn't his. That broke him. Braden threw her out, let his hand have a few words, and tossed a few of her clothes and items out with her, vowing that it'd be a cold day in hell before she came back. Cheryl and her lover took off in the car Braden bought for her and flew down the road, disregarding the icy conditions. They took a bend too hard, her Jaguar landing upside down in a ditch. They were both rushed to the hospital, but she was DOA. Her lover, on the other hand, had a spinal cord injury he'll never heal from."

"And the baby?" Andrea edged.

"Died along with its mother. Twenty-one weeks along. But Braden did ask for an ultrasound and a prenatal DNA test. It was going to be a girl, but it was just as she had said. The baby wasn't his, and even though he had the true results, it has haunted him. Regardless who fathered it, Braden had his hopes on that child in wanting to give it a childhood he never had. After that incident, he buried his feelings and became what he is today. As the years passed, he let no one near him. And we had all lost hope that he would ever reach out to someone else. Until now."

Andrea's brow furrowed as Shelley stared at her, all the optimism within those eyes.

"He wouldn't be doing all of this if he didn't care about you."

Andrea, startled by what she was told, stumbled from her chair, reaching back to the counters for support. That couldn't be true. "You think he cares about me?"

"It's obvious. He's willing to sacrifice his life to protect you. He wouldn't do that for just anybody if he didn't care." She lifted her coffee cup to her lips. "Might even be in love with you."

Andrea laughed. "Love? That man wouldn't know the concept of it." She glanced toward the floor. "Love and lust aren't the same."

Shelley set her coffee cup down. "It goes beyond lust, honey."

"Really? He has a good way of showing it."

The older woman watched as the younger started pacing back and forth, wringing her hands. It was enough just trying to decipher these emotions by herself when she only had her input, but to have an outside source reinforcing what she was thinking...

"But now you know the reason why. All of these emotions he's feeling are new to him, too. Give him time to adjust."

"How much time? I don't know if my heart can do that..." Andrea glanced outside the window, watching the daylight waning from the sky. She went over to the refrigerator. She had to do something, anything to keep her hands and her mind busy and off Braden. "I have to make dinner."

Andrea took down the ground meat and got a few potatoes from the bin. Shelley stood and went over to her. "Andrea, stop. Stop." She placed her hands on Andrea's to still the paring knife. "Honey, why is it so hard for you to accept that as a possibility?"

Andrea's bottom lip quivered as tears dared to surface again. "I don't see it," she said, her voice faltering. "I think part of me is scared to."

"How do you feel about him?"

Andrea glanced out the window without focusing on anything. "I don't know," she replied, then shifted her eyes to Shelley. "I couldn't sum up in one word how I feel but...I want him. I'm fascinated by him. I love to watch him out in the field. The way he speaks and carries himself, despite that he does come off as an arrogant bastard. I'm drawn to him. But I can't love him. I can't."

"Why?"

"Because I couldn't bear it if he could never love me back."

Shelley forced Andrea to turn to her, although Andrea's shoulders were slumped in defeat. "You shouldn't lose heart. I know it's hard to give all your emotions to someone when you're not sure how they feel or if those feelings will ever be reciprocated." She stroked Andrea's dark tresses from her brow and cupped her face. "If it's to happen, it will. Just wait it out."

Andrea nodded before going into Shelley's arms, choking on the tears that came as she released the gale of her emotions.

The porch swing rocked to no particular rhythm later that evening while its occupant stared off into the distance as dusk settled around her. Her mind was elsewhere, reflecting on every little tidbit Shelley had told her about Braden. Her outburst made it appear as if she was in love with the man. She begged to differ. She felt appreciation for what he was doing for her, and she still desired him.

Desire wasn't love.

Braden didn't seem like a man capable of that emotion, receiving or giving it. It was one thing to be impassioned with uncontrollable carnal desires, but love? Andrea didn't think he could ever love anyone, though that was something he couldn't help. His mother was the only one who had shown her son any love or compassion, and she was just a small beacon of light in the darkness of Braden's soul.

So much damage had been done. So much. None of it could be reversed. Braden carried all those demons inside him, refusing to let anyone help him exorcise them. For the first time since she'd been there, she felt sorry for him. She might have considered him as a man without feelings, but she knew he had them or else he wouldn't be safeguarding them to prevent them from being hurt by anyone.

Braden Sutherland was a conundrum. How can someone so cold manage to make her melt as he did? And it seemed everyone assumed that Braden had deep regard for her. Andrea felt that wasn't it but couldn't put another emotion as to why he was doing all of this for her. Maybe he expected some sort of payback when it was all said and done.

She trembled, imagining what kind of payback that would be. She didn't esteem her body as the only thing he'd want in exchange for his protection, but it made her curious if her innocence would be the price he asked of her in the end and how she would pay without complaint.

"You seem to have a lot on your mind."

Andrea smiled as she saw the old ranch hand at the bottom of the stairs. "Hi, Handy."

"Mind a little company?"

Andrea scooted a little bit to make room. "Not at all."

The old hand made his way up and settled in next to her. They remained quiet for a spell. Andrea's eyes seemed occupied in studying the wooden planks of the porch while Handy glanced at her, reflective.

"Penny for your thoughts?" She smiled again at him and shook her head. "Come on. You can tell ol' Handy anything."

"I couldn't even begin to form into words what I'm thinking. I just need some time to figure it out on my own. But if I ever need an ear, I know who to go to."

Handy nodded and silence fell between them again. He set them to rocking, each enveloped in their own thoughts. Sal, who was the designated watch at that hour, greeted them as he passed by.

"It's so quiet here," she commented, making small talk. "Reminds me of my grandmother's house in the country. I remember when I was little, my mother would bring me there, and about five o'clock every evening, they would put on coffee and sit out on the porch, enjoying the quiet, waving to cars passing through. Back then, I used to hate going there because there was nothing to do, but as I got older, I came to appreciate that kind of life you don't get in Austin." She stared up. "Especially get a clearer view of the stars."

"I've always liked to take a gander at them myself. Me and Mrs. Gemma would just sit out here and point them out to each other. I'd always tried to show her how smart I was about that stuff, and she'd always listen with a smile."

It almost broke her heart to see Handy so sullen. Ever since Mrs. Gemma left, he had this smidgen of sadness he carried around with him. "You love her, don't you?"

Handy allayed a heavy sigh. "I've been in love with her for years, Miss Andrea. Before she got married. I wanted to ask her then, but Turner Upshaw got to her first. And after all these years, I still love her, even after I had married Sarah. But Sarah was good to me, as good a wife a man could hope for, but I felt bad for the longest that I couldn't devote all my emotions to her."

"I'm sure she understood," Andrea replied. "Why didn't you tell her how you felt after you were both widowed?"

"I was afraid. I don't take rejection very well, especially rejection from her. So I've been too afraid to ask."

Andrea felt sorry for him. She saw both sides of the equation. She knew how to want something and be wanted. Despite that Braden made sure to never touch her, she knew the tension remained between them. It was still evident anytime she had grazed her body against his by accident, the way he'd become motionless every time. That same war was going on within her, and with the new intel she received, she wasn't sure which side would be the victor in this.

Her gaze flitted away, only to collide with that of Braden at the base of the porch and seeing him with new eyes. A very faint smile appeared on his mouth as he regarded her company. "What are you up to, you old flirt?"

Handy rose from his seat. "Nothing but talking with a pretty young woman for a spell, which I hope I may have the pleasure again?"

Andrea smiled as she squeezed his gnarled hand. "Anytime, Handy."

He eased down the stairs, giving Braden a pat on his sturdy shoulder as he passed. "You old softy," Braden commented, following the older man until he rounded the corner and was out of sight. Andrea lifted her eyes to the man Handy left her with and was unnerved with the way he eyed her now. Lord, she was how young, and yet she felt like she had started menopause. One look from him was all it took to start the hot flashes.

She was stunned when he came to sit beside her and rocked them in their silence. He took care to sit as far apart from her as possible, and she did likewise. She supposed it was for them to be as careful as possible not to end up stripping and having sex right there on the swing. The palpability was still there and potent.

"You respect him a lot," Andrea pointed out.

"Shows, don't it? Handy is one of those men I respect, and they come few and far between."

"Unlike your father?"

His eyes cut to her, though she didn't dare peek at him to read the emotion on his face. "He told you?"

"Shelley did, and then some, but please don't be mad at her. I asked. I wanted to know."

Braden released a heavy sigh from his chest as his gray eyes focused on the horizon. "I guess if everyone in town knows, I suppose you should too. My life hasn't been a happy one. I don't expect it to get much better, but I try to squeeze what pleasure I can out of it before it dries up and wastes away to nothing."

So much bitterness. So much pain and grief dwelling in him. She felt helpless, wishing she could put a stop to all those cynical feelings. But Andrea ended up surprising him and herself by leaning across the imaginary line between them to press her hand against his scrubby jaw. His eyes caught hers, unable to shield the astonishment registering on his face.

"I'm sorry, Braden."

His eyes darkened, and as she took that as her cue to withdraw, he took a gentle hold of her wrist. Almost as if trying to prolong that tender moment for as long as possible. She was sure his rough fingertips could feel the erratic strum of her pulse beneath them, her blood rushing hot in her veins. But instead of going with her impulses to ride him like no tomorrow, Andrea moved to stand but felt resistance when he refused to release her.

"Where are you going?"

"I-I'm g-going inside," she stuttered, searching her mind for an excuse, any excuse. God, his touch rendered her mind to mush. "I have some things to get out of the dryer."

"Just another excuse to run away from me, isn't it?"

Andrea withdrew her hand, her body rigid and regal. "You can think of it however you like."

She half expected him to follow her to the laundry room, but no heavy footsteps came behind her. Andrea didn't understand herself. She knew what was passing between them. She wanted him, and he wanted her. He had told her as much all those nights ago. Why did she keep refusing him? Was it to keep her heart on lockdown? She refused to be one of those women who confused lust for authentic affection. She refused to be an empty shell wasting away and yearning for a man she could never have outside of sex. She would want nothing more than to have him spread her over the washing machine and worship her body, but she could not admit that to him. As she took the clothes out, she knew without a shadow of a doubt that the day of reckoning between her and Braden would be coming sooner than later.

Oh, I'm gonna getcha, Andrea promised a dust mite that was a little out of her reach. She balanced with as much grace as she could on the stepladder, her left leg pointed out in a pose a ballerina might give her props for. If she were destined to fall, at least she'd have Braden's couch to cushion her.

Her tongue stuck out in gritted determination as she dared to step closer onto the arm of the couch to stretch herself to her limits. Andrea tilted a little more, her duster a centimeter away from claiming another dust bunny.

Almost there...

"What the hell are you doing?"

She whipped her head to see Braden scowling at her from the entrance, but the turn of her head was enough to send her body off-balance. She went flying backward, not toward the couch, but to the unforgiving wooden floor. She screamed, bracing herself for impact, but her hard landing never came. She opened her eyes and they encountered Braden's intense face. He was none too happy about her little stunt. It had been a little over twelve hours since their time together on the porch, and that moment was awkward enough. Being in this man's arms triggered a memory of what had happened the last time she was there. Right before he carried her to his bed and proceeded to eat her like his favorite dessert.

Andrea cleared her throat and her mind of the memory, pushing against his unmovable shoulder, flaring her legs with pleas for him to put her down. "Damn foolhardy woman," he griped in a tight voice as he placed her down to sit on the couch. "If it's not a loan shark that'll kill you, your own stupidity will." He paced, allowing Andrea to notice the dark gray pinstriped suit he had on, black polished boots and Stetson to match. Seeing him in his business suits made her just as hot as seeing him in his work clothes. But in his business attire, Braden seemed more unapproachable and distant compared to the other aspects of him.

His hands came to his hips, a stare hard and penetrating focused on her. "Tell me, what the hell were you doing?"

Andrea lifted her chin, not backing down from his tone. Like he had any right to be angry at her for doing her job. "If you're too stupid to notice, I was trying to get a dust bunny before you surprised me, and I lost my footing. That's all."

"That's all?" he parroted. "Woman, you're lucky I was here. You would have busted your ass if I weren't."

"What do you care if I did?" she bit back.

"I have the mind to bust your ass myself. I think that's long overdue."

Andrea balked. "You wouldn't dare!"

"Wouldn't I?" he countered, and before she could scramble away, Andrea found her wrist captured in a tight, unrelenting grip as Braden settled down on the couch and forced her face down over his lap. She squirmed, kicking and screaming. What kind of kinky shit was this? Braden shifted beneath her, and she couldn't mistake the solid ridge against her stomach. He was turned on as hell, and that knowledge quieted her to where she stopped struggling to get off his lap, but to push him as far as she could.

It didn't matter that Braden was dressed to the nines as Andrea began to rock as best as she could against him. Feeling the hardness thicken and stir beneath her. A shudder went through her, along with a tiny groan which seemed to have vibrated from her body to his.

At that moment, his hand did come down on her ass. Not too hard but the sound was deafening in the room. It remained there to keep her still, but not before it tested the plump bounty there. Andrea heard the ragged intake of breath, his exploration of her ass becoming more eager as he studied every delicious curve of her.

Another slap came on her other cheek with the same amount of force. Andrea was sure Braden was fascinated by the slight jiggle of it. The thought couldn't stop her from breathing his name.

"I've got a prospective client to see down in Laramie," he started, his tone thick like it was a trial to talk. "I need to go, but I don't want to. Not when I want to fuck you so bad." His hands kept touching her ass, his thumb now daring to stroke her through her jeans between her legs. She shivered. "And you'd let me, wouldn't you, baby?"

She bit her bottom lip. Andrea didn't say a word. She wasn't sure why it was so damn difficult to say yes. To give in to what they'd been craving. It would be so simple. So easy to let him. Deal with the consequences later. But her mouth remained shut due to the fear. Due to the prospect of falling in love with him with no return on investment. She had no idea how she could survive that.

Another blow to her ass came, harder, as if to punish her for her reticence. "Say it, Andrea. Say you want me to fuck you right here, right now."

She bit her lip almost to the point of drawing blood. She wouldn't give in. She wasn't ready. But those denials did nothing to quiet the hot rush of her blood in her veins, wishing to accommodate Braden in every possible way.

Her silence fed into the sexual frustration of the male who had her so enraptured. With a growl, Braden pushed her off his lap and stood. He straightened his suit, checking it for wrinkles. But it seemed like a superficial action to disguise that he was still hard for her.

Andrea glared up at him, her chest heaving with fury and the same sexual turmoil flowing through her own body.

"You won't budge an inch, will you?" he said. Andrea still sat there seething. Braden sighed as he lifted his Stetson to smooth the chocolate curls of his hair before placing it back on his head. "I need to get the hell out of here," he muttered, mostly to himself. "I shouldn't be gone long, but don't do anything rash." Braden lifted her chin, his stormy mercury eyes warring with hostile brown. "Do you hear me, Andrea?"

Andrea jerked her head away. "Sorry. I don't speak or understand asshole."

Silver eyes flashed lightning before Andrea was pulled to her feet and dragged until her back met the wall. His hands shot out, positioning themselves beside her arms to hold her there. She had no choice but to stare into turbulent steel-colored eyes that spelled her doom. He edged in closer, and she breathed in his cologne and the pheromones that were still surging.

"*Don't...play...with me,*" he threatened in a soft, unmoving voice. "You might not believe it, but I'm as calm as I can stand it so I wouldn't recommend pushing your luck. I went light on you with this spanking bullshit, but trust and believe, your sweet little ass will tremble as I take it."

Andrea's eyes widened, his meaning dawning on her. He didn't mean...there?

Braden smirked as he nodded. "When I said I wanted you, I meant *all* of you. Every inch, every hole. Every*thing*."

Her gaze narrowed. "I'm not something for you to own and use like one of your mares. No aspect of me belongs to *any* man, much less you."

"Not yet, but I *will* have you, Andrea, in every sense of the word. It's only a matter of time. This...thing between us has been building since the moment we laid eyes on each other, and it's eating us alive."

Andrea rolled her eyes as she tried to push him from her. Braden grabbed her wrists and held her arms wide as his eyes traced down her curves. He saw everything she kept denying in her words or lack thereof. The signs were all there. Her nipples were peaked into fierce points through her shirt, her breasts feeling swollen and heavy, desiring his hands on them. Her pussy was beyond wet and pulsing, and no doubt his thumb had already felt her steamy snatch when he had stroked her through her jeans. Her knees clenched together in a pitiful attempt at self-preservation, but they were quaking to keep her upright. She could even detect her scent wafting in the air, taunting her, daring her to dismiss it. Her breathing was labored, her flesh breaking out in goosebumps. All the signs of her need were alive, aching to be met. And she said nothing. Her immediate impulsion was still to lie even though Braden already knew everything.

He smiled with knowing. "I'll give you a couple days." His eyes took another languid tour down her body, his thumbs brushing against the insides of her wrists, feeling her erratic pulse. "Maybe not even that long. You're about to break, and it's damn obvious. But I can promise you this: once I get inside you, baby, you won't be able to love me enough."

"You can't force me," Andrea seethed, finding the fight within her. "I won't sleep with you just because you tell me to."

Braden released her. "That's the thing. I won't have to. When you're ready, you'll tell me yes." He adjusted his Stetson on his head and straightened his suit. "Stay out of trouble now. I should be back before supper."

Andrea was angry. Angry to have been found out and dismantled so well. Angry because what he said was true. "To hell with you," she said.

Braden took hold of her chin, his cold eyes warring with the venom residing in her own. His thumb traced the soft texture of her lips, feeling them tremble beneath it. "I have plans for that pretty mouth. Maybe if it was wrapped around what I've got for it, I won't have to hear it."

He started to leave when she fired off, "You're not big enough to silence me."

"Oh, honey. I'm more than willing to put my cock where your mouth is, but I doubt that's a wager you're willing to fulfill tonight." Braden dipped in to place a kiss on her lips that sealed this promise between them. "But you will." And with that, he walked out of the study, leaving Andrea in a state of undoing. She didn't know how to react, but she couldn't breathe for the longest time. How did all of this come about? Weeks had gone by since the night his fingers explored her naked flesh, and the yearning was still there.

Braden was right. There had been feelings mounting between them since they locked eyes on each other, and the culmination was for them to bang it out. Andrea felt in the very marrow of her bones that it was going to happen sooner than she was prepared for. She shuddered in anticipation, wondering how he would act when he got home. Would he leave her alone with the heightened awareness of what was to come, or would he immediately come for her, bending her over any surface she was near to slide his dick into her, slow and deep? Andrea wasn't sure she could handle either scenario, as both held the promise that Hurricane Braden was going to breeze through and leave nothing in his wake.

Andrea had no idea how to please a man, and she was at a bigger loss for how to please someone with Braden's sexual appetite. Would she be enough to satisfy? What would he expect of her? She had little expertise in anything past what they had already done. She had felt secure in the moment, but the aftermath had gone to hell. It was due to her own fears, but her desire for Braden was outweighing them.

She finished with his study and tidying and dusting the foyer before returning to the kitchen to prepare lunch. Her hands fixed what she was preparing, but her heart wasn't into it. His words echoed in her mind, and she found herself grabbing a hold of the counter to steady her buckling knees.

This was getting ridiculous. She couldn't allow a man's words, let alone Braden's, to weaken her like this. Andrea hated Braden more because of it. She never thought in a million years that a man could make her feel like this. So vulnerable. To turn her on with just words or a look. This man was out of her league. Out of all the women he could have, why her? She always considered herself pretty with an average figure. But she realized she had enough desirable qualities to make Braden Sutherland hard for her. She wished it were for more than what was between her legs.

She got her food together, settled it upon the table outside, and rang the bell. Andrea waited for the men to surface from the stables. Cooper led the way, followed by Handy, Dane, Russ, Sal, and J.D. They took their places and proceeded to dig in.

"Where's the rest of the guys?" Andrea asked.

"Still in there, I imagine. Daredevil's being his namesake today," Dane informed.

"Why?"

"He got a whiff of one of the mares we were training and broke loose. Before we could stop him, it was too late. He had already mounted her. I know the boss is gonna throw a fit when he gets back, not to mention the owners if she winds up pregnant."

Andrea's body flooded with heat. Again, her knees weakened, forcing her to grip the edge of the table. She might have told him she wasn't a mare for him to own, but damn if she couldn't resist the visions that assailed her mind of Braden mounting her from behind, fucking her with wild abandon as she...

"Miss Andrea, are you okay?"

Her eyes went to Cooper who glanced at her with concern. "Do you need me to take you inside? Call for a doctor?"

She shook her head, faking a smile as she covered her out-of-control thoughts. "I'm fine. Just a little flushed. It was so warm in the kitchen." She stepped around the table. "I'm going to get them before the food gets too cold."

Andrea walked with as stable feet as she could manage. She focused on keeping one foot in front of the other all the way to the corral and into the stables. Buddy was tending to the mare that Daredevil had gotten to. Daredevil was off in another corral being detained. She had seen him prancing back and forth, almost as if he were indecisive of whether to break free again.

"Lunch is ready, guys, and I'd hate for you to eat it when it's cold."

"We're just about finished, Miss Andrea," Kel remarked. He took off the mare's bridle and saddle and put it up while Buddy led her to her stall. He stroked her before closing her door.

Buddy turned to Andrea, rubbing his hands together. "So, what are we having?"

"Fried chicken, fried okra, black-eyed peas, and cornbread."

He placed his hand to his heart. "Lord, Miss Andrea. You know the way to a man's heart. I swear I'd marry you just for your cooking."

She struck him on his arm. "Go on. I cooked plenty for you. You too, Kel."

"Yes, ma'am," he chirped as he rushed after Buddy. The rest of them followed until she was alone in the stables. She took a moment to meander. It had been a while since she had been alone here, a place she had often gone to when she wanted peace or time away from Braden. From anyone. She sometimes came out and settled in a pile of hay and allowed her mind to wander. A good deal of it wandered to the first time Braden had touched her. Tasted her...

Andrea shook. She hated him! She wanted him, but she hated him! Why must all the men in her life have something wrong with them? She lacked for choices, but there was one, despite the conceited nature, who had merit within him that surpassed all others.

Her eyes lit on a bridle and saddle hanging from their respective hooks and racks. A yearning blazed within her. Everywhere from the house to the stables had Braden written all over it. She couldn't stare at anything without it bringing him to mind. Where could she go to break from that? To have her thoughts to herself before the man who occupied them came home? It was as if her subconscious was answering her desire to be free of the Braden fog for a minute. Her body was on autopilot, not registering what she was doing as she placed a saddle blanket, the saddle, and bridle onto Samson and led him out the back. She mounted once she was clear and rode toward the beckoning woods, relishing freedom while her heart and body were still her own.

Braden's large truck pulled up beside Andrea's Toyota later that evening. He jerked the burgundy Sierra into park, resting his head against the headrest and squeezing his eyes tight. The meeting didn't go very well. The prospective client took a good look at the contract and what price Braden was willing to breed his horses and told Braden in not so many words to go to hell. Although Braden gritted his teeth to keep from shooting his mouth off, he told the man his offer would stand for a time until he withdrew it and left it at that. After all, business was business, even if the man had been an overbearing jerk-off who would like most services free if he could get them. Braden understood that times were tough, but that was the way of business. He had to make money, too.

He grabbed his Stetson from the dashboard and jumped down from his truck. Braden entered the house after waving to Russ doing his tour around the home. He loosened his tie in the dark foyer, tossing his hat upon the coat rack. It was quiet which was unusual. It was about dinner time. He smelled nothing coming from the kitchen except for the stale remnants of lunch. Andrea might have fallen asleep and forgot to set an alarm. Or maybe she was revolting against what he had promised her before he had left.

And he had meant every word of it. Braden was a man who preferred to resolve his conflicts quickly and upfront, and this was one conflict that had gone a minute too long. Who would have thought his beautiful conflict was so eager to be resolved? If he had known how his meeting was going to go, he would have stayed to put them both out of their misery. Her response to him was too potent to be ignored, and Braden was a moth to her flame.

God help him, he'd tried to be patient these last few weeks. Finding out she was a virgin and the reason why she was here, he decided to give her space. She would have kept the truth of a loan shark chasing her forever if she had it her way. He didn't hold that against her considering how desperate she was to escape, and he didn't regret her being there. Braden had never wanted anyone so much in his life. When he had married, he loved Cheryl to the depth of what he believed was love. He had wanted her, but it wasn't with the all-consuming desire ravaging him every time he thought of Andrea. It made him delirious.

Now, his lust demanded to be satisfied.

His every restraint went to hell after her soft, pliant curves were against him after he had caught her when she fell. When she squirmed against his lap… Goddamn, he almost came. It took the entire drive for him to think of all the turnoffs this side of the moon to cool his libido. Anything to keep from turning the truck around.

It was time. Long past time. Each time he had come to her, she had turned him down. It seemed she was willing to fight until the bitter end, but Braden was tired of it. By all that was holy, she was going to tell him "yes" before the night was done.

He went to his room to change into a button-down shirt, jeans, and boots. His mind was narrowed, his eyes on the hunt for her. Braden walked down the hall to peek into her room, not bothering to knock. Her room was neat, pristine, and vacant.

He called her name as he searched throughout the house, coming into the kitchen last. No sign of her. An uneasy feeling slinked in his gut as he went outside. The table still had the dishes leftover from lunch. A thunderclap echoed in the distance, a foreboding sign that reflected Braden's mood.

Braden strode to the stables, glancing about at the solemn faces that greeted him once he arrived.

"Where is she?"

All of them exchanged nervous glances with each other, as if trying to see which of them would be brave enough to be the spokesman for the group.

"Someone better answer me now, or I'm about to fire every goddamn one of you."

Wringing his cap in his hands, J.D. shrugged. "We don't know. She's been missing since lunch."

Braden's jaw clenched. "She's been missing for six hours and all of you are still here?"

"Buddy, Cooper, and Sal have gone out to search for her. We stayed on as a diversion just in case those scum who are looking for her showed up."

That was a good plan, but it didn't ease the pace of his heart. "Then how did she leave?" His eyes scanned the place until it came upon a stall that was now empty. His blood boiled as he figured the answer out for himself. This incident wasn't any of his men's doing, or even the loan shark who was after her. No. This was a classic case of a woman's stupidity, and she was about to pay for it.

Another thunderclap sounded. "Saddle Daredevil for me."

Handy glanced around at the stunned faces before going up to Braden. "Boss, I don't think it's wise. It's about to storm real bad, and we already have three men out there looking for her. We should just wait and pray for her safe return."

Braden didn't say anything more. He grabbed a saddle, blanket, and bridle and marched toward the far corral where the black Arabian was being kept. Daredevil calmed at the sight of his master and waited as he was adorned with his riding gear. Braden mounted and wheeled him to the direction of the woods. Even as the rain started to fall from the sky in earnest, Braden didn't flinch. His mind, as his mood, was black as coherent reason went out the door and only one thought remained.

I'm gonna kill her. When I find her, I'm gonna kill her.

Chapter Eight

Braden was going to kill her. A slow, deliberate, methodical killing. Not only did she leave the house, she ended up losing his most valued horse.

Out of all the *Lifetime* movies she had seen, she had just lived through one of those ill-fated moments where her pride overshadowed common sense. Now that she thought about it, her stupidity led to this moment of regret. Yes, she had left to get peace of mind, but Andrea also knew that it was to spite Braden. She thought she'd be back from her ride before Braden came home, but this situation was proof that God had jokes, and she couldn't imagine the hell she would catch returning home without Samson.

The more she searched for Samson, the deeper she strode into the brush. It never ceased to amaze her the acreage this man had, and Samson could be anywhere. She glanced up at the sky as it thundered above her, the clouds in dark, foreboding formation. She heard the distant sound of a whinny coming from a thicket close by. She hated to even think about going there, but she worried if Samson's reins had become ensnared.

What have I got to lose? Andrea swallowed her fear to venture forth. She could either die here or die at Braden's hands. Either way, she had lived a good life.

She followed the noise of the whinnies as much as she could before it was all drowned out by the piercing rain that came down in a relentless torrent. She called for Samson, her voice straining over the thunderous sound of nature unleashing its fury upon the earth, and it seemed the more she called, the more her four-legged companion eluded her, and the more she got lost.

It rained so hard Andrea couldn't see a few feet in front of her. It was also getting darker, so dark it seemed like nighttime. She would have to find somewhere to wait for the storm to lessen.

A cove of tree branches formed a natural awning as shelter from the rain. She sat beneath it, resting her head upon her knees as she waited for the right moment to leave. After a few, uneasy minutes, her ears picked up the sound of a horse whinnying. Andrea perked up, her eyes straining to see through the thick curtain of pelting rain. Then came the sleek, black coat of an Arabian, and he was not alone.

Her eyes widened at the sight of Braden scoping the area before his gaze locked onto her. His scowl deepened, his eyes remained cool and incisive as they watched her from amidst the brush. Despite her heart's elation, his visage said it all. She was a hassle. Chasing after a woman during a thunderstorm was far from his top priority. If he thought that, why did he come after her at all? He could have just let her drown and never be bothered with her again.

Andrea was galvanized, unable to move as he nudged Daredevil into a trot toward her. He glared down at her from his lofty height, scolding her without saying a word. Andrea would prefer if he told her off. Those gleaming, quicksilver eyes were more damning than any words could ever be.

She stood by him, her head bowed, waiting for something, anything to come. Braden reached down to lift her to sit in front of him, wheeling Daredevil around to navigate out of the thicket. She shifted, but with nowhere to move, she had no choice but to feel him behind her in all his callous masculinity and the warmth he exuded.

Minutes passed without a single exchange. Andrea kept moving away from him in the saddle. He wasn't having that, and his firm hand splayed against her stomach to keep her anchored. The contact made her jump, a few inches away from sinking down and touching her in a place that was throbbing in her jeans. Doubtless, Braden was not in the frame of mind to finger her while on the saddle, but she held herself on edge, wary of anything he might do to her.

And she was aware of everything. Aware of her ass being in the niche between his powerful thighs. Aware of his warm breath teasing her neck. The jolting trot of Daredevil didn't help. Between straddling him and with Braden to the back of her, she didn't know if it was just her or a sadistic version of foreplay.

They left the thick brush of the woods until they came to a clearing and an abandoned barn. Andrea eyed the graying, splintered wood that made up a structure that had seen better days. She did catch a few newer boards that attested to recent repairs.

Braden dismounted, leaving her to balance on the horse while he opened the door and guided them in. He helped Andrea down before placing Daredevil in a stall.

Andrea examined the place. There were cobwebs in dark corners and no doubt other creepy-crawlies and rodents, but there was fresh hay on the ground, a small buildout for a firepit, and a couple of tree logs for sitting. Andrea rubbed her arms, but despite her efforts, she couldn't diminish the chill she felt.

She watched as Braden took off Daredevil's bridle, his back turned to her as he stroked the horse's snout.

"Braden...I'm...I'm sorry."

He stopped mid-stroke as if realizing she was standing behind him. He turned his head a quarter of the way. "Where's Samson?" His voice was quiet with a hard edge. It struck her like the lash of a whip.

Swallowing, she glanced away. "I don't know. He...he wandered off."

Braden turned, his face black with mutable anger. He closed the door to the stall and walked toward the entrance. He gave a shrill whistle and a few more between intervals. Andrea frowned, thinking it was impossible for a horse to hear him, but she was astonished at the distant whinnying that soon came closer. A couple minutes of waiting and after Braden's last whistle, a drenched horse came up to the door. Braden grabbed his reins, stroking his snout as he guided him into a stall next to his brother. Once he got Samson settled, Braden went over to the barn door to close it, shielding them off from the world.

Now no one would hear her scream.

Though it was too dark for her to see anything but the outline of him, she could feel his eyes burning into her. She fidgeted beneath that intense glare, glancing everywhere else but him. She was waiting for him to blow up.

Instead, Braden went to some wooden bins in a corner and fished for some blankets, matches, and lighter fluid. He grabbed some wood stacked in another corner and took it to the firepit. Soon warmth and light flared into the room. Braden then stood, his eyes running down her soaked form in a harsh study before he began to unbutton his shirt. "Get undressed. The last thing I need is you getting sick on me."

Andrea didn't see why she should bother. The anger in his tone seemed like he wouldn't have cared if she caught pneumonia and keeled over. But she didn't want to get any more on his bad side and began to unbutton her own shirt.

Braden tossed his shirt aside and undid his belt. He dragged it from the belt loops of his jeans and bent it so that it doubled over. His eyes ran the length of it, admiring the quality of the strong leather.

She almost stopped breathing when he lifted that unbendable silver gaze to her, nailing her to the spot. Then he dropped the belt and crossed the distance between them. She tried to run to avoid him, but his tread overtook hers. He grabbed her by her upper arms. "What the hell do you think you were doing? You could have been kidnapped or killed! How can I protect you if you keep being stubborn about it?"

Braden released her, backing away as he ran tense fingers through damp, dark brown hair. Andrea fought back tears, biting her trembling bottom lip at hearing the anguish beneath his contempt of her. "Braden, I'm sor—"

"Don't." He went over to fetch one of the blankets and tossed it to her. "Wrap yourself in that when you're done." And he motioned to one of the stalls.

Andrea went inside one and proceeded to undress, wrapping the blanket around her but hesitated to come out. She knew she deserved this rage, but she still didn't want to face it.

"I know you're done. Get out here."

She shook her head, despite that he couldn't see it. "No!"

"If you don't come out, I swear I'll come in and get you."

That was the last thing she needed. Taking a calming breath, she gathered her clothes and exited the stall like a virgin bride facing her groom on her wedding night. Braden had his blanket wrapped around his waist. Her eyes dragged the length of him, at the dark hair sprinkling a well-structured chest, and how the blanket he wore rode low on his hips. She did her best to ignore the way he glared at her now, getting used to the fact that he was going to do that for however long he planned on them staying there. Or for however long he planned on keeping her alive.

Andrea organized her clothes on the stall door to dry, nervous when she hung her bra and panties last. She caught Braden's brief interest in them before his eyes flickered to her, something unreadable crossing his features. She didn't want to study the meaning behind that look and went to sit by the fire, keeping her attention to the flames. He settled across from her, doing the same. From time to time he would poke the flames with a stick.

Andrea buried herself in the blanket, unable to stop herself from glancing at him and the way the orange glow from the fire illuminated his sun-kissed skin, highlighted the masculine structure of his muscles.

Her thirst was palpable, and she was still too much of a coward to show it. She would glance away every time he would catch her, but her eyes never strayed from him for long. The process cycled until she couldn't stand it. Her gaze flitted about, trying to find words to occupy the quiet. "What is this place?"

"My secret hideaway. Found it when I was eleven after wandering too far. I fixed it up through my teens. Then I started using it when I needed to get away from home."

She wondered if he'd ever considered staying for days at a time. "It seems like it's been used recently."

"I was here a couple weeks ago. Stayed the night here to think things over."

Andrea thought back to the night she watched Braden ride out from the ranch. The night before Gaines' henchmen came. She had always wondered why he left. Where did he go? Was she right in assuming that what she had said that night affected him?

"I know what you're thinking," he said, his tone cruel. "The answer's no. I didn't come out here because of you."

Her eyes cut into him, the pity she felt for him withdrawn. "Did I ask?"

"Didn't have to. Your face is like a book, sweetheart. Pretty cover but an easy read."

A frown marred that pretty cover. "You're a bastard."

"And you're fucking stubborn as all get-out. What did I tell you? If I remember, I *told* you to stay at the house. Why did you disobey me?"

"Disobey you? I'm not a child."

He scoffed. "Could've fooled the hell out of me, 'cause what you pulled back there was a childish stunt."

Andrea could feel the anger inside her simmer. "Look, you don't have to be bothered with me anymore. I'm going to do what I should have done weeks ago. As soon as we get back to the house, I'm leaving."

The glint in those eyes faded. "Who said you're going anywhere?"

"*I* said. I'll have a better chance out there by myself than with you."

Intense eyes raked over her, stopping at the hint of a shoulder not covered by the blanket. "And how do you plan on surviving out there? Hmm? Flatter them with your pretty looks? Some men can be ruthless enough to take what's offered, intentional or not."

"What about you spying on me when I was taking a bath? You all but pounced on me!"

"Bullshit, honey, and you know it. Your body told me otherwise, and if you were concerned for your virginal state, you wouldn't have followed me." Warmth seeped into his gaze like hot mercury, lingering on spots of her becoming aroused by his study. "Since that night, I've wondered."

"What?" Andrea asked, her voice breathy.

"If your virgin alarm hadn't gone off, would you have stopped me from fucking you?"

Andrea took a quick intake of breath and held it captive in her lungs. She could count her heartbeats thundering against her ribcage. He was right. She was far too easy to read by the way he gazed at her with smug knowing.

"Judging from your reaction, you wouldn't have. Even now while you're sitting over there high on your pride, pretending to have the goodness and restraint of a nun when I know you'd want nothing more than to finish what we started that night."

Andrea shut her eyes, willing him to disappear like a bad dream. But Braden Sutherland couldn't be wished away like in a fairy tale. She was losing the fight against her body every minute, and she would give almost anything to have him put it anywhere he wanted.

"Stop," she whispered, a demonstration of how much of her will remained. "This is wrong."

"To who? You?" His voice was mocking. "I know this goes against the grain of your moral fiber, honey, but I'm not going to sit here like a damn monk and play off that your body has no effect on mine. Not when, after all this time, I've thought of little else."

His hard mouth set into a mutinous line, his quicksilver eyes scrutinizing a body he had already seen naked and trembling at his whim.

"It's hard to forget the essence of a woman. Your moans sounded so sweet, your juices even sweeter as you came. For days, I swear, I could still taste you." He paused, a glimpse of his tongue skimming across his lips followed by a small, impish smile. "Sometimes, I still think I can. But that came second to the moment I was inside you. God, I've almost gone crazy in the last few weeks. You have no idea how many nights I've wanted to come to you. I've surprised myself at how much restraint I've shown so far. But no more, Andrea. I've waited long enough."

Her gaze kept level with his, unable to break away as she remained mesmerized.

"I don't hear one of those classy comebacks of yours," he taunted. "So what's it going to be? Are you going to be woman enough to say yes?"

Andrea's ire boiled within her veins. "I'm woman enough without having a jackass like you pawing at me for his own satisfaction. I still have no idea why you want to sleep with someone you don't even like."

"I'll take whatever I can get any way I can get it."

"And who says that I'll let you when I hate you?"

"You say that, but your body doesn't. And deep down, baby, you know everything within you wants me, too." Andrea took a shallow breath as Braden tilted his head, considering her. "You know, by the time I had gotten home today, I had already resolved myself to being with you tonight. Fully with you in *every* capacity. You left me so hard when I left. Remembering you rubbing against me. And you knew what you were doing. Pushing me to my limit and damn near coming in my pants. That's asking for a fucking, and it was only amplified with this shit you just pulled."

"It's not my fault you don't have self-control."

Braden's eyes flashed before he popped to his feet, prompting Andrea to do the same. His pace was predatory as he stalked over to her. There was no place to go. She could either face the harsh storm still raging outside or the brooding, all-encompassing one that was surging forward to claim her in his devastating wake. Andrea swallowed her fear and stayed rooted as he continued toward her with an unhurried air, his silver eyes heated and direct.

"There's more electricity between us than all outside. It's been there since the day you set foot in Rock River."

Andrea shook her head even though she knew it was true. Her response came out whispery and unsure. "You didn't want me then."

"You had no idea what I wanted. I was a bastard to you to hide it. But I've wanted you the moment I saw you." Another step. "And I want you now." The last step had him a breadth away, his strong chest almost brushing her. The look of him was ardent, his gaze tracing over her. "Tell me yes, Andrea."

Fingertips reached out to stroke her face, but she bowed her back to avoid contact. He tried to grab ahold of her, but his fingers remained empty.

"Andrea."

"No."

"Andrea!"

"No! I...I can't."

"Why?"

That single-worded question reverberated in the room, but it carried so much weight for answers Andrea couldn't give him. She stumbled toward the stall where she had every intention of sealing herself away from Braden for the rest of the night. A fruitless run from what she knew was in vain. Because he was right. Every look, every word, every stroke was leading to this inevitable moment. As she fumbled to open the door, Braden's hand enclosed her arm to spin her around. He held her close, trapping her arms between their bodies.

"Let me go."

"Not until you tell me why. Why are you fighting this? Fighting me? What's got you so goddamn terrified?"

"That you'll use me!" she screamed, shoving him off. She felt the burden loosen as she revealed her innermost fears. "That you won't care afterward. That you fucking me would be all I'm worth. That my job, my *life* will depend on this." *And that you would never love me.* She couldn't say the last part. Andrea already felt embarrassed by her emotional outburst and couldn't bear it if Braden knew of the last thing that would break her.

But that emotional outburst had Braden's features register in shock. "I'd never use your body as a condition. I've always given you a choice."

Andrea rolled her eyes. "You've preyed on me, and you know it. Cornered me. Given me no choice in anything."

"Like hell," Braden growled, turning away for a moment as he got his frustration under control. "I stopped from fucking you every time you've asked." Andrea opened her mouth to counter, but Braden pressed on. "I've kept to myself, but then the whole lap incident this afternoon? I left you alone when I could have fucked you then."

"Because you had to leave! You wouldn't have stopped if this was any other day. What you've been telling me this whole time is that you're done waiting and that you'll force your hand one way or another."

"All I've ever wanted you to do was tell me yes. Yes, you're ready for me to do everything I've been dying to do to you. Yes, you're curious to see how the rest of me would feel so deep inside you. And yes, I'm the only man you want and trust to give that to you." He gazed at her with the assurance of a man who owned his shit and knew what he was about. And, it seemed, he wanted to be all about her.

She was startled when he smiled as he put his hands up in surrender and backed away from her, the aura of him leaving her personal space to allow her mind to return to some functionality. "You're right on something. I want you, and I've been an asshole to get you, but we won't do anything you don't want." He lowered his arms. "Whenever you want me, you can have me. At your own pace." His eyes diverted to the stall. "Go in there, baby. Get some rest."

She watched, stunned, as he turned from her, his hands going to his hair as he walked away to the other side of the barn. The sleek lines of his back flexed as his fingers clasped and unclasped his wet curls. He was showing restraint, showing a form of goodwill toward her at the expense of himself. So used to getting his way. So used to doing things, seductive things, and willing females to bend. Aggressive in his desire. Hard-edged in his want. But still, at the crux of it all, he was giving her a choice. He still wanted his answer. He still wanted his yes.

Andrea entered the stall, resting her head against the wall as the door closed, astonished by the reprieve. Her body was on edge, trying to sense his movement. Hushing her breathing to hear anything from him. The red thread of fate encircled them both in a trap. Braden had already stopped struggling while the war in her raged on. But it had accumulated to this point where denial was fruitless. She was a grown woman with her own desires, and those desires reached for Braden. Wanted…Braden. And she would swallow all the fears that were still staunch in holding her back.

No more. No more waiting. No more denying. She would own that fear and allow herself to feel, even for one night. A night where Braden would belong to her.

"Braden?"

Her voice seemed hollow, but Andrea knew that she was loud enough to be heard. She waited for his response, but the seconds ticked on without him saying anything. Her nerves were on edge, and she closed her eyes, readying herself.

"Yes."

She jumped when the stall door opened with tremendous force, her head popping up. It appeared that her agreement broke him, all traces of control gone. His chest heaved as his stare bore down on her, his passion turning her on and scaring her at the same time. Andrea backed up as he crowded her, the stall door slamming behind him.

Despite her backing away, Andrea was at a loss on how to proceed. Braden knew the perfect segue as he hooked her quivering frame with his strong, hair-roughened arm, bringing her into the humming heat of him. Their eyes remained locked as they started the slow, sensual tango of him leading her back until she met the wall. He smoothed his hands up her body, along her shoulders, her neck, until he cupped her face.

Thumbs stroked her mouth, eyes promising he'd not only give them what they both wanted, but that they would be satisfied.

He teased the corner of her mouth with a brief kiss. His lips trailed to her cheeks, down along her jaw to nip at her ear. The warm, damp heat of his breath sent a shiver through her, followed by a husky command.

"Say it again."

She didn't know if she had the capacity to say anything. As she hesitated, he reacted, latching his mouth onto her neck, and suckled with ravenous zeal. The tension ebbed out of her, her body feeling boneless as her eyes fluttered closed. Braden switched sides, marking her with equal fervor as his mouth made its way up to her other ear.

"I didn't hear you," he crooned. He retreated, but still within kissing distance. "Do you want me?"

Andrea swallowed, her throat dry. "Yes."

Smiling and with a seductive gaze, he captured her hand, bringing it up to kiss before returning it down to guide her between his legs. She gasped at feeling the thickness still protected by his blanket, the only thing separating her itching fingers from embracing it.

"Fuck," he panted. "God, Andrea, you have no idea how long I've wanted you to do that. Do you want to touch me, baby?"

"Yes."

Braden laughed like it was painful. "I believe I like you telling me yes just as much as you saying my name." He dipped his head against her neck and groaned. "Touch me."

With the confidence he instilled in her, her fingers found where his blanket was tucked and tugged, and her hand encased the throbbing cock. He tensed as her fingertips explored the veiny, daunting length of him, holding him firm as she stroked. Braden cursed in her ear, drawing her hand away and turning her loose.

She frowned at his change, and he shook his head. "It's too soon for me to come," he admitted as he proceeded to unwrap the blanket that hid her from his eyes and dropping it to the floor. "I'm not done with you yet."

His rough hands found the ample mounds of her breasts whose nipples sent immediate shockwaves from their tender points to her burning pussy. His mouth brushed against the curve of her neck again before trailing upward, leaving fiery, bite-sized kisses as the path ended at her trembling mouth. His tongue traced her plump lips, the tip of it dancing along the pursed seam before diving inside. Andrea couldn't resist the artful stroke of his tongue against hers, and the feelings it elicited within her. She moaned into his mouth, her arms surrendering around his neck and bearing herself more into him.

Braden's hands traveled over the warm, satiny flesh of her back before one of them moved again to her left breast. Andrea gasped as he plucked and pinched, squirming against him.

"No, no," he cooed as he lifted her generous breasts upward, his thumb passing along the straining tip. "Don't fight me, baby. Just...let me..." Braden then ducked to inhale the swelling bud past his lips. Andrea cried out, supported by his resilient arms as he bit, nipped, and suckled her aching dark nipples as if he'd die of hunger.

He tugged at it with his teeth before he released it and proceeded to engulf its twin. His groans were content as he drew on the stiff point, reverent in his worship. Andrea's hands tore through his hair as his head started to venture downward. She rested her upper back against the wall, allowing Braden to rest her long legs over his stalwart shoulders before he dove face-first into her dripping snatch.

Andrea's knees weakened as his tongue dipped in, flicking out to tease her. His seduction was ardent and meticulous. He lashed at her hardening bud, tentatively at first, a few licks before darting his tongue to lure her honey from deep within her. She panted his name, squealing with feverish delight when he come back to her throbbing clit to lick or suck it with ravenous, open-mouthed adoration.

"Fuck, so good. So fucking good..." he purred as he ran his thumb along the quivering, slick pearl as he stared at her swollen flesh. "So beautiful and ready to come."

He dove back in to resume his onslaught, drawing hard on her inflamed clit. Andrea screamed as she began to slip down the wall, unable to support herself as her orgasm drew near.

She was in for a rude awakening when his mouth ripped away from her. Her hazy eyes stared at him in disbelief and anger at being cheated. Braden rose to take her mouth in a savage kiss. He grabbed a handful of her generous ass, lifting her so that her long, brown legs wrapped around his waist and her pussy brushed against his pulsing cock.

"I want you to come, but I want you to come on this dick," he breathed as he notched himself against her slick entrance. "Can you do that for me, baby?"

Andrea couldn't answer, not as Braden would slip the tip in, withdraw, only to do it again. It was driving her out of her mind.

"Tell me," he demanded between clenched teeth. "Tell me yes."

To hell with pride. The only thing that mattered was that the man standing between her legs was about to give her the fucking of the century. "Yes...please," she implored.

In the next second, Andrea couldn't hold back a scream once Braden drove through her hymen. The breath rushed from her body, and her lungs failed to function. The only thing she could do was feel, feel her encompassing the thick girth of him. She was caught between a rock and a hard place in every sense.

Braden summed up the sensation in one gritted word. "Jesus."

Andrea couldn't find any words to say. His body was drawn tight, his fingers tense as they dug into her thighs as he fought for patience and control. She was just full, so full. Her tight tissues were unsure of how to proceed with the foreignness of him. When she clenched around him, Braden's lean hips nudged forward, pushing all the way into her. Andrea's distress became apparent as she began pushing at his shoulders and flailing her legs. Braden tried to placate her, but Andrea wasn't hearing any of it. She didn't want this. She was a fool for telling him so, but she was unaware that her jolting movements only succeeded in having him slide in and out of her and tossing most of his restraint out the window.

Braden's right hand slammed against the wall, mere inches from her head. "Goddammit! Don't do that!"

She stopped, and as they both waited endless seconds for her to adjust, the pain faded to where it felt uncomfortable and strange. Andrea shifted, her inner muscles constricting around him again. She heard a gruff, guttural groan coming from the back of his throat. His masculine frame shook, his forehead resting into the curve of her neck as he fought to give her as much time as he could. When it happened again, Braden was lost.

He released a frustrated grunt as he lifted his head to gaze down at her, his primal stare telling her that any control he had was gone. "To hell with it," he grated as his arms wrapped around her thighs to hold her in place. He drove inside of her. His hips moved rapid-fire, plunging in as he sought to be buried deep into her snug, wet heat.

"Fuck, you're tight." His voice was hoarse and labored. "So damn tight."

Braden, getting carried away with his lust, increased his pace, pounding into her as he nailed her to the wall. Andrea took the wild thrusts as she hung there. The climax she almost had now seemed like an unreachable goal. Cries did break from her throat, but not from bliss. His drive was brutal and relentless. She couldn't handle the girth of him that proceeded to stretch her wide. The time he gave her to adjust hadn't been enough. Now it glided in and out of her with relish but afforded her little comfort or pleasure.

Andrea squeezed her eyes shut, braving the pummeling until it was over. However, she opened them again to realize Braden had stopped, his mercury gaze zeroing in on her. She remained speechless, getting lost in those eyes that were overcast with the passionate storm brewing in them. He shifted her upward, stealing one of her nipples into his mouth. With each deep draw, Andrea could feel the fire that she had thought was snuffed out flare back to life. One of his hands maneuvered down between their bodies. His thumb found her swollen nub and flicked it, coercing with ease her feminine moans to flow from her throat. He watched with awe as she writhed in ecstasy, the orgasm she hadn't gained before in sight again.

"There it is. Closer, baby. I want you to come with me."

She *was* so close. Her quaking thighs encompassed him. Getting her closer to the peak, he withdrew his hand and braced her legs farther apart. Her swollen, damp folds had no choice but to open, leaving her at his mercy. He angled her enough to have his manhood graze the vulnerable little bud as he eased out then back into her with a single stroke, gaining the reaction they had both been waiting for.

Braden went back to work, pushing in and out of her body as if to make up for lost time. It was like lightning each time his hard dick brushed against her clit. The feeling was so intense, it felt as if her body couldn't handle it. Her nails found his back and raked without qualms. She gave a sweet little cry that was answered with a groan of his own.

"That's right, baby," he coaxed. "Give it to me. Let me have it."

Andrea tossed her head back as he pushed into her again and again. The horses were startled by the moaning, groaning and panting coming from them, but the two lovers were lost in the heights they were achieving together. Andrea burned, so hot from the sensation Braden was feeding her. She shook, her shaky cries and coos echoing. Each dulcet sound propelled Braden's hips faster, bringing her to the pinnacle of her overpowering climax.

Her body bowed away from the wall. She became rigid, releasing a long, throaty moan as she quivered around his still-driving cock.

"Fuck, bab—Oh, shhhi…God, Andrea!"

Braden sagged against her when his orgasm hit and then subsided, crushing her to the wall. Andrea clung to him, her heartbeat thundering against his as they waited to come down from their ultimate highs. After a while, he stood back, allowing her naked and well-satisfied frame to slide down the length of him as she was placed on unsteady feet. She collapsed as soon as he released her. Braden, also appearing off-balance, braced himself against the wall.

They exchanged a look of wonder and realization. A realization of how much everything had just changed.

God, he felt so good as he moved inside her. She mewled as she arched her hips to meet his, trembling and eager for release. Her nipples grazed the strong structure of his chest, grating against the brown chest hair and setting her ablaze.

"Look at me, baby. Look."

His husky command lured her eyes to open. Green ones gleamed as they hovered over her, their owner grinning with evil intent. Andrea screamed, her balled fist striking at any available place she could. "No! Get off me!"

Braden shook her, jostling her from her nightmare. Andrea stared wildly into solid gray eyes that were filled with concern.

Samson. The thunderstorm. The barn. She was tucked in a part of the world with Braden on a makeshift bed of hay and blankets.

"It's okay," he pacified. "It's me."

Tears ran down her cheeks as a sob broke from her. He frowned, brushing an ebony tendril of hair from her forehead.

"What is it, baby?"

Andrea couldn't answer. She collapsed into his arms, Braden stroking her hair as she cried for several minutes. Soon her sobs quieted to hiccups as she rested against his chest, comforted by the resounding thump of his heartbeat.

"He tried something, didn't he?" Andrea nodded. A vicious curse flew from Braden's mouth. "When?"

"The day I turned eighteen," she murmured. "He came to my father with a proposition. Because of the debt, he knew my father wouldn't be able to put me through school on his own. He had already burned through my college fund. He proposed to wipe Daddy's slate clean if I were offered to him in exchange."

Braden tensed, his breathing deepening as anger surged.

Andrea teased her bottom lip. "Daddy refused him and told him to leave. He left my father's study but sensed I was around the corner, listening. He was in front of me before I knew it, backed me into the dining room, and kissed me."

She squeezed her eyes shut, reliving that moment in her mind as if it happened twenty minutes ago. "I managed to push him away before he could try something else. He left the house before Daddy saw. But he knew. I hadn't seen him around after that except…I could swear I saw him watching me go to class or my study groups, or even when I went to work. I know it was him. I could recognize those eyes from anywhere. They've been watching me since I was fourteen."

Andrea scoffed, her fingers tracing invisible patterns on his chest. "But I knew even then that I refuse to be a victim. His or anybody's."

Her fingertips circled his nipple hidden beneath the dark chest hair, her mind not paying attention to what her fingers were doing until he grasped her hand, startling her. His smoldering eyes connected with hers as he rolled their bodies so that she was positioned beneath him. On instinct, her legs parted to permit him between them.

Braden cupped her head in his hands. "You won't be," he promised as his hard cock eased into her. She gasped as the exquisite length of him plunged deep. "I'll kill the bastard first. I won't let anyone have what's mine."

Andrea's brow furrowed. "I don't belong to you."

His head dipped low, his lips a hair's breadth from her own. "Not yet."

But you will. An unspoken vow that he sealed with a kiss.

Braden made love to her until the matters of her mind faded.

Chapter Nine

For the first time in her life, Andrea awoke next to a man. His hand propped his head while she remained on her back on their rough and ready-made bed. Despite the fact he was naked, and with the help of his five-o'clock shadow, he appeared dangerous. But that was before a genuine, lazy smile surfaced on his lips, and seeing that was enough to send her heart into overdrive.

"Morning, baby," Braden drawled.

Her insides stirred at hearing the sexy roughness in his voice. "Morning," she demurred. His eyes drew down her body with appreciation, taking in the sight of her uncovered breasts.

Andrea gasped, attempting to jerk the blanket up until he placed his hands on hers. "Uh-uh," he chided. "What did I tell you about covering yourself?"

"Sorry, but I don't do this on a regular basis."

His eyes flashed. "Good thing you don't. I like that I'm the only one who's seen you like this." His hand caressed the tender skin of her stomach, causing her to jump. He smoothed up to cup a breast and leaned forward. "Can't imagine who wouldn't want to wake up every morning next to these babies."

Andrea gripped the blanket, her back arching as he took a dark tip into his mouth, greeting each one good morning. Andrea sighed his name, drawing his head closer. He eased out of her grasp, taking one of her hands to place a light kiss on the pulse at her wrist.

"If I had my way, we wouldn't leave this place for days."

Andrea moved to put her arms around him. Braden shook his head.

"No, baby. It's too soon for you. Maybe after you've gotten a good soak in the tub, we can play later." He gave her a couple of lingering kisses. "Let's get dressed. We need to get back."

He withdrew with reluctance and got to his feet. Andrea admired the view of his tight, corded ass which he wasn't ashamed of showing off. The last time they made love, she had grabbed hold of it as he rocked within her, feeling the muscles undulate beneath her hands as he fulfilled both of their pleasures.

Andrea dawdled for a moment before she rose. Almost every single one of her muscles was against the idea. She put her best face on to disguise the pain when she walked out of the stall. She grabbed her things, then cut a sly eye to Braden. He had just slipped into his pants and was now working on placing his belt through appropriate loopholes, those keen silver eyes of his not straying an inch from her body.

She proceeded to get dressed, casting occasional glances his way. Braden finished buttoning his shirt and readied the horses. Andrea gathered the blankets, folding them and placing them back in the bins. She grabbed the can of lighter fluid and turned it over. What reflected on the lackluster surface was the image of a woman who had been well fucked. She still had the same eyes, but she felt different. She was a woman of passion, although nowhere equal to the man who made her insides burn to cinders.

Andrea's hands smoothed down scattered strands of her hair. Rain notwithstanding, her scalp still tingled from the countless times Braden's fingers ran through it, cradling her head as he stared down at her, his hips going a hundred miles an hour to bring her orgasm after orgasm after...

She growled as she fingered an uncooperative curl.

"Your hair looks fine." Andrea spun around to see Braden with a bemused look on his face. "We're just going back to the ranch, honey. Not a country social." He faced Daredevil again, tightening the saddle back in place. "Besides, I'm starting to love what my loving's done to you."

Despite everything they had done last night, Andrea was mortified. Braden glanced back to catch it. "The former virgin's embarrassed. That's unusual, considering all the times you've jumped down my throat."

Embarrassment gave way to anger. "Like you didn't deserve it."

Braden turned away, stroking Daredevil. "I did," he admitted. He didn't see the astonishment on her face, but her silence was surely enough. He grabbed Daredevil's reins and the leading rope attached to Samson. "You ready to go?"

Andrea shrugged. "Why not? It's not like I have to wait for the concierge to bring my luggage."

Braden released a husky chuckle. "Come on, honey."

She followed him outside and waited as he secured the barn then mount Daredevil. She moved toward Samson, placing a foot into the stirrup.

"Uh-uh," Braden reproached. Andrea glanced over to him. He crooked his finger. "Come here."

She stood beside him before she was lifted in front of him. "Braden…"

"Hush," he murmured. "It wouldn't be a good idea. Not when I rode you so hard last night. Better if you sit in front of me. And hold on tight, baby. I promise I won't let you fall."

Andrea did, wrapping her arms around his waist. Braden gave slack to the lead rope, wrapping it around his hand before starting off. They trotted back as if they had all the time in the world. Andrea closed her eyes, snuggling close to him as her head rested against his chest. Braden had his left arm enclosed around her waist, his hand holding Daredevil's reins with careful ease. His jaw rested against the crown of her head. This was how they stayed on the journey back home, not as if Andrea minded. She lost herself in his scent, his warmth, and his protection.

The reverie came to an end when the ranch was in sight. Andrea was jolted from her dreamlike state, reality kicking in. Braden dismounted then helped her down. He led both the horses into the stables, and then they were greeted by faces that could have used about forty winks, but life and relief poured into them at the sight of the couple.

"Thank the Lord you're all right, Miss Andrea," Handy said, lifting her hand and giving it a comforting pat. "You had us beyond worried."

"I'm sorry, guys. What I did was stupid, and I didn't mean to worry you."

"We're just glad you're all right," Cooper confided. "The way the boss-man rode out of here, we're relieved you're back and not buried somewhere in the woods."

Andrea blanched. As blatant as that statement sounded, she didn't glance to Braden for a denial when she knew firsthand how angry he was when he discovered her.

Cooper fumbled for a subject change. "When did he find you?"

"Last night, just as it was getting dark. We stayed in a barn to wait out the rain."

"We're sure you did," Dane supplied, although he, like the rest of the men, now glanced at each other, suppressing chuckles. And the ever-crude Dane wasn't done. "If I had a beautiful woman alone to myself in the middle of nowhere, and I hadn't fucked one in years, I'd spend all damn night letting my dick warm her up. Judging by the look of her, boss, you did a mighty fine job in that."

Andrea could have died. What happened last night seemed like a dream. This was reality, the real world where all their problems were visible, and their actions were transparent to others. Dane, always having the capability of shooting his mouth off first before thinking, evidently didn't realize how far he had gone until he saw her reaction.

She excused herself, stepping around the group of men and out the door. As they watched her, they didn't notice Braden until he grabbed Dane by the collar and propelled him hard against the wall. "Goddamn you, Dane!" he gritted. "*When* will you learn to keep your mouth shut? You say another thing like that to her, I'll string you up by your dick. You hear me?"

Dane stuttered out an affirmative, and Braden strode away, leaving him to face the goading jeers and teases of the men.

Andrea leaned back in the tub, sighing in relief. It felt good to soak to ease the tender ache in her body. Her hands ran over the sensitive tips of her breasts, still sore from Braden's constant worship of them. She shivered, her nipples hard again due to the thought.

He had called after her. She had ignored him. As he had mounted the stairs, she waited against her bedroom door, heart drumming in her chest. His steps paused before turning left to his room, and she breathed easier. She would have to confront him sooner or later. She just wanted some time to herself before she had to. The wall she had built around herself was gone. Everything she had kept secret had been laid bare. She had been on her guard for so long, it was hard to accept that this man had penetrated her defenses.

Andrea never thought she'd see the day that she'd be able to trust a man in this way. To trust anyone. But Braden was becoming something Andrea never expected. She was starting to see a decent man who was capable of feelings. The way he had soothed her were indications that the coldness was a hard shell to the emotions he didn't want anyone to see. Last night, he had allowed her to take a glimpse of a different Braden. A Braden whom she could fall hard for. Or was already in love with.

She held her face in her hands, tormented by her feelings. Andrea couldn't be in love with him. It was just a fantasy of wanting to fall in love with her hero. But there wouldn't be a happy ever after. Not if Edward Gaines or Braden had anything to do with it. Even if Gaines weren't in the picture, Andrea believed Braden could never love anyone. Sure, he was capable of tenderness and regard, but he'd never be interested in nothing more than what had been consummated last night.

Her mind was so preoccupied, she didn't hear her door open until she glanced up to see Braden, his silver gaze filled with heat as he stared at her. He was leaning against the doorjamb with his black Stetson in hand, dressed in a casual sports coat, a crisp white shirt, jeans, and a shiny pair of boots.

Andrea gasped, her arms crossing over her chest on instinct. "Braden!"

His eyes diverted down to her arms, then back up to her gaze before doing it again. Understanding his unspoken wish, she lowered her arms back down to her sides.

"Smart girl," Braden praised. "You'll get accustomed to being naked around me. Lord knows I could look at every sweet inch of you forever."

He glanced down when she didn't answer, facing straightforward in the bath. He turned his hat in his hands as if to keep them occupied instead of filling them of her. "I know you heard me. Why didn't you answer?"

"I'm surprised you didn't come after me."

"You didn't answer my question." He paused. "Look at me."

She turned her eyes into his direction. "You know why."

Braden didn't seem concerned. "What's to be embarrassed about?"

A fierce, irritated growl sounded from Andrea's throat. "What do you think? Every one of them knows what happened last night. They're not stupid. God, they must think I'm a whore or—"

"Don't."

She stared at him, those doe-like eyes shimmering behind a wall of tears. "I am."

"No, you're not. Baby, we know that you've only been with me. Regardless, who you're fucking is your own damn business."

"But wouldn't it seem strange how I went from someone you hated to your fuck buddy?" She shrugged. "I can't deny that I didn't want last night to happen. I'm woman enough to admit it, but now we've come back to where judgments are passed. I still care about what people may think. How guilty I'll feel to go to church with you on Sundays then you take me to a pasture to screw me afterward. If you had feelings for me, this would be better for me to swallow. But since our personal relationship won't go beyond the bedroom, it makes me wonder what'll happen after all of this. If you'll keep me on as a pity case or tell me to leave when you're angry or bored."

"I told you, it won't be like that.'

"Then what?"

Braden rotated the hat again, quiet for a spell. Andrea's idle fingers drew over the surface of the water, his response what she knew it would be. Even though her face didn't show it, she was disappointed that he had a conviction for everything else except for this. Then again, she was terrified to hear that she wasn't worth anything past the tip of his dick.

"I'm going to be gone for most of the afternoon," he murmured. "I'm expecting a couple of people for dinner tonight. Make sure to prepare a nice dinner, the dining room's ready and everything."

Andrea nodded, not sure what else could be expressed between them.

"Andrea."

She turned back to him. Braden neared the tub, bending over to lift her chin, and for the longest time, he got lost in her sparkling, dark eyes.

"Do you trust me?"

As if in a trance, she nodded. He then closed the distance between them, his tongue surging deep once his mouth connected with hers. It was a kiss that was subtle, yet she still saw starbursts behind her eyelids each time his tongue brushed against hers.

Braden withdrew, his fingertips skimming her cheek. "I'll be back before dinnertime."

He gave her another sweet kiss before leaving, leaving its occupant alone again to her thoughts. Hopeful thoughts of what would never be.

Andrea was in a dreamlike state for the rest of the day, analyzing every glance, touch, and the breathless murmurings he had told her last night. She kept telling herself not to read too much into anything except that their bodies were attuned to each other. No other emotions needed to be involved.

But how could she downplay her emotions each time they came together? How could she dismiss the curiosity in her mind that wondered what her children would look like with Braden as their daddy? What it would be like to have him as hers? It would never happen. After his first wife, she was sure the thought of marriage didn't sit well. Why would he ever want to go through it again?

Andrea understood that people were capable of change, but she had high doubts that Braden was able to do that even in the smallest increment. His soul seemed impenetrable; his feelings buried deep. But she had witnessed small flashes of a well-meaning man. He had lived up to the fixed opinions of everyone who knew him to be a cold son of a bitch, doomed from the beginning because of a harsh father and a cruel wife. And it seemed that everyone was expecting her to be his saving grace but trying to preserve what feelings were left in the man could very well jeopardize her own. She feared she didn't have the strength, and it scared her witless to try.

Andrea prepared a pot roast big enough for the guys and their guests. She had already straightened the dining room, dusted and polished. While the roast cooked, she tried to occupy her thoughts as best she could with making new notations into the books. However, her gaze kept flying to the clock on the mantel above the great, stone fireplace in Braden's office. It was a little after four. Braden had placed his coming back around dinnertime. Andrea couldn't help but feel anxious in catching a glimpse at him.

The fantasy played out in her mind, hearing his truck roaring up the driveway. She'd come running out into his embrace. He'd swing her around, give her a long, sweet kiss, and tell her how he loved her.

The dream faded when she *did* hear the roaring of a truck in the driveway. Andrea tossed her pen down and ran toward the study door but, catching herself, tried to dim the smile that stretched across her mouth. Her heart almost dropped when she heard a voice unfamiliar to her. A female voice.

Andrea almost jerked the front door open to see who this woman was and greet her with a slap. How dare he? How dare he do this after what happened last night?

Her mood blackened, and not-so-healthy thoughts flew through her mind. She busied herself with straightening things in the foyer and hallway to make it look like she was doing her job, not waiting at the door like a puppy. If he wanted to bring his lovers home, fine, but she would never give in to him again.

The front door opened, Braden's larger frame lumbering through, followed by a shorter, plump woman. His eyes locked with hers, and despite her building anger, she couldn't help but stare at Braden with profuse hunger. His own gaze told her without words what he would do if it wasn't for the company.

Her eyes followed back to the woman who came after him, carrying a bag that told Andrea she wasn't there for a day trip. The woman was in her mid-fifties, with blond hair that was short and styled to accommodate a heart-shaped face full of good humor. The older woman peered at Andrea and dazzled her with the warmest smile. Every bad thought went out of her head. With a smile like that, Andrea couldn't think badly of her to save her life.

Braden closed the door and walked up to her. He glanced back, stretching out his hand. "Andrea, I'd like you to meet my mother, Ms. Gale Sutherland. Mama, this is Miss Andrea Banks, our house and bookkeeper."

Andrea cleared her throat as she extended her hand to the woman who had given birth to such a handsome man. "It's so nice to meet you, Ms. Sutherland."

"Oh, it's Gale, dear. Please, call me Gale."

Andrea smiled. "Gale."

Braden started for his study. "I got a business call to make. Been playing phone tag with a client all day." He gave Andrea a brief nod and a prolonged look before shutting the door behind him.

Andrea was determined not to let her smile show and become too giddy. She turned her attention to his mother. "I can make some coffee, if you like, Gale?"

"Good, I could go for some, especially if it's not made by my son. No offense, but he has enough sludge in his coffee to coat a highway."

"I heard that," came the muffled reply behind the study door.

"It doesn't make it any less true," Gale Sutherland countered in a louder voice, smiling at the younger woman. "Why don't you make us some coffee, honey, and I'll go upstairs to put my things away."

Andrea watched as Gale made it up the stairs with no problem, just in time to see Braden opening his study door. His eyes zeroed in on her as his body followed suit. Her eyes widened as she took a precautionary step back. "Braden!" she squealed as he hauled her against him. "What are you doing? I thought you said you were about to make a call?"

"I am, but I couldn't make it until I did what I've been thinking about all damn day...amongst other things." He dipped down to sample her mouth, his tongue reaching in to sweep against hers. His kiss bent her, her knees giving as her body rested against his. She had a death grip on the front of his shirt by the time his lips parted from hers. For a few seconds, they lingered in each other's arms. His lips brushed against her temple, huffing a ragged sigh. "God, you're so sweet, baby. So sweet. What I wouldn't give to carry you upstairs right now."

"Your...mother," Andrea replied breathlessly.

He scoffed. "It's not like she's never heard the sounds of fucking before."

Andrea sobered at the crass statement and pulled herself out of his arms, a frown displaying her mood. "I refuse to do that while your mother's in the house. I might not have met her until now, but I'm determined to respect her while she's here."

Braden studied her for a long time. "That kind of respect is rare these days. Most females would love the opportunity to jump my bones regardless if she's here."

"I'm not like most females."

His eyes glimmered as they took a brief tour down her body. He gave a small, wolfish smile. "No, you're not," he agreed, "but I also know that with enough persuasion, you would…and you will."

"That's what you think," Andrea countered. "I refuse to sleep with you just because you say so. I still have pride."

"Oh, I know all about your pride, sweetheart, but that pride gave way to me last night, didn't it?"

He was goading her again. The merriment lodged in his face, dancing in those mischievous silver eyes showed it all. She started walking back toward the kitchen. "I need to put on coffee before your mother comes down."

"Andrea."

She turned to him, fighting the shiver that raced down her spine.

"This is a formal dinner. I want you to dress up."

Andrea blinked. "What for? I haven't joined your dinners before."

"This time, my mother's here, and I'm sure she'll like another woman to talk to at the table instead of shooting the breeze with us males. Wouldn't you think so?"

Andrea glanced away, rubbing the chill bumps on her arms that appeared out of nowhere. "I guess so."

He said nothing more and returned to his office. Andrea walked into the kitchen on shaky legs, still trembling from the kiss, the man, and the words. She was amazed she managed to hold onto the coffee pot. The coffeemaker was bubbling to the brim by the time the older woman had made her way to the kitchen.

Andrea proceeded to pour the coffee into their respective cups then carried them over to the table. "Cream? Sugar?"

"Cream, no sugar, please."

Andrea added it then settled down in a seat. For several minutes, they sat in silence. Andrea studied her coffee, stirring it with her spoon as she felt the eyes of Braden's mother on her. Features-wise, there wasn't much that suggested she was the woman who brought him into this world, however, she could tell where he got his eyes.

It was funny how eyes so similar could be so different. They harbored and projected different feelings. Braden's, even at their warmest, still had traces of coolness in them. It was strange to see them in the face of Gale Sutherland, whose eyes were jovial and kind. But she could also see the intensity Gale was capable of.

Gale set down her cup, volunteering to be the first to break the quiet. "My son was right. You're a beautiful girl."

Andrea almost choked on the coffee going down her throat. "He said that about me?"

"Oh, yes. He talks about you every time he calls."

Andrea snorted. "I bet it was to complain about how difficult I was or insulting my cooking and cleaning."

Gale shook her head. "Most of his comments have been good. He speaks more of you than he ever did of Cheryl. He couldn't sum up what he could say about her on a bumper sticker, good or bad."

"What did you think of her?"

If Gale was surprised by the question, she didn't show it. Andrea could see where a little of Braden's coolness came from when questioned about personal opinions. "Well, she came from good people. Too bad good morals were lost on her. She did a number on him. You've seen the effects of it. Braden's willing to make every woman pay for her sins." Gale sighed. "Situations like these happen, but I hate that it happened to him. My son's more sensitive than he'd like anyone to know.

His father tried to beat that out of him, grinding into his skull that no man should be vulnerable. He would shut himself down to never have someone do that to him again, but I know it's also to placate the ghost of his father."

"Then why does he keep a picture of his father in his study?"

Every time she had to dust and clean around it, the hairs on her neck would stand on end. She had wanted to ask him why he kept it there but then resolved that he had his reasons. She couldn't understand why someone would want to have that as a constant reminder of the hardships they endured growing up.

The older woman shrugged as she took a sip of her coffee. "God only knows. I've often asked him why he keeps that godforsaken picture, but I've realized it's a reminder of the man he could be."

Gale's speculation made sense. "If he was such an evil man, why did *you* remain married to him?" Andrea asked.

Gale's face changed color but soon she had it under control. She had years of practice schooling her emotions, keeping them concealed from a public curious to see them.

"I stayed with Braden's father because…I guess there's no real reason that could justify staying in an abusive relationship. Not because of love or even necessity." She paused. "When people bring you down enough, you tend to believe it. That you're never good enough beyond the bar they've set. Cash wanted your classic trophy wife, and showing my spirit earned me a beating each time. But I did finally get the nerve to tell him I had enough. He told me that if I left, he'd take Braden out of his will, cut all ties, and pretend that our marriage never happened. I didn't care what he did to me, but I refused to let him punish my son. This is his birthright."

"But Braden wouldn't want you to sacrifice your life for it," Andrea debated. "If it meant that much to him, you both could have taken him to court to contest it."

"Honey, you were fortunate enough not to have known Cash. He was good at getting what he wanted, and if he didn't want Braden to inherit South Land, then that was how it was going to be. He would have paid anyone to lie, cheat, and whatever else. But soon the beatings stopped when his affairs took most of his time. He died not long after that, and I left without looking back."

"Until now," Andrea supplied. "I know you haven't been back here. I can imagine that just by being in this house, it's conjured so many bad memories for you."

"It does. You try not to focus at certain spots. I'm sure from your experiences, you understand."

Andrea couldn't hide her surprise. "You know?" Gale nodded, and Andrea laughed, indignant. "Of course, you do. Everyone to the state line knows."

"No different from you knowing what happened to me and Braden. People who've had hard times come together because they understand." She placed her hand on Andrea's. "Your situation may not be the same as mine, but I know. You still have that same fear about your future, and that's enough to scare anyone." Gale squeezed. "It's funny how life can be. To have a thousand good memories to be marred by a handful of bad ones. It can change the outlook of your perception. Just like it did for Braden."

The grim tone of that last sentence told of a mother's sadness for her son and the helplessness of not being able to save him from despair.

"Do you think he'll ever be capable of love?"

Gale sat, lost in thought. "To be honest, I haven't heard my son tell me he loved someone in over twenty-five years. His father's doing. However, through his actions, it shows a man's love for his mama, even if he can't express it the way she wants. But the question should be if you love him?"

Andrea's cheeks flamed when the question rebounded. She found it funny that a couple days before, sitting at the same table, Shelley was fishing for the same. Except now, they had slept together, and new emotions stemmed from that experience alone. Even pondering her feelings all day, Andrea hadn't reached an answer. Or perhaps she did, and she was afraid of the possible repercussions of that truth.

"I don't know. There's a war going on inside me. It's difficult to explain."

Gale drew her hands up. "No rush, honey. It's just motherly instinct that has me wondering who has made my boy this animated in a long while. It might not seem much to you, but it's a huge improvement compared to before. You know, even after all these years, I still want what's best for my son. I still worry for him, wanting him to finally settle down with someone he deserves and show him that he's worthy to love."

Andrea shook her head, whispering, "I don't think I'm that person, Gale. It's not my job to fix him."

"How would it affect you if he brought another woman into the house? Any woman can be jealous without being in love, but a jealous woman in love can be a tragic thing to behold. Especially if it's felt for the first time."

Andrea exhaled long, dabbing the tears away. "You should have your own talk show and bestselling books."

Gale waved her hand in a dismissive gesture as she gathered her empty cup and went over to the sink. "Some things are better from a regular person. That's how I deal with all the women at the center I work with back at home. I give them advice on how to handle their relationships, abusive or not. The question is if they want to be at a place where they're happy? It took me a while to gain that knowledge myself, but it made me stronger once I knew." She placed her washed cup into the nearby draining board and dried her hands. Gale turned back toward the table. "Now, let's change the subject from all this dull stuff. Unless my senses have failed me, you're cooking a roast?"

Andrea smiled before proceeding to fill Gale in on the rest of the menu, although the previous subject of their talk still loitered around in her thoughts. Was she in love? She didn't want to build a fantasy on the broken wings of something that wasn't meant to take flight. To be in love was to surrender her trust, her entire self, but Andrea wasn't sure that was something she wanted to give.

Andrea took dinner out to the men at six, leaving the rest to simmer on low heat as she raced upstairs to hop into the shower and get dressed. She even took the time to place curls into her hair and applied a little makeup. First impressions were everything, and even though she was nothing but Braden's current bedmate, she would give their guest a show of being a true lady.

She peered at the simple, sleeveless sundress resting upon the bed. It was the last gift her father had given her. By that time, she had already sold most of her clothes to resale shops, and they scraped by with as little means as necessary. The gesture had made her cry when she received it, and that sentiment remained every time she laid eyes on it. Andrea had never worn it. After her father died, she had a hard time looking at it, but she couldn't bring herself to get rid of it.

She sighed, fighting back the sentimental tears that stung her eyes. "For you, Daddy," she murmured as she shrugged on the dress, caressing her like it was a warm hug from her father. A perfect fit. She slipped on some white ballerina flats, spritzed some perfume, and went downstairs.

It was a few minutes 'til seven, and their guest hadn't arrived. She proceeded to search for Braden. His study was empty, so she continued to the kitchen to witness a well-dressed Gale popping between the stove and the island.

"Gale, what are you doing?" Andrea came around the island. "You're our guest, too. I should be doing all that."

Gale hushed her as she bustled over to drain the potatoes in the colander she had sitting in the sink. She nudged Andrea away with her elbow as she proceeded to pour the potatoes out. "You've done enough already. Plus, you won't impress anyone if you get anything on that dress. It's far too pretty to ruin. But if you want to help, you can get the china out of the buffet in the dining room and set the table."

Seeing that she wasn't going to win this battle, Andrea went into the dining room. She hummed a tune as she arranged the dishes and silverware in their appropriate places. It was in her last place setting that Braden marched into the room. Her eyes drew to him, drinking in the delicious sight. He was dressed to the nines, from his polished alligator boots and neatly pressed black suit to the dark brown hair that was slicked back and damp from his shower. She loved the curling hair at the nape of his neck that refused to be tamed.

Much like the man himself.

For a long time, Andrea did nothing but stare at him. Braden returned the compliment, his silver eyes sweeping the length of her, fascinated by the dress that accentuated the curve of her hips and came to a stop a couple of inches above her knee.

"Come here so I can get a closer look at you," he burred.

Reticent, Andrea set down the remaining silverware and inched her way toward him. He took her hand and lifted it, prompting her to do a twirl. When she faced him, her heart almost stopped at seeing the pleased smile that stretched his mouth. God, if that man knew what his smile did to the floodgates of her being. Andrea had to clench her inner muscles to keep from making a mess on the floor.

"You look good, honey. Very nice."

It seemed he was saying that to her lips, his eyes telling her that he'd love nothing more than to kiss and lick off every trace of her lip gloss. Andrea started to inch away despite her hand still in his grasp. "No, Braden. Not here," she said in a low voice.

His callused thumb traced over of her hand before letting go, though his face told of his displeasure. "Don't worry, sweetheart. I'll behave…for now."

She gulped, knowing full well what he meant. He had promised her as much in the hallway earlier that afternoon, and Braden wasn't a man to be denied for what he wanted.

When they heard footsteps, they separated. Andrea occupied herself by straightening the silverware on the table while Braden adjusted a cufflink. Gale came into the room, eyeing them as she settled the potatoes and salad on the table. "Everything's ready." She glanced toward the grandfather clock. "Where is that man? I swear, for as many years as I've known him, Clayton wouldn't know the meaning of being on time if it slapped him."

Andrea frowned as she glanced at Braden. "Clayton?"

"Just an old family friend, honey. No worries."

She wasn't worried but more curious than anything. Her curiosity was about to be satisfied when the doorbell rang. Braden excused himself while Gale brought in the roast. Soon, Andrea perceived a man who was coming in behind Braden. A somewhat stout man in his mid-sixties, he was balding with salt-and-pepper hair and a kind face. He greeted Gale with a hug and a kiss on the cheek then turned his twinkling brown eyes to Andrea.

"Clayton, let me introduce you to Andrea Banks. Andrea, this is the honorable Judge Clayton Merrill."

The man greeted her with almost as much vigor as he'd greeted Gale. They went to the table, Judge Merrill escorting Gale to her chair, Braden to hers, then the men sat down. With bowed heads, they blessed the food before digging in.

Andrea, who thought she'd be an outcast, found that she was included in every topic and discussion, where her opinions were valued. At times, the dining room rang with rounds of laughter. The bulk of it dealing with childhood stories Gale dished out on Braden like the time he went to church with her on Easter Sunday and ended up getting into a fight with Caid in the mud, ruining his new clothes. Gale then proceeded to chase him all over the churchyard.

"You were so bad," commented Gale as they all leaned back in their chairs, letting their dinner digest.

"Yeah, but I won," rejoined Braden, "even though he damn near knocked my ass out the next day at school and cracked my tooth. God, that was hard as hell to live down, considering I got four years on him."

"Wasn't a fair fight to begin with since you are older," Gale pointed out. "And should have known better. You were a junior in high school."

"But what's all this talk about you two getting along after all these years?" Judge Merrill asked. "Every time y'all saw each other, you'd start swinging. What's brought about this truce?"

Silver eyes glinted over to Andrea, and she was captivated to hold them. A sly smile registered on his mouth. "For the protection of a certain interest."

Andrea couldn't contain her smile as she gazed down to her plate. Gale cleared her throat and slid her chair back. She began collecting the dishes. "I'll start some coffee and bring some dessert. Shall we move into another room?"

Braden scooted his chair back as well. "You can bring it to my office." He gestured for Judge Merrill to follow him. Andrea brought the dishes into the kitchen. Gale fussed at her for doing her job and shooed her out. Andrea ambled down the hall where she was greeted by Judge Merrill as he came out of the hallway bathroom. He charged her to come into the office while they waited for Gale to join them.

She came in ten minutes later, balancing her tray of goodies as she placed it down on the coffee table. They enjoyed

Andrea's blueberry crumb pie with a side of whip cream. When he was done, the judge leaned back into the sofa, patting his protruding belly.

"That was a wonderful dessert, Miss Andrea. I hate to say it, but you put my wife's cooking to shame. God love her, she tries, but even after all these years not much improvement. Perhaps I should send her over here for lessons?"

"This one hasn't always cooked perfectly," Braden teased. "Her first night here, and she managed to burn most of the dinner."

Andrea gasped, then her brow furrowed. "That was that first time. At any rate, you're not exactly a pleasant man to cook for on a trial basis. I almost lost my religion when you poured that coffee down the drain. Thank God Mrs. Gemma was there. I was close to letting you have it."

"I don't doubt it." Braden chuckled, staring at her as if she were the only one in the room. The man drew her in without moving a muscle. It was frightening, the power he had over her, and not just in the physical sense. For endless seconds, he made her forget about their guests until Judge Merrill got to his feet. He clapped Braden on the back.

"Well, a hearty congratulations must be said again. Now I've seen with my own eyes the reason you're willing to rush into such a commitment. With such a pleasant and beautiful young woman, I'm surprised it didn't happen sooner, despite the circumstances."

Andrea blinked as she tried to process what the older man had just revealed. Her heart thundered within her as she stared, dumbfounded, between Braden and Judge Merrill.

"What?"

Looking uncomfortable, Braden approached her with caution, his hand rubbing the back of his corded neck. "I've thought this over, Andrea. You came here seeking protection, which I can give you, but I could do a hell of a lot better if you had my name."

Her eyes widened, her stomach dropping inside her. "What?" she repeated.

"Goddammit all, woman! I just asked you to marry me!"

Andrea had to fight sinking to the floor, although her face told everyone how floored she was.

Hours before, she had resigned herself that their compatibility in the bedroom would be all. Now he was thrusting something more permanent at her. And how ironic that out of all the colors this dress could have been, it had to be white just for the occasion. Believer of fate, it almost seemed as if her father had been in on this in advance.

Andrea cast her eyes to Gale who didn't seem at all shocked. "You knew?"

The older woman stood up from the winged chair. "Not until today when he called me on his way to Cheyenne."

She should have suspected. His mother, who had never set foot in the house since she'd buried her husband, decided to pop up for a visit? No, not without motivation. The sudden marriage of her only son would prompt any curious mother to see the woman who had ensnared him.

But it wasn't going to be her. Andrea almost freaked out when Braden withdrew the velvety, black box from his coat pocket and opened it. Brandishing in the light were two exquisite bands of gold, waiting for their new owners to claim them.

No, this wasn't a dream.

"Oh, my God!" Andrea backed away. "You people are crazy!

"Andrea!" Braden barked.

No. She refused to take part in this shotgun wedding. She ran for the door but didn't clear the threshold. Her arm was detained in a strong grasp. She fought against Braden as he escorted her down the hall. He braced himself against the wall beside her while Andrea's back was against it, wishing she could melt into it. It took some time for her to glance up at him again. When she did, she witnessed the roiling passion in his look, swirling and accumulating into a huge storm.

Andrea slid along the wall away from him but made it a fraction of an inch before his left arm shot out to land beside her, stilling her movements.

"What the hell's the matter with you?"

"The matter with me? I should be asking you that question about this bullshit."

His façade darkened. "Asking you to marry me is far from bullshit. I'm dead serious."

"I know you are, but you couldn't talk this through with me before you brought your mother and a JP here? Where in the confines of your mind did you think I would be all gung-ho for the idea in the first place?"

Braden blew out a huff of air. He was losing his patience. "This is the most ideal solution to our problems."

Andrea crossed her arms with what little space he allowed her. "Ideal for what? So you can take me to your bed without a guilty conscience? Really, you don't sacrifice yourself for my sake."

"Goddammit!" he bellowed as he stepped away. He raked his fingers through his scalp, then whirled back to aim those churning, turbulent eyes on her. He was quiet as he regained control of his sensibilities.

Braden strode back, his finger pointed at her. "Listen, just listen to what I have to say. I know this isn't what you'd think is the answer to all our problems, but it can fix a couple of them for a little while. Yes, I want you like hell, baby, and there's no secret between you and me of how deep that wanting goes. But, despite that fire flaring in you, I still can see that part of you that would become resentful and resigned to an arrangement that doesn't suit you. You deserve more than a tumble in the sheets every night. Second, this would legally bind you to me. As your boss, I could only do so much, but as your husband, there could be less red tape for us to deal with in the end."

It was so strange to hear those words. *Your husband.* Everything was. It was difficult to evaluate a situation of this magnitude in such a small timeframe. Again, all she had to do was say "yes" and she would belong to this man. But possession went both ways, and she could have him in a way no woman had since his first marriage. But at what cost? Could she be happy with Braden for the rest of her life?

She studied his serious features, trying to discern anything outside of just wanting her. To see if any part of him only wanted to be with her because he cared and not necessarily because he was in love with her. No. That was one reality that would never come to fruition.

"And what's in it for you?" she inquired. "What are you getting out of this?"

"Honey, I've been a lonely man for years. It's a miracle you were thrown my way, and you're the first woman I've ever desired like this." Andrea glanced away, but not long before he lifted her chin, prompting her to gaze back at him. "God, you have no idea what just looking at you does to me, woman. You draw me with that fire in your eyes. If I could keep that in my bed every night, then it'll be a worthy sacrifice."

Braden backed away, a small smile registering on his lips.

"Besides, I'm old-fashioned. We can't be living in sin if what we did last night will be evident in a few months."

Andrea grasped her stomach. "I'm *not* pregnant!"

"You don't know that."

"Neither do you."

"Then what's the problem with preparing for contingencies? No harm in that."

"But we don't have to get married over it," Andrea debated. "You'll still have legal rights to the child without a marriage certificate *if* there is one."

"But no legal rights to you," he clarified. "You don't have to run anymore. Not from me, not from Gaines, not from anyone. Isn't that what you want? To finally be in a place where you can feel safe? Why not let me give that to you? Marry me, Andrea."

Andrea held his weighty stare for a couple minutes as turmoil raged within her. She could have the best of two worlds. She could have Braden and a home with children. He was offering her more than she thought possible. Why not accept it?

Because it seemed like duty and obligation spoke for him rather than simply wanting to. She wanted to marry for love, to love and be loved in return. That was the fantasy ingrained in her mind since childhood. To think that after years of wanting to plan a wedding of her dreams, the bubble popped because of the wrong choices made by a father and two men who desired her. Except one had her best interests at heart. The others did not.

"Can't I have time to think it over?"

Braden shook his head. "Tonight, or we'll have to wait. I'd rather it be tonight." He embraced her hands with his. "Are you willing to take a chance with me?"

"Who's to say you won't change your mind tomorrow?"

"I won't. I want you, Andrea. I want you to stay with me."

"Even if Gaines wasn't in the picture?"

"Even then."

"What if we don't suit? This would be wasted."

His gaze at her was level and staunch. "No time spent with you would be wasted. I wouldn't do this if I weren't sure. I'm a hard man to please, and I doubt I'll be made happier by anyone else."

"You don't know me enough to determine that. We will make each other miserable in the long run. What then?"

"They hand out divorces like candy. If we don't pan out, so be it." His hand cupped her cheek. "But you're wrong. I already know your mettle, Andrea Banks. I know that you're a woman who wants me. That you're not Cheryl. That you care for me in some way. Even now, your eyes tell me that."

"I don't want you to use that against me."

"Never," he declared. "It's the best weapon you got. I'm defenseless against it."

His confession astounded her, his look sincere. He cupped her face with both hands, almost as if he could feel her slipping through his fingers. "Just marry me. Please."

Her heart was overflowing with emotion, her mouth empty of words. She just stood there, surveying his face to detect any deception to why this successful man would want her. Andrea thought having Braden was a long shot. But here he was, earnest in his appeal in wanting to make her his wife. Part of her felt that she wasn't supposed to have him. This wasn't supposed to be home. This was a temporary stop in her journey to God-knew-where. But the other part of her was selfish and wanted to live in the lie. The lie that this was home, and she was marrying a man who loved her as much as she loved him.

She stared into his eyes and gave a brief nod. Her voice was still absent, her smile weak. His face brightened, happiness emitting from him like a beacon of hope.

God, let me bask in that light for a little while.

He kissed her hands before leading her back to the office where Judge Merrill stood, with Gale, by the desk.

"Is everything all right?" the judge asked.

Braden nodded. "Just a bout of cold feet. We're ready now."

"Are you sure? As much as I respect you, Braden, it would go against my office if the young lady is unwilling. Are *you* ready, my dear?"

She was starting to lose her nerve. "Yes, sir."

The judge wasn't convinced, but a resolved look from Braden swayed him to continue. Before the marriage got underway, Braden fetched Handy to be their second witness, who was just as stunned as the bride at the spur-of-the-moment event.

The next few minutes were a blur and Andrea felt more like a prop than a participant. She couldn't keep her gaze away from the band of gold Braden slid onto her finger in a perfect fit. With a brief kiss at the end and the signing of the marriage license, the deed was done. Her stomach turned with regret.

What had she done? In a moment of selfishness, she felt like she had signed Braden's death certificate instead of a document that bound her to him. This wasn't how she imagined her wedding to be, a quickie shotgun type like she was guilty of a crime. But she was. For wanting to hold onto him for as long as she was able.

It was done. He was hers.

Andrea worried at how long he would be hers, either from his abandonment, hers, or some force taking him from her. That was the point that pained her the most. She didn't know how she'd continue if something happened to Braden. She'd leave him before that ever happened, though her heart and soul would remain forever with him.

She was a fool, even more foolish to love him.

There it was. The truth of why she rushed headlong into marriage with selfish zeal. She loved Braden, and she wanted to hold onto him. Andrea worried that she wouldn't be able to maintain her grip on him for long. The words he had said with assurance inflated her confidence, but now fear soured her mood, and nothing but regret remained.

Andrea withdrew herself after she received hugs from Gale and Handy. She dashed upstairs as Braden shook Judge Merrill's hand and showed him out the door. She locked her bedroom door behind her as her mind raced. She had to leave. It felt like the walls of the room were enclosing on her. Yes, she would leave and somehow get an annulment. Carry the trouble far from the man she loved. She was a whirlwind around the room as she began shoveling clothes from drawers, tearing them from hangers in the closet, all arcing to land on the bed. She didn't hear the muffled calling of her name until there was knocking. Andrea froze.

"Andrea?" The doorknob rattled, followed by a series of impatient knocks. "Andrea!"

"Go away!"

"Dammit, Andrea, open the door!"

"You can't make me!"

The muttered phrase "the hell I can't" was heard right before the door was kicked open on the first try. Andrea hid a pair of shoes behind her back like she was hiding a broken toy as her husband filled the doorway. Simmering silver eyes zeroed in on her before trailing over the clothes thrown in disarray on her bed. His chest moved up and down as if trying to keep his emotions in check.

"What the hell is this?"

Her mouth opened then shut. She couldn't find anything to say. It was all too evident what this was. Without another word, he marched toward her. Andrea squealed, jumping on the bed to climb over it, but she became entangled in her clothes. She cursed, and Braden was upon her. He helped her get free, then lifted her over his shoulder and left the room.

"What on earth is going on up there?" cried Gale from the bottom of the stairs.

"This is between me and my wife," Braden answered, placing her down once he reached his room.

Andrea paced from him, then whirled to face him as he locked the door. Her temper was through the roof. "You are *freaking* insane. Not only did you break my door in, you hauled me in here like a Neanderthal. What's wrong with you?"

"I'll be damned if there'll be any locked doors between us." Braden shrugged off his coat and unfastened his cuffs. "And where did you think you were going?"

Andrea couldn't answer him. Even she didn't know.

"Nowhere, huh?" Braden whipped off his tie and tossed it aside. "Well, I can guarantee you're not going anywhere now. Not on our wedding night."

Andrea scoffed. "You think just because we're married that you own me? That you can tell me what to do?"

"No, but I sure as hell didn't expect to find my wife packing minutes after the ceremony."

Andrea threw her arms in the air. "A lot of things weren't exactly planned. This... I... I didn't expect you to propose marriage a day after we slept together."

Braden scowled. "What difference would it have made? You seemed hell-bent on running regardless of the answer you gave. But it doesn't matter. You said yes. It's done." Part of his mouth tipped in a wolfish smile. "You're mine."

Andrea rolled her eyes, buying her brain time to form lucid thoughts. It was short-circuiting, unable to withstand the way Braden eyed her with an insatiable hunger. And her body was reacting in kind.

Oh, my damn.

"As I told you," Andrea countered. "I'm not yours. My body, my holes, my every*thing* belongs to me, so you can keep your kinky ideas over there."

Braden chuckled as he started toward her, his pace languid. "I won't go for *that* hole tonight, but I may change your mind about it later." He leveled his heated gaze down to the V of her legs. "Now, I wager that the rest of you is something you're willing to share with me?"

Her mind was slipping, unsure of how to react. "Share?"

"Yes, like those sweet-tasting nipples peaking beneath your dress?"

Andrea peered down to witness, to her horror, her stubborn nipples blazing hard through the fabric of her bra and dress. She covered her breasts with her hands, the contact of it sending ripples down her spine. They were still sensitive from the night before, and they got heavier as those ravenous silver eyes of his bore into her.

He was keen on her reaction, and still stalking his way closer to her, his humorless smile ever-present. "I bet you're wet down there, aren't you, baby?" he burred, his tone intimate. "You're soaking, aching."

She was. Oh, God, she was. It was insane to her how little it took for him to get her going.

Braden halted in front of her, waiting on any kind of response from her. Andrea licked her lips, feeling her mouth go dry. "And what do you propose to do about it?"

"Touch you… if you'll let me."

The voice was thick with a hint of impatience like she couldn't answer him fast enough. Like his need to touch her was a burden he could no longer bear. And Andrea was kidding herself if she could deny him. Or herself.

"Yes."

Braden groaned as he reached for her. His hand cupped her throat in a silken embrace, his fingers fanning over it. His other arm wrapped around her body, backing her up until he hit a wall. Andrea had no idea what was up with Braden's obsession with pinning her against walls, but that thought flitted away as his hard body pressed into her. His knee wedged itself between her thighs while one arm wrapped around her waist.

Andrea's erratic pulse strummed beneath his callused fingertips as her body trembled more in anticipation than fear. His hands traced down the length of her, brushing against her throbbing nipples on the way to the hem of her dress. He traced the skin of her outer thigh before jerking her dress up to her waist. A shaky breath tumbled past her lips, his fingers edging to the front of her to feel the sodden lace panties that told him what he already knew. She couldn't quell the shudder that wracked her body as his forefinger traced along the damp, swollen lips beneath the lace.

"Fuck, so wet, and I've barely touched you," he uttered, though sounded triumphant at his discovery. His hand shifted inside her panties to cupped her for a few seconds before removing it, holding it to her eye level to see the puddle she made in his hand. She wasn't sure if she should have been embarrassed or aroused, but arousal won out when she spied the languid smile Braden wore. "I've been dreaming of getting you so wet that your sweet honey would be gushing down your thighs, and my tongue chasing every single drop."

He sucked up the pool her juices made from his palm, licking and savoring before his hand returned to her. She grasped his arms as he moved the damp layer of her panties aside, baring her to the cool air and his expert fingers. God, just having him touch her was enough to make her come as he teased her by slipping the tip of his index finger inside her. Andrea whimpered, her body consumed with fire, but she remained spellbound as his glittering eyes held her captive.

Braden's breathing was like hers, turbulent and harsh, and determined to see if he could fulfill the goal of getting her to come harder than before. While his finger toiled inside, his other hand worked on the hard tips of her nipples. His thumb stroked across her thickening nubbins through her clothes, pinching them to the point that Andrea could almost die if he didn't take them in his mouth.

Braden's lips fastened to the drumming pulse at her neck as he eased down the zipper of her dress. Her skin burned where his strong hand touched her naked lower back. It smoothed up and pulled the straps off her shoulders, leaving her upper body shielded by only her bra. It was hardly a deterrent to Braden. His lips traced down to her shoulders then to her breasts.

Andrea's throat freed a moan as Braden inhaled her clothed nipple past his lips and drew deep. The dual stimulation of his mouth and his finger plunging inside felt so divine that she couldn't stand. Braden held her up, his arm a strong anchor around her waist, and he held her closer to his hungry mouth.

"Braden," she whimpered against his bent head. God, every time the man's mouth was on her body, she went limp. He paid equal attention to her right nipple, laving and loving it like its twin until her bra stood the testament of his aggressive love, two damp spots of where his lips had been. He stood away, breathless for a moment as he watched her expressing her desire for him, the need swirling in her gaze.

Andrea was reflexive as she moved against the finger that had never eased its journey inside her. She felt bereft when Braden withdrew, her eyes catching more of her glistening wetness that was dripping down his hand and wrist. He stuck his honey-dipped digit into his mouth again like an addict, starved for the taste of her that drove him crazy each time, licking the rest from his hand and the racing drops going down his forearm. Andrea was mesmerized by the action, the way he eyed her as if he could devour her whole.

Braden swooped in for another kiss, tasting herself as his tongue plunged in to caress her own. His deft hands reached around to unfasten her bra and flung it across the room. Andrea drew away from him, but he urged her hands to the top of his shirt.

"Undress me, baby," he implored against her jaw. Andrea wasn't certain her fingers were going to work. Her nerves were so jittery that she felt like jelly thanks to his touch. But, with tempting kisses in between, she managed to unbutton her husband's shirt, revealing the corded muscles that jumped when her hands smoothed over them. Braden shrugged out of it as she dropped to her knees, unfastening his belt and unzipping his trousers. The bulge against his dark briefs was undeniable, and she lowered his pants and underwear to release it. Andrea balked at the encompassing size of it, in a state of wonder that he had managed to fit it inside her at all. It stood erect and unashamed, a clear measure of his arousal. Such a beautiful tool of masculinity, Andrea's mouth watered in wanting to pay it homage.

She eased her lips around the thick shaft, and his body lurched forward. Braden balanced on the wall with his left forearm while his other hand plunged into her long, ebony tresses, winding in the soft mass. His body went taut from her curious exploration, his fingers tensing in her hair as Andrea took him as far as she could, drawing out long, deep groans from him.

His breathless urges encouraged her to continue. She licked him from root to tip, giving the mushroom head deep suckles between swallowing him. Andrea even worshipped his balls, taking them past her lips, and tongued them with loving attention. His cock jumped, Braden's sentences sounding like garbled nonsense before he ripped her from him, his delicious length slipping from her mouth. Andrea stared up at him, puzzled. His chest was heaving, his gaze frenzied. Braden raked a hand through his hair before pulling her to her feet. His tongue was inside her mouth before she could think twice, bearing her closer.

"God, you're gonna kill me," he whispered against her lips once his broke contact.

His hands eased her dress and panties over the generous swell of her hips and down her long, brown legs courtesy of a booted foot, and he eased away to let her step out of them. He discarded the rest of his clothes and shoes, and clothed only in her white ballerina flats, Andrea was whisked in his arms and carried to the bed. Braden rested her on the edge and guided her back. She lifted her right leg where he seized a shoe-covered foot and eased it off, kissing around her delicate ankle and heel. He also did the same for the other, keeping her legs splayed a little before dipping down to run his tongue along with the wet opening of her entire universe. But he didn't visit long. His mouth journeyed upward to her soft belly, the valley of her breast, the smooth column of her neck and the sweetness of her lips.

She never knew there could be such beautiful joy in kissing someone, naked and so attuned to the other's physical needs. Her dark legs entangled with his hair-roughened limbs, her hard nipples rasping against his chest as his mouth slashed over hers again and again. Their kisses were ravenous, as if they were lovers who hadn't had each other in a decade instead of a mere twenty-something hours.

With a hand between them, Braden teased her with his erection, stroking the head against her puffy nether lips. The tip of it caressing her throbbing clit hidden beneath the hood. Andrea's back arched against it. His hot mouth trailed down to engulf her tender nipple, drawing on it deep and hard.

"Braden!" she cried out, her nails digging into his biceps.

He hovered over her, caressing and pinching a nipple, keeping the blaze within her simmering. "God, I love hearing you say my name, baby. Say it again."

Andrea leveled her gaze at him as she whispered his name again, and he groaned in reaction. Braden made sudden movements, leaning back to urge her legs wider. Andrea lifted herself on her elbows but was on her back a second later.

"Braden…" was all she could get out before he sank deeper into her. They both moaned, grabbing ahold of each other to wait until the sensation was bearable enough for him to continue. Braden positioned her legs until they almost reached her chest, but he went to work, his lean hips hammering home. He gritted and groan with each gleeful glide. Andrea held onto his wrists, whimpering and writhing with each powerful push. A fine sheen of sweat formed on his body, his hips never slowing.

"Goddammit," he gritted between his teeth. "Fuck, how my dick loves the feeling of you, holding me deep inside like you never want to let go."

Andrea felt close to exploding. Her hips followed his tempo, her prospering love button trembling each time he brushed it. Braden was alternating looks between his rapid moving dick and her face. When her eyes rolled back, Braden became undone, propelling him to thrust faster.

Andrea arched her back, calling his name as her orgasm came so close, she could almost brush it with her fingertips. But Braden soon withdrew, and she whined from her lack of fulfillment. He placated her by kissing her before persuading her to get on her hands and knees facing the foot of the bed.

He nudged her upper back until her ass was in the air. A hand plopped hard on his thick backside before squeezing. "What I would love to do to this fine ass of yours." His fingers brushed her throbbing pussy before he slid his thick cock back in. "All in good...time," he gritted. Andrea's fingers dug into the footboard of the king-sized bed, almost choking at how full he made her feel. Braden resumed his rhythm, the swift slapping of damp flesh meeting echoed throughout the room followed by guttural grunts and sweet screams of pleasure. Braden reached around to fondle her throbbing button, and she died.

"Braden! Oh, God, Braden!"

"That's right, baby," he grated. "Say my name." His hand wound into her hair, pulling her head back. "Scream it, baby."

His other hand moved between her thighs like a blur, flicking her engorged clit until it triggered her orgasm. Andrea screamed his name as she clamped hard around his driving cock, persuading him to follow into that blissful oblivion. Braden placed his hands on either side of hers along the footboard, careful not to crush her as they slowly descended from heaven. His lips brushed against her neck as they regained their breaths and full consciousness.

Braden moved, detaching her fingers from the footboard to lie back with him. Her body rested on his while he remained sheathed within her. Her hand reached up to caress his sweat-drenched hair while his ran along her soft curves.

"God," she replied, her voice hoarse.

"Hmm?"

"Me kill you? I wouldn't be surprised if I'm battered and bruised come morning."

"Every bit of my loving would be worth it."

Andrea turned her head so that he could place a kiss on her brow. "Cocky, much?"

Braden chuckled. "As many times as I've made you come, I have every right to be." His assertive fingers trailed down to her drenched pussy, full of their mingled love. He strummed her sensitive clit, wrapping his free arm around her as her body bowed and bucked. And with his cockiness intact, had her shatter again in his arms.

Braden stared into the dark distance. His thoughts kept him from slumber, and they were full of nothing but her. Although he thought they were all-consuming before, last night started an epidemic of his soul that was raging out of control. And he wasn't sure if he wanted that to stop.

The feelings he felt for her were foreign, beyond the limit of anything he had ever felt for anybody. Hearing of her plight roused a need in him to be her champion. Braden had never been needed beyond the use of his monetary abilities for most women. They grinned and bore his crass, hard-ass nature if it ensured a higher way of living. Cheryl didn't think twice about it.

Cheryl was the main reason for his resistance of women. Through a resentful perspective, Braden had pinged most women who showed an interest in him as manipulative and insincere. He didn't mind the occasional fling, but marriage had been out of the question until Andrea Banks blazed into his life like a firestorm.

He glanced down to see the odd gold band encircling his finger. It was odd because he never thought he'd ever wear one again. Within a blink of an eye, she had reversed years of stubborn thinking in a handful of weeks.

She was worth casting off his previous mindset. Braden had been tempted to say yes to anything she wanted just to have her. His attraction to her had been instantaneous. It was his pride that had led him to hire her on, but it was desire that prompted him to make her his wife. Not just the desire for her body, but the desire to have her with him always.

He had never admitted it to anyone, but he looked forward to coming back from business trips or the field to see her. Lived for even her glares when they weren't talking. At first, even those smaller pieces of her seemed to be enough until they weren't. Until the selfish part of him had to have all of her. He had realized this when she was taken, and how bereft he felt by her absence.

And that was a few minutes. He couldn't imagine a lifetime without her.

Braden turned from the window, folding his arms and leaning against the wall as his eyes studied the fine figure lying beneath his sheets. She appeared helpless, a hand tucked beneath her chin while the other reached out to the space he no longer occupied.

What made her so different from the rest? For sure, she was nothing like Cheryl. Money had been the start of her troubles, and she wasn't afraid to work for an earnest living. She was like an open book when it came to reading her desires. But she, like him, became powerless when her skin came in contact with his. The fiery passion he stoked in her was real. His first wife could fake an orgasm before leaving his bed to occupy another.

But Andrea…

His wife shifted in her slumber, rolling onto her side away from him.

His wife.

Braden drew in a quick breath, his body still aching from the loving she gave him. Her body was so exquisite and honed with graceful lines and curves. His hands always felt starved of her. The need to hold her would never leave him, and he'd be damned if someone forced him to give her up.

The moment she had said "yes" was the gap in her armor. Now Braden was inside her defenses, raging a battle for her unconditional surrender. He had changed battle strategies on her, pulling strings with Judge Merrill and bribing the county for a marriage license without her knowledge or presence. Even called his mother ahead of time to find rings for them while he drove to get her. He had orchestrated it all within a day, and even in this, Braden wasn't sure if he had done this more for her protection or his selfishness.

It was by pure providence that she had chosen Rock River, of all places, to run to. He had always questioned why, suspecting the reason to be more than money. But in the end, it didn't matter. Her misfortune had been his gain. The guilt he should have felt about that should have been insurmountable, but he wasn't sorry. Through her tragedy and his own selfish behavior, Andrea was now his wife. He didn't regret the decision. He just couldn't let her go. His cold arms refused to relinquish her sensual fire.

He refused to be cold ever again.

His thoughts were turbulent. Too heavy for his wedding night, a night he was eager to resume. His gaze swept over the enchanting form waiting for him. A beauty to whom only he had the privilege of seeing, touching, tasting, and being inside. Every night for the rest of his life.

His wonderful, brave wife.

Braden slipped back into bed, settling beside her before she turned over, using his chest as her pillow. He held her, sleep eluding him but his thoughts brought up a memory he didn't realize until now. When he brought his mother home, she had been waiting for them in the foyer. He was sure he had read her eyes, seeing that same need he knew well. Was it possible that she could see through his mounting faults?

Could she love him?

Braden snorted to himself. He wasn't lovable by any definition, but there were some enduring qualities that she could find attractive, whatever they were. And as he tried his best to count some on his right hand, Braden thought of their future, and what a privilege it would be, if possible, to be loved by her.

Chapter Ten

A dreamy smile stretched Andrea's mouth, still wrapped in dreams which were full of nothing but the man who had satisfied her throughout the night. She turned over, her arm reaching out to feel the warmth of her husband. Her eyes flew open, staring first at the unoccupied, wrinkled sheet beside her, then at the clock.

8:31 blazed in angry, red, digital numbers. And upon seeing them, Andrea bounded into a sitting position. Her eyes adjusted to the sunlight falling through the eastern window, wondering why Braden didn't wake her.

He strode into the room from the huge walk-in closet, bare-chested and donned in a pair of black slacks and a pressed dress shirt in hand. That very shirt was tossed to the foot of the bed the second her bedroom eyes met his, and the next thing she knew, her husband had yanked the blanket down, hauled her against him, and made love to her mouth.

Her insides curled at the intimate sweep of his tongue against hers. He tasted of cool mint and smelled of heady aftershave, drugging her senses and driving her desire to have more. She felt the stirrings within her and moved against him, gripping his shoulders as he nibbled on her plump bottom lip.

Andrea soon drew back, giddy from the experience. She freed a short laugh. "Well, good morning to you, too, cowboy."

Braden braced his hand on the other side of her. He tucked back a strand of her hair behind her ear. "How did you sleep, love?"

Andrea was so astonished to hear the endearment that she stared at him, dumbfounded. He frowned as his forefinger and thumb skimmed the soft curve of her jaw. "What is it?"

Andrea glanced away. If she kept this up, he'd be able to read her emotions faster than she could deal with them. "Nothing."

His eyes told of disbelief. "That's some nothing. I thought I asked an easy question, but you stared at me as if I said it in another language. You sure you're okay?"

"Yeah. I think I've slept better these past two nights than I had in a while. I'm surprised you didn't wake me. I missed making breakfast. What are they going—"

"Don't worry about that," Braden cut in. "I've already told them that my wife will have the day off, and they're capable of cooking for themselves. But I hope I won't see any dead of starvation when I get back."

Andrea sat up. "Where are you going?"

"Dallas," Braden divulged after a pause. "I've been invited to see a Thoroughbred I've bred do its first major run, and I promised my client that I'd attend."

"But we…we had just…"

Braden placed a hand to her cheek. "I know, but these plans were made long before you came here. It's a little late to back out."

The bottom lip he had sucked on a minute ago stuck out in a full pout. "How long will you be gone?"

"I have some other clients in the area, and the race isn't 'til Saturday. Probably won't be back until next Monday."

Andrea's features fell. He'd be gone for a little over a week. She wasn't expecting her husband to be gone the morning after their wedding. Then again, she wasn't expecting to have a husband. Then she recalled him mentioning how he'd rather marry her last night because they would have to wait. Now she understood why.

Braden's mouth set into a grim line as his gaze traced over her solemn features. "You have that pouting thing going on, almost as if you'd miss me."

"You're going to Texas."

"You're concerned that I'll run into Gaines?" Braden scoffed, unimpressed. "There's nothing to worry about."

Her eyes regarded his, serious. "But he's dangerous."

"He's nobody I can't handle. And you know the men will be here protecting you around the clock." He gave her a small smile, his fingertips grazing her jaw. "So, no worries now."

"I know," she said, despondent.

"Do you?" He glanced her over. "Is this how you're going to act while I'm gone?"

Andrea shrugged a shoulder. "I don't know. It's just that we just got married, and you're already leaving."

"As I remember, I had to drag you to the altar, but I see your point." He paused. "Would it make you feel better if I asked you to come along?" Andrea's hopes elevated, then she remembered something that eclipsed her joy. Her husband sighed. "What now?"

"I don't have anything to wear. The dress I wore last night is the nicest thing I have. The last thing I received from my father. I had to sell all my clothes to resale shops to keep us going toward the black."

"Easy solution. Why don't I just buy you some new clothes?"

"You don't have to do that."

He frowned, his face transforming back into the Braden she recognized. Seeing him so jovial was perturbing. "And why the hell not? It should be a man's right to buy clothes for his woman if he wants to, and I want to."

Andrea smiled a little. "You mean it?"

"Every bit of it. You can shop anywhere you like. Neiman-Marcus, Nordstrom's, hell, even Walmart. Wherever you feel comfortable. After all, I want you to be the envy of every woman there, and have every man wishing they had you."

Andrea lifted a brow. "The other day, I was all but a pain in your ass."

"That's still debatable but fortunes change, baby. Despite me being a hard-ass, I vowed to take care of you. Do you trust me?"

Again, asking her about trusting him, as if she never did. She wasn't sure why, but even back at the diner, she trusted him enough to choose him over Caid. Not to mention, the man was consistent in putting his life on the line for her. The only thing he wanted in return was her. Rather her body, but he wanted her beyond protection. That had to mean something, and perhaps in the future, he would be receptive to her love.

Seeing that he was still waiting on her answer, Andrea nodded. Braden took her lips again in a brief but dire kiss before withdrawing, allowing fleeting breath to return to her.

"So, how long do you think it'll take you to get ready?"

Andrea glanced down her body which was covered by his strapping weight. "Depends. How long do you plan on staying on top of me?"

"I don't know, honey," he replied, his features meditative. "Somehow, I'm thinking a lifetime wouldn't be enough."

An hour later, they were on the road to Laramie. Packing took no time at all, considering Braden had promised to take her shopping, but she brought a couple of her nicer outfits just in case. Her new mother-in-law waved them off, assuring her that the house and guys would be taken care of, and the men would continue to circle the place like vultures to appear as if she had never left.

For the first time, they had a conversation that didn't deal with their current troubles. He inquired after what she liked to do, her hobbies and favorite pastimes. While she divulged these tidbits, it was hard to get used to a Braden who smiled. Hell, he even laughed on occasion. Life hadn't given him a good reason to smile, but it was good to see.

What started off as a tiny seedling grew into something wild, forbidden but abiding that would last for the rest of her life. She wasn't sure of when it took root, but she felt it there all the same. Andrea could tell by the way she looked at him, and her heart felt like it could burst. Of course, they pushed each other's buttons to the fullest, but the passion was undeniable between them.

Her loving him would have to be something that was kept to herself. That love could be exploited. Andrea couldn't imagine anything happening to him, and she'd sacrifice the chance of remaining by his side if it meant saving his life. How it hurt to see this side of him, aware of the warmth he could extend. She had to keep back stinging tears, not wanting to say goodbye to that dream just yet.

They reached the Laramie Regional Airport and proceeded to the onsite FBO service center, Cowboy Aviation, where they were greeted by the manager. Braden's Piper Seneca was already fueled up and ready to go. They retrieved their things from the truck and walked over to the plane now sitting by the runway.

Andrea was in awe. "I didn't know you could fly," she said, handing him her bag.

"You didn't ask," was the dry answer, though he graced her with a roguish smile.

"You're not exactly the talkative type."

"Oh, I beg to differ." He wrapped an arm around her to bring her close. "I'd say that I'm damned good at saying things that get you wet. Last night, you proved my theory, unless..." His right hand filled itself with her generous bottom. "...you want me to test that hypothesis again?"

God, the gruffness of his voice zipped sweet zings throughout her body because the telltale signs of her ever-dampening panties were true. Her breathing became shallow, ninety-eight percent of her mind losing touch of reality. She almost forgot they were standing in front of Cowboy Aviation, focused on this man who held her so entranced.

"In public? You crazy bastard."

"Baby, I've been called a bastard lots of times, half the time by you. But I'd bet my ass there's a part of you that would be crazy enough to do some...public displays of affection if I got you there. Isn't that right?"

God, yes! She'd christen everything from here to Albuquerque if he came, in every sense of the word. Though her mind screamed yes in every language she knew, somewhere along the channel from her brain to her mouth, there was a failure. All she could do was stare at his eyes and mouth, trying to express what she was thinking.

Braden bent to kiss her until they heard a throat clearing. They turned to witness Caid standing there with an amused expression on his face, his own luggage in tow.

"If you two newlyweds are going to induct yourself into the mile-high club, don't mind me. I'm only a guest."

"You?" Andrea asked, finding the will to pull away from her magnetic husband. "You're coming?"

Braden became serious, his gaze hooded as he stared at Caid. Even though they were getting along better than they ever had, they were still wary of each other. After all, Rome wasn't built in a day.

"Just as a precaution."

Caid strode up to them. "Luckily not chaperone. Voyeurism's not my thing." He tossed his bag which Braden caught on reflex. "Load this, my good man. And I'll expect my newspaper to be served with a glass of bourbon, on the rocks."

Braden leaned in close to Caid after Andrea boarded, his demeanor hostile. "Do yourself a favor, Marshall. Get in the plane, sit down, and shut up, or you'll fly to Texas duct-taped and unconscious. Got me?"

Caid clicked his tongue, shaking his head. "I'd thought married life would have softened you a bit, Sutherland."

"Been married for only fourteen hours, Marshall. No effects yet."

"I hope, for your sake, you take your wife to the hotel and not leave for a couple of days. You've got some pent-up frustration to work out. I'm sure with enough begging, Andrea will let you, so you won't be a complete asshole for the rest of the trip. Wouldn't want to lose any more customers."

With that, Caid entered the plane, and Braden rolled his eyes heavenward, dreading that this was going to be the longest trip of his life.

They made great time as they landed at the Fort Worth Alliance Airport a couple hours later. Caid separated from them when he was approached by a beautiful blonde who greeted him as if they were exclusive. Caid didn't waltz around Rock

River with a steady date, but it didn't mean he didn't have others wherever he went.

With a promise to meet them later, the blonde whisked him off in her cherry-red BMW. Braden rented a Range Rover, and as they made their way to the hotel, Andrea couldn't help but notice the way her husband seemed at home in the SUV as if he'd always owned it. Just like he seemed at home in his truck, riding a horse or riding her.

Andrea was enthralled at where they were staying, although calling it a hotel didn't seem appropriate. The way it sat off Grapevine Lake was like a small version of the Palace of Versailles done Texas-style.

The Gaylord Texan was already buzzing with business, bracing for the mass of visitors they'd receive once school was out and the summer began. Andrea heard the planes above screaming as they landed at the DFW Airport across the highway. Her eyes were drawn everywhere, to the vibrant colors and vegetation once inside. Seeing things that blazed Texas pride ate at her, and her homesickness resurged at seeing the replica of the Alamo and their Riverwalk Café. She wrapped her arms around one of her husband's. She never thought she'd be this close to home ever again.

Braden's gray eyes scanned her, taking note of how her eyes were swimming in unshed tears. His brow scrunched. "What is it? You sick?"

Andrea shook her head, taking her thumb to wipe the wetness away. "No, it's just that I love this hotel. Reminds me of home."

He glanced around before he scoffed, though a small smile appeared. "In love with a hotel at first sight, but no love for me. If I had feelings, knowing that would hurt more."

But even Andrea detected the hurt in his eyes at acknowledging that. However, if his eyes had stayed on her a second more, he could have witnessed all the love a woman could have for a man.

Never, she thought. *I could never love anything more than you.* The truth resonated inside her like a keening knell, which gave her both comfort and concern.

They checked into an executive suite Braden always stayed in and made sure that he booked it months in advance. Even though they were here on business, Braden had promised to give her a better honeymoon than this spur-of-the-moment ordeal. She wondered what aspects of intimacy he had in mind.

A woman, who Andrea surmised was the manager of the place, came around the corner, and her defenses went up. She was a striking brunette who appeared professional with her hair swept back in a tight bun, pearl earrings, and navy-blue suit. The woman's smile made it known that she was glad to see Braden. Too glad. She even had the gall to walk past Andrea like she was nothing but vapor and hug him.

"So good to see you again, Braden," she purred in a seductive voice. She went to her tiptoes to give him a brief kiss on his unshaven jaw which made Andrea balk. Wasn't this woman at work? The lady drew back, although her hands were still on him. "I was wondering why you haven't called me."

As he detached her straying hands and tossed them down, his gray eyes flickered to a fuming Andrea who was about to snatch a handful of coiffed hair. "That's the reason why," he indicated with the point of his head.

The woman whirled, eyeing Andrea up and down in disbelief. But she remained civil, though those crystal-blue eyes flashed the word "enemy" within them. "Oh? Don't tell me your secretary is your only excuse, Braden?"

Andrea's eyes narrowed. She was a second away from losing her religion. But she had been raised with class. A class that was being challenged by her temper.

Braden stared the woman with disinterest. "Not by a long shot. But I suppose introductions are in order. Kit Davenport, this is Andrea, my—"

"Secretary. Got it."

"It's *Mrs.* Sutherland to you…uh, what's your name? Bitch, wasn't it?"

The tight smile the woman wore didn't waver, but those blue eyes became ice-cold as they narrowed. "It's Kit, but you can refer to me as Ms. Davenport."

Andrea returned a cold smile. "How unfortunate. I think I like Bitch better."

Those blue eyes, to Andrea's glee, told of her shock, but soon mellowed back into that condescending gaze that would do all in their power to save her wounded pride.

"Well, a hearty congratulations to you both," she said with forced cheer. "And Braden, you must tell me when it's due."

"Excuse me?" Andrea countered.

"Why, I'm sure Braden wouldn't have married you unless he knocked you up."

Andrea's anger raged. Her right hand balled into a fist. This bitch was asking for a broken nose. Before she could take two steps, Braden stepped between them, his silver eyes gleaming down at Kit. "That's enough and low, even for you."

"I apologize." Kit's vengeful eyes lit on Andrea, not the least bit penitent. "I have other things to do. May you both enjoy your stay."

She stalked away while Andrea wished the she-devil's heels would break and her face would greet the floor. Hard. The nerve of that woman! And she gritted her frustration aloud as they went to their room.

"How dare she?" Andrea fumed. "That bitch had some nerve. The audacity to look down her nose at me as if I'm nothing. She's not a high-and-mighty socialite herself." She began pacing as Braden watched her, amused. "I mean, I know I don't really belong in your social class, but still, what gives her the right to judge? Then she dared to insinuate that you knocked me up."

"Which is possibly true, baby," Braden supplied.

"She doesn't know that!" she yelled before glancing over to see the grin on his face. Andrea proceeded to pick up the nearest thing to her, a pillow from the couch, and hurled it at him. "How can you think it's so damn funny? Your wife can possibly be arrested in the next couple days from knocking her out. And she was fawning all over you like she wanted to be your personal fluffer."

"Hm, that would be an idea," he reflected, his tone teasing.

She came at him, struggling to strike him with her fists, but he held onto her wrists. Braden released a deep chuckle, entertained by the whole thing. Then it dawned on her.

"You ass!" she exclaimed. "You did this just to get me jealous."

"Kit was solo on this trip, but I confess that I was waiting to see your reaction. And you were jealous, weren't you?"

She pushed against him, trying to get free. "I hate you."

"Nuh-uh. We've already been through this before. But I am sorry for how you were treated." He paused for a second before lifting her into his arms. "I think I know how to make it up to you."

Andrea gave a start, holding onto his broad shoulders as he carried her into the bedroom. "What are you doing?"

"We got some honeymoonin' to do."

He placed her on the bed, her legs dangling over the edge as he proceeded to get out of his sports jacket and shirt. Andrea rested herself on her elbows. "But what if I don't want to have sex with you right now?"

He picked up her legs one at a time, taking off her shoes and tossing them over his shoulders. "We're not going to have sex. I'm just going to put my tongue inside you, have you come five or six times, then if you're still conscious, fuck you for the rest of the evening." He unfastened her pants and pulled them off along with her lace panties. His forefinger ran along the damp opening to her world. Andrea couldn't resist a shiver as he pushed inside, her slick walls caressing his searching digit.

"I've been dying for another taste of you, honey." He took out his finger and placed it into his mouth, savoring the sweet, saccharine flavor. He got down on his knees beside the bed, placing her legs over his shoulders as he stared straight on at her glistening lips. "I don't think I've ever enjoyed pleasuring a woman this much."

"Not even Kit?"

"Baby, Kit couldn't even get a dinner date out of me, as much as she tried. But..." He took a moment to take her slick love button into his mouth and suckled. Andrea's back arched, a long moan sailing past her lips. Braden withdrew, a corner of his mouth lifting as those eyes flickered to her. "...if you want me to be your personal fluffer, baby, you wouldn't have to ask. I'd do it willingly."

And that was the last rational thing she thought of before his tongue dove back inside.

To say her husband catered to her every whim was an understatement. Their first night was spent with him buried between her thighs in some fashion. But he was considerate enough to put brakes on their marathon to order room service to build her strength. He even ran her a nice bath, and she leaned against him while they soaked in a genuine, tender moment. His hands were everywhere, touching while his mouth would kiss her temple or nibble her earlobe or neck.

The next day, he took her shopping for new clothes. Even though Braden had said she could shop wherever she wanted, it was apparent that he had narrowed the choices down to the Galleria and *only* the Galleria.

Andrea crossed her arms, glancing at Braden. "What, no Walmart?"

He ignored her as he guided her in the mall. He led her into places that had clothes she couldn't even dream of affording a year before. And Braden stood so close to her like she was a shoplifter who'd steal the nearest thing and take off for the exit.

Some items she fell in love with, but she didn't want to overindulge. She wasn't comfortable spending someone else's money despite being married to it. She'd pick up outfits then put them down once she saw the hefty price tag. Andrea stuck to clearance racks, searching for clothes that was youthful and didn't have a rip from here to Russia. She selected her three favorites while Braden picked up the rest. She contested seeing the clothes she had put down that were now slung over his arm. He ushered her to the checkout counter and laid down a couple of grand without blinking a lash.

This was repeated from store to store. The amount he racked up on her alone could almost buy a brand-new car, and he did so without complaint. They left the Galleria loaded down with purchases. Andrea glanced at all the shopping bags and boxes piled in the back.

"You've just spent the amount of a small country's deficit back there. How in the hell am I supposed to pay this back?"

"Easy." He put the car in reverse. "You don't."

"But I would've been more than happy to shop at Target or something."

"Last time I checked, it wasn't against the law for a husband to want to buy some things for his wife."

Some things. They bought more items than she could count on her fingers and toes four times over. "No, but..." She sighed. "I'm coming off as ungrateful, aren't I? It's just that the price for two outfits is the value of my entire wardrobe. I'm so used to bargain shopping for things. It's been a while since I've bought anything high end, but I've learned to do without."

He turned onto the interstate taking them back toward Grapevine. "What, is it a sin for wanting to have nice things?"

"No, but it's something I'm not overly concerned about. Expensive shirts or pants can stain or tear. That sucks at all walks of life, but the value of it means different things to people, is all."

Braden glanced over at her, his curiosity piqued. "Suddenly you're a philosopher? You're, what, twenty-three, and so pessimistic on life and possessions?"

"I would add that neither should you, but I understand why you are. My life's like *Sesame Street* compared to the one you've had."

"Yours hasn't been easy, either. I guess that's one field we're level on." He glanced at her. "I know you, honey. Even with the lemons life's given you, I know you wouldn't fuck me over as my money-hungry ex."

"Money's the last thing I want. After what happened with my father, it was tiring because it was all we worried about. Just made me sick of the concept."

"What do you want?" Braden asked.

The simple question caught her off-guard, but she searched a bit until she found a suitable answer. "A life where I don't have to worry about who's following me. I want to be with someone I love and who values me. But apparently, that's too much to ask."

Braden didn't respond as they drove back to their hotel in reflective silence.

Andrea called Ella the next day. She hadn't talked to her since last week but kept silent about the whirlwind affair that was Braden-gate. Her best friend expressed her eagerness to see her before they headed home.

Andrea brought the matter to her husband who recommended that Ella could come up on Friday and spend the weekend with her. He even agreed to front the cost for her room and any additional accommodations, within reason. After hugging and kissing Braden in gratitude a dozen times, she called Ella back with the news.

In the meantime, as she waited for Friday to come around, she hung close to her husband. The rest of that Tuesday was spent about Dallas. The places he took her were surprising: the aquarium and the art museum. The art museum still had the King Tut exhibit, and she had been wanting to see it since it was on its last world tour.

Andrea wasn't the only one fascinated by the showcase. Braden seemed to know more about ancient Egypt than she did and kept her enraptured by his knowledge and his theories of how the king had died so young.

"You don't think Ay killed him?" she asked him as they left the exhibit.

"It sounds better to say he was murdered than gangrene killing him. But I've read books and seen a lot of documentaries, and all bring interesting points. Everyone will have their difference of opinion of how it happened. That's why no real consensus will come about."

"You're a man of many talents. You claim to be a reader, yet I haven't seen you lift one book, not even to throw it at someone."

"Ah, but you're not around me all the time, are you? I mainly leaf through a few pages before bed if there's time. Just goes to show that there's more to me than breeding and training horses."

At first, it seemed that he wasn't into anything else but his profession. Not to mention making love to her until her eyes rolled to the back of her head. Braden took pride in his work, but he was adjusting well to the new role as her husband. It was just odd that he showed more enthusiasm in the change of their relationship than she did. She wasn't sure if it were to play his part or if he cared about her. Until she knew for certain, she would shelve her thoughts behind a smile and trudge through their fun-filled week. Wednesday, he left to visit a couple of clients, and entreated her to a day at the soothing Relâche Spa. By the time they were through with her, Andrea felt like she was on cloud nine.

She went back to her room, lay down on the bed, charged her phone, and was asleep in seconds. That's where her husband found her a couple hours later. Braden woke her, reminding her of their dinner invitation with Bill Rafferty and his family before they went to midweek service. They met Asa Updike, the jockey, and the horse that Braden had come to see race, a three-year-old chestnut mare called Hadassah's Faith.

Thursday's outing involved going to see the Fort Worth Stockyards, then downtown's Sundance Square and a nice steak dinner.

When Friday arrived Ella burned up the highway to see her. She arrived a bit after eleven, bringing her latest boyfriend or friend with benefits. Andrea wasn't sure which title the man was going by, for he was someone she hadn't met before. When she introduced her husband to her best friend, Ella almost fell over, her features telling of profound shock. Andrea couldn't blame her. She had been married to Braden for a week and still didn't quite believe it herself. Ella was cordial, giving her "what the hell" stares between the light conversation she was having with Braden. Once they were alone, Andrea had some explaining to do.

After getting Ella and her man settled in, Braden visited an old friend and a potential client for lunch. Ella's boy toy went to hang out along Lake Grapevine, and the two women settled down for lunch at the Riverwalk Café, picking a table far from the prying ears of the public. Andrea had no idea how to begin, but true to form, Ella dove in headfirst.

"Explain, missy. When were you going to tell someone that you got married?"

Andrea shifted in the chair. "I would have, but there's been so much going on in the past week. Just been so preoccupied."

Ella lifted a knowing brow. "Well, if I was married to a man like *that*, I could understand why. Now, this *is* the same bastard you've been telling me about?"

Andrea stirred her pink lemonade. "One and the same."

Ella squeezed a lemon resting on the rim of her cup into her sweet tea. "Doesn't seem that way now, does it? He's certainly a nice, tall glass of water. But curious minds are wondering...can the man bone?"

Andrea almost choked on her lemonade. "Girl!"

"Just a simple question, doll, that requires a simple answer."

Thinking about all the times they'd made love in the past week, Andrea's cheeks flamed as she grabbed the nearby drink menu and fanned herself.

"He can," Ella confirmed.

Andrea placed the menu back. "But that's not the only thing he's capable of. If he's not spending time screwing me stupid, he's got his head buried between my thighs."

Ella's eyebrow lifted. "So, your cowboy's a bit of a pussy freak? Lucky! It's a miracle to find a man who can stay down there for more than a minute."

"That's something to be happy about, I guess?"

"Aren't you?"

"I'm not knocking it. The man is phenomenal in *and* out of bed. It's just..." She tapered off to find the right words. "It's just that I'm not sure if getting married was the wisest thing for us to do."

"Why not?"

"Because I want to be more than someone's piece of ass every night."

"Thing is that the man didn't have to marry his piece of ass. I mean, you must have put the moves on him good for him to put a ring on it. He may already be in love with you."

"I doubt it."

"But why?"

"After what his father and his ex-wife did, I'm not sure if he has anything left to give."

"The man's willing to lay down his life for you."

"All the guys at the ranch and Caid are willing to do the same thing."

Ella stared at her best friend, incredulous. "God, got all of them sprung on you, huh?'

"I'm being serious!"

"Well, Braden was the one who orchestrated all of this. He didn't have to. He could have tossed you out two seconds after you told him everything. But no, he took it upon himself to look after you."

Andrea shook her head, despite smiling. "Why is everyone trying to make him redeemable?"

"Your call," Ella replied. "I ain't the one married to him. But if I were in your shoes, I'd give that man all the lovin' he could handle…and then some. Plus, it seems like he needs a good dose of it."

"I'm sure he doesn't."

"Well, I'm outright positive he does. Case in point, that wedding band he's sporting has certainly been the talisman that's turned him from brooding asshole to doting husband."

"Which has been hard seeing him this way. I'm so used to him being so imposing. Now it's as if the old Braden never existed."

"Maybe this is his true nature coming out. Just give the man time. He's had to repress his feelings his whole life. But it seems to me, he's already opening to you. It shows promise."

"I suppose you're right." Andrea was startled by the homicidal rampage occurring on Ella's plate as she stabbed her fajitas. "What's the matter with you?"

Ella stopped. "Ever heard the expression 'denial ain't just a river in Egypt?' You have denial tenfold when you could have true happiness with a man who loves you. Everyone in the world can see this but the two of you." She shook her head. "God, I'm never going to fall in love. Just dealing with your problems gives me a headache."

Andrea smiled, but still faced inner turmoil. Love could be the most torturous emotion. It had driven individuals crazy for less, while others had killed for the sake of it. However, when it was heartfelt and returned, couldn't it bring the greatest pleasure?

The greatest pleasure she wished Braden would be brave enough to show.

That weekend, they all congregated at Lone Star Park for the annual Lone Star Derby. The day was beautiful, sunny and clear with a slight breeze to keep them cool. Andrea was dressed to impress in a red halter dress with white tropical flowers and white peek-toed slingbacks. Her hair was done up to fit into the matching red, wide-brim hat. This hot little number was chosen by her husband who had gotten the reaction he wanted. Walking into the park garnered the attention of men who wished they had such beauty on their arm. Some of them suffered instant reproofs from their significant others for staring longer than they should. Even some women were green with envy as she linked arms with her handsome husband. But they also got a lot of glares that signified they were tolerated but not quite welcomed. Braden ignored the unspoken negativity. Wrapping his arm around her waist, he leaned over to her and said, "They're the ones who have a problem with it, baby. We don't."

It was true. Their relationship wasn't based on race. They wanted each other as a man would want a woman and vice versa. Except now that she thought about it, even their relationship was growing deeper than just the basis of desire. She had been thinking a lot about what Ella had said the day before, and the possibility of gaining Braden's love. Her husband was a man of action rather than words, and through that action could be the way he expressed his care. Andrea prayed she wasn't reading too deep into every little gesture. She hated to think that for the rest of her life, she would only be regarded as a wife of convenience than of love.

They were directed to the seasonal box with Braden's client, Bill Rafferty, owner of Pilot Knob Farms, his family, Ella and her boyfriend Chris. Caid was around doing some mingling with woman number four. Or was it five? Andrea had seen so many on his arm this past week it was hard keeping tabs. But it seemed he was now with the daughter of one of his local clients, and the family was pushing her at Caid for marriage. Andrea wished them good luck. Caid seemed to be interested in doing a lot of things but marriage wasn't one of them.

There were eleven races lined up for the day, and all the while, Braden was explaining to her about horseracing. She learned that the race Hadassah's Faith was running in was where about twenty-five horses were nominated but only seven were chosen to compete. They were competing for the largest purse out of the three major stakes races that day, but it would be split amongst the seven competing horses with the winner taking the biggest slice.

The announcer declared the starting of the ninth race, and the second of the three stakes races. It was then that Braden asked if she would like to make a wager. The question caught her off-guard. She hadn't felt comfortable about gambling since it was what consumed her father. She didn't want to be in that same boat.

"It's really simple, honey. No skill involved."

"You should go ahead and give it a try, Andrea," Bill urged. "The least you can be out of is a couple dollars."

Andrea glanced at her husband, who gave her a comforting smile. "You don't have to, baby, if you don't want to."

She shrugged. "I don't know…"

"Well, if you don't mind, Braden, could you make a wager for me on Hadassah's Faith?" Bill asked as he gave a few bills to Braden.

Braden stared down at her. "Wanna accompany me?"

She took his offered arm, and they walked to the betting booths. Along the way, she asked, "So, how do you wager, anyway?"

"Depends on what sort of bet you want to make."

"What if I want to make a wager on Hadassah's Faith? What are the rules?"

"Well, when betting on a horse, there are four straight wagers: win, place, show, and across the board. Bet to win is if your horse wins. Bet to place is if your horse places first or second. To show includes third place."

"What if your horse wins first and you made place and show bets?"

"You'll only get those payouts."

"And what about across the board?"

"You're making three bets for win, place, and show. If your horse wins, you'll get all three payouts. If it comes in second, then you'll collect place and show and so on."

They got into line and waited as the people in front of them rattled off their bets.

"Wanna press your luck? My treat."

Andrea rubbed her arms. "I don't know. I'm still leery of all this gambling stuff, you know?"

"You're not like your father, love," he replied as his forefinger drew an invisible line down her nose. "You're a saint compared to most people in my life, but I wouldn't have you any other way."

Those were perhaps the sweetest words he had ever said to her. Andrea couldn't do anything but gaze back at him with a dazed appearance on her face, enthralled. Was that her sign? The long-awaited signal that he was willing and capable of loving her? She bit her lip to keep from blurting out words that could seal her fate. The moment just didn't feel right, telling him "I love you" while in line at a horse race. The past few days, the compulsion to reveal her feelings grew stronger, and she felt that she should be able to have the strength to tell him. All in good time.

As they neared the betting counter, Braden got Bill's wagers ready. "What do I say when I get up there?" Andrea asked.

"How much do you want to wager?"

"I don't know. Ten bucks, maybe."

"Daring, aren't we?" he teased. "Say, 'Lone Star Park, tenth race, ten dollars to win on number four.' And always check your ticket before you leave to make sure it's right. They won't issue you another one once the race begins." He reached into his pocket for his wallet and took out a ten-dollar bill. "Are you sure you don't want to wager more?"

"I'm sure. You've already spent a fortune on me this trip."

"You're worth every penny, sweetheart. The pleasure's mine."

There it was again, right on the tip of her tongue. *I love you, Braden.* But she was distracted when he urged her up to the counter to make her bet. Andrea then waited as Braden made his and Bill's wagers, then they went off to the side to examine their tickets.

Her face scrunched, and she handed her ticket to her husband. "Is this right?"

He studied it for a second. "Looks good, sweetheart. Now, let's get back to the box unless you'd like to— What?"

Andrea's entire frame stilled. She could feel herself hyperventilate, her mind in panic mode. Braden was trying to snap her out of it, but she didn't hear anything past "Lone Star Park, tenth race, five thousand dollars to win on number two."

That voice. She recognized that voice that oozed charm and seduction, but to Andrea, if she could picture the Antichrist, Edward Gaines' face would appear in her mind's eye. To be so close to the man who had ruined her life standing a few feet away from her was too much. How she tried to end that chapter of her life, but she supposed it would never end due to him still breathing. But although she had the displeasure of sharing oxygen with the vile bastard, she was comforted to know she didn't have to face him alone. She had her savior, her knight to come to her aid, and he had vowed to be there to protect her.

Gaines drew nearer to them, his stare gravitating to Andrea. They told of the lascivious things he'd love to do to her as he took in the dress that molded to her fine curves. The glimpse of desire, that same desire that had haunted her since she was fourteen, made her quiver in revulsion.

"Well, well, well," he began with a grin. "Isn't this a pleasant surprise?"

"Sorry I can't say the same," Andrea bit back. "What are you doing here? Got a customer to rip off? Another one to blackmail? Or maybe someone has a date with a car and a lake tonight?"

Ever cool, he didn't rise to her baiting and responded as if she were flirting with him. "I have many interests, little one. My investment in horseracing is just one. But in fact, I am here on business. One of my clients has a horse running in the Lone Star Derby. I believe my namesake, Gainer's Fortune, will sweep the race. I've never seen a horse so conditioned since birth to be a champion. If I overheard you though, you were betting on a mare in the same race?"

Both husband and wife remained silent, glaring hard at their unwanted company.

"Good luck to you. I hope for your sake, she wins, although, I'm surprised to find you gambling at all, considering your father's unfortunate bout with the habit."

Her eyes narrowed but she remained silent. Gaines' gaze shifted to Braden, as if noticing him for the first time, despite his arm around Andrea's waist.

"And who's this?" he asked with an unconcerned air. "Your lover?"

"Her husband," Braden replied in a low, no-nonsense tone. Like an experienced poker player, Gaines didn't betray his emotions. He kept his engaging smile, even as his eyes turned spiteful.

"When did all of this take place?"

Braden edged in front of his wife. "I don't think that's any of your goddamn business."

Andrea stiffened. She knew Gaines wasn't the sort of person you'd want to affront without paying the consequences. God, if anything happened to Braden…

She tugged on his arm. "Let's just go. Please?"

"I should be the one to rush off. I should return to my client." Gaines' gaze lingered down her body. "Until we meet again, little one." He departed, leaving a fuming Braden and a stunned Andrea behind. But Braden wasn't immobile for long, his feet heading in the direction the bastard went.

"No! Braden, please. Don't do this!" She dug her feet into the pavement, her arms fastened around one of his to deter a man who had his sights on committing murder.

"Goddamn that fucking cocksucker!" he roared, not caring if the entire world heard him. "I'll kill the son of a bitch!"

She rushed in front of him, standing in his path despite his own determination to walk past her. She pulled at his arm again. "*Please*, Braden. Not here."

He stopped, turned around to stare at her, reason lost on him. "Why the hell not? I could put an end to this right now."

"Are you crazy?"

"Enough to twist his nuts off and stuff them down his throat? Damn straight."

"You think he's not armed? And I'm sure he's surrounded by at least a dozen men today. Men who'll kill you in an instant."

"Maybe," Braden replied as he continued walking.

Andrea ran in front of him again, this time wrapping her arms around his waist. She glanced up into his eyes, her determination shining through. "If you want to die today, fine. They'll have to shoot me, too. I refuse to be made a widow today."

Andrea wasn't sure if her words would penetrate through the intense, black hatred coursing through his body. She could feel it humming within him as he remained tense. The day may have been ruined by Gaines, but she didn't know what she would do if Braden did something rash to get himself killed. She couldn't bear it. She just couldn't.

She could feel the deep breaths he blew stir her hair, his body relaxing.

"You won't be a widow today, baby," he burred at last, hugging her back. "Do you want to get out of here?"

Andrea nodded.

"Then we'll make an excuse and go back to the hotel, okay?" He wiped away some of the tears, gave her a brief kiss, and guided her back to the box. Upon seeing Andrea's tear-stained cheeks and leaning against her husband, her best friend reacted.

"Andrea, are you feeling okay?"

"I'm afraid she's feeling a little under the weather," Braden replied, handing Bill's ticket back to him. "I'm going to take her back to the hotel and put her to bed. Let us know how Hadassah's Faith does."

As everyone wished for Andrea's recovery, Braden leaned toward Ella, whispering in her ear before they said their goodbyes. After they left the box, Andrea asked him, "What did you tell Ella?"

"That Gaines is here and to be on their guard." Braden dug out his cell to call Caid but it went to voicemail. He left Caid a message about Gaines and that as soon as Caid was done cavorting, he was to meet them back at the hotel.

Braden ushered Andrea to the car, guiding her to her seat before rounding to the driver's side.

"Shouldn't you check whether or not it's been tampered with?"

Braden shook his head before staring into the rearview mirror. "If he's doing all this just to get to you, he wouldn't want his prize damaged, even if it guarantees taking me out. He's been patient so far. We just have to wait until he makes a move."

"I'm scared," she confessed in a shaky voice. This week had been wonderful but was ruined in a matter of minutes. "I don't know what I'll do if...I couldn't stand it if you died because of me."

Her husband reached over to take her chin so she'd look at him, even though she was halfway blinded by unshed tears. "And I won't." He took her hand, entwining her fingers with his. "I want you to know that none of this is your fault. I chose to protect and marry you out of my own free will." He squeezed, and she felt comforted by the security presented in that gesture. "We'll survive, baby." He guided the car to the interstate and hauled it back to Grapevine.

Braden was sitting by the lake sipping on Glengoyne whiskey as his eyes studied the mirror-like surface. It was so beautiful at night, tranquil as the water rippled, the moon casting its radiance upon it. A few late-night boaters disturbed the peace, but Braden was too preoccupied to notice. The events of today replayed in his mind.

Gaines was here. It made Braden wonder if the visit was planned or by coincidence. Either way, it was an inconvenience for them. He wanted to hunt Gaines down, but now it would be like searching for a needle in a haystack.

They had made it back without a hitch, although Braden took the "scenic route" in case they had followers. Andrea stayed in Caid's room with Ella as soon as she returned.

He didn't dare move her yet for ulterior reasons. One was that he wasn't sure if Gaines was tracking them. The second was that he had taken the liberty of setting up a meeting with an old army pal in the morning. His life after his brief stint in the army hadn't been full of catastrophes he couldn't handle. But this was something bigger than him, and he needed help to put an end to it. His future depended on his success. His future with her…

Call him a vengeful bastard, but he was waiting for Gaines to make a move. Just one. Gaines had constructed a successful business built on schemes and blackmail that had involved the destruction of Andrea's father. And the man still had his mind set on her.

Braden would be goddamned.

He had too much at risk. He had a wife who was willing to die with him, telling him with eyes and mannerism what her mouth wasn't willing to say. But he knew she loved him. It warmed his soul. Her body, her mind, and her love were his. She, despite everything that had occurred between them, still had the ability to love him. She was wary to lay all her cards on the table, fearing rejection. But Braden swore that when this was all over, he'd demonstrate just how much in love a man could be with his wife. Because he loved her beyond everything, and he'd sacrifice all that he had to never be deprived of her.

Braden heard the shuffling of footsteps behind him. He had a mere second to glance over his shoulder before a gun was placed point-blank against his temple. He turned back as the man of the hour took a seat on the opposite side of the table.

"You don't mind if I sit here, do you?"

Braden glimpsed sideways at the gun aimed to blow his brains out at any sudden movement. "Apparently, I'm not supposed to."

"This is a beautiful hotel," Gaines replied. "It's nicely situated to the lake and the golf course across the way. Although—"

"Cut the bullshit," Braden grated. "I know what you're here for, and it'll be a cold day in hell before I fork her over."

Gaines' smile remained in place, although his eyes cooled to a frosty gaze. "Not many would defy me, even unarmed with a gun in their face."

There was a brief *click* from beneath the table, the sound stemming from Braden's thumb pulling back the hammer of his Smith & Wesson.

He smirked as the bastard's smile faded, unease setting in. Braden might have been drinking and a bit cocky because of it but he was far from incompetent.

"Now, I'm itching enough to get my gun off, despite the risks. Unless your boy wants to seek new employment, ask him to back off. You and I talk privately. Maybe by the end of this conversation, I won't have a bullet in my head and your dick won't be blown off. Fair trade if you ask me."

To ensure that his body parts remained attached, Gaines signaled for his bodyguard to fall back. Braden's finger remained on the trigger. He had a fast reaction time, and if he were destined to die, he prayed his blood wouldn't be the only one shed.

"Now, what do you want with her?"

Gaines' eyes glimmered in the lamplight. "Not your concern."

Braden searched deep within himself to stay calm. He was caressing the trigger like a lover, so tempted to pull it. "What will it take to buy you off?" He was bluffing. It would be a long time before Gaines saw a dime.

Gaines sat back in the chair, cocking his head to the side. "If it were only money I was after, I would have taken the millions she already paid. There's not a price in this world, Sutherland, that could match what she's worth. As her husband, I thought you'd already notice that potential."

"I have or else I wouldn't have married her, much less fucked her." Again, Gaines kept smiling as if the barb didn't faze him. "I have to hand it to you. You're a persistent son of a bitch to pursue something that was never yours."

"Just like you?" Gaines countered. "She's belonged to me far before you knew her, Sutherland. Your marriage is only temporary, I promise you. I've waited nine years to collect what I'm owed. I won't wait anymore."

"You sick son of a bitch," Braden muttered with disgust. "Having it for a girl that young. She was just fourteen."

"And you're full of shit if you didn't have one lustful thought when you first saw her."

His impulse was to lie, but Braden tempered his denial. When he had seen her for the first time, it was like an out-of-body experience where he envisioned a swirl of sheets around their entwined, naked bodies as he fucked her. The need was immediate and instinctive, and he damn near went crazy with wanting her.

Gaines stared back with those knowing green eyes as if his thoughts were parallel to the ones flashing through Braden's head. "I didn't think so. You felt it, too. The desire to do anything to have her."

"There's a difference. I didn't lust after a child. But I'm sure there have been many other beautiful women in your life. Why waste your time on her?"

"Because I've already had enough of those women. All of them cut from the same cloth. Then I see this girl who's lovely, sweet and pure, a complete opposite to what I usually get. Not that I've never tried women close to Andrea's age. None of them appealed to me, so I've bided my time, waited until she was older, and her father no longer dictated her."

"And is that why you had him killed?"

Still, nothing. The man was impenetrable. "Her father was a drunk with a gambling habit. Stress could drive a man to suicide."

"You urging him on didn't help matters."

"He could have stopped any time. After all, I'm a businessman who is concerned about what's due to me."

"My wife isn't part of the debt."

"I'm sure you thought it noble to protect her by marrying her. You're a brave man, Sutherland. I'll give you that, but I can't congratulate someone who stole what was mine to begin with."

"You've caused her enough grief. You stay the hell away from my wife, or I'll make you regret the next time you see me."

Those green eyes darkened and warred hard with Braden's. "I don't respond well to threats, Sutherland. When I want something, I do everything in my power to get it."

Braden grinned as if he were responding to a compliment. "So do I, and it'll be over my dead body before I'll let you have her."

He heard the shuffling of feet before they were joined by a fourth. But the addition to their party was on Braden's side. There was the flash of a gun lifting in his peripheral, pointing at one of Gaines' henchmen.

"Everything okay here, Sutherland?" Caid asked.

"Couldn't be better," he replied, his eyes narrowing back on Gaines. "I believe our guests were about to leave."

Gaines' face flashed his displeasure. He eased out of the chair and buttoned his jacket. He motioned with his head to his henchmen that it was time for them to leave. Before he left, he said, "You know, 'over my dead body' was what her father told me once when I propositioned for her." The older man's mouth lifted. "It would be a shame for Andrea to mourn not only the loss of her father but that of her husband just mere months from each other."

Braden's face hardened.

"I'd watch my back if I was you, Sutherland, and if you have any concern for your own life, you'd give me what's mine and walk away." He gave a brief nod. "Have a nice night, gentlemen."

Gaines walked off into the night, and Braden and Caid remained bathed in the lamplight with their guns still leveled at the places their enemies had been.

"As much as I appreciate the backup, Marshall, you shouldn't have left her."

"She's in good hands. Turns out the boyfriend's on the Austin S.W.A.T. team. If that doesn't mean the man's qualified, I don't know what does."

Braden lowered his gun. "You trust him?"

Caid did the same. "Probably more than I trust you."

The other scoffed. "Point made."

"So, what's the game plan?"

Braden stared out into the distance. "I hope you brought more ammo, Marshall. It looks like we're going to war."

Chapter Eleven

When Andrea stirred the next morning, she was shocked to find herself dressed only in her underwear. The remainder of the previous day was a blur, her mind wishing to omit that the meeting with Gaines ever happened. What she did remember was coming back to the Gaylord, and Braden securing an arm around her as she curled next to him on the couch. No words were exchanged, each buried in their own turbulent thoughts until everyone returned. Then she was whisked into Caid's room with Ella and Chris while her husband went off to do Lord-knew-what.

The guys and Ella did an adequate job of distracting her for a while. Caid coaxed her into playing poker, which she tried to get into, but they weren't blind to her anxiousness; her gaze watching the door. Caid, unable to bear her pitiful state, excused himself to find Braden. Neither man came back for a while. Andrea couldn't fight the pull of her eyelids after bawling her eyes out on Ella's shoulder. She supposed her husband had come back and took her to their room. At least, she hoped it was her husband. He wasn't in bed.

Andrea shrugged on a terry-cloth robe and made her way to the living room. She was relieved to discover Braden lounging low in a chair by the door, asleep with his pistol on his thigh. She clutched the lapels of her robe together. Guns made her uncomfortable, but this was the protective side of Braden she could trust would never hurt her.

"Braden?" she whispered as she neared him. She was cautious in resting her hand on the side of his downturned face. His eyes opened, and she witnessed the cool grayness of them bloodshot. Her hand fell to his shoulder and rubbed. "Hey, did you get any sleep last night?"

"A few minutes here and there. I can be a light sleeper when need be." He groaned as he leaned forward, rubbing his hands over his face. "What time is it?"

"A quarter to nine." She ran her fingers through his hair. Braden closed his eyes, relishing the sweet contact. "Go to bed, get more sleep."

Braden shook his head, placing the gun on a nearby coffee table. He took hold of her wrist and guided her to stand between his legs. "I should but can't afford to. I'm meeting with someone in a little more than an hour."

"Who?"

"Just an old friend I haven't seen in a while."

Braden unraveled the belt of her robe and parted it, beholding her in her red satin panties and nothing else. He drew her close, resting his head in the valley between her breasts and released a soft groan. "God, it was hard as hell putting you to bed last night." His rough hands smoothed down her sides and up again before standing to his feet. "I'm going to jump into the shower. Wanna join me?"

He flashed an impish, heart-fluttering smile, which was added to Andrea's growing list of weaknesses as far as Braden was concerned. He steered her to the bathroom, releasing her to make quick work of his clothes. Andrea followed suit, causing Braden to hesitate when her panties slipped down her legs, revealing the sweet treasure to her entire universe.

Andrea grinned as her husband remained mesmerized by the sway of her hips as she came toward him. He had stopped at unbuckling his belt, but Andrea was eager to take over the task. She lowered his pants and underwear, his dick throbbing at the ready. She gave it a quick kiss and drawn suckle on its crown, making Braden relinquish a deep, guttural groan from the back of his throat.

He was quick in stepping out of his remaining clothes before hauling her to her feet. Andrea witnessed the fierce, turbulent swirl of desire in his silver gaze that was ready to unleash its fury upon her. She stood and took it, his lips sinking down to devour hers in an impassioned kiss.

She loved his warmth enveloping her, making her hot and flustered. Andrea moved against him in seductive want, her hard, dark nipples grinding into his rough chest hair. Braden resisted the sweet torture of her body, drawing out of her arms to step into the shower, the steam enveloping them both like a misty fog. It drifted between them but not enough that she couldn't see the hand he lifted to her.

"Come to me, baby. Come on."

She took his hand and was pulled into his embrace. Andrea didn't know what it was about him, but Braden was her muscled security blanket, and nothing beyond the threshold of their paradise existed.

Her hands traced the muscles of his biceps that bulged beneath his sinewy, tanned skin as his own moved along her curves. She couldn't believe that this man in all his delectable glory belonged to her. That she had the privilege to have and to hold what others could not. That she was the woman he chose. He lifted her chin, and Andrea swore she saw a kindred emotion in that swirling, silver stare. An emotion beyond lust, a yearning for more than her body. A desire to belong to her in every capacity he could allow himself. But Andrea wasn't sure if she was reading too deep into what she wished was there. For now, she would wrap herself in the pretense of a husband in love. Thinking otherwise would have her miss the heady effects of Braden sweeping back the now dampen tendrils of her hair, and him lowering his face so her mouth received his. Every one of her taste buds tingled from tasting him. She moaned with each possessive sweep of his tongue against hers, her body in blissful communion with his.

Braden's left hand smoothed down her side and around the back to massage her generous ass. He leaned back, taking a playful bite out of her bottom lip before letting go and bidding her to her turn around. He walked her forward, urging her to splay her hands against the cool tile. Braden's callused hands reached around to cup her bountiful breasts, stimulating her poor aching nipples as he kneaded them. Despite the water running hot, it could do nothing to retain the tremors dancing up and down her spine.

They traveled again to her backside, pulling her hips until she was nestled against his keen, twitching cock. She bit her lip when the tip of him brushed her, a tremulous moan falling from her mouth. God, she was dying to have him, and the anticipation drove her mad. His fingers explore her from behind before inching inside her. His hands guided her into a tender but torturous rhythm, goading her to take the lead.

She steered the course of their pleasure, sliding along the hard length of him. She relished the control, to have him at the mercy of her drive. Her torment of him was rewarding, hearing the throaty groans she loved as sensation conquered him.

"Oh, fuck me, baby. Fuck me good."

Andrea's face contorted at his guttural words, her will faltering. She voiced her ecstatic response with each deep plunge. Her hands clawed at tile, her nails biting into her palms. She was starting to lose it, her body unable to keep up with the intensity it desired. The slick walls of her clenched around him, and Braden made a choking sound before crushing her to the wall.

His takeover was immediate, pummeling into her hard and fierce. His hot breath stirred at the delicate nape of her neck, his front flushed against her back as his warmth and strength surrounded her. He brushed her hair aside, his lips fastening to her fluttering pulse at the side of her neck. His fingers entwined with hers against the wall, Andrea wanting to have something to hold on to through this cyclone of chaos and elation.

He whispered encouragements that spurred her to come. Still entwined with hers, Braden took her right hand on a journey down her body and between her legs. Pressing her fingers against the expanded bud nestled there, and with the help of his own, he encouraged her to rub it. God, it was like mating with lightning. Brushing against it achieved more moans and sighing of his name. Her legs quaked as the heat and fury were fast upon her.

Braden stood back and administered a few more hard thrusts. "That's it, baby. That's it. Come for me."

Andrea was there, her screams of delight harmonized by the rough ones from Braden. She sagged against the wall while he sagged against her, and for the longest time, neither one of them moved. The hot water raced down his back while he shielded her from it. But Andrea was so enamored by the way he felt as he nibbled on her supple shoulder.

God, she never thought she could achieve something like this in her life. She had achieved love and happiness with a man whom she had hated but was intrigued with from the start. Ever masculine and protective but loving and caring. This was what it was like to be content. As devastating as the past year had been, being in Braden's arms after such a beautiful joining was rewarding enough. She couldn't ask for anything greater.

"You all right?" he grumbled after a few moments.

"No. You?"

"No." He smothered kisses along her shoulder blades. "We keep having showers like these, we'd drown. I could stay in here with you all day."

"Then why don't you?" Andrea turned around to face him. Her fingers teased his wet, curling hair. "Do you have to go to your meeting?"

"Yes," Braden confirmed, his face solemn. He cupped her cheek, his fingers spearing into her hair. "In the meantime, I want you to get ready and packed. When I get back, I'm going to have Caid fly you home."

Andrea's insides dropped. She was still a little dizzy from the loving he had just given her, but the moment wasn't lost on her. Her hands clutched his wrists. "No. Braden, no. Please let me stay with you."

He shook his head, as if fortifying himself from her pleading. "I can't risk it. I can't risk you. I'll be damned if I have to."

"But it's fine for me to go home to worry to death?" She paused. "That's what this meeting is about, isn't it? Braden…"

"If I don't do anything about it now, we'll never have peace." He stroked her hair. "If I'm unable to give you anything else, at least I can try and give you that."

Your love would be enough. But perhaps she was being too greedy to require that of him when he had just revealed his intention to secure their happiness forever.

"You understand, don't you, baby?"

"Yes. I don't like it, but I understand. I couldn't talk you out of it if I tried." Her morose gaze traced over his beloved features as her hands did the same. God only knew how much she loved and cherished this man. "Promise you'll come back to me."

Braden gave her a gentle kiss before taking her into his arms. A huff of air blew past his lips as he caressed her, resting his cheek against the crown of her head. "I promise."

After their tender moment, Braden left Andrea to wash her hair. He was dressed and gone in minutes but not before kissing several more times. In between drying herself and her hair, Andrea began packing her clothes and toiletries. When she was dressed, she curled her hair then applied makeup. While putting on her lipstick, she heard the room door open. It was earlier than she would have expected him, but Andrea eager to greet her husband. She sprayed perfume to her neck and chest area, straightened her clothes and came out to the living area.

"Braden?" she called with a smile. But that smile dimmed when she witnessed Gaines standing at the threshold. The man of her nightmares had breached her defenses when her husband was nowhere to be found.

On impulse, Andrea lunged for the phone on an end table. Too late. Gaines had his gun aimed at her heart.

"Uh-uh. None of that." He gestured with his gun to get her away from her lifeline. "I want a word with you."

"You need to leave. My husband will murder you if he finds you here."

"Your husband is the reason why I'm here," he pointed out, stepping in her direction. He stopped when Andrea stiffened. "I haven't harmed him. Not yet. In fact, I probably know more about his whereabouts than you do. Visiting a Randall Quinn at the Texas Rangers branch in Garland, and he probably won't be back for some time…if ever. I have people waiting to take him out as soon as he walks out the door."

Andrea closed her eyes, breathing deep to help alleviate the fears inside her. "What do you want?"

"Why ask a stupid question when you know the answer? At any rate, I'm done waiting."

"You'll wait a long time yet if you hurt Braden," Andrea threatened.

Gaines chuckled. "You don't have the means to make threats."

"Do I?" Her smile was malicious. "I'd gladly kill myself just to spite you. After all, what do I have to lose?"

"What about your husband?"

"I won't see him again anyway."

"I'd still kill him if you did, and wouldn't you want your husband to live?"

That gave her pause, and her bravado tapered.

"I'm a nice guy," Gaines began again after she remained quiet. "I'm willing to cut a deal. You convince your husband to let you go, and I'll make sure he walks away without a scratch. You have my word as a gentleman." He extended his hand.

Andrea scoffed at it. "Your word means nothing to me."

"But your husband does, and that'll be enough." He put his hand down. "You have until you leave Dallas. If you're seen boarding his plane, my men will take him out. That's including the little bodyguard you two brought along." Another step toward her. "And I know you'll want your best friend to get home safe…"

Andrea's hands balled into fists, anger and anguish warring within her, but there was little she could do. She had to protect the people she loved. "All right," she conceded, her voice soft.

"See? I knew you could be reasonable." He strolled up to her, fishing out his card and held it out to her. "You get to a place and call me. I'll take care of you."

"Drawing up divorce papers can take a long time."

"I'm not waiting for the ink to dry. You finalize the divorce or funeral arrangements. It doesn't matter to me which happens first. The result will be the same." She flinched when his hand reached out to stroke a strand of her hair. "You'll finally be mine."

Andrea wanted to vomit. The fire wasn't out of her yet. She remained submissive as he lifted her chin to kiss her. She waited for the brush of his mouth, and the sweep of his tongue before she chomped down on it, hard.

He bellowed as he jerked his head away, his tongue bleeding. Andrea was repaid with a fist slamming into her left cheek, sending her to the ground.

"Come here!" Gaines raged. "Get up, you little bitch!" She didn't have a chance to crawl away before Gaines grabbed her by her hair and wrapped his fingers around her throat before slamming her against the wall. Then came a foot-long KA-BAR he brandished in the dim lamplight. He pressed the flat side of the cool blade against her cheek. "I've had women killed for fewer affronts."

Despite her fear, Andrea glared down her nose at him. "But it takes a *real* man to hit a defenseless woman."

Gaines trailed the knife down her neck to trace the heaving swell of one of her breasts, causing her breath to catch. "I'm man enough to let you know that I'm not someone to fuck with. And you *will* learn your place, or you can bury your husband. Pick any path you like, little one. I'll still win."

Andrea sunk her head, fighting back tears. She refused to let the bastard see her cry. "All right," she breathed. "Just call off the guy. Please?"

Gaines studied her, appearing satisfied by her brokenness. He dialed the guy and smiled at her when it was done, returning his phone back to his pocket. "Happy?"

Andrea glared at him. Gaines reached over to touch her again, but like before, she turned her head away.

"Trust is something we'll eventually work on, little one. You'll grow accustomed to your new life."

Andrea had to hold her tongue from saying something that would endanger Braden's life. Gaines moved in to give her a sweeping kiss on her neck, but she drew away as if he had bitten her, placing her hand up to her neck and staring at him with such horror.

"Remember our deal and don't get cute." He stroked her jaw. "Until later."

Andrea waited until Gaines left, agonized at what his interference was going to make her do. God, she didn't need this, but her hands were tied. She was sick and tired of him threatening to take away the people she cared about. As much as Braden took pride in protecting her, it was time she did something for him.

Andrea knew what she had to do. She just prayed it would buy her enough time.

Much to her relief, her beloved husband came back in one piece and in good spirits. Andrea hadn't done much since Gaines left, sitting in a chair to wait for Braden's return. She was sick to her stomach while the minutes ticked by. But he came back to her, and it took all her restraint not to charge the door and wrap her arms around him, all the while weeping and thanking God for his safe return.

Instead, she stayed seated in a dark corner of the room, her face in profile to him almost as if she weren't acknowledging his presence at all. The room was illuminated by one lamp on a sideboard, giving off an ominous vibe.

Braden took it all in as the door closed behind him, his curious gray eyes sweeping down her perfect posture as she continued to stare straight ahead.

"Baby? You okay?"

Andrea peered into her lap, teasing her quivering bottom lip. "I think we need to talk, Braden."

She waited, but he didn't give a response, although he stood still as he waited in the tension-filled silence for her to continue. After gathering some courage, she did.

"I've been thinking. Perhaps…perhaps this isn't the best for us. I've been having second thoughts about our marriage since day one, and…I think it's best to just call it off."

"Call it off?" Braden's tone was sharp. "Woman, you were willing to ride my dick just a couple hours ago. Now you've suddenly had a change of heart?"

"There should be more to our relationship than sex," she argued. "A woman can get tired of you rutting on her all the time."

Braden exhaled as he paced about the room, his emotions roiling. The next time he gazed at her, his stare was incredulous, not to mention hurt. It almost broke her.

"Rutting. Rut…rutting?" he stammered out. "You describe my lovemaking as rut— What the hell's wrong with you?"

She said nothing.

"You're willing to pull insults at my expense but not once are you able to look me in the eye. I think I deserve to know why."

She was done for. Andrea could no longer hide behind the cracking, icy exterior, and she hated being cruel to him.

"Please, Braden." Her voice cracked. "Don't make this harder than it already is."

"You're the only one making it hard, and I'm not giving up." His face morphed, suspicious. "Did he put you up to this?"

"No!"

Braden stalked toward her, seized her by her upper arms, and pulled her to her feet. Andrea turned her head where her husband caught a glimpse of the swollen, discolored cheek. His face softened before eclipsing into a black rage. His hands increased pressure on her arms, causing her to cry out. He released her and started toward the bedroom.

"Goddamn that motherfucker! Dared to lay hands on *my* woman!"

Andrea chased him, watching as he checked his gun and placed extra rounds in his pocket. "What are you going to do?"

"Do? I'm going to put so many bullets in the bastard, he'll still be shitting slugs after I've sent him to hell."

Braden tore out the room without another word, leaving Andrea to process everything. She couldn't stop him. He was too far gone. But she already knew by now that Gaines had left town. Braden didn't.

There was but one play left in her cards.

Andrea sat down at the desk and took out a couple of sheets of paper and wrote two letters. One she folded and addressed to Caid and the other to Braden. She gathered her things and made it down the hallway. Reaching Caid's door, she passed the notes beneath it, not waiting around to see if he was in or not. Her next stop was Ella's room, where she and Chris were packed and readying themselves to go back to Austin.

Ella started at seeing her best friend's bloodshot eyes and swollen cheek. A barrage of questions was asked rapid-fire. Andrea informed Ella of what had happened, and what she was about to do.

"Honey…are you sure?" Ella asked, stroking back Andrea's ebony hair as she cried for the hundredth time in the last hour. "I mean…you don't…"

"Ella…please don't." She had to do this. She had to save him.

Ella, despite her objections, no longer pushed or tried to persuade a mind that was firm in its resolve. They went downstairs to the lobby where Chris checked them out. Andrea was in her own world, watchful of the exit just in case Caid or Braden came blazing through. She was startled when she heard an accusatory whisper in her ear.

"I know why you're leaving, slut. Couldn't wait until Braden left to fuck your lover, could you?"

Andrea's vacant visage remained that way. She didn't owe this bitch an explanation, but now she knew the culprit who helped the viper get into her nest.

Her dark brown eyes cut hard into the icy blues of Kit, right before Andrea planted a hard slap on her cheek. It was the slap heard 'round the hotel. The patrons and staff gasped from the sound of Andrea's hand meeting flesh.

Kit stood back, holding her cheek and looking horrified. "You slapped me!"

Ella came up to wrap an arm around Andrea. "No less than what you deserve, you dick-hounding ho."

She ushered a silent Andrea to the exit and away from a man she'd never see again.

Braden returned three hours later. He knew he had been searching in vain, but he had been so pissed off that he wanted instant retribution. The bastard dared to hurt something precious to him. Braden wanted to rip him limb from limb. His poor baby. Her cheek swollen; her eyes red from tears. There was no evidence that he had done nothing more than hit her, but that was enough. Gaines would never get another opportunity.

He walked into the lobby; his face strained with weariness. Seeing a grim-looking Caid didn't ease matters. His entire body seized; his heart beat sporadic. From his very marrow, Braden knew what had occurred in his absence.

"When?"

"A couple hours ago. She left with Ella and Chris. I found these beneath my door when I got back. One's addressed to you."

Braden eyed the letter and took it with hesitance. "The other?"

"Just instructions and thanks. Making sure you don't do anything rash."

His inside churned, not sure he even wanted to see her words of goodbye, but his anticipation got the better of him. He unfolded the letter and read.

Braden –

> *You're probably not going to approve of what I'm about to do, but believe me, this is the hardest decision I've ever had to make. But I know why I'm leaving you now. I had come to grips a while ago that I would sacrifice a lifetime of happiness with you for your life. A small sacrifice on my part...so I thought. I just can't bear to have your death on my conscience...*
>
> *God, it's difficult to write this. In the last few days, you've shown me just how much of a loving husband you can be. I appreciate all the care you've given for my protection. Now it's time for me to repay you in kind.*
>
> *I can't thank you enough for all you've done. You're a remarkable man, and I know I'll never love again for the rest of my life because I've given all my love to you.*
>
> *With that, I beg you, please don't try to find me. Trust me, this is for the best.*

Love Always,

Andrea

Braden read the tear-stained letter multiple times, his eyes hanging on one part now engraved into his memory.

I've given all my love to you.

Reading those words was torture, but he got confirmation of what he knew all along. He had her love, a selfless, hard-earned love, but the knowledge did little to placate him. Braden felt betrayed that she underestimated his vow to protect her. He'd sacrifice anything to keep her. He also realized how he failed in making his intentions to her clear. That he wanted her for a lifetime. Would always want her despite the circumstances that brought them together. Braden loved her, and he would not go home without her.

"Pack your things," he told Caid, folding the letter back in half and placing it into his pocket. "We're going to Austin."

Caid nodded. "Give me twenty. I'll meet you down here."

As they headed upstairs, Braden arranged for an extension on his rental. It would be easier to drive than to wait for his plane to be ready. By the end of the transaction, he was opening his door in time to see the generous curves of a woman rising from the same chair Andrea had occupied earlier. Kit had her long hair down from its usual bun, her jacket's top button undone to display a bit of her black, lacy bra covering her fulsome breasts, a coy smile teasing her mouth and her eyes ready to play. However seductive she wanted to be, Braden wasn't playing along, nor would he even if he had all the time in the world.

He glowered. "What the hell are you doing here?"

She was undaunted by his simmering hostility, instead coming closer to him. "Oh, I'm here to give my condolences. I imagine it's difficult to get over your whore of a wife cheating on you, but I wish to only comfort you any way I can."

Braden stared at her hard. Of all the stupid, plotting women…

"God, I'm sorry," she said with fake compassion. "I thought you knew."

"With who?"

"Some guy." She ran her hands up his chest to rest on his broad shoulders, sporting a sure smile. "He came to the hotel earlier looking for her."

Braden seized her wrists, his grip on them tight. "Who?"

Kit frowned as Braden's demeanor shifted to something dangerous. "What does it matter?"

His hands constricted, shaking her once. "Who, damn you!"

"I don't know who he is!"

"And you gave him a key to the room, didn't you?" He shook her again when she refused to respond. "I didn't hear you."

Kit stared at him, her blue eyes wide. "She was cheating on you! I was only trying to make you see—"

She was cut off by Braden's anguished scream as he threw her away from him. He kicked over the coffee table. Kit backed up to a wall, and Braden pursued, crowding her in. He was livid. If she hadn't let Gaines in, then the bastard wouldn't have hit Andrea and convinced her to leave. Leave him to deal with this calculating bitch who'd set into motion the ruination of his marriage.

His stony face bent to her. "You don't have the brain capacity to understand what you've done, but I promise I'll make you suffer as much as I can."

Kit appeared terrified. "Are you going to kill me?"

Braden gave her a wicked smile. "No. Even that's too merciful for the likes of you. But I happen to know a couple of your bosses. I will have you fired before you even get downstairs. Count on it."

"You wouldn't! You're going to turn me down for some whore who—"

She shrieked as Braden's fist came flying past her and embedded into the wall inches from her head. Kit was on the verge of fainting, her features ashen. Braden extracted his hand, bits of the wallpaper and crumbling drywall coming with him.

"You can put that on my bill, which will be the last thing you'll do at this hotel. You'll regret pissing me off." He eased away from her. "Get out of here."

He waited a few seconds while Kit recovered from the shock of having her life in shambles before she made her exit.

Braden closed his eyes at the quiet shut of the door, trying to find that calm and steady place in him that would help quiet the riot of emotions.

But damn her! A relationship that had taken him all this time to build was demolished in less than twenty-four hours. Gaines was the dynamite to Kit's wrecking ball to cause the biggest destruction in Braden's life.

Out there was a woman who loved him enough to put her own life on the line to save his. No woman had ever put his needs before theirs. Perhaps no woman ever would again.

Andrea was his woman. His wife. His everything. Now she was gone.

Gone. God, Andrea...

Braden reached for his phone. He had plans to formulate and a marriage to save. He just hoped he wasn't too late.

Chapter Twelve

Andrea was in a state of depression over the next two days. She was inconsolable on the car ride down to Austin. Part of it because of her conscience. The rest was for feeling stupid for leaving the one man she would ever love.

He either hated her or was glad he wasn't saddled with her problems anymore. He was free. She imagined he had already contacted his lawyer to draw up divorce papers to put an end to their short-lived marriage.

If it was supposed to be for the good of them both, why did she feel so terrible? She supposed it was because she was haunted by memories of him. The look of sincerity in his eyes tortured her, along with the pain and hurt when she insulted him.

Now she was paying for it. Being away from him was destroying her. But the deed was done, and there was no going back. As for her future, there was no such thing as happiness after Braden. She would have to live with that decision for the rest of her life.

She stayed on Ella's couch, wallowing inside and not eating a thing. But toward the end of the second day, her emotions had numbed enough that she didn't break into tears every five minutes. Andrea worked on steeling herself for what she had to do. She was determined to seek justice. She had sacrificed a lifetime with Braden. She wouldn't let that sacrifice be in vain and wanted to make damn sure that no one she loved was ever threatened again.

Chris was quick to hook up a meeting with a detective to question her the next day. She went to a seafood restaurant downtown and waited until Chris showed up with the detective in plain clothes to give the illusion of him being a friend in case Gaines' men were lurking about.

From him, she learned they had gotten a call from the Texas Rangers' branch in Garland the day before, and that the case was now being handled by them and the Travis County Sheriff's Department.

Andrea recalled the ranger he'd spoken to. Randall Quinn was the name Gaines gave her. The man her husband met with. Despite that the case wasn't in their hands, the detective insisted to have any information that would be vital to pass along. She relayed all she had and after business concluded, Andrea made her way back to Ella's apartment.

Her mind was still trying to wrap around the fact that Braden's actions was already gaining momentum and trickling all the way down to Austin. It was startling, but at the same time, such a relief. But her question was if Braden still had a hand in this or was his buddy at the Texas Rangers handling this solo? Was there any chance of reconciliation since she abandoned him? Was she stupid for holding out hope?

Andrea got out of Ella's car and burst through the door. "Ella, you wouldn't believe…"

She stopped in her tracks once she witnessed Ella sitting across from the man who hadn't left her thoughts since she physically left him.

"Braden!" she exclaimed, her mind racing. Andrea moved to place her hands on the nearby bar to steady herself, placing a hand over her pacing heart. Her entire body was trembling, her legs about to give. She had to wait until she found her voice which was buried somewhere in her throat. "What are you doing here?"

God, he was so beautiful...and so here. Despite his glowering features aimed at her, she couldn't help but be thankful to see him.

Ella cleared her throat when neither of their eyes strayed from the other and nothing was being said. She stood to her feet and gathered her house keys. "I think I'm going for a walk. Lord knows I need to. I'll be back to check on you two lovebirds in an hour."

"You don't have to go, Ella," Andrea voiced in a quivering half whisper, her gaze still magnetized to his.

Ella knew better. Looking at the way Braden's hard, quicksilver gaze remained cool and unwavering was an indication that this was one storm she didn't want to be in.

"Yeah," Ella replied, inching toward the exit. "Sorry, chick. You're on your own." She shook her head as she went out the door, but not before Andrea heard a mumbled, "Lord, they're going to tear up my house."

The slamming of the front door broke the trance Andrea was absorbed in. Her eyes broke contact as she placed her purse and spare keys onto the bar before turning to him again. She attempted to give off a casual air of indifference once she got past the initial shock of Braden sitting mere feet from her, unsure if she was at all convincing.

"I suppose Ella's the one I should thank for you being here?"

Braden nodded, rising to his feet. "But I guess you're going to pretend that you're not happy to see me?"

"I'm not pretending. You shouldn't be here."

She was lying, and he knew it. Braden edged around the couch that seemed a paltry wall between them. His entire magnetism rolled off of him to where she felt crushed by the presence of it.

"I'm not going anywhere."

"You fool. You stubborn fool."

"I'm a fool? Why? For not cowering?" Braden stepped nearer. "I already told you, honey. I'm not afraid of the motherfucker. Neither should you be."

"He told me he'd kill you for interfering. I couldn't let that happen!"

"So you said in your letter. Is that your justification for running away? To sacrifice your happiness with me for my life?" He shook his head, indignant. "You blind little martyr. Can't you see that I don't have a life without you?"

Andrea almost couldn't breathe after hearing that. She stared at him in disbelief, her chin on the ground. It was what she had always wanted to hear, but it couldn't have come at a more inopportune time. Not while his life was still in danger.

She rounded the other end of the couch to set some distance between them. Him just standing there, earnest and unwavering, tore down her feeble defenses. She was on the verge of tears, hating that Braden would soon see them as a testimony of how he always weakened her resolve. That he was her weakness, and he was about to use it against her.

"I just…I just wish you would have left well enough alone. Just go."

She ran for Ella's bedroom, but within a few strides, Braden cut her off before she reached the hallway. Her body rushed into his, the impact registering as nothing significant. Her body's contact against his brief but detrimental to her senses. The smell and heat of him had attached itself to her, filtering into her clothes as if his essence were tracking hers.

Her dark gaze saw the intense gleam of dilated pupils that made her aware of the same transference happening to him. Except with Braden, he had no desire to ignore it, and the knowing, wolfish smile he displayed confirmed what he had in store for her.

Oh, shit.

"We're not done yet."

Andrea backed away from him, and he followed her step for step. Her mind was scrambling, trying to think of anything to detract him from his purpose of making his dick the mediator of their fight. Nothing came to mind outside the thought of how she had missed said mediator and its intimate negotiations.

Oh, shit, shit.

Her backside met the back of the couch, and a couple of steps later, her husband loomed inches away. His stance indicated he was ready for her if she bolted, but he stood steadfast as if he waited for her surrender.

How close she was to giving it.

She licked her dry lips, her mouth parched. "I'm sure he knows you're here."

"I don't give a good goddamn if he does. He dared to put his hands on my woman. I'm going to repay the bastard in kind. It's as simple as that. And I won't let anyone take you away from me. Not him. Not even you."

Andrea remained quiet; her eyes cast down to the floor. She heard Braden exhale long.

"Look at me."

Despite her desire to resist, she couldn't slow the long climb up his body to stare into the face of the man she loved. "Look me in the eyes and tell me that letter was bullshit. Tell me you were lying when you said you love me." He leaned in closer, engulfing her entire vision with himself. "And don't lie because you think it'll save me. It won't."

Large tears formed and rolled down her cheeks, betraying what she wanted to keep under wraps. "I don't want you to die," she whispered, her tone pitiful. "I couldn't bear it if anything happened to you. It'll...kill me." She was unable to stop the sobs tearing from her. "I love you too much."

His face softened, and through the blinding wall of her tears, Andrea was immersed into his strong, robust arms. She made desperate grasps at his shirt, hot tears soaking into it. Braden held her closer to his heart, stroking her back as his lips graced kisses into her hair.

"It would kill me to lose you. I don't have a life without you, baby, and I mean it." She lifted her head to stare up at him with luminous eyes that beheld the pure anguish embedded in his own. He cupped her face, his thumbs wiping away her tears. "I couldn't bear not seeing your face for the rest of my life." His thumbs caressed her plump, quivering mouth. "Or tasting you."

His subtle seduction subdued her, Andrea melting at his touch with his mouth over hers. It was brief, and she was swaying toward him when he withdrew, her lips reluctant to let go. He steadied her, and she tingled from where his hands rested on her shoulders. His thumbs stroked her neck before smoothing down her arms to land around her waist. He bore her against him again in another hug. "Or holding you."

Her nose went straight into his shirt where the top two buttons were undone. She was drifting through the fog of his heady scent, luring her awareness back to everything about him that was familiar. His warmth, his strength, his love. Rather, what she would imagine his love would be if he had given it to her. On that fulfillment, she still turned up empty.

Andrea started to shrug off the haze, coming back to herself to regain ground, but Braden was quicker. He had slipped in, his fingers in stealth mode as they stole beneath the elastic band of her pants, searching for her aching spot that was always ready for his touch. She descended back into the mist of his ministrations, her legs spreading apart without him asking her to. It was as if her body no longer obeyed her as it fell in line under his command. Callused fingers slipped beneath her cotton panties, streaking past to massage a clit that was already prospering and slick. She grabbed the back of the couch as he strummed her, watching with rapt fascination as if he would never get tired of seeing her being pleasured at his mercy.

His hand departed from her love button, continuing further to push two thick fingers inside her. Andrea gasped, her hands latching onto Braden's arms as he pulled her hips to his crooked hand like she was caught on a hook.

"Oh, my G— Oh!"

The last word came out in a squeak she never knew she could make. If he didn't have her so strung out, she might have been half embarrassed by it.

"You feel that? So sweet, tight, and wet for me. All for me." His voice was thick with a variety of emotions Andrea couldn't pin down. His jaw flexed as his fingers moved in an agonizing pace, torturing her in ways she couldn't handle. Sounds of frustration sounded from her as his thumb stroked her clit like a casual afterthought. As if he was giving her enough fuel to stoke her fire but not enough to consume her.

She tried to move to dislodge his fingers. "Braden…"

"Everything about you drives me crazy. Your sounds, your body, that glorious spitfire nature of yours…" The intensity of him slipped, and for a moment, he appeared stricken. "I *need* that in my life, and I'll be damned if I have to be without it."

A part of Andrea's heart crumbled. His need wasn't directed to her a whole but to pieces of her. She had taken a chance with Braden because she was in love with him, even married him without the promise of him ever returning her affection. Their passion together was beyond anything she had imagine, but she knew it wasn't enough to sustain her for the rest of her life. He may have needed her body, but she needed his love.

As a quivering moan slipped out of her, Andrea snagged his wrist, pulled his hand from her dripping snatch. She bit down on her lip as she drew his hand out of her pants, missing the warmth of his fingers. But she continued to follow through, sidestepping away from him and throwing his hand down.

Braden looked floored by her audacity, catching her before she could take another step, his well-built frame heaving from being denied.

"Why?" His voice was low but sharp. She still retained her glare at him as she fought the longing flowing through her own body. He pulled her back in front of him, trapping her between the couch and his solid form. "*Why?*"

She heard him but still said nothing, even when he held his slick fingers aloft for them both to see.

"You can't say you *don't* want it."

"I can't."

"Then what is it?"

Her eyes glazed with tears. "Is screwing me the only thing you want?"

Braden blinked. "What?"

Her blood was hot from more than the lust, which was the push she needed. Andrea edged around him, finding her words. "What do you want from me, Braden? I don't want to be just a fuck buddy to you. I deserve better than that, and I refuse to settle for less."

Andrea turned to leave, but Braden enclosed her in his arms. She struggled against him to no avail. The look in his eyes stilled her to listen.

"You think I would do all this because I want you? Hell, are you so naïve that I have to spell it out for you? Even the blind can see how much I love you. Why can't you?"

There they were. The words she had assumed Braden wouldn't have the capacity to say. And the moment left her dumbfounded as her wide eyes stared up into those beloved quicksilver ones that shone sincerity. She closed her eyes, allowing the feeling to envelope her. Braden cupped her head between hands that had adored and explored her body time and time again. A small smile creased his mouth as she continued to stare at him with awe.

"Wanna hear that again?" he coaxed. She nodded. "I love you, baby. More than my own life."

His face was no longer hidden behind its standard mask of stone. Andrea was able to witness it all, from vulnerability to earnestness. Braden, her Braden, was a man of action, yet he swallowed his pride to tell her what she needed to hear.

Because he loved her.

Andrea smoothed back the renegade curl of dark brown hair that fell on his forehead, her fortitude weakened. Braden took her into his arms, crushing her to his heart, vowing to never let her go. "God, I've missed you. It's been two days, and I've missed you like crazy."

She reveled in him embracing her. "I've missed you, too."

Braden scoffed but then released a brief chuckle. "You've got a funny way of showing it, running off like that." Andrea's head lifted to stare up at the man who belonged to her in every sense. "I understand why you did it, baby. You'd sacrifice your life and then some for me, which makes me mighty humbled that you would. But I wish you would've trusted me more to protect you. You know I would do anything for you."

"I know. And I'm sorry, but I just didn't want you sacrificing your life for me."

"Life's like hell without you. Putting my life on the line is nothing if it means I can hold you until the end."

Andrea frowned, worry still wearing at her. "Braden...what are we going to do?"

Some of the warmth ebbed out of his mien as he held her close. His hands came up to stroke her long hair, his chest allaying a heavy sigh.

"Anything we have to, baby. Lord knows I refuse to lose you now."

It wasn't just the Texas Rangers and the sheriff's department involved. The Feds also wanted a piece of Gaines. Between the three, no one had been able to get a scrap of proof to bring him down, either from his shakedowns or his money laundering. Whenever he was brought to justice, either his lawyer would get him off scot-free or one of his men took the fall. They had to get a confession out of him somehow. Now they had the very thing he wanted, and she could prove to be the vital weapon to be wielded against him.

Before he had left her that day, Braden had deemed it necessary for them to stay away from each other. He knew Gaines would have his sentinels watching their every move, so it was best if they looked the part of the separating couple. Braden, along with Caid, returned to Fort Worth and flew home.

As the days went by, Andrea became irritable. She longed to see her husband. It felt as if she were going at this alone, but not a day went by without a secret message of his love. In those messages, she found strength. The strength to know that as soon as this was over, she could be with him, free and clear.

Two weeks after they had parted ways, she met with a lawyer who had been a friend of her father's. He was notified prior to her meeting with him what was going on, and he agreed to assist. He had knowledge of her dealings with Gaines since he was the one who helped with her father's affairs.

The lawyer drew up paperwork that leaned more toward an annulment than a divorce. Once all was processed with the promise that her husband would be served, she waited for the next step, which was to contact Gaines. Randall Quinn arranged to have her conversation recorded from her cell. She dreaded ever having to see the snake again, let alone talk to him. Braden wasn't too keen about the idea, either, but Andrea knew Gaines wouldn't be drawn into the open unless his prize was there for the taking.

The call took place while her husband was still away since Quinn knew if Braden overheard the conversation, he would blow their cover in his rage. Andrea mustered her nerve to dial the number, praying it would go to voicemail. She was disappointed when he answered, his tone gloating with a hint of acidity.

"It's taken you a while to call me. Almost as if you were stalling for time."

Already, he was suspicious. She didn't hide the uncertainty in her voice to play innocent. "I had some loose ends to tie up."

"Like your husband?" Her eyes widened at that drop of detail. "I heard he paid you a visit a couple days after you left Dallas. And don't try to lie. I already know."

"He came to get me back, I refused. If one of your brain-dead lackeys had stayed behind long enough, he would have seen Braden leave empty-handed."

"Not to mention a little disheveled," Gaines supplied with sarcasm. "You gave hubby one last ride before sending him off?"

Andrea gritted her teeth. He was slicing into her bit by bit, and it made her uneasy of how aware he was. She wondered if he knew of her meetings with law enforcement. They had been discreet, but now she wasn't sure if it had been enough.

Her best strategy was to match his demeanor. A malicious smile crossed features he couldn't see, all in an attempt to steel herself. "Why not? I'm only preparing myself for my new life. Crawling from one bed to another."

"Just to mine. I don't share."

Gaines being monogamous was far from endearing. Andrea would rather be riddled with every disease known to man than be his one and only.

"You still haven't answered my question. What has taken you so long?"

"Don't you already know? You've been tracking me."

"Yes, but I want to hear it from you."

Her mind pasted together reasons that would pacify him. She couldn't lose it. Not yet. "Then you should know that I was getting my affairs in order. And, to tell you the truth, I've been milking my freedom for what it's worth before I become a kept woman. You wouldn't begrudge me that, would you? After all, you know I wouldn't come to you without a fight."

Andrea heard him scoff. "You've been fighting me for years. I wouldn't expect anything less. But I hope that delightful fire of yours won't burn out once you finally give yourself to me."

"Would hate to disappoint. But I do have some terms to be met."

Gaines chuckled. "You have some audacity, girl, to think you could negotiate anything. As I've said, you have no grounds for it."

"We meet on my terms or not at all."

A pause. "All right. I'll play. What are your terms, little one?"

She sighed in relief. Andrea thought she had blown everything when she became hotheaded, seconds away from telling him to play in traffic.

"One, I want your guarantee that nothing will happen to Braden, Caid, Ella, or anyone else I know and love. Because if it does, I swear to God I'll drown myself in the same lake my father was found in."

She said the last sentence with bitter conviction, which was met with brief silence before he said, "Done. Next request?"

"I have your word on that?"

"No one has died recently, have they?"

Except for her father, unless he were exempt from what this man qualified as recent. Andrea was still edging on trust but continued. "I want our meeting place to be The Driskill."

"Why?"

She searched her mind for an excuse that wasn't far from the truth and would sound authentic. "I love the architecture, and I've been dying to stay there since its renovation. Just never had the opportunity."

He sighed into the receiver. "Seems suspicious to me. Are you sure you won't have the cavalry there?"

"Why risk it? Braden and Caid left for Wyoming, and I've already exhausted any type of help I could get. Austin PD is willing to write off everything I've told them, so I have little ground to stand on. And I'm willing to do anything to protect who I love, even if it means sacrificing myself to the likes of you."

"Fair enough," he answered, her last line not fazing him. "Then I'll see you Friday at eight. Wear something sexy and eat ahead of time. You'll need all the strength you can get before I'm finished with you. Until then, little one."

Her eyes lit on Randall Quinn as the call ended. "Two days. We don't have much time."

Despite Braden's protests, they prepared for the confrontation at The Driskill downtown. Rangers, agents and police came in one or two at a time over the next two days to make it appear as if they were guests instead of trying to set up a sting. Even Braden and Caid came in under the radar with fake wigs, beards and prosthetics noses, but when her husband bent her over backward in a soul-searching kiss, Andrea felt complete at having her love near her again.

Gaines had booked their reservation for the luxurious Lyndon B. Johnson Suite, so the base of operations were set in the suite next to it. Even with them being close by did little to quell Braden's volatile mood, asserting his need to be within the suite in case Andrea needed him. And his adamant stance accumulated into a standoff with Quinn.

"I'm not leaving my wife!"

"You'll jeopardize the whole damn thing with you being hotheaded! Your wife will be well-protected…"

"Protected like hell, Randall! Not when she'll—"

The argument raged on for twenty minutes until they had to separate before an old fashion duel took place in the hallway. But once they were able to calm down, Braden conceded, considering there was nowhere for him to hide without him being discovered.

Andrea got prepared for the meeting with Gaines down to the questions she would ask and the clothes she would wear. In a black negligee, Andrea appeared every bit the seductress. The padded bra molded and pushed her breasts to where they were on tempting display, her matching black lace panties with her legs encased in a pair of thigh-high pantyhose. Her long, ebony hair was teased and tousled with cascading curls hanging loose over a delicate shoulder. Her makeup had her with dark, smoky bedroom eyes with a hint of scarlet staining her lips.

Braden seemed so jealous, he shielded her from the gazes of others, growling at anyone who stared a second too long.

"Stop that," Andrea chided, despite her stomach doing somersaults. She toyed with the buttons of his shirt. "You're making them uneasy."

"*They're* uneasy? My wife's decked out like a sacrificial lamb to Satan himself."

"They're only trying to help."

"Looking at you sure as hell don't help my temper." His eyes, stirring with a mixture of emotions, slipped to display flecks of desire. "Not when your body is for my eyes only."

Her nails dug into his forearms as she stared up at him with yearning.

"Of all the inopportune times to get a hard-on," Braden quipped before seriousness appeared again. "I wish you didn't have to do this."

"I have to. It's the only way I can go home with you without this hanging over us."

His thumb and forefinger traced her jawline. "And you will." Braden glanced over his shoulder when the rangers and agents were wrapping up and leaving the room. "I'll be next door if you need me."

She nudged her forehead against his chest, curling her arms around him. "I know."

"Come on, Braden!" Caid gestured from the door.

"I love you," he said before kissing the crown of her head.

Braden pulled away from her, pausing when he reached the suite's threshold. He gazed back at her with a face that said to hell with it. But Andrea stood firm, radiating strength as she mouthed, "I love you," before he closed the doors behind him.

Andrea turned to walk into the separate living area, blinking back tears to prevent damage to her makeup. She couldn't afford to break down when it was too crucial for her stay strong for the both of them. But she couldn't handle it if that would be the last image she had of Braden, his reluctant face radiating a love that floored her.

She teased her bottom lip, her palms sweating as she checked herself in the mirror thirty times in twelve minutes. When a knock sounded at the door moments later, she hesitated in answering it. She wanted to backstep, ignore what was about to happen. Gaines was not only the one who stood between her and Braden, but he also held answers to what happened to her father.

She had to do this.

Blowing out her held breath, she strode to the door with confidence she didn't feel. She opened it and was greeted to the sight of Gaines, along with four men. Horror and disgust choked her as green eyes crawled down her body, his study licentious and possessive. He leaned against the doorframe, reaching for a curl of her hair and rubbing it between his fingertips. She continued to stand compliant, gritting her teeth.

"All this for me?"

She ignored him, her eyes swiveling to the four unexpected guests.

He smiled at her discomfort. "Like I told you, little one. I don't share." He crossed the threshold to stand in front of her, dipping his head close to her ear. "Your body is for my eyes alone."

To hear Braden say that line drove her to her knees. To hear Gaines say the same made her skin crawl.

He straightened. "Sweep the room."

The men scattered to perform a thorough search, all the while, he kept his eyes on hers, his eyebrow quirking as if he were trying to call her bluff. But she remained calm and composed, giving away nothing.

Within three minutes, one of them shook their head. Gaines' green gaze lit back on hers, and with a gesture of his head toward the door, his men followed suit until they were alone. Andrea was vigilant, heading into the living area to avoid being close to him.

"Would you like a drink?"

"Not of liquor." Andrea threw a questioning look his way. He raised his hand, crooking two fingers.

"Come here."

He wanted to get straight to business instead of attempting to sweet talk her out of her panties. Not that she minded. She was ready to express lane the whole affair.

After dawdling for a few more seconds, Andrea took her time until she was before him. An arm slithered around her waist, keeping her anchored to his side. The two fingers he had used to summon her smoothed down the same cheek he had struck weeks ago. Andrea flinched away from him.

"You'll forgive me losing my temper and hitting you, won't you?"

"And if I don't want to?"

"I'll have to persuade you to change your mind." He leaned in toward her. "Kiss me."

No, no, hell no! She'd rather hurl herself out the window to greet the unfortunate pedestrians treading 6th Street.

He smiled as she continued to stare at him with indecision, knowing her obedience was key but she didn't want to overplay her hand. His hand moved to caress the small of her back as if trying to soothe her when it was doing the opposite.

"I suppose it was wishful thinking that you'd be more pliant. But you're not running from me now. That's a start." He nudged her. "Kiss me."

She rocketed onto her tiptoes to plant a quick one on the mouth, but once their lips met, he held her hostage. Andrea was getting lightheaded as she held her breath, keeping her mind on Braden, imagining him tossing furniture next door in his fury.

Through her struggles for air, her clamped mouth weakened, which gave him the access he longed for. She almost gagged as his tongue darted inside, trying to take what didn't belong to him. Her eyes were squeezed shut, wishing her tastebuds were numb against the slimy taste of him.

The offending appendage slinked back from whence it came. Her eyes opened as a finger traced down her nose and to the plump mouth his just abused. "You taste sweeter than you did years ago." His hand coasted down to grab a handful of her ass, causing her to gasp. "And I'm sure you're just as sweet everywhere. Tight as hell, too. My cock is dying to find out." Andrea grimaced, and he released a breathy laugh. "You'll enjoy it, little one, and by the end of the night, the entire hotel will know just how much."

By the end of the night, she was praying his cock would be on lockdown if Braden didn't get to him first. Andrea twirled out of his arms, but he grabbed hold of her wrist.

He drew her back to him. "Where do you think you're going?"

She shrugged. "There's no place for me to go. You've ensured that."

"You're right." He paused to study her. "You must love him very much to sacrifice your body and freedom to keep him safe."

"You've also threatened Ella and Caid, but I refuse to let what happened to my father happen to them."

Gaines still remained impassive at her gentle prod, but now she figured it was time to lay all her cards on the table. She was done biding her time to lure answers out of him. Her sense of urgency was heightened now that he wanted her naked within a few minutes.

She had to act.

"Since we're on the subject, I really would like to know what happened that night."

"What about it?"

Gaines tried to pull off a cool demeanor, but he appeared uncomfortable when faced with a question he didn't wish to answer. Instead of being dick-deep in his so-called seduction, she hit him with a boner killer. It suited her fine since she was past caring. Because of him, she had lost her father. She was going to earn her truth.

"You know what I mean. I want to know what happened to my father."

"You already know what happened to him. There's no need to bring it up now."

He was eluding her on purpose, and Andrea's temper didn't appreciate it in the least. "Don't try to bullshit me. You can lie about everything else, but at least let *that* be the truth."

He shook his head. "I have far too many skeletons in my closet. You knowing any of my sins...the truth will only make you hate me more than you already do."

She'd hate him regardless, and him attempting to garner sympathy out of her fed her growing animosity. "I only care about this one sin against me."

He was quiet for a second before beginning with, "I didn't have anything—"

"Don't...lie!" Andrea bellowed. Her enraged outburst resonated in the room, followed by her mind short-circuiting in her anger. He was lying! Her entire body reacted as much with her free hand curling into a fist. Said fist flew, striking him wherever she could. At first, Gaines took her infuriated blows, his other hand doing its best to shield him from her onslaught. She didn't think about keeping her composure or the other questions she was supposed to ask. Her combined feelings of loss and loathing were offloaded with each hit, and her mind narrowed on retribution.

Gaines reached for her flailing battering ram. But when she connected with his jaw, he repaid her with a fierce backhand that landed her on the floor. It felt like her cheek exploded. Andrea placed her hand against the throbbing area as she glanced up to the fuming creature hovering over her. His green eyes blazed hell within them, as if he were on the verge of killing her. She recoiled as he reached down to grab a handful of her hair, persuading her to stand. His features were now maniacal, far removed from charming. His fingers wrapped around her throat, tightening until she started to choke. He then slackened to keep her conscious.

"You're too curious for your own good. Suppose I have that bastard you married to thank for that. But no matter. Now that I have you, I'll make sure he dies, just like your father."

Her eyes widened in alarm as his smirk expanded, turning his face cruel. It was frightening that he managed to turn at the flip of a dime, but she had done herself no favors by provoking him.

Gaines spun her into him, her back facing his front and his hot, searing breath at her ear. "You want to know what happened to your father?" With his tone, she almost didn't. "I'll tell you."

He took her earlobe into his mouth, suckling on it. When Andrea tried to move, he bit down on it hard enough for her to cry out. "Your father made it too easy, you know. Practically handed his life over to me on a silver platter. He came to my house dead-drunk and dared to threaten me. Then the stupid fool passed out. It would have been easy to let him sleep it off, but if he were gone, there would be nothing standing between us."

The hand that had a death grip on her hair came to rest at her thighs. It trailed upward, rising the hem of the negligee until his fingertips brushed against the delicate folds between her legs still encased in the thin, black lace. Andrea shook in repulsion, jerking away but his hand tightened around her throat.

"Uh-uh," he chided. "Don't you want to know how the story ends? How I had my men drive his car out to Lake Travis, placed him inside and let it roll down the embankment? I guess he just couldn't get out in time."

Andrea struggled, trying to land her elbows anywhere, sobbing under the weight of his confession.

"You might have thought you could escape your fate, little one," he muttered, a finger following the trail a large, wet tear had made. "But you belong to me. You've always belonged to me." He spun her around to face him, Andrea's eyes wide with fear as she beheld his wild, sadistic state. A finger passed over her trembling lips. "I could have taken you when you were fourteen, but I waited. Nine years is a long time to be patient." He seized her by her hair again. "Now it's time to be rewarded."

Gaines dragged her into the bedroom, flinging her hard toward the bed. The momentum sent her headfirst into the headboard, the impact leaving her dazed. By the time she came to, he was on top of her. She squealed and screamed, flaring her hips to buck him off. He slapped her hard before tearing at her negligee, one of her breasts bounding free.

He descended upon the now-available nipple, sucking on it before the door exploded and quick footsteps soon revealed the tall, statuesque frame of her fuming husband. His silver eyes were roiling and she knew a catastrophic disaster was about to go down.

When he was next door, Braden was either pacing or spewing a litany of curses that never seemed to end. He had shown remarkable self-control when he overheard from the recording equipment of the bastard commanding Andrea to kiss him. He couldn't stare at the camera footage, knowing that a glance at it would send him through a wall. Instead, he mouthed curses, ignoring Caid and Quinn trying to calm him, shaking them off as he resumed pacing. He couldn't stop moving, and he didn't want comforting. His wife was all alone with a monster, and he was powerless.

He did stop when he heard her screaming at Gaines, his skin prickling as an uneasy feeling settled in his gut. That unease was confirmed by a sharp sound, followed by something dropping to the floor. Like a body. Her precious body…

Braden roared as he bounded toward Quinn, who harbored the key to the LBJ suite. He clutched him by the shirt collar, knowing that Quinn would fight him tooth and nail to regain control. Caid and a couple of others were on him, imploring and trying to pry his hands away. But Braden was past reason.

Past placating. And he didn't have to say a single word to convey what he wanted.

"Braden..." Quinn struggled for breath as the raging man before him tightened his hold like a tourniquet.

A guy at the recording equipment shouted, "We got something! Sounds like he's confessing to murdering her father..."

Braden dragged Quinn out of the room like a dog on a leash before he could hear the rest. He didn't care if he had to hurl Quinn through the doors. His wife needed him, and he was going to do everything to get to her.

He spied Gaines' henchmen guarding the entryway. He didn't wait to throw Quinn in front of him, demanding for him to open the door as he rushed forward and clocked one of the men in the jaw.

Another fist was thrown at the man, this time, landed by Caid, and a scrimmage broke out. Braden ducked and swung at opponents, pulling back to keep them away from the door, all the while eyeing Quinn scrambling to get the keycard out of his pocket. A couple of other agents came to help subdue and handcuff the struggling men. Braden had his attention on one thing, and as soon as he saw his green light, he leaped over a man rolling in pain on the floor and raced into the room.

Now he stood at the threshold to the bedroom, seeing the new bruises his wife sported and her scared expression. His gaze narrowed on her torn negligee as she covered herself. Braden's hands balled into fists so tight, his knuckles crackled in anticipation of beating Gaines down to nothing. He might have been in Texas, the land of capital punishment, but killing the bastard would be well worth the death penalty.

"You get off her right now, you dickless motherfucker."

His words were barely above the hum of the air conditioning but were apt in conveying that Braden was on the far, far side of livid. His anger was hot, surging fierce, and if not appeased with murder, it could burn the entire city of Austin and its suburbs down to ash.

When Gaines didn't move, the younger man started into the room to haul the bastard off his wife but hesitated when his ears picked up on a muffled *click.*

"Or you'll what?" Gaines dared from over his shoulder, the barrel of a gun sticking into Andrea's side. Braden froze when he witnessed the horrified look etched on his wife's face followed by a flinch of pain.

"If you're determined to kill her, Sutherland, keep coming. Her blood will be on your hands."

"And yours," Braden stated as he held up his hands in surrender. "You won't kill her. Not after all the sacrifices you've made to have her."

"I would to save my life." He took a glimpse down at the petrified young woman beneath him. "But it would be a waste of a perfectly good fuck. Perhaps you could tell me just how good she was from your personal experience."

Braden was set to charge. "You son of a b—!"

A muted discharge of the gun resonated in the room. Gaines had shot into the mattress just inches away from Andrea, who couldn't hold back a startled scream. But it got the reaction Gaines seemed to want. Braden didn't move.

"You're determined to be a widower tonight. That can be remedied." Gaines vaulted over the side of the bed farthest from Braden, dragging a paralyzed Andrea along by her wrist. "Get up, bitch. Now!"

With a hard jerk, Andrea bumped into him, her legs unstable. The collision put him off-balance, and as he adjusted his hold on her, Andrea attempted to run to Braden.

"No, you don't! Come here!" Gaines snarled as he dragged her back to him, striking her head with the side of his gun.

Braden reached for his own sidearm to blow the bastard away but fumbled in his quickness. Gaines nestled the gun back into Andrea's side. "Drop it, or I drop her."

Braden's mind raced, grasping at thoughts on what he could do to turn the situation back into his favor. Where the hell was Quinn? It shouldn't take this long to round up a few guys, and Braden was losing a war against Gaines and his emotions. Staring at his wife's terrified tear-stained face killed him. The gun Gaines wielded could put a bullet in her the size of Travis County, and Braden itched to have that gun directed anywhere else. Even if that target was him.

He had always been ready to give his life for her without compulsion. Always preferred that it was him instead of her. After discovering the warmth of the sun, he refused to descend back into the darkness he had wandered in. She was his sweet, sensual fire, the flame that kept him going. He'd rather that light continue to shine long after he was gone.

Finality filtered through him; his mind settled on doing whatever he had to do to ensure her safety. But before he could react, footsteps raced in, and soon the doorway to the bedroom was filled with a disheveled Caid, Quinn, and an FBI agent.

Quick to access the situation, Quinn eased out in front of the crowd; his unarmed hands stretched out in front and behind him as if to temper both sides. "You're surrounded, Gaines, and killing her would only get you into deeper trouble." He edged out more. "You don't want to do anything stupid, now."

There was a brief glimpse of consideration in Gaines' eyes before they eclipsed back into the haunted, cornered creature he was. But there was something else that flashed in that gaze Braden didn't like. Something that seemed akin to desperation and resolution.

Gaines glimpsed down at his long sought-after prize, taking in every beautiful angle of her countenance to the curled wisps of her hair. A smirk appeared on his face as he studied her for long beats, as if for the last time. Then his green gaze moved to Braden, a sharp contrast to the almost sickening sweet regard he had for Andrea. Focused on him were eyes that blazed with intense loathing accompanied by that look of resolve again. The smirk remained, and his entire composure was adding up to something drastic.

Something finite.

Something...

Every proceeding second seemed like eternity. Braden reacted, thoughtless, though everything in him urged him to the forefront to stop him from shooting her. He could see Gaines' finger about to pull the trigger, while in the same instant, Andrea seized his wrist and jerked it forward as it fired in a downward trajectory. Braden went down with a grunt of pain.

"No!" Andrea screamed in horror as she lunged toward her fallen husband.

Braden grasped his thigh, the gunshot mere inches from his groin. But all his attention zeroed in on his wife. She struggled against Gaines, even attempted to headbutt him which only succeeded in the gun connecting with her temple, knocking her out cold. Braden bellowed as he watched Andrea fall to the ground but was soon quieted by a loud *pop*! His eyes flew to Randall Quinn, his service revolver at the ready. He then glanced over to Gaines, who had a bullet wound in his shoulder, shock residing on his face.

"That's as good a warning as I can give you," Quinn advised. "Don't make me warn you further. You might not live for the end result."

Gaines blinked once, twice, before he shifted his gun toward Andrea's head. Another shot rang out, Braden seeing Gaines' chest marked red before he collapsed. Quinn made his way over to Gaines, checking for signs of life. After a moment, he shook his head.

"Braden," Caid started. "You okay, man?"

Braden disregarded any concern for himself. His leg could have been taken clean off. He could have been shot ten more times. There was only one thing in the room that he cared about. The only thing in his life that had priority over all else, and he crawled with care toward her. "Andrea."

Caid tried again. "Braden, you'll need to get that leg looked at."

"Andrea," he said again, settling beside her. His wife was tucked into herself on her side, still unconscious. But she was alive, which was the most important outcome he could wish for. He stroked her forehead before lifting her into his lap, balancing her as much as he could on his good leg while cradling her to him.

His poor baby. He cupped her face which was starting to swell, his thumb skimming her bruised cheek which seemed to trigger her to wakefulness. Her eyes strained against the light as she opened them, pain registering on her features. Her head had to be pounding from being struck. Braden was glad the bastard was dead for that reason alone. Now he could never hurt her again.

Andrea attempted to lift her head but soon surrendered it to the brawny mass of his arm still supporting her. "Braden?" she croaked.

Braden hugged her to him, placing kisses along her face, careful of her cuts and bruises. "I don't know what I would have done if I'd lost you."

Andrea pulled away, her hazy mind trying to piece together the chaos around them. Agents, rangers, and officers were everywhere, securing the scene as they remained situated on the floor as if their world remained still. She glanced over her shoulder to the form lying inert next to her. She saw Gaines, eyes wide and vacant as he stared up at the ceiling. It troubled her how he was alive just seconds before. Andrea had missed the whole transaction, but she surmised from the gunshot on his chest that his last-ditch effort wasn't a wise one. Her reaction to seeing him was visceral, her body stiffening as she stifled a sob.

"Hey."

She couldn't tear her gaze away, her eyes soaking up the man who had threatened so much. Taken so much. Now he was gone. He was gone, and she was free. Free to choose her path, free to go wherever she wanted. She was free to love.

"Hey."

Her husband cuffed her chin to make her look away. Her dark brown gaze lifted to stare into eyes she adored. Stormy grays showered her with the affirmation she needed. She no longer needed to worry, and soon she would be able to go home with the man her heart had chosen.

Relief flooded Andrea as she collapsed into her husband's arms, breaking down into tears while ignoring the people around them. None of them mattered.

It was over.

Epilogue

It was a wonderful affair that people from miles around came to see. Almost every business had closed in Rock River to attend the renewal of the vows a full year later. If there was any proof of a couple being in love, it was apparent in the way Braden Sutherland stared at his wife as they exchanged words of love with family and friends present. The event took place outside on a gorgeous day, destined to be the talk of the town for years.

The guests congregated inside for the reception, everyone mingling and spreading good cheer to the couple. Not only did everyone in town show up, but so did Braden's mother, Mrs. Gemma Upshaw, Andrea's best friend Ella and her boyfriend, Chris, who were still going strong. Caid was also there, and he sat off apart from the festivities, not his usual jovial self. He studied the happy couple as if trying to decipher through them the puzzle that is love.

It astonished him how Braden, though he still had his moments, was almost the very antithesis of the man he had been a little over a year ago. Andrea had changed him, and part of that change boiled over to Caid. It was funny that after numerous generations of feuding, Andrea managed to put that to bed in the first few weeks she arrived.

Braden had been changed for the better, and Caid envied that.

He had been cynical about love. His bedroom pursuits proved a testament to that. But the process was turning stale. He was thirty-two, by no means old but then again, each day placed him further away from twenty. He had yet to look at a woman with the promise of loving her until the breath in his body was gone. No woman had persuaded his thoughts to matrimony, and he believed no woman ever would.

The chime of the doorbell interrupted his musings. Braden's mother attempted to rise from her seat, but Caid stayed her. When he opened the door, he half expected it to be a belated guest but was bewildered when it was someone he had never seen before.

It was a girl in her late teens with alluring sepia features and large, expressive eyes to match. He stood stone still when those very eyes locked onto him and the breath stole out of his body. He surmised she had no idea what those eyes could do to a man. They could make him want to give her the world without asking for it.

Her dark hair was in a tight, kinky curl style that framed her round face, coming down just past her ears. She had a bulbous nose above a mouth that was a tad wide with a fleshier lower lip encased in gloss, enhancing the lush dark pink of them. Then his eyes dragged the length of her. She had some meat on her bones, but it was proportioned and fleshed out into curves that were womanly and enticing.

He forced himself to stop, disgusted with his reaction. She appeared to be a kid with her foot just over the threshold of adulthood, and he was imagining all the ways her eyes and body could get him ready.

Hell, he already was.

Caid had never felt something so immediate, an attraction so spontaneous, and it was with a child. Life was indeed cruel.

Regaining his wayward thoughts, his hazel eyes leveled back to hers. "Yes?"

The girl swallowed at the awkwardness, darting her gaze around the imposing rancher taking up the doorway. "Does Andrea Banks live here?"

"Maybe, maybe not, but if you're trying to sell something, honey, we ain't buying."

She licked her lips, jerking her head to get a tendril of short, natural curl out of her eyes. "I'm not. My name's Camille Davis. I think she knows my mother." She became even more nervous when she got nothing but a frosty glare. The girl quivered under the magnitude of it. "Is there any way I can speak to her? It's really important."

Caid's arms crossed over his chest like a bouncer at a club's entrance. "I'm sure it is."

"Look," she began, reaching into her back pocket. "I've got something to show her if you could—"

Her sentence was cut short by her startled yelped. Caid's reaction was quick, grabbing her by the arms and twirling her until her back met the wall beside the front door. Her fingers bit into his brawny muscles through the crisp fabric of his dress shirt, those soulful brown eyes staring up at him. He didn't know why he was manhandling her, but perhaps it was of the impulse to place his hands along curves he knew it was a sin to touch?

He was a sick bastard.

"So, this is how you get women to go home with you, right, Marshall?"

They both glanced over to see Braden standing in the doorway. Andrea was behind him, peeking around her husband's statuesque frame. "What's going on?"

Caid backed away, staring at their visitor. "I don't go about making love to children."

"No, you just like roughing them up a little," Braden countered.

The girl frowned, straightening her light, beige jacket. "I'm not a child. I'm eighteen."

Caid snorted. "Yeah, and that's a child in my book, honey."

"Leave her alone, Caid," Andrea interjected, coming around her husband. "Sorry about that. Some up here lack home training…" Andrea froze when she caught sight of the younger woman. "How can we help you?"

"Are you Andrea Banks?"

"Andrea Sutherland as of a year ago today."

The girl winced. "And I've interrupted your anniversary party. I'm so sorry."

"It's okay, Miss…"

"Camille. My mother sent me. Do you remember Yvonne Davis?"

"Yeah, vaguely. I know she was my mom's best friend. They went to college together at UT. God, I haven't seen her in ages. She moved to California sometime before my mom died. How is Miss Yvonne?"

The girl's pretty visage became despondent. "She's dying. Cervical cancer."

Andrea's bright smile faded. "Oh, I'm so sorry to hear that. I know how it feels to lose a mother to cancer. But is there a reason why your mother would want to connect with me after all these years?"

Camille's eyes lit on Braden, then Caid who was all but scowling at her. "That's what I need to talk to you about," she replied. "Is there somewhere we can talk privately?"

"Yeah. We can go into the study, can't we, baby?"

"Sure thing, honey," Braden replied, easing himself to one side of the porch. "No one should be in there." Andrea gestured for the girl to go ahead of her, but before she followed, Braden detained her. "You sure you want to do this alone?"

She smiled through her apprehension. "It'll be okay." She kissed him before ushering the girl into the study.

The gentlemen went inside where the party wound down due to whispers of curiosity sweeping the crowd, wondering who the girl was and why Andrea appeared so grim.

Thirty minutes later, they knew the reason why. The two women came out of the study, holding hands. Braden gave a start when witnessing his wife's puffy, red eyes. Her companion hadn't weathered any better, her eyes weary from excessive crying.

The whole house quieted as Andrea's mouth curved into a smile, despite being on the verge of tears again. "Everyone, I'd like you to meet...my sister, Camille."

"Sister?" Braden and Caid parroted.

Braden went to her, taking her shoulders into his hands. "Baby, you're sure?"

"Positive. I thought it was coincidental, but she looks exactly like my father."

Braden's eyes moved over to the girl standing behind her. She looked as if she might faint trying to endure the intensity of his gaze.

But like the sun coming out from the clouds after a turbulent storm, his face softened, and the most handsome smile streaked across his mouth. "Welcome to the family, kiddo," he said as he engulfed his new sister-in-law into his arms.

Once he stepped away, everyone, one by one, came up to greet the girl. All except for Caid, who watched her from the hallway. He was the sole killjoy of the group. It wasn't for the reason of two sisters reuniting after all this time. It was because the girl intrigued him, pure and simple. It felt strange, as if his entire universe were shifting, all because of meeting this girl. He didn't like it. Didn't like it at all.

The couple of the hour observed as everyone greeted the new addition to their family. Braden had his arm around his wife, and she had one curled about his waist.

"You don't mind if I go back with her to California, do you?"

Braden cocked a brow.

"I'd really like to see her mother and learn more about Camille. I'll even take one of those DNA kits from one of those genealogy sites."

"And if it turns out she's not? Are you sure you could handle it?"

"She is," said Andrea. "I can't even explain the connection I instantly felt when I saw her."

"Hm, sounds like the feeling I had when I first saw you, but I think I was hornier than anything else," Braden teased.

Andrea playfully slapped him across his abdomen. He held his stomach as if she had done a number on him. She giggled. "You deserved it."

"The abuse is a small price to pay for loving you." Braden stroked the cheek of the woman who had given him the happiest year of his life and hoping several more of the same nature would follow. Along with a handful of children that would fill their home with light and joy that had never resided there before. Braden was determined to make it so, now that he had the best woman by his side.

"Happy anniversary, baby," he endeared, heartfelt to his very soul. "Thank you for loving me."

Andrea wrapped her arms as far as they could reach around his broad shoulders. "Thank you for doing the same."

Braden embraced his wife, overjoyed that he had found a woman he could spend the rest of his life with. There were no more complications from outside forces or internal conflicts within himself. Because even the most callous heart can be receptive to love, and Braden was thankful to be given that chance.

Next in Series

The Rancher's Searing Touch
A Ranchers Hot & Cold Duology: Book Two

Camille wasn't expecting life to hand her a basket full of lemons without room for sugar. Years after meeting her sister have added some sweetness, but her encounters with Caid Marshall leave a sour taste in her mouth. Camille wishes to forget him, but his searing touch won't let her…

Caid has always been the golden playboy. He's had enough women to host his own beauty pageant, but none of them compare to Camille Davis. She's younger and not his usual type of pretty, yet Caid craves to touch her every moment he can to melt her hardened resolve, and his own…

Now read the first chapter of
The Rancher's Searing Touch

Chapter One

Camille dared not feel at ease around the sea of happy, unfamiliar faces surrounding her. Most were cordial and receptive, already accepting her into their close-knit community. But she couldn't get too comfortable. She was here on a what-if possibility that everyone questioned, including herself.

Was Andrea Sutherland her half-sister?

She hadn't had time to dwell on that bit of mind-blowing news. Her mother had told her less than a week ago when her condition had taken a nosedive. What Camille didn't understand was why Yvonne hadn't been forthcoming about this when she had been candid about everything else. Yvonne made no secret of who Camille's father was or how she came to be. But it was hard to fathom that in her eighteen-year existence, Camille had no clue that she had a sister.

Yvonne still had a number for Andrea's aunt who lived in Alabama. From her, Camille learned that Andrea had married a rancher in Wyoming then proceeded to book a plane ticket for the upcoming weekend.

Her grandparents, or rather her grandmother, was staunch against her going. But the dying wish of her mother overrode any trump card her grandmother threw down. So Camille took a chance, armed with a picture of her father at his wedding reception. It wasn't much, but it was all she had.

It had been enough. Andrea Sutherland, without hesitation, had held her in a tight embrace as they both wept over the past and what might have been if they had known of each other sooner.

Andrea answered whatever questions Camille had about their father and divulged what had happened to him. Camille already knew that Darren Banks was dead. The day she found out was the day her mother's sunny disposition went away for good. Now all that was left was the shell of what Yvonne Davis used to be as she endured her terminal fate.

Camille glanced down as tears dared to surface again. She had been the epitome of everything brave for her mom. Today was the first time Camille had been able to cry in a long time, to express her vulnerability with someone who empathized. How was she going to face the future without her mother?

She squeezed her eyes shut, floating her thumb along her long eyelashes to collect the tears that formed.

"Camille, are you okay?"

She peered up to dark brown eyes staring at her with concern. Eyes that shared genetic similarities with her own. Andrea was so open, smiling at her with heartwarming comfort as she accepted Camille without question.

"Yeah," Camille replied with a minute, reassuring smile of her own, even though the smile was nothing short of a lie. "I'm sorry, where's your bathroom?"

"There's one right through there." Andrea pointed to the hall that led toward the study. "Hmm, looks like someone's using   it.

Why don't you use the one upstairs? Turn right, go down the hall, and it's the last door on the right."

Camille nodded, excusing herself as she walked up the stairs. She glanced over the crowd, her gaze drifting over the jovial faces of strangers. Then her eyes collided with hazel ones that gleamed at her as their master leaned against the doorway to the hall, arms folded and face impassive.

A peculiar flutter occurred inside her, and she almost missed the next step. Lord, she was about to kill herself! Camille craned her neck away before she broke it and concentrated on making it up the stairs with the little dignity she had left. And she felt that stare burning into her with each committed step.

Once on the landing, Camille made a beeline to the bathroom, slamming the door with more haste than she intended. She ran a trembling hand through her shoulder-length, kinky hair. The fluttering wouldn't stop. Camille was already a jumbled mess of nerves with meeting her sister. Her nervousness increased tenfold all because of a statuesque stranger who had manhandled her at the front door.

When Camille's nails dug into his bulging biceps after their introduction went to hell, she felt the power within them as he restrained from crushing her. But with a face and body like that, he wouldn't have to put his hands on a woman who wouldn't want them there, touching, caressing.

Loving.

Her eyelids drifted closed, and she licked her lips as she searched her mind for a name.

His name.

Marshall. No. It was something like…Caid.

Caid Marshall.

She could only imagine how a man like that could be with a woman. Even a child like her could dream since that's all he thought of her.

I don't go about making love to children.

There was nothing childlike in the way she had to grow up since her mother had gotten sick over two years ago. Camille had worked to help with the bills, her schooling paying the price for her negligence. But her maturity in life's experiences never prepared her for the shockwave of sensation Caid Marshall placed within her. Every one of her adolescent relationships were infantile compared to what she felt about this man, which was in every way, very real and *very* adult.

And it terrified her at how instant and intense those feelings were.

Camille rubbed her face. Why was she fantasizing over a man who didn't like her? His stance and demeanor said it all. Even with that steadfast resistance on his end, she felt the pull on hers. Maybe it was all those wistful romantic notions of handsome cowboys that had her in such a state.

Camille strolled over to the sink and stared into the mirror. Reflecting back at her was someone with a girlish face but possessed a body that belonged to a woman. Her sepia-hued features were full, soft, and pretty. Her body was a couple dress sizes past ten, her breasts and her ass overabundant, not to mention her belly that she cinched in with shapewear for more flattering outfits. Even though that shapewear was fighting against her for the ability to breathe every time she conjured thoughts of Caid Marshall.

Lord, that man took her breath away.

She sighed, knowing she couldn't stay in the bathroom all day. Tidying her clothes and swiping at her hair, Camille came out of the bathroom in a rush, her gaze downward. She didn't see the wall in her path until it was too late. She rammed into it, bumping her forehead before straightening up and falling back. But she gasped as the wall's strong hands shot out to steady her while she held on for dear life.

She closed her eyes, waiting for her equilibrium to be restored. And then she realized that unless she was in

Wonderland, walls didn't have hands. Or muscles. Or smell so… fucking good.

Her eyes followed up along his white dress shirt, to a structured neck unveiled by a couple of loose buttons, to a scrubby jaw and fine, kissable lips. Camille licked her own as she dared to travel the rest of the way to find those same unreadable hazel eyes narrowed down at her.

And this was the way they remained, unable to move, unable to speak. Breathing seemed the only plausible thing to do to fill the time.

Camille noticed that her hands were fastened to his biceps while his hands rested at her waist. She gasped as she felt them constrict before letting go. She widened the distance between them, standing against the bathroom door.

However, the one step she took back, he took forward, filling her vision of nothing but pure virility. She could faint from the magnitude of it.

His golden-brown gaze that drifted down her frame before lifting to her face again.

"You all right?"

Camille nodded since her voice did a vanishing act.

"What, can't speak now?" he replied, his tone haughty. "I know you're itching to tell me off." Caid placed his forearm against the door and leaned against it. "Let's hear it, honey."

Camille's dark eyes flashed, not only because of his arrogant attitude, but what he was trying to do. "You're looking for a fight. You won't get one."

"Why? Not woman enough?"

She gave him a cool smile, ignoring the prod. "No. Because fighting is for children, and I don't fight with children."

His eyebrows shot upward before he moved until his face was an inch from hers. She stayed still despite wanting to hightail it down the hallway. She was giving off signs of her uncertainty, and she knew Caid sensed it as his gaze caught on her full, trembling mouth, advertised with tinted lip gloss.

Camille's weight surrendered to the door when his thumb came up to smooth along the area beneath her pouty bottom lip. Her eyes closed to absorb the invigorating emotions zipping inside her, but when she opened them, he was watching her, his eyes indiscernible.

Then his attention turned down the hall. There were footsteps coming up the stairs. Camille glanced at Caid who appeared as if he wanted to say something, to keep the moment intimate. Camille couldn't afford to hear it, slipping around him. By now, the footsteps had stopped, and the perpetrator stood there, smiling at her.

"I was checking to see if you were all right?" Andrea inquired.

"Yeah. Just got a little detained."

Andrea peeked behind her, her smile dying a little before her attention shifted back to Camille. "Some of the guests are beginning to leave. Once everyone's gone, we'll get your things. I'd like you to spend the rest of your time here with us."

"I'd like that."

Andrea turned to go down the stairs. Camille found herself glancing down the hall to see that intriguing male staring back at her. Her gaze lingered before following her sister down, feeling deep down the alteration that had occurred. That this man, this Caid Marshall, might be her everything or downfall if she wasn't too careful.

And Camille feared it could be both.

Acknowledgments

As mentioned in my note at the beginning, getting something written and published has been years in the making for me. From story theft, life's ups and downs, writer's doubts, and the blessings in between, I'd like to take a moment to thank everyone who has encouraged me along the way.

My Hubs

I've thanked you more times than you can count, but it needs to be said again. You have been my driving force to get this done and to no longer put off a dream that has been a long time coming. Thank you for being my beta reader, my sounding board, my advisor, my cheerleader, and my constant support. Your Casa loves you beyond anything in the universe, and she is so happy that she has found you.

Mrs. Abt

You were the first teacher who truly helped foster my writing. You personally gave me my first writing guide because you believed in what I could do. I've never forgotten it or your encouragement. Even after all these years, I've never stopped writing in some form, and I want to thank you for instilling that in me. Although this is the sort of story I could have never turned in to you for an assignment.

Mia

Our writing weekends brought the best out of us. From writing stories in school, podcasting, gaming, your Sim videos, and other projects, we've never stopped being creative together. These last few years have been gold. Thank you for being one of the best encouragers I could have to finally get across the finish line. And you know I'm cheering for you, too!

Michelle

Thank you so much for editing this manuscript and writing for the better. I appreciate you still remembering me from all the years prior when I first contacted you. Thanks for being a great resource for me.

Summer

You inspired me to write in high school and beyond. Came to bat for me when people posted something negative and stole work. Read every single chapter as soon as I was done with it. That was the foundation that started all of this, and this victory lap is just as much mine as it is yours. Thanks, boo.

Parents

Thanks to my mother for giving me some creative gene, even if it's not cooking. To my stepfather who always demonstrated how a gentleman treats his lady. Thank you for taking care of my mom.

Crystal

You publishing your book after so long made me get my butt into gear. And you had recommended my editor, which I'm thankful for. Congratulations on your own success and many more to come.

Mama Jane

I appreciate you, Mama Jane, for your support in this and trying to read this book despite it not being your cup a tea. I love you for it.

Texas Rangers

Thanks for responding back to my inquiry. I'm glad you didn't pay me a visit.

Stephany Esposito

Thank you for your awesome proofreading skills and getting my first manuscript finalized.

LJ Anderson

Special shout-out for the awesome cover designs and ads.

All That Jazz

Jazz Matthews has been writing ever since she was little, from *Star Wars* fanfiction to being published in *Dragon Tales* twice when she was in the eighth grade. She wrote her first full-length novel when she was a senior in high school and has written ever since. A few of her stories were published on websites such as Romance at Heart and Literotica.

Jazz lives in Fort Worth, Texas, with her husband and their three adorable but needy dogs. She is a nerd who loves to play video games, go to fan conventions, read fanfiction, and listen to podcasts and audiobooks. She is also constantly in her feelings when watching Asian and Turkish dramas.

Website   Goodreads

Facebook   Instagram

TikTok   Twitter